IVAN SERGEEVICH TURGENEV (1818–83) was brought up on the estate of his mother at Spasskoe-Lutovinovo and educated at the universities of Moscow and St Petersburg. In 1838 he went to study in Germany and became a convinced believer in the West, or a Westernist (*Zapadnik*). On returning to Russia he gradually turned to literature, first as a poet, then as the author of the famous *Sketches* (*Zapiski okhotnika*, 1847–52), in which he exposed the evils of serfdom. He also began to make a name for himself as a playwright (*A Month in the Country*, 1850), but his life had already become dominated by his devotion to the famous singer, Pauline Viardot. Arrested in 1852 and exiled to Spasskoe, he turned to the larger genre of the short novel, publishing *Rudin* (1856), *Home of the Gentry* (1859), *On the Eve* (1860), and *Fathers and Sons* (1862). The hostile critical reaction to the nihilist hero of this last novel, Bazarov, and his own desire to live close to Pauline Viardot made him choose to live abroad, first in Baden-Baden, then, after the Franco-Prussian War, in Paris. Two further novels (*Smoke*, 1867, and *Virgin Soil*, 1877) followed, in addition to many short stories. By the end of his life his reputation had become overshadowed by his great compatriots, Tolstoy and Dostoevsky, but as the first Russian writer to gain recognition in Europe and America and as a master of the short socio-political novel and the lyrical love story Turgenev still remains matchless among Russian writers.

RICHARD FREEBORN, Emeritus Professor of Russian Literature, University of London, has published several works on Turgenev and the Russian novel. His translations of Turgenev include *First Love and Other Stories* in Oxford World's Classics. He is also the author of several novels.

OXFORD WORLD'S CLASSICS

*For over 100 years Oxford World's Classics have brought
readers closer to the world's great literature. Now with over 700
titles—from the 4,000-year-old myths of Mesopotamia to the
twentieth century's greatest novels—the series makes available
lesser-known as well as celebrated writing.*

*The pocket-sized hardbacks of the early years contained
introductions by Virginia Woolf, T. S. Eliot, Graham Greene,
and other literary figures which enriched the experience of reading.
Today the series is recognized for its fine scholarship and
reliability in texts that span world literature, drama and poetry,
religion, philosophy and politics. Each edition includes perceptive
commentary and essential background information to meet the
changing needs of readers.*

OXFORD WORLD'S CLASSICS

═══

IVAN TURGENEV

Fathers and Sons

═══

Translated and edited with an Introduction and Notes by
RICHARD FREEBORN

OXFORD
UNIVERSITY PRESS

OXFORD
UNIVERSITY PRESS

Great Clarendon Street, Oxford OX2 6DP

Oxford University Press is a department of the University of Oxford.
It furthers the University's objective of excellence in research, scholarship,
and education by publishing worldwide in

Oxford New York

Athens Auckland Bangkok Bogotá Buenos Aires Calcutta
Cape Town Chennai Dar es Salaam Delhi Florence Hong Kong Istanbul
Karachi Kuala Lumpur Madrid Melbourne Mexico City Mumbai
Nairobi Paris São Paulo Singapore Taipei Tokyo Toronto Warsaw

with associated companies in Berlin Ibadan

Oxford is a registered trade mark of Oxford University Press
in the UK and in certain other countries

Published in the United States
by Oxford University Press Inc., New York

Translation and editorial material © Richard Freeborn 1991

The moral rights of the author have been asserted

Database right Oxford University Press (maker)

First published as a World's Classics paperback 1991
Reissued as an Oxford World's Classics paperback 1998

British Library Cataloguing in Publication Data

Data available

Library of Congress Cataloging in Publication Data

Data available

ISBN 0-19-283392-8

7

Typeset by RefineCatch Limited, Bungay, Suffolk
Printed in Great Britain by
Clays Ltd, St Ives plc

CONTENTS

INTRODUCTION

It is the pleasure and the responsibility of a translator to enter very fully into a writer's consciousness while never overtly seeming to do so. The translator should ideally be as invisible in the translated text as the conductor is inaudible in his orchestra's playing of a piece of music. Needless to say, neither ideal is always achievable in practice, but the ideal is worth respecting, and the closeness of the translator to the text as of the conductor to the music involves a very precious and sensitive intimacy of feeling between the creator's intention and the interpreter's role as medium for its expression.

As translator of Turgenev's masterpiece, *Fathers and Sons*, I have been privileged to experience a little of this not merely through close study of the published text but also through having had the good fortune to look at the working manuscript when it first came to light in London, in the summer of 1988. It had been assumed that this manuscript was lost. Only the fair copy which Turgenev had prepared for the printer was known to survive. This was located in the Bibliothèque Nationale in Paris. It had first been described by André Mazon in 1930, but it did not become available for scholarly study until a photocopy was made in 1961 and Soviet scholars were able to analyse it.

Then, in 1984, Professor Patrick Waddington of the Victoria University of Wellington, New Zealand, published the sketches which Turgenev had made for his novel. If examination of the fair copy of the novel had laid to rest many speculations about the role of Turgenev's so-called advisers in determining controversial emphases in the portrayal of the novel's hero, the publication of the sketches for the novel has helped to elucidate this issue—and many others—in a quite remarkable way.

We need no longer doubt that, as Turgenev frequently insisted, it was characters, not ideas, that came first for him—those characters of whom Henry James records him saying: 'If I watch them long enough I see them come together, I see them *placed*, I see them engaged in this or that act and in this or that difficulty. How they look and move and speak and behave, always in the setting I have found for them, is my account of them.' The sketches for his novel amply bear this out. Turgenev *saw* his characters—the Kirsanov brothers, Arkady, Bazarov, Sitnikov, Fenechka (or Fenichka as he spelt her name then), Odintsova, Katya, Kukshina and the servants at Marino—with extraordinary clarity, in terms of their ages, biographies, characteristics, mannerisms and even living prototypes. From here, for example, we know that Bazarov was compositely based on the famous critic Dobrolyubov (1836–61), on a Dr Pavlov (1823–1904) whom Turgenev knew in Orël, and on a certain Preobrazhensky (Nikolai Sergeevich), a friend of Dobrolyubov and a contributor to the radical journal *The Contemporary*. Yet if Turgenev *saw* his characters, as the character sketches testify, he also saw them *placed* and in action. The sketch of the novel's content demonstrates that he appears to have had a clear idea of the way in which the plot of his novel was to develop before he actually began writing, right down to the calendar chronology of the events throughout May, June, July and August (Bazarov dies on 25 August, for instance) of 1859 or such a detail as the kiss between Bazarov and Fenechka which was to be the pretext for the farcical duel between the representatives of the 'fathers' and the 'sons'.

Such, very briefly, may be the salient insights offered by Turgenev's sketches for his masterpiece (they are translated in part in the Appendix to this edition). What happened during the actual composition of the novel is only revealed by the working autograph manuscript, and this dark-green ledger-type volume (18 cm × 30 cm), containing 180 pages of 33 ruled lines per page, with a red vertical line on the left-hand side of each page approximately 4 cm in width, tells us chiefly with what extraordinary care Turgenev corrected, reworked and refined his novel. It also tells us two very important things. Firstly, that some of the most politically sensitive and polemical parts of the novel—the confrontation, for example, between Bazarov and Pavel Petrovich Kirsanov in Chapter 10 or Bazarov's conversation with the peasant in Chapter 27—are written in extremely tiny handwriting in the narrow margins or are even in very faint pencil jottings. Constricted space obviously dictated this. Judging by the sketch of the novel's content, the ideological confrontation between the generations in Chapter 10 was an addition to his plan and required to be inserted, for the greater part, into what had already been written. Perhaps Turgenev also used such tiny script in order to hide from inquisitive eyes the extent of his novel's polemical—not to say seditious—character. Secondly, the autograph manuscript also reveals the difficulty he faced in developing the relationship between Bazarov and Odintsova into a love story. There was no real sign in his sketch of the novel's content that this was ever intended. Chapter 17 of the autograph manuscript, so full of revisions and corrections, crucially shows that the whole nature of the relationship underwent a change at this point, dictated seemingly by the characters themselves. Similarly, the character of Bazarov clearly appears to have grown beyond what the sketches intended, so that the scene of his death as well as the famous final paragraph of the novel are no more anticipated than are the tragic dimensions which his portrayal acquired during the writing of the novel.

Most of all, of course, the working autograph manuscript reveals the struggle of the author to establish and refine the detail. The 'realism' of the work can literally be sensed in the minute changes, the finessing process of introducing the right descriptive adjectives into depictions of landscape or clothing or facial appearance, whereas for the greater part the dialogue (except in some of the polemical passages) received far less revision and can therefore be supposed to have formed the voiced or dramatized structure of the fiction, its inner core, the characters themselves being often signalled by no more than initials. The dramatist's art, the sheer theatricality of so much nineteenth-century realistic fiction, reveals itself here as structurally having priority over practically all other *realia*. But it is in the amplifying process, when detail becomes so important, when the *placing* of the characters in their respective worlds assumes such significance, that the continuing trial and error of the author's struggle to body forth and make real turns his manuscript into a haphazard battlefield of uncoiled barbed-wire scribblings, skirmishings of alterations among the serried ranks of words, phalanxes of new material brought in from the margin and wholesale deletions of hard-won literary text.

The first page of the autograph manuscript states that the novel was 'conceived in 1860, in the summer, in England. For a very long time I was unable to sort out the subject and began it in the autumn in Paris, wrote it slowly and finally finished it on 30th July, 1861, on a Sunday, in Spasskoe.' The beginnings of the novel—and Turgenev's first attempts to *see* his new type of hero—belong to a period of three weeks in August 1860 when he was staying at Ventnor on the Isle of

Wight. He had gone to Ventnor for a holiday, partly because in mid-Victorian England the Isle of Wight was a popular venue for the better-off holidaymaker, easily accessible from London by train and ferry; partly because, of course, Queen Victoria went to Osborne; and partly because, in Turgenev's case, friends of his among the so-called London émigrés, particularly Alexander Herzen, had been there earlier. But on this occasion Turgenev visited Ventnor for business reasons as well as pleasure, and the business he had in mind was closely connected with the political state of Russia on the eve of the Emancipation of the serfs.

The defeat of Imperial Russia in the Crimean War (1854–5) and the death of Nicholas I at the height of the hostilities precipitated a crisis in Russian domestic affairs. The thirty-year reign of Nicholas I (1825–55) had ended with seven years of extremely oppressive government when no reform of any kind was contemplated. Once the war was over, it became clear that internal reforms were essential. Alexander I, the new tsar, seized the initiative by declaring the need to 'liberate' his people from serfdom. Instantly a liberal spirit spread abroad among the educated classes of Russian society. In this context—that of the intelligentsia, as it was known—Turgenev already had a special reputation and place. During the 1840s he had associated with Belinsky and other leading Russian Westernists (i.e. those educated Russians who believed that Russia should follow the example set by Peter the Great and support greater closeness between Russia and the West). Then in 1852 he had published his famous *Sketches* (1852) about peasant and rural life (I have translated them as *Sketches from a Hunter's Album*), and suffered official government disapproval and exile to his estate. In the immediate post-Crimean War period he was therefore regarded as the champion of the oppressed peasantry and to that extent 'progressive'. Politically speaking, though, Turgenev was 'liberal', one who believed in gradual reform, and the talk of revolution which formed part of the atmosphere of the times held no great appeal for him. He was, in short, a representative of the 'fathers', a 'man of the forties', dedicated all his life to the ideals of Western civilization and the values, political as well as aesthetic, which he considered best exemplified it.

Opposed to him, principally in a social sense, were a younger generation of the Russian intelligentsia who first became prominent in Russian life after the Crimean War. Their leading spokesman was

N. G. Chernyshevsky (1828–89) who helped to turn the journal *The Contemporary* into the foremost radical publication of the day. His advocacy of scientific materialism, utilitarian aesthetics, rational egoism and a variety of other ideas (mostly drawn from the left-wing Hegelian Feuerbach) educated a whole generation of intelligent young Russians in the need to criticize and reject everything—social institutions, the church, the political status quo and so on—which did not conform to the laws of the natural sciences. Allied to all this was the belief that, if only society were changed on rational, socialist lines, human beings could be changed also and a 'new man' could be created. Even more outspoken and radical (though naturally within the constraints of censorship) was Chernyshevsky's young protégé and collaborator, N. A. Dobrolyubov. Through his criticism he called on the younger generation to repudiate the liberal, aesthetically based values of the older generation of the intelligentsia. Largely drawn as they were from among what might be called a socially rootless meritocracy—the sons of priests, doctors and officials in the different ranks of the tsarist civil service—this younger generation was known not altogether flatteringly as the *raznochintsy*, sing. *raznochinets* (meaning 'those/someone of different ranks'). Because they were neither of the peasantry, nor of the landowning class (to which the older generation of the intelligentsia, the 'fathers', mostly belonged) they were unfettered in their desire for change and could contemplate revolution with equanimity. Indeed, the overthrow of the tsarist autocracy had been on the agenda of Russian internal affairs ever since the Decembrist revolt of 1825. Echoes of it are clearly to be discerned by the attentive reader in *Fathers and Sons*. For Turgenev such an expectation and such attitudes were potentially dangerous by-products of the reformist euphoria of the times.

Turgenev may have intended to relax at Ventnor in the company of an attractive young authoress, Marko Vovchok (who in fact never arrived), but his trip to Ventnor in August 1860 was partly dictated by a desire to discuss the likelihood of political changes in Russia in the wake of the Emancipation edict, scheduled for the following year. Also gathered in Ventnor were several other Russian liberals, acquaintances or friends of his. We know that he stayed initially at Rock Cottage, Belgrave Road (next to the Marine Hotel) and later moved down to Belinda House on the Esplanade. We know that the weather changed shortly after his arrival from being hot and sunny to something more typical of an English seaside August—storm and rain. He was obliged to stay indoors, caught a cold, occupied himself with talking to other compatriots, notably his friend Pavel Annenkov, and with the drafting of a programme for primary education in Russia, visiting the local museum and undertaking an excursion to Blackgang Chine and finally making a trip to see his friend Herzen, who was renting a holiday home near Bournemouth (or 'Bonmuss', as he called it). But more important than these occupations, though reflecting them in some ways, was his writer's concern with what he called in his memoirs the 'living person' of his newly conceived hero, Evgeny Bazarov, based on the personality of a young provincial doctor who had much impressed him. As Turgenev went on to write in his memoirs:

In this remarkable man were embodied—in my eyes—that scarcely conceived, still fermenting principle which later received the name of nihilism. The impression produced upon me by this person was very strong and at the same time not entirely clear; at the start I was myself unable to define him—and I listened to and studied intently everything around me, as if wishing to endorse the truthfulness of my feelings. I was upset by the following fact: not in a single work of our literature did I come across so much as a hint of what I sensed everywhere . . .

What Turgenev sensed about this 'living person' was, above all, his 'nihilism', his commitment to science and materialism, his negative cast of mind, his self-assurance, cynicism, energy, repudiation of aesthetic feeling and everything 'romantic'. He sensed, in fact, the reality of the 'new' man whom Chernyshevsky and Dobrolyubov had been so keen to foster through their radical journalism. Turgenev insisted more than once in his memoirs that he portrayed his hero from life, even claiming that 'I had to depict him precisely *that* way', regardless of his personal feelings in the matter. His Bazarov emerged as the most 'modern' as well as the most memorable of Turgenev's heroes and a figure who, in terms of literary influence, was a source of inspiration for Chernyshevsky's hero Rakhmetov in his novel *What is to be Done?* (1863), Dostoevsky's Raskolnikov and Ivan Karamazov, Goncharov's Mark Volokhov and many other 'positive' heroes. Bazarov became the epitome of the 'thinking realist' for the critic D. I. Pisarev (1840–68); later, especially in Soviet criticism, he tended to be treated as a hero whose nihilism had obvious revolutionary implications; and more recently, for Sir Isaiah Berlin, he was a new Jacobin, a type whom Turgenev could grudgingly admire but whom he also feared as one of 'the young iconoclasts bent on the total annihilation of his world in the certainty that a new and more just world would emerge.' And as Sir Isaiah Berlin also put it so eloquently, in his assessment of Turgenev's overall achievement:

If the inner life, the ideas, the moral predicament of men matter at all in explaining the course of human history, then Turgenev's novels, especially *Fathers and Sons*, quite apart from their literary qualities, are as basic a document for the understanding of the Russian past and of our present as the plays of Aristophanes for the understanding of classical Athens, or Cicero's letters, or novels by Dickens or George Eliot, for the understanding of Rome and Victorian England.

To the extent that Turgenev *saw* his characters and, what is more, saw them *placed*, he constructed his novel according to certain principles. The first of these dictated that his characters should be 'explained' (in a manner which we may nowadays find old-fashioned) by the addition of fictional biographies. This was usually his habit as a novelist. He never pretended to be completely invisible in his fiction and he never supposed that the novelist should abrogate his responsibility as a historian. The second principle was that the character should not only be *placed* in a historical sense, but he should also occupy a place or setting, have surroundings and an ambience. In this sense, the Kirsanovs have their biographies, their setting of Marino, their particular world. Within this world, also given an individual setting, is the peasant girl Fenechka. Similarly Kukshina and Sitnikov (the latter, admittedly, in a caricature, near-satirical fashion), Odintsova and Bazarov's elderly parents all have their places in time and space. The sole exception to this rule is the hero, Bazarov.

His role in the fiction illustrates a third principle: that the presence of the hero as a stranger or unknown quantity in the carefully drawn setting of the novel provides the novel's motivation. His portrayal through a graded sequence of settings—Marino, the town, Nikolskoe, his parents' estate—turns the novel into a many-faceted biography of the hero, in which Marino serves to expose his socio-political meaning as a nihilist (in the confrontation with Pavel Petrovich), the town highlights his superiority to other members of his generation, Nikolskoe reveals the romanticism in his supposedly strong character and his parents' estate forces him to confront his mortality, his insignificance in relation to an indifferent nature and a limitless eternity. Returning for a final visit to each of the three major settings, he resolves the ideological conflict between himself as a 'son' and Pavel Petrovich as a 'father' by participating in a farcical duel at Marino; at Nikolskoe he acknowledges that his destiny is not one of love and happiness (as it is for Arkady), but a rejection of any collaboration with the nobility in anticipation of his solitary destiny as a *raznochinets*; and on his return to his parents' estate he faces the fact of his superfluity in life and dies from a typhus infection, cut down tragically in his prime with so much of his potential unrealized.

The novel's structure exhibits various parallelisms and contrasts, just as the characterization may be studied in terms of groups. Bazarov, Pavel Petrovich and Odintsova, argues David Lowe, the American critic, 'all belong to the camp of the strong, the egoistic, and the sterile', whereas Arkady, Nikolai Petrovich and Fenechka (not to mention Katya and Bazarov's parents) can be said to be characterized by timidity and therefore belong to a 'believers' group who are more often than not 'observers rather than the observed'. Such an approach enriches one's appreciation and understanding of the novel's complexity and depth, but it would be wrong to assume that it takes precedence over that fundamental contrast between generations and types signalled by the novel's title—'fathers and sons'.

Arguably the greatest achievement of Turgenev, one which earned him the lasting opprobrium of the younger generation of the Russian intelligentsia and can still stimulate heated debate, is that he, a writer of the generation of 'the fathers', was so successful in portraying— intuitively but sympathetically—a representative 'son'. That he brought a kind of paternal affection to his task is reflected in the way he emphasized so warmly—far more than in any other novel of his— the theme of fatherhood and paternal love in the affection which unites Nikolai Petrovich Kirsanov and Arkady, or Nikolai and his little son Mitya, or Bazarov *père* and Bazarov himself. The balance in the viewpoint of the author towards his hero, for all its 'objectivity', is discernibly of the older towards the younger, the establishment or upper-class towards the *raznochinets* or radical. But the sympathy between creator and creation is equally discernible. A reader may increasingly feel that the difference between generations yields thematically to an emphasis on the ever deepening affection between old and young and to stressing the need for such universality of feeling. The novel's tragic dimension, the ultimate condition of things in which all generations are equal, is demonstrated by the hero's final need to 'die decently', as he puts it. Here each individual's confrontation with death and 'that great peace of "impassive" nature' which the novel celebrates in its final words turns what is essentially a work of realistic literature into a tract for all times.

Universal though its implications may be, *Fathers and Sons* has a particular historical setting and in striving, as a work of realistic literature, to describe what Turgenev liked to call 'the body and pressure' of the time, it is concerned with particular social issues and particular conflicts between the generations. It opens on a specific day—20 May 1859—with Nikolai Petrovich Kirsanov awaiting the arrival of his son Arkady home from university. In a Russia of serfdom Nikolai Petrovich is unusual for having redrawn his boundaries with his peasants and altered the relationship between master and serf by establishing a farm on which the workforce is ostensibly hired. Obtuseness on both sides in this equation has frankly produced few results in what, agriculturally speaking, is an impoverished region. Arkady, travelling homewards from the post-station, acknowledges to himself that reforms are essential. But how to go about them, how to start? he wonders. His generation's answer is epitomized by his taciturn, strangely dressed friend Evgeny Bazarov, whose difference is first clearly signalled by his shout from the tarantass in Chapter 3, deliberately interrupting Arkady's father in the latter's recitation of Pushkin's encomium to Spring as the time of love. For him nature is unlovable, a workshop, and a thick black cigar, not poetry, is all he permits himself in the way of sentiment.

'He behaves in this way', the radical critic Pisarev noted in March 1862, 'not out of principle, not so as to be completely candid every minute of the day, but because he considers it entirely superfluous to restrain himself in any way, for the very same reason that Americans throw their legs over the backs of chairs and spit tobacco juice on the parquet floors of posh hotels.' The observation is acute and legitimate. One real aspect of the difference, in class terms as well as character, between Bazarov and his hosts at Marino is nicely caught by the contrast between free-and-easy American ways (always assuming there are stereotypes in such things) and European, particularly English, stuffiness. A translator no doubt can legitimize this by emphasizing the brashness. Take the delightful little scene when they reach Marino, the Kirsanovs' estate:

'Here we are at home,' said Nikolai Petrovich, taking off his cap and shaking his hair. 'The chief thing now is to have something to eat and relax.'

'Food's a real good idea,' remarked Bazarov, stretching himself and dropping on to a divan.

'Yes, yes, let's have some food, let's eat as soon as we can.' For no visible reason Nikolai Petrovich stamped his feet. 'By the way, here's Prokofich.'

The 'no visible reason' for Nikolai Petrovich's behaviour charmingly assumes the reader's understanding. Though Bazarov exposes the affectedness of etiquette—something the elderly retainer Prokofich resents instantly—he does so not out of principle, it seems, but out of a natural negativism, a cast of mind which can be labelled nihilist pure and simple for want of any more elaborate definition. 'He doesn't like standing on ceremony,' explains Arkady (Ch. 5) because, in so many words: 'He is a nihilist.' Pavel Petrovich Kirsanov, when he hears this over breakfast, his knife raised in the air with a piece of butter on the end of the blade, caustically re-emphasizes the brashness by supposing the term denotes someone 'who doesn't respect anything'. But Arkady corrects him by asserting: 'A nihilist is a man who doesn't acknowledge any authorities, who doesn't accept a single principle on faith, no matter how much that principle may be surrounded by respect.'

Principles, then (pronounced as *principes*) are the armour which Pavel Petrovich straps on himself for the forthcoming ideological fray, but Bazarov, having learned from Arkady about his uncle's past and the reason for his retirement to the depths of the country, at once repudiates anything that is educationally prescriptive, any idea that people are at the mercy of the period in which they live. 'Each man's got to educate himself,' he says (Ch. 7), '—well, as I do, for instance. As for the period—why've I got to depend on it? It'd be better if it depended on me. No, my friend, that's a lot of sloppy thinking, a lot of nonsense!' Such Quixotic independence of mind in defiance of cliché is Bazarov's principal weapon. It may make him scornful of the romantic scars borne by his opponent—and in that he is probably being unfair—but his disregard of proprieties enables him to thrust more vigorously and accurately when the jousting begins, even though in the end he may have been competing with nothing more serious than a windmill of words.

The confrontation in Chapter 10 clearly reveals the differences. Pavel Petrovich's Anglophile, beautifully manicured and well-suited advocacy of principles, however purblind in its unselfcritical stance, attempts to justify individualism and the conviction that 'personality must be strong as a rock, because everything is built on it.' Theoretically there might seem to be little difference between this and the individualism evident in Bazarov's independence of mind. Bazarov's criteria, though, are utilitarian. He dismisses aristocratism, liberalism, progress and principles as so many foreign and useless words. They are wholly inappropriate to a situation in which human needs, meaning the needs of the Russian peasantry, are at a basic subsistence level. To Pavel Petrovich this betokens a rubbishing of all the most sacred shibboleths about the Russian people—their traditionalism, patriarchalism and religious faith. Bazarov is unimpressed. Under the nagging pressure of his opponent's reproaches, he may be driven to claim that he understands the peasants better than Pavel Petrovich; equally he may enumerate the various ills in Russian society which deserve severe censure; and he may be forced into a corner eventually when he is driven to admit that his nihilism amounts to no more than so much impotent invective. But he is not prepared to advocate any action beyond the purely practical and useful. It is his disciple, Arkady, who inadvertently hands his opponent the potentially most damaging weapon. 'We smash things because we're a force,' says Arkady. Pavel Petrovich's answering tirade against such a threat to civilization (introduced, incidentally, by Turgenev into the fair copy of his manuscript under the influence of his friend Pavel Annenkov) is the single most eloquent testimony in the novel to the values of the 'fathers', of Turgenev's own generation, and of the way in which the younger generation's nihilism could so easily end up as revolution and so much mindless and aimless destruction.

As for the Russian people, the peasantry, the ultimate pretext for the quarrel, Bazarov easily dismisses Pavel Petrovich's arguments. He possesses, after all, a superiority which Nikolai Petrovich admits to himself when he muses over the apparent rift which has opened between himself and his son (Ch. 11). 'No, it's not youth by itself,' he thinks. 'Doesn't their superiority lie in the fact that there are fewer traces of class-consciousness and privilege in them than in us?' But if such democratic feeling may be Bazarov's asset, his handicap is a lack of precisely that feeling for poetry and nature which Nikolai Petrovich experiences and holds so dear as he surveys the beauty of the surrounding evening and remembers the joy of his marriage. Admitted as we are at this point into a greater intimacy with a character than at any other time in the novel, we are also for the first time made aware of the inevitable transience of the human condition when Nikolai Petrovich poses to himself the equally inevitable ques-tion: 'But . . . those sweet, first moments, why shouldn't one live with them in undying, eternal life?' Life, not as social difference or economic struggle, but as the temporal yearning for the eternal, or as light forever burning against an engulfing darkness, like an icon flame, is part of a recurrent symbolism of hope in the novel.

Bazarov's indifference to individuals, to their feelings and to art-istic sense in general makes him declare, on the first occasion that he discusses anything with Odintsova at Nikolskoe that 'all people are alike in their bodies as in their souls.' His fondness for formulae and generalities has a kind of simplistic appeal. In so far as physical ailments can all be amenable to diagnosis and cure, so moral diseases can be put right by reforming society. As one who disbelieves in medicine and even makes fun of it, he hardly convinces as a social reformer ('Believe me or not, it's all the same to me!' he seems to be saying). As a counterpoint to his offhandedness is the growing awareness between his erstwhile disciple Arkady and Odintsova's younger sister which presages his own growing awareness of self and the emotional changes occurring within him. Bazarov is to discover that he was too right by half: moral diseases may supposedly be put right, but there is no cure for love. There is only a cure for the kind of extreme intellectual arrogance he displays when, in speaking to Arkady about the newly arrived Sitnikov (Ch. 19), he compares himself to one of the gods. Strong, independent-minded and self-assured though he may be, his arrogance at this point seems to epitomize the hubris of all those who challenge fate and bring about their own ruin.

In his relations with Odintsova the need for affection, flippant at first and little more than a bandying of words, quickly becomes a need for commitment and sacrifice. Her philosophy of 'a life for a life'—quite just in Bazarov's estimation—does not exactly correspond to his previous assumption that women should be easy targets for masculine desire, to be used offhandedly or discarded if difficult. She forces him to confront the likelihood of personal happiness, to acknowledge the emotional turmoil, the revolution that is literally occurring within him, and in so doing she provokes both his violent admission of love and her own sudden, shameful realization that 'peace of mind', the most treasured asset of her comfortable life, had been imperilled by her thoughtlessness. The result, for Bazarov, is an equally sudden recognition that life is precarious—'Every single man hangs by a thread,' he tells Arkady on the way to his parents' estate, 'a bottomless pit can open beneath him any minute . . .'. His reassertion of his masculine independence ('In my opinon it's better to break stones working on a road than to let a woman control so much as the tip of your finger') has a hollow ring about it at this stage. The Hamlet-like characteristics, which Turgenev believed coexisted with the Quixotic as opposed poles in the human personality, now rise to the surface in Bazarov and gradually assume a dominant role.

His return home marks not only the final stage in Bazarov's friendship with Arkady, but also the moment when, confronted by memories of childhood and the overweening adulation of his parents, he sees himself no longer as one of the gods, nor even as the potentially great man of science (as Arkady's prediction suggests), simply as a 'tiny little place', an atom in which blood circulates and the brain works and even desires something. It is a vision of human insignificance which owes something to Turgenev's reading of Pascal. But if the intellectual arrogance is displaced by this philosophical nihilism, Bazarov as a human being governed by sensations and given to hatred of, say, the peasantry, for whom he must supposedly work his fingers to the bone, or Arkady's highflown 'poetic' language, which he should presumably respect, is a Bazarov become more himself, more unaffected in his class attitudes and his honesty, than at any previous point in the novel. He distresses his parents beyond measure, of course, by his decision to leave so soon after arriving home, but he is rootless, he recognizes, superfluous, an ostensible Quixote now flawed by the melancholy of a Hamlet.

The brief visit to Nikolskoe is a mistake; the return to Marino, the

Kirsanovs' estate, is a disaster. Solitary now, no longer accompanied by his disciple, who has been drawn back to Katya in Nikolskoe, Bazarov finds himself toying with death during the farcical duel with Pavel Petrovich. The outcome does him every credit, but his unwise kissing of Fenechka did quite as much to provoke it as did his opponent's misguided gallantry. When he next sees Arkady, he wryly admits: 'You drop in on feudal lords and you find yourself taking part in knightly tournaments.' Bazarov's sense of humour has an ironic, if caustic, dryness that nicely contrasts with the straitlaced and often rather boring niceness of his hosts. He has been out of his element, he confesses to Odintsova. 'Flying fish', he says, 'can keep in the air for a short while, but they're bound to flop back into the water pretty quickly. Allow me to flop back into my element.'

His 'element' is the solitary one of an unmarried, harsh existence, with no prospect, it seems, of that family happiness which awaits Arkady and Katya in the conventional sub-plot of their relationship. What reads in many ways as a family chronicle, or an episode excerpted from such a novel, has in Bazarov himself a character whose strength lifts the fiction and its message out of a mould. In doing so the true revolutionary heroism of the character is revealed. In his statement of farewell to Arkady, Bazarov makes clear that his personal destiny is to fill up the luggage of his own life with something or other (love, as both he and Odintsova prefer to think, being an overblown emotion); and, in any case, the nobility cannot endure what *he* has to endure. 'You're not made', he tells Arkady,

'for the bitter, sour-tasting, rootless life of people like me. You haven't got the daring, you haven't got the anger, all you've got is youthful courage and youthful fervour—and that's not enough for what I've got to do. Aristos like you'll never go beyond noble humility or noble indignation and that's all nonsense. You, for example, won't fight—and yet you think you're fine chaps—but people like us, we want to fight. And we will! The dust we kick up'll eat out your eyes, our mud'll get all over you . . .' (Ch. 26)

As a political judgement, the implication is obvious. As a defiant statement of personal destiny, it is strong but by no means certain, and as the return to his parents' estate shows Bazarov appears to lose interest quickly enough in all his former scientific pursuits. The fond, uneasy banter between father and son—a relationship always beautifully suggested by Turgenev, if mostly from the father's point of view—highlights the 'need', which is almost a compulsion, for Bazarov to occupy himself with something. The truth is laid bare that Turgenev allows only two real choices in life, strictly speaking: happiness in love leading to marriage or a kind of extinction in life (such as the life of Pavel Petrovich in his Dresden exile) which leads inevitably to death. Bazarov, as he puts it himself, has been 'run over'—accidentally and tragically, for sure, but for someone who has been so obviously independent in life and so ready to challenge convention and orthodoxy and cliché the irony in the old joke of death is especially poignant. His medical knowledge tells him that he is doomed. It is as a doomed man with a caustic and self-deprecating sense of humour that he acknowledges to Odintsova, the only woman he has ever loved, that he, the supposed giant, is not 'needed'—not by her, not by Russia. 'And who is needed?' he asks in his dying breath, 'The shoemaker's needed, the tailor's needed, the butcher . . . he sells meat . . . the butcher . . . Stop, I'm losing my way . . . There's a forest here.'

The imagery surrounding Bazarov's last moments significantly contrasts light and dark, the life-enhancing and the life-extinguishing. If the forest suggests the blackness of death, echoed in his very last word 'darkness', then his final predicament is compared in his own words with that of a dying lamp which Odintsova's kiss will extinguish, much as it might seem that the failure of their love had been the cause of his rapid loss of interest in life and precipitated a death from surgical poisoning so quick it might almost have been self-induced. As for the last light he sees—that of the candle before the icon—to one who had repudiated religion and assuredly remained in death as independent of superstition as he had been in life, it horrifies with its threat of divine consolation; but that does not deny the hope of everlasting life promised in the novel's last words.

The moral of *Fathers and Sons*, whether as a realistic novel concerned with reflecting its historical period or as a family chronicle devoted to showing how one generation succeeds another while naturally contrasting with it, emphasizes continuity, even unchangeability; in such aspects it has the necessary trappings of a fine novel, if not of an enduring masterpiece. Where it transcends convention and touches greatness is in the masterly portrayal of a new type of hero. In his independence of mind and scientific respect for truth, in his anti-aestheticism and pragmatism, Bazarov offers more than the simple recalcitrance of a younger generation reacting against the 'truths' of an older. He is not only sceptical of such truths, not only anti-establishment through background and cast of mind, he is also essentially different in his common touch, his practicality, his readiness to test and experiment, his denial of authorities and his awareness of freedom as a habit of mind and a way of living. Together with such virtues come, of course, a brashness that is close to bullying and an arrogant uncouthness that shows an unpleasantly intolerant and insensitive side to his nature. Perhaps as a nihilist he is politically a revolutionary, or as an anti-liberal meritocrat he may seem to foreshadow the Jacobinism associated with today's technocracy, or as the archetypal doctor-figure he may be committed as much to the healing of society as to the alleviation of human sickness; but as a heroic type he offers a vision of human self-reliability and potential that has a modern appeal to it and suggests both the power of man when armed with scientific understanding and the Frankenstein-like fate awaiting him if the power is abused.

As translator I have taken certain minor liberties with the punctuation. The semi-colon so beloved of the nineteenth century has been replaced by the full stop, with a resultant shortening of the sentences. In translating dialogue I have tried to emphasize the difference between the language of Bazarov and that of practically all the other characters, especially those from the nobility, by including slang expressions and some American idiom. As for the title of the novel, I have chosen to translate *Ottsy i deti*, which means literally 'Fathers and Children', as *Fathers and Sons* because it seems to encapsulate the novel's meaning more directly. Otherwise accuracy, allied to sensitivity, has been the aim at every stage; and it is an aim which, to my regret, I cannot always be sure of attaining.

NOTE ON THE TEXT

Fathers and Sons was first published in March 1862. The text used for this translation is taken from I. S. Turgenev, *Polnoe sobranie sochinenii (Sochineniya*, vol. 8, Moscow-Leningrad, 1964), supplemented by I. S. Turgenev, *Polnoe sobranie sochinenii*, second complete revised edition (*Sochineniya*, vol. 7, Moscow 1981).

SELECT BIBLIOGRAPHY

1. ENGLISH TRANSLATIONS

There have been many translations of Turgenev's masterpiece, but the first worthy translator of Turgenev into English was Constance Garnett, whose *The Novels of Ivan Turgenev*, 15 vols (London, 1894–9) established a standard which few have bettered. Although Isabel Hapgood, Bernard Isaacs, Rosemary Edmonds, Richard Hare and Bernard Guilbert Guerney, to name only a few, have translated the novel, the thorough revision of the Constance Garnett translation by Ralph Matlaw for the Norton Critical Edition (New York, 1966; 2nd edn, 1989) remains especially noteworthy, particularly as it is enhanced by the inclusion of a large and well-chosen range of critical materials.

2. LETTERS

Turgenev's Letters, tr. A. V. Knowles (London, 1983)
Turgenev: Letters, tr. David Lowe, 2 vols (Ann Arbor, 1983)

3. BIBLIOGRAPHIES

Royal A. Gettmann, *Turgenev in England and America* (Urbana, Ill., 1941)
Rissa Yachnin and David Stam, *Turgenev in English: A Checklist of Works by and about him* (New York, 1962)
Nicholas Zekulin, *Turgenev: A Bibliography of Books 1843–1982 by and about Ivan Turgenev* (Calgary, 1985)

4. BIOGRAPHIES (in Chronological Order)

Avrahm Yarmolinsky, *Turgenev: The Man—His Art—and His Age* (New York, 1926; London, 1927; rev. edn, New York, 1959; London, 1960)
V. N. Zhitova, *The Turgenev Family* (London 1947)
David Magarshack, *Turgenev. A Life* (London–New York, 1954)
Lenard Schapiro, *Turgenev: His Life and Times* (New York, 1978)
Henri Troyat, *Turgenev*, tr. Nancy Amphoux (London, 1989)

5. CRITICISM (in Chronological Order)

J. A. T. Lloyd, *Two Russian Reformers: Ivan Turgenev, Leo Tolstoy* (New York–London, 1911)
Edward Garnett, *Turgenev* (London, 1917)

Harry Hershkowitz, *Democratic Ideas in Turgenev's Works* (New York, 1932)

J. A. T. Lloyd, *Ivan Turgenev* (London, 1942)

Henri Granjard, *Ivan Tourguénev et les courants politiques et sociaux de son temps* (Paris, 1954, 1966)

Gilbert Phelps, *The Russian Novel in English Fiction* (London, 1956)

Richard Freeborn, *Turgenev: The Novelist's Novelist. A Study* (Oxford, 1960; repr. 1963, 1970, 1978)

Jane Wexford, *Turgenev's Fathers and Sons*, Monarch Notes (New York, 1966)

Denis M. Calandra and James L. Roberts, *Turgenev's Fathers and Sons. Notes* (Lincoln, Nebr., 1966; Toronto, 1979)

Sir Isaiah Berlin, *Fathers and Children* (Romanes Lecture, 1970) (Oxford, 1972)

Charles A. Moser, *Ivan Turgenev* (New York–London, 1972)

Marina Ledkovsky, *The Other Turgenev* (Wurzburg, 1973)

Eva Kagan-Kans, *Hamlet and Don Quixote. Turgenev's Ambivalent Vision* (The Hague–Paris, 1975)

Dale E. Peterson, *The Clement Vision. Poetic Realism in Turgenev and James* (Port Washington–London, 1975)

Peter Brang, *I. S. Turgenev. Sein Leben und sein Werk* (Wiesbaden, 1977)

V. S. Pritchett, *The Gentle Barbarian. The Life and Work of Turgenev* (London–New York, 1977)

Robert Dessaix, *Turgenev: The Quest for Faith* (Canberra, 1980)

Victor Ripp, *Turgenev's Russia. From 'Notes of a Hunter' to 'Fathers and Sons'* (Ithaca, NY, 1980)

Patrick Waddington, *Turgenev and England* (London, 1980)

David Lowe, *Turgenev's Fathers and Sons* (Ann Arbor, 1983)

Ivan Sergeyevich Turgenev: 1818–1883–1983, ed. Patrick Waddington (*New Zealand Slavonic Journal*, Wellington, 1983)

Transactions of the Association of Russian-American scholars. Vol. XVI: Turgenev Commemorative Volume, ed. Nadja Jernakoff (New York, 1983)

A. V. Knowles, *Ivan Turgenev*, Twayne World Authors (Boston, 1988)

Jane T. Costlow, *Worlds within Worlds: The Novels of Ivan Turgenev* (Princeton, 1990)

A CHRONOLOGY OF IVAN TURGENEV

1818   28 October: born in Orël, Russia, second son of Varvara Petrovna T. (*née* Lutovinova), six years older—and considerably wealthier—than Sergei Nikolaevich, his father.

1822–3   Turgenev family makes European tour. Ivan rescued from bear pit in Bern by his father.

1833   Enters Moscow University after summer spent in dacha near Moscow which provided the setting for his story 'First Love' (1860).

1834   Transfers to St Petersburg University. 30 October: father dies.

1838–41 Studies at Berlin University and travels in Germany and Italy. Friendships with Granovsky, Stankevich, Herzen and Bakunin.

1842   26 April: birth of illegitimate daughter. Writes master's dissertation, but fails to obtain professorship at St Petersburg University.

1843   Enters Ministry of Interior. Meets Belinsky. Long poem *Parasha* brings him literary fame. Meets Pauline Viardot.

1844   'Andrei Kolosov', first published short story.

1845   Resigns from Ministry of Interior. Meets Dostoevsky.

1847   First of *Sketches from a Hunter's Album* 'Khor and Kalinych' published in newly revived journal *The Contemporary*.

1847–50 Lives in Paris or at Courtavenel, country house of the Viardots.

1850   'The Diary of a Superfluous Man.' Completes only major play, *A Month in the Country.* 16 November: mother dies. Inherits family estate of Spasskoe-Lutovinovo.

1852   *Sketches* published in separate edition. 16 April: arrested for obituary on Gogol, but really for publication of *Sketches*. Imprisoned for one month. Exiled to Spasskoe till November 1853.

1855   Meets Tolstoy.

1856   *Rudin*, first novel, published in *The Contemporary*. Travels widely, visiting Berlin, London and Paris. Till 1862 is abroad each summer.

1859   *Home of the Gentry.*

FATHERS AND SONS

Dedicated to the Memory of
Vissarion Grigorevich Belinsky*

'NOTHING to be seen yet, Peter?' was the question asked on 20th May 1859 by a landowner of a little over forty, in a dusty overcoat and checked trousers, as he came out on to the low front steps of a post-station on the * * * highway, addressing his servant, a young, round-cheeked fellow with some whitish fluff on his chin and small, lacklustre eyes.

The servant, in which everything (the turquoise ring in one ear, the pomaded multi-coloured hair, the unctuous body movements), literally everything bespoke an example of the newest, absolutely perfect generation of gentleman's gentlemen, glanced superciliously along the road and pronounced in reply:

'Nothing to be seen, sah.'

'Nothing to be seen?' the landowner repeated.

'Nothing to be seen,' the servant pronounced a second time.

The landowner sighed and sat down on a bench. We will acquaint the reader with him while he sits there, tucking his feet in beneath him and looking thoughtfully around.

His name is Nikolai Petrovich Kirsanov. About ten miles or so from the post-station he has a good estate of two hundred serfs or, as he puts it since he redrew his boundaries with his peasants and set up a 'farm', an estate of some five thousand acres. His father, a general who had seen active service in 1812, a Russian gentleman, semi-literate, coarse-grained, but without malice, had been in the army all his life, first in command of a brigade, then a division, and had lived all the time in the provinces where, on the strength of his rank, he had played a fairly significant role. Nikolai Petrovich had been born in the south of Russia, like his elder brother Pavel (about whom later), and had been educated at home until the age of fourteen, surrounded by cheap tutors, free-and-easy but obsequious adjutants and other regimental and staff types. His mother, from the Kolyazin family, known as Agathe before marriage but as Agafokleya Kuzminishna Kirsanov in her capacity as a general's wife, belonged to the tribe of 'matriarchal battleaxes' and wore sumptuous bonnets and noisy silk dresses, was always the first in church to go up to kiss the cross, talked loudly and a great deal, permitted her children to kiss her hand each morning and gave them her blessing each night—in short, lived her life to her heart's content. As the son of a general, Nikolai Petrovich, although he not only did not excel in bravery but even deserved the nickname of 'cowardy custard', was intended for the army like his brother Pavel, but on the very day when news of his call-up came he broke his leg and, after spending a couple of months in bed, remained all his life 'a bit of a cripple'. His father dismissed him with a wave of the hand and let him be a civilian. He took him to St Petersburg the moment he reached eighteen and entered him for the university. Meanwhile, his brother had just become an officer in a guards regiment. The young men started a life together in the same apartment under the distant guardianship of a second cousin on their mother's side, Ilya Kolyazin, a high-ranking civil servant. Their father returned to his division and his wife and only occasionally sent his sons large quarto sheets of grey paper covered in his flowing clerkish scrawl. The end of these sheets was always graced by the words: 'Piotr Kirsanof, Major-General', assiduously surrounded by embellishments of squiggles.

In 1835 Nikolai Petroch graduated from the university, and in the same year General Kirsanov, having been forced to retire after a disastrous inspection, came with his wife to St Petersburg to find somewhere to live. He was intending to take a house by the Tauride Gardens and join the English Club but suddenly died of a stroke. Agafokleya Kuzminishna soon followed him: she couldn't stand the dull life of the capital and the anguish of a life of retirement became insufferable to her. In the meantime Nikolai Petrovich succeeded, even in the lifetime of his parents and to their no small distress, in falling in love with the daughter of an official called Prepolovensky, the previous owner of his apartment, an attractive and, as they say, well-developed girl who used to read serious articles in the 'Science' sections of journals. He married her as soon as the mourning was over and, having given up his job in the Ministry of Crown Estates, where his father had found him a place, enjoyed a life of bliss with his Masha, first of all in a country cottage near the Institute of Forestry, then in the city itself, in a small, pretty apartment with a clean staircase and a chilly sitting-room and, finally, in the country where he settled at last and where his son Arkady was soon born. The married couple lived together extremely happily and

calmly, hardly ever apart, reading together, playing duets on the
piano and singing songs; she was fond of planting flowers and looking after the poultry, he occasionally went hunting and looked after
the management of the estate—and all the while Arkady went on
growing and growing, just as happily and calmly. Ten years went by
like a dream. In 1847 Kirsanov's wife died. He scarcely survived the
blow and went grey in a matter of weeks. He was planning to go
abroad to distract himself a little—but then along came 1848.* He
returned willy-nilly to his estate and after a fairly long period of
inactivity set about making changes. In 1855 he took his son up to
university and spent three winters with him in St Petersburg, hardly
ever going out and endeavouring to get to know Arkady's young
friends. He wasn't able to make the journey the previous winter—
and so now we see him in May 1859, already quite grey, chubby and
a bit bent, waiting for his son who had just graduated, as he had
once himself.

  His servant, out of a feeling of propriety and perhaps because he
didn't want to remain under his master's gaze, had gone out of the
gates and lit up a pipe. Nikolai Petrovich bent his head and began
studying the ancient verandah steps. A plump young chicken in
motley plumage strutted self-importantly along them, tapping away
firmly with its large yellow claws. A bedraggled-looking cat, curled
up foppishly against the railings, eyed it in an unfriendly way. The
sun burned down. From the shadowy entrance to the post-station
wafted the smell of hot rye bread. Nikolai Petrovich fell into a day-
dream. 'My son . . . graduated . . . my boy Arkady—a graduate . . .'.
He went over and over such thoughts in his mind. He tried to think
about something else, but again and again his thoughts returned to
the same thing. He recalled his late wife. 'She didn't live to see it!' he
whispered aloud despondently. A large grey dove flew down on to
the road and hurriedly set about drinking from a puddle beside the
well. Nikolai Petrovich started watching it and then his ear caught
the sound of approaching wheels.

  'Seems they're coming, sah,' the servant announced, plunging in
from outside the gates.

  Nikolai Petrovich jumped up and gazed along the road. A tarantass came in sight drawn by a troika of post-horses. In it could be
glimpsed the band of a student's cap and the familiar outlines of a
dear face . . .

'Arkady—my boy, my boy!' exclaimed Kirsanov and ran forward and waved his arms. In a matter of moments his lips were pressed to the beardless, dusty and sunburned cheek of the young graduate.

2

'LET me give myself a shake, dad,' said Arkady in a loud, youthful voice, slightly husky from the journey, happily responding to his father's embraces. 'I'll make you all dusty.'

'It doesn't matter, it doesn't matter,' repeated Nikolai Petrovich, smiling tenderly and brushing the collar of his son's greatcoat and his own coat once or twice with his hand. 'Give me a good view of you, come on,' he added, taking a step backwards, and then and there he hurried off towards the post-station, saying commandingly: 'Over here, over here, bring the horses quick as you can!'

Nikolai Petrovich appeared a great deal more flustered than his son. It was as if he'd literally lost control of himself a little and become embarrassed. Arkady stopped him.

'Dad,' he said, 'allow me to introduce my good friend Bazarov, about whom I've written you so often. He's been kind enough to agree to stay with us.'

Nikolai Petrovich turned quickly round and, going up to a tall man in a long, loose, canvas garment with tassels who had just that minute stepped out of the tarantass, firmly squeezed his ungloved red hand, which the other had not immediately offered him.

'Sincerely glad,' he began, 'and grateful to you for kindly intending to stay with us. I hope you'll . . . Permit me to ask your name and patronymic?'

'Evgeny Vasilev,' answered Bazarov in a lazy but manly voice and, turning back the collar of his coat, gave Nikolai Petrovich a view of his entire face. Long and thin, with broad temples, a nose flattened at the top and sharp towards the tip, with large greenish eyes and sandy-coloured drooping sideburns, the face was enlivened by a quiet smile and expressed self-assurance and intelligence.

'I hope, my very dear Evgeny Vasilev, you won't be bored with us,' Nikolai Petrovich went on.

Bazarov's thin lips made a slight movement, but he didn't answer and simply raised his cap. His somewhat dark fair hair, though long and thick, could not conceal the large protuberances on his extensive skull.

'So what do you think, Arkady,' Nikolai Petrovich began saying again, turning to his son, 'shall we get the horses harnessed right away? Or would you like to have a rest?'

'We'll rest at home, dad. Have them harness the horses.'

'Will do,' his father agreed. 'Hey, Peter, d'you hear? Get a move on, lad.'

Peter, who in his capacity as an absolutely perfect gentleman's gentleman, had not approached the young master to kiss his hand but had simply bowed from a distance, once more disappeared beyond the gates.

'I came here in the carriage, but there's a troika of horses for your tarantass as well,' said Nikolai Petrovich in a concerned way while Arkady was having a drink of water from an iron cup brought by the post-mistress and Bazarov lit up a pipe and walked over to the coachman who was unharnessing the horses. 'The trouble is that the carriage is only a two-seater and I don't know how your friend . . .'

'He'll go in the tarantass,' Arkady interrupted under his breath. 'Don't please stand on ceremony with him. He's a splendid chap, doesn't give himself any airs—you'll see.'

Nikolai Petrovich's coachman led out the horses.

'Well, turn around, big-beard!' Bazarov said to the driver.

'Didya hear that, Mityukha,' cried another driver standing there with his hands stuck in rents at the back of his sheepskin coat, 'didya hear what the gentleman called you? You are a big-beard, you know.'

Mityukha simply tilted his hat slightly and flicked the reins off the sweating shaft-horse.

'Look lively, lads, give 'em a hand!' shouted Nikolai Petrovich. 'There'll be something for vodka!'

In a few minutes the horses were harnessed; the father and son were settled in the carriage; Peter had climbed up on to the box; Bazarov had jumped into the tarantass and buried his head in a leather cushion—and both vehicles had set off.

3

'So here you are at last, graduated from university and back home,' said Nikolai Petrovich, patting Arkady on his shoulder and on his knee. 'At last!'

'How's uncle? Is he well?' asked Arkady who, despite the sincere and almost childish joy which filled him, wanted to alter the mood of their conversation from one of excitement to an ordinary and everyday one as soon as possible.

'He's well. He'd wanted to come and meet you, then for some reason he had other ideas.'

'Were you waiting for me long?' asked Arkady.

'About five hours.'

'Dear old dad!'

Arkady turned smartly to his father and kissed him loudly on the cheek. Nikolai Petrovich chuckled softly.

'What a fine horse I've got ready for you,' he began. 'You'll see. And your room's been given new wallpaper.'

'Will there be a room for Bazarov?'

'We'll find one for him.'

'Be nice to him, dad, please. I can't tell you how much I treasure his friendship.'

'Have you got to know him quite recently?'

'Quite recently.'

'Somehow I don't remember seeing him the last winter I was with you. What's he do?'

'His chief subject is natural science. But he knows all sorts of things. Next year he hopes to qualify as a doctor.'

'Ah, I see, he's in the medical faculty,' remarked Nikolai Petrovich and fell silent for a moment. 'Peter,' he added and stretched out his hand, 'those aren't our peasants, are they?'

Peter glanced in the direction his master was pointing. Several carts harnessed with unruly horses were bowling along a narrow sidetrack. Each cart contained at least one, most two peasants in unfastened jackets.

'They are, sir,' Peter declared.

'Where are they off to? To the town?'

'I suppose they're on their way to town. To the inn,' he added contemptuously and inclined slightly towards the coachman as if he were soliciting his opinion. But the latter did not move at all. He was a man of the old school who didn't share the latest ideas.

'I've had a lot of bother with the peasants this year,' Nikolai Petrovich went on, turning to his son. 'They're not paying their rent. What can you do about it?'

'But are you pleased with your hired labourers?'

'Yes,' said Nikolai Petrovich through his teeth. 'The trouble is they're being stirred up. And, well, there's no real effort put into their work. They don't know how to treat the equipment. Still, they did the ploughing well. It'll all work out in the end. Does the running of the estate interest you now?'

'You've got no shade, that's the pity,' remarked Arkady without answering the question.

'I've had a large awning put up over the balcony on the north side,' said Nikolai Petrovich. 'Now we can have dinner outside.'

'It'll be a bit like being on holiday—still, that's nonsense. How marvellous the air is here! What a wonderful scent it's got! It really does seem to me that nowhere in the world smells as good as here! And the sky here . . .'

Arkady suddenly stopped, threw an oblique glance backwards and fell silent.

'Of course,' remarked Nikolai Petrovich, 'you were born here, so that everything here must seem special to you . . .'

'Well, dad, it doesn't matter where a man's born.'

'Still . . .'

'No, it simply doesn't matter.'

Nikolai looked sideways at his son and the carriage travelled approximately a quarter of a mile before their conversation was resumed.

'I can't remember whether I wrote and told you', Nikolai Petrovich began, 'that your former nanny, Egorovna, had died.'

'Really? Poor old lady! Is Prokofich still alive?'

'Yes, he's alive and not changed at all. He grumbles away as much as ever. Generally you won't find any great changes at Marino.'

'Is your bailiff still the same one?'

'That's one thing I have changed—the bailiff. I decided not to keep by me any longer any of the freed former houseservants, or at least not to give them any jobs involving responsibility.' (Arkady deliberately directed his eyes towards Peter.) '*Il est libre, en effet*' muttered Nikolai Petrovich under his breath, 'but he's just a valet. Now my bailiff's a chap from the town—he seems businesslike. I've assigned him 250 roubles a year. Besides,' Nikolai Petrovich added, wiping his forehead and eyebrows with his hand, which was always a sign with him of inner turmoil, 'I said just now you wouldn't find any changes at Marino. That's not quite right. I consider it my duty to warn you, although . . .'

He checked himself a moment and then continued in French:

'A stern moralist would find my candour out of place, but, firstly, I can't hide things and, secondly, you know that I've always had particular principles about the relationship between a father and a son. However, you are of course quite within your rights to condemn me. At my age . . . In short, the, er, the girl you've probably already heard about . . .'

'Fenechka?' asked Arkady blithely.

Nikolai Petrovich went red.

'Please, not so loud . . . Well, yes . . . She's now living with me. I've brought her into the house . . . there were a couple of small rooms going spare. However, all that can be changed.'

'But, dad, why?'

'Your friend will be staying with us . . . it'll be awkward . . .'

'So far as Bazarov is concerned, please don't worry. He's above all that.'

'Well, I mean, there's you as well,' said Nikolai Petrovich. 'The trouble is that the little domestic quarters are in a bad way.'

'Really, dad,' Arkady pointed out, 'it's as if you were apologizing. You ought to be ashamed.'

'Of course I ought to be ashamed,' Nikolai Petrovich responded, growing even redder.

'Please, dad, enough of that, enough!'

Arkady smiled warmly. He's got nothing to apologize about! he thought to himself, and a feeling of indulgent fondness for his kind and soft-hearted father, mixed with a sense of secret superiority, filled his heart to the brim.

'Please, not another word,' he repeated, delighting despite everything in a sense of his personal maturity and freedom.

Nikolai Petrovich glanced at him from beneath the fingers of the hand which he was continuing to use to wipe his forehead, and he felt a sharp pain in his heart. But he blamed himself for that.

'Look, we've reached our land already,' he said after a long silence.

'Isn't that our woodland up ahead?' asked Arkady.

'Yes, it's ours. Except I've sold it. They'll be cutting it down for timber this year.'

'Why did you sell it?'

'I needed the money. In any case, that land's going to the peasants.'

'Who don't pay you any rent?'

'That's up to them, but they will have to pay eventually.'

'I'm sorry about the woodland,' Arkady remarked and began surveying the scene around him.

The places through which they were travelling could hardly be called picturesque. Fields and still more fields stretched right away to the horizon, slightly ascending or descending. Here and there could be seen small woodlands and, covered in sparse, low-lying shrub, winding gullies, reminiscent of the way they were depicted in the old maps of the time of Catherine the Great.* Small streams with hollowed-out banks came in sight, and the tiniest mill-ponds with frail dams, and little villages with low peasant huts under dark roofs, often with half their thatch gone, and small threshing barns all tilted to one side with walls made out of woven brushwood and gaping openings beside dilapidated hay-barns, and churches, either of brick from which the stucco had fallen in places, or of wood with crosses all higgledy-piggledy and graveyards gone to rack and ruin. Arkady felt a gathering pressure on his heart. As if deliberately, all the peasants they came across were in ragged clothes and riding clapped-out nags. The roadside willows were like beggars in tatters with torn bark and broken branches. Emaciated, rough-coated, almost bare bones, cows hungrily munched at the grass in ditches. It was as if they'd only just that minute escaped from the clutches of some fearful, deadly claws—and, summoned into being by the miserable sight of these enfeebled cattle, there arose in the midst of the fine spring day the white spectre of endless, joyless winter with its blizzards, frosts and snows . . .

No, thought Arkady, this isn't a rich region, it doesn't strike one as either prosperous or industrious. It can't, just can't stay like this. Reforms are essential. But how to go about them, how to start?

Those were Arkady's thoughts, but while he was thinking them spring began to come into its own. Everything around glinted green and gold, everything softly and expansively waved and shone under the quiet breath of a warm breeze, everything—the trees, the bushes, the grass. Everywhere skylarks poured out their song in unending, resonant streams. Lapwings cried as they circled above the low-lying meadows or ran about silently among the tufts of grass. Rooks wandered about, darkening beautifully among the soft green of the low spring wheat and disappearing in the rye, which was already beginning to whiten, their heads showing here and there among its smoky waves. Arkady gazed and gazed and his thoughts, gradually diminishing, finally vanished completely. He threw his greatcoat from him and looked at his father so happily, so like a small boy, that his father embraced him once again.

'It's not far now,' remarked Nikolai Petrovich. 'We've only got to get over the next rise and the house'll be in sight. You and I'll get on splendidly, Arkady. You'll be able to help me run the estate, if that doesn't bore you. We've got to be close now, got to get to know each other well, don't you agree?'

'Of course,' said Arkady. 'But what a marvellous day it is today!'

'Specially for your return, dear boy! Yes, spring is here in all its brilliance. Besides, I agree with Pushkin. Do you remember in *Evgeny Onegin*:

> How sad to me is your appearance,
> Spring, O Spring, the time of love!
> What—'*

'Arkady!' came Bazarov's shout from the tarantass. 'Let me have a match, I've got nothing to light my pipe with.'

Nikolai Petrovich stopped speaking, while Arkady, who had begun listening to him not without a certain astonishment, but also not unsympathetically, hurriedly reached into his pocket for his silver matchbox and sent it across to Bazarov via Peter.

'Would you like a cigar?' Bazarov shouted once again.

'Hand it over,' answered Arkady.

Peter returned to the carriage and handed over to him along with the matchbox a thick black cigar which Arkady lit up at once, spreading around him such a strong and acrid smell of raw tobacco that Nikolai Petrovich, who had never been a smoker, had to turn away his nose, although he did so unobtrusively in order not to offend his son.

A quarter of an hour later both vehicles came to a stop before the entrance of a new wooden house, painted white, with a red iron roof. This was Marino, known also as New Place or, as the peasants called it, Fieldless Farm.

4

No crowd of servants poured out of the front door to meet them. Only a girl of about twelve appeared and she was followed out of the house by a young lad looking very like Peter, dressed in a jacket of grey livery with white buttons embossed with a coat of arms: he was Pavel Petrovich Kirsanov's servant. In silence he opened the door of the carriage and undid the apron of the tarantass. Nikolai and his son, together with Bazarov, crossed a dark and almost empty hall, beyond the door of which there flitted momentarily the face of a young woman, and entered a drawing-room furnished in the very latest taste.

'Here we are at home,' said Nikolai Petrovich, taking off his cap and shaking his hair. 'The chief thing now is to have something to eat and relax.'

'Food's a real good idea,' remarked Bazarov, stretching himself and dropping on to a divan.

'Yes, yes, let's have some food, let's eat as soon as we can.' For no visible reason Nikolai Petrovich stamped his feet. 'By the way, here's Prokofich.'

A man of about sixty entered, white-haired, thin and dark-complexioned, in a brown frock-coat with brass buttons and a pink cravat at the neck. He gave a grin, approached and kissed Arkady's hand and, bowing to the guest, withdrew to the door and placed his hands behind his back.

'Look at him, Prokofich,' began Nikolai Petrovich, 'he's back with us at last . . . So? How do you find him?'

'Looking well, sir,' declared the old man and grinned again, but at once knitted his bushy eyebrows. 'Will you want the table laid?' he intoned impressively.

'Yes—yes, please. Would you prefer to go to your room to start with, Evgeny Vasilich?'

'No, thank you, there's no need. Simply arrange for my trunk to be taken there—and this thing as well,' he added, removing his tasselled canvas garment.

'Very well. Prokofich, take away the gentleman's greatcoat.' (Prokofich, as if he didn't know what to do with it, took Bazarov's 'thing' in both hands and, lifting it high above his head, went out on tiptoe.) 'And you, Arkady, will go to your room for a moment, will you?'

'Yes, I must go and clean up,' answered Arkady and was on the point of going towards the door but at that moment there entered the drawing-room a man of average height, dressed in a dark English suit, a fashionably low-hanging cravat and patent-leather shoes: it was Pavel Petrovich Kirsanov. To all appearances he was about forty-five. His short-cut grey hair shone with a dark brilliance like new silver. His face, looking peevish but devoid of wrinkles, was unusually regular and pure of line, as if literally carved by a delicate and fluent scalpel, and retained traces of remarkable beauty; particularly striking were the bright, dark, elongated eyes. The entire outward appearance of Arkady's uncle, so elegant and well-bred, preserved a youthfulness of figure and an upward striving, away from the earth, which tends for the greater part to vanish after one's twenties.

Pavel Petrovich removed from his trouser pocket his beautiful hand with its long pink fingernails—a hand which seemed still more beautiful in contrast with the snowy whiteness of his cuff, fastened with a cuff-link containing a solitary large opal—and offered it to his nephew. Having done with the preliminary European 'shake hands'*, he kissed him in the Russian fashion three times, that is to say he brushed his cheeks three times with perfumed whiskers and said:

'Welcome home.'

Nikolai Petrovich presented him to Bazarov. Pavel Petrovich slightly inclined his elegant waist and gave a faint smile, but he didn't offer his hand and even put it back in his pocket.

'I'd already been thinking you wouldn't arrive today,' he began in a pleasant voice, swaying amiably, slightly shrugging his shoulders and displaying fine white teeth. 'Did something happen on the journey?'

'Nothing happened,' Arkady answered, 'we just got a bit delayed. Which is why we're now as hungry as wolves. Chivvy up Prokofich, dad, and I'll be back in a moment.'

'Stop, I'll come with you,' called Bazarov, suddenly tearing himself away from the divan. Both young men went out.

'Who is that person?' asked Pavel Petrovich.

'A friend of Arkady's, a very clever chap, according to him.'

'He'll be staying with us?'

'Yes.'

'That long-haired person?'

'Well, yes.'

Pavel Petrovich drummed his fingers on the table.

'I find that Arkady *s'est dégourdi*,'* he remarked. 'I'm glad that he's back home.'

Over the meal there was little talk. Bazarov in particular said nothing, but ate a great deal. Nikolai Petrovich related various incidents from what he called his 'farmer's' life and talked about the forthcoming governmental measures,* the committees, the deputies, the need to introduce more machinery and so on. Pavel Petrovich walked backwards and forwards across the dining-room (he never had supper), occasionally sipping from a glassful of red wine and even less frequently uttering some remark or exclamation such as 'Ah! Ehe! Hmm!' Arkady contributed a few pieces of St Petersburg news, but he felt a modicum of embarrassment, the kind of embarrassment which usually seizes hold of a young man when he has only just stopped being a boy and has returned to the place where everyone is still accustomed to look upon him as a boy and consider him one. He needlessly strung out his speech, avoided using the word 'dad' and even once substituted the word 'father', pronounced, to be true, through his teeth. With excessive expansiveness he poured himself a much larger glass of wine than he wanted and drank it all down. Prokofich never took his eyes off him and simply chewed his lips. After the meal they all went their separate ways.

'What an oddball of an uncle you've got!' Bazarov told Arkady as he sat in his dressing gown beside his bed and sucked a small pipe. 'Such dandyism in the country, just think! His fingernails, fingernails like that, they could be put on exhibition!'

'Yes, but you don't realize,' Arkady responded, 'he was a lion in his time. One day I'll tell you his story. He was very handsome and turned women's heads.'

'Is that so! It means he can't forget the past. It's a pity there's no one here he can charm. I couldn't take my eyes off him—such an amazing shirt collar, looking as if it was made of stone, and his chin's so exquisitely shaved. Arkady Nikolaich, it's ridiculous, isn't it?'

'Maybe. Honestly, though, he's a good man.'

'An archaic phenomenon! But your father's a splendid chap. He wastes his time reading poetry and he's hardly got any idea about running a farm, but he's a really good type.'

'My father's twenty-two carat!'

'Have you noticed how shy he is?'

Arkady shook his head as if he weren't shy himself.

'Astonishing,' went on Bazarov, 'these olde-worlde romantic types! They'll cultivate their nervous systems to the point of irritability . . . well, all sense of balance is destroyed as well. Anyhow, goodnight! In my room there's an English washbasin but the door won't lock. Still, one's got to encourage that sort of thing—English washbasins, that's progress!'

Bazarov went out and Arkady was overcome by a feeling of happiness. It was lovely to be sleeping in his own home, in his familiar bed, under a quilt which had been worked by loving hands, perhaps the hands of his nanny, those hands that were so tender, kindly and tireless. Arkady recalled Egorovna and sighed and made a wish that she should have her place in the Kingdom of Heaven. He said no prayer for himself.

Both he and Bazarov fell asleep quickly, but other people in the house were a long time awake. His son's return had excited Nikolai Petrovich. He got into bed but did not put out the candle and, supporting his head on his hand, thought long thoughts. His brother sat until well after midnight in his own room in a wide Hambs* armchair, facing a fireplace in which coal glowed feebly. Pavel Petrovich had not undressed but had simply replaced the patent-leather shoes with red heelless Chinese slippers. He held the latest copy of *Galignani's Messenger** in his hands, but he wasn't reading it. He gazed fixedly into the grate where a bluish flame flickered, occasionally guttering into life and then dying down. God knows where his thoughts wandered, but they weren't all concentrated on the past. The expression on his face was intent and sombre, which is never the case when a man is occupied solely by memories. And on a large trunk in a small back room sat a young woman, Fenechka, wearing a light-blue jacket and with a white kerchief thrown over her dark hair, and from time to time she listened attentively or dozed or glanced through the open door, where a child's cot could be seen and there could be heard the even breathing of a sleeping baby.

5

THE next morning Bazarov awoke earlier than everyone else and went out of the house. 'Hey,' he thought, looking round him, 'this quaint little place ain't up to much!' When Nikolai Petrovich had redrawn his boundaries with his peasants, he had been obliged to allocate to his new house about ten or so acres of completely flat and featureless land. He had built a house, outhouses and a farm, laid out a garden and excavated a pond and two wells, but the young saplings hadn't taken well, very little water had accumulated in the pond and the wells yielded water that tasted salty. Only a small arbour of lilacs and acacias had grown up satisfactorily; sometimes that was where they had tea or a meal. In a matter of minutes Bazarov had gone round all the paths in the garden and visited the cattle sheds and stables and come across two small local boys, with whom he'd at once made friends, and set off with them to a small area of marshland about a mile from the house, to look for frogs.

'Wotcher want frogs for, sir?' asked one of the boys.

'It's like this, see,' said Bazarov, who had a special flair for eliciting the trust of the lower orders although he never indulged them and treated them rudely. 'I dissect the frog and have a look at what's going on inside it. Because you and I are just like frogs, 'cept we walk about on legs, I'll be able to find out what's going on inside us as well.'

'Wotcher want to know that for?'

'So as not to make a mistake if you fall ill and I've got to cure you.'

'Is you a docture?'

'Yes.'

'Vaska, didya hear what the man said, he said you and me's like frogs! It's cra*zee*!'

'They're scary, them frogs are,' remarked Vaska, a boy of about seven, with fair hair pale as flax, in a grey smock with a stand-up collar and bare feet.

'Wot's scary 'bout 'em? They don't bite, do they?'

'Well, you philosophers, into the water with you!' said Bazarov.

Meanwhile, Nikolai Petrovich also woke up and went in search of Arkady, whom he found already dressed. Father and son went out on to the terrace under the marquee awning. Beside the railings, on a table, surrounded by large sprays of lilac, the samovar was already bubbling. A little girl appeared, the same one who had met them on their arrival the previous day, and said in a small voice:

'Fedosya Nikolavna is not quite well and can't come. She told me to ask, will you do the tea yourselves or shall we send for Dunyasha?'

'I'll do the pouring myself,' Nikolai Petrovich said hurriedly. 'Arkady, how do you have your tea, with cream or lemon?'

'With cream,' Arkady answered and, after a short silence, inquired: 'Dad?'

Nikolai Petrovich glanced at his son in confusion.

'What?' he asked.

Arkady lowered his eyes.

'Forgive me, dad, if my question seems out of place,' he began, 'but you yourself, with the frankness you showed yesterday, make me want to be frank . . . You won't be annoyed, will you?'

'Go on.'

'You give me the courage to ask you—doesn't Fen . . . is it because I'm here that she's not coming to do the tea?'

Nikolai Petrovich turned away slightly.

'Perhaps,' he said at last, 'it's because she assumes . . . because she's ashamed . . .'

Arkady cast a rapid glance towards his father.

'She's got nothing to be ashamed about. In the first place, you are familiar with my way of thinking.' (It was very pleasant for Arkady to pronounce these words.) 'In the second place, would I ever want to put any constraints on your life and your way of doing things in the very least? Besides, I'm sure you couldn't make a bad choice. If you've permitted her to live with you under the same roof, it means she deserves to. In any case, a son should never be a judge of his father, especially I of such a father as you, who've never in any way put any constraints on my freedom.'

Arkady's voice was unsure when he began speaking. He felt he was being magnanimous, though at the same time he realized he was reading his father a kind of lecture; but the sound of one's own speech always has a strong effect on a person and Arkady pronounced his final words firmly, even with a certain rhetorical effect.

'Thank you, Arkady,' Nikolai Petrovich started saying in a hollow voice, and again his fingers began running over his eyebrows and temples. 'Your assumptions are well and truly just. Of course, if this girl hadn't merited . . . It's not a fanciful whim of mine. I'm embarrassed to talk about it with you, but you understand that it was hard for her to come here while you're here, particularly on the first day after your arrival.'

'In that case, I'll go to her!' exclaimed Arkady with a new access of magnanimous feeling and jumped up from his chair. 'I'll make it clear to her that she's no need to be ashamed in my presence.'

Nikolai Petrovich also got to his feet.

'Arkady,' he began, 'please don't . . . how's it going to be . . . there . . . I haven't given you any idea . . .'

But Arkady wasn't listening to him any more and ran from the terrace. Nikolai Petrovich followed him with his eyes and dropped back into his chair in confusion. His heart was beating rapidly. It would have been hard to say at that instant whether he imagined the unavoidable strangeness of the future relations between him and his son, whether he was aware that Arkady would have shown him even greater respect if he'd never touched on the subject at all or whether he was blaming himself for his own weakness—all such feelings were inside him but in the form of sensations and therefore unclear. His face remained red and his heartbeat fast.

There was a sound of hurrying footsteps and Arkady came on to the terrace.

'Father, we've met!' he cried with a look of rather fond and good-natured triumph on his face. 'Fedosya Nikolaevna is really not quite well today and will be coming a little later. But why didn't you tell me I had a baby brother? I'd have kissed him last night just as I've kissed him now.'

Nikolai Petrovich wanted to say something, wanted to rise and open his arms in an embrace . . . Arkady flung himself at once on his neck.

'What's this? Embracing again?' resounded the voice of Pavel Petrovich behind them.

Father and son were delighted at his appearance at that moment, because there are touching situations from which one is always glad to escape as soon as possible.

'Are you surprised?' asked Nikolai Petrovich happily. 'I've been waiting for Arkady to return here for such ages. Since yesterday I've not had a chance to see enough of him.'

'I'm not at all surprised,' remarked Pavel Petrovich. 'I'm not even against embracing him myself.'

Arkady went up to his uncle and again felt the touch of his perfumed whiskers. Pavel Petrovich sat down at the table. He was wearing a stylish morning suit in the English fashion, his head crowned with a small fez. This fez and a loosely tied cravat suggested the free-and-easy ways of life in the country, but the tight little collar of his shirt—not a white one, true, but multicoloured, as befits morning dress—bit as unmercifully as ever into his well-shaved chin.

'Where is your new friend?' he asked Arkady.

'He's not here. He usually gets up early and goes off somewhere. The chief thing is not to bother about him. He doesn't like standing on ceremony.'

'Yes, I've noticed that.' Pavel Petrovich began, without hurry, to spread butter on bread. 'Will he be staying with us long?'

'It depends. He's dropped in here on his way back to his father.'

'Where does his father live?'

'In our province, about sixty miles from here. He's got a small estate there. He was previously a regimental doctor.'

'Yes, yes, yes, yes . . . I've been all the while asking myself where I've heard the name Bazarov before. Nikolai, do you remember that father's division had a doctor called Bazarov?'

'Yes, it seems there was.'

'Exactly, exactly. So that doctor's his father—hm!' Pavel Petrovich waggled his moustache. 'Well, this gentleman, this Bazarov, is what precisely?'

'What is Bazarov?' Arkady grinned. 'Do you want me, uncle, to tell you precisely what he is?'

'Please be good enough, nephew.'

'He is a nihilist.'

'What?' asked Nikolai Petrovich, while Pavel Petrovich raised his knife in the air with a piece of butter on the end of the blade and remained motionless.

'He is a nihilist,' repeated Arkady.

'A nihilist,' said Nikolai Petrovich. 'That's from the Latin *nihil*, *nothing*, so far as I can judge. Therefore, the word denotes a man who . . . who doesn't recognize anything?'

'Say, rather, who doesn't respect anything,' added Pavel Petrovich and once more busied himself with the butter.

'Who approaches everything from a critical point of view,' remarked Arkady.

'Isn't that the same thing?'

'No, it's not the same thing. A nihilist is a man who doesn't acknowledge any authorities, who doesn't accept a single principle on faith, no matter how much that principle may be surrounded by respect.'

'And that's a good thing, is it?' interjected Pavel Petrovich.

'It depends on who you are, uncle. It's a good thing for one man and a bad thing for another.'

'Is that so! Well, I can see it's not for us. We, men of another age, we suppose that without *principes* . . .' (Pavel Petrovich pronounced the word softly, the French way, while Arkady, by contrast, pronounced it 'principles' with the accent falling hard on the first syllable) '. . . without *principes* accepted, as you put it, on faith we can't take a single step, we can't even breathe. *Vous avez changé tout cela*, so God grant you good health and the rank of general* and we'll all admire you from afar, you gentlemen—what do you call yourselves?'

'Nihilists,' Arkady pronounced clearly.

'Yes. Previously there used to be Hegelians, now there are nihilists. Let's wait and see how you get on in a vacuum, in airless space. Now, please, brother, Nikolai Petrovich, ring the bell, it's time I had my cocoa.'

Nikolai Petrovich rang and shouted: 'Dunyasha!' but instead of Dunyasha it was Fenechka who appeared on the terrace. She was a young woman of about twenty-three, of fair and soft complexion, with dark hair and eyes and bright red, childishly full lips and tender, delicate hands. She wore a neat cotton print dress. A light blue scarf covered her sloping shoulders. She was carrying a large cup of cocoa and, having set it down in front of Pavel Petrovich, blushed scarlet, the hot blood spreading in a crimson wave under the delicate skin of her pretty face. She lowered her eyes and stopped beside the table, leaning slightly on the very tips of her fingers. She appeared chastened at having come and at the same time she showed she felt that she had a right to be there.

Pavel Petrovich frowned sternly and Nikolai Petrovich was covered in embarrassment.

'Hello, Fenechka,' he said through his teeth.

'Hello, sir,' she answered in a quiet but resonant voice and, with a sideways glance at Arkady, who gave her a friendly smile, she quietly left them. She had a slight waddle in her walk, but it suited her.

Silence reigned for several moments on the terrace. Pavel Petrovich sipped at his cocoa and suddenly raised his head.

'Here's our nihilist gentleman coming to pay his respects,' he said under his breath.

And indeed Bazarov was coming through the garden, stepping across the flowerbeds. His linen coat and trousers were spattered with mud and a clinging marsh plant wound its way round the crown of his old round hat. In his right hand he was holding a small bag; the bag had something alive inside it. He came rapidly up to the terrace and, with a nod of the head, said:

'Hello, gentlemen. Forgive me that I'm late for tea, but I'll be back in a moment. I've got to see to these little captives of mine.'

'What've you got there—leeches?' asked Pavel Petrovich.

'No, frogs.'

'Are you going to eat them or breed them?'

'They're for experiments,' Bazarov said indifferently and went into the house.

'He'll start cutting them up,' remarked Pavel Petrovich. 'He doesn't believe in principles, but he believes in frogs.'

Arkady gave his uncle a look of pity and Nikolai Petrovich gave a covert shrug of the shoulder. Pavel Petrovich himself felt he'd made a bad joke and started talking about the estate and the new bailiff who'd come to him to complain the day before that a worker called Foma was 'libauching himself' and had got out of hand. '"He's a right old Aesop," he said among other things. "He's everywhere making himself out to be a no-good, so he'll stay around here a bit and then when something silly happens he'll be off."'

6

BAZAROV returned, sat down at the table and started to gulp down his tea. Both brothers watched him in silence while Arkady looked covertly first at his father, then at his uncle.

'Did you have a long walk?' Nikolai Petrovich asked at last.

'You've got a bit of marshland there, by a grove of aspens. That's where I started up half-a-dozen snipe. You can go and kill them, Arkady.'

'You're not a hunter yourself?'

'No.'

'You personally occupy yourself with physics?' asked Pavel Petrovich in his turn.

'With physics, yes. With the natural sciences in general.'

'They say the Teutons have been very successful recently in that sort of thing.'

'Yes, the Germans are our teachers,' Bazarov answered casually.

Pavel Petrovich had used the word Teutons rather than Germans for the sake of an irony which, however, no one seemed to have noticed.

'You have a pretty high opinion of the Germans, do you?' said Pavel Petrovich with studied courtesy. He was beginning to feel a secret annoyance. Bazarov's completely free-and-easy manner upset his aristocratic nature. This apothecary's son not only didn't know his place, he even responded to questions curtly and unwillingly and there was something vulgar, even rude, in the sound of his voice.

'The experts over there know their stuff.'

'I see. So you no doubt don't have such a flattering opinion of Russian experts?'

'Could be.'

'That's very praiseworthy self-effacement,' declared Pavel Petrovich, straightening his back and throwing back his head. 'But wasn't Arkady Nikolaich telling us only a moment ago that you don't recognize any authorities? That you don't believe in them?'

'And why should I? What should I believe in? They tell me what it's all about, I agree, and that's all there is to it.'

'So the Germans tell you what it's all about?' declared Pavel Petrovich and his face acquired such an impartial, distant look it was as if he'd gone off into some heights beyond the clouds.

'Not all of them,' was the yawning reply from Bazarov, who clearly had no wish to continue the discussion.

Pavel Petrovich glanced at Arkady as if wanting to say to him: Nice and polite, your friend, isn't he?

'So far as I am concerned,' he began again, not without a certain effort, 'sinner that I am, I don't have much sympathy with the Germans. I'm not thinking about the Russian Germans. We all know what sort of bird they are. But I can't even stomach German Germans. The ones in the past were passable. Then they had, well, Schiller, for example, oh, and *Goethe* . . . My brother's particularly keen on him . . . But now they only seem to have a lot of chemists and materialists . . .'

'A good chemist's twenty times more useful than a poet,' said Bazarov.

'Is that so!' murmured Pavel Petrovich and just as if he were on the point of going to sleep raised his eyebrows slightly. 'So you don't recognize art, is that it?'

'The art of making money, or no more haemorrhoids!'* exclaimed Bazarov with a contemptuous grin.

'Really, sir, really! I see you're one for a joke. Shall we suppose that you dismiss everything, in that case? Which means that you believe only in science?'

'I've already told you that I don't believe in anything. And what's this thing called science, science in general? There are sciences as there are trades and vocations. But science in general doesn't exist at all.'

'Very well, sir. As for other ordinances accepted in day-to-day life, you maintain a similar negative attitude, do you?'

'What's this—a cross-examination?' asked Bazarov.

Pavel Petrovich paled slightly Nikolai Petrovich considered it time to intervene in the conversation.

'We'll discuss this subject with you in more detail at a later date, dear Evgeny Vasilich, and we'll hear your views and express our own. For my own part I'm very glad you're concerning yourself with the natural sciences. I've heard that Liebig* has made some remarkable discoveries in regard to field fertilization. You can help me in my agronomical work by giving me some useful advice.'

'I'm at your service, Nikolai Petrovich, but Liebig's got nothing to do with us! First of all you've got to learn the alphabet and then start on books, but we haven't so much as clapped eyes on the letter "A" so far!'

Well, I can see you really are a nihilist! thought Nikolai Petrovich. 'Still, you'll allow me to come running to you when the occasion arises,' he added out loud. 'But now, brother, I suggest it's time for us to be going off to have a talk with our bailiff.'

Pavel Petrovich rose from his chair.

'Yes,' he declared without looking at anyone, 'it's a great misfortune to have spent five years or so in the country far removed from great minds! In a flash you become a perfect fool. You try not to forget what you've been taught and then—just like that!—it turns out everything you've been taught is nonsense and you're told sensible people don't concern themselves with such rubbish any more and that you're, so to speak, old hat. What's to be done! Evidently the young are more intelligent than we are, that's a fact.'

Pavel Petrovich slowly turned on his heels and slowly walked away. Nikolai Petrovich set off after him.

'Is he always like that?' Bazarov asked Arkady cold-bloodedly as soon as the door had closed behind the two brothers.

'Listen, Evgeny, you were too harsh with him,' said Arkady. 'You offended him.'

'As if I'm going to play along with these provincial aristocrats! After all, it's just a matter of their self-esteem, their acting like society lions, their being such dandies! Well, he should've kept up his career in St Petersburg if that's what he likes . . . Anyhow, to hell with him! I found a fairly rare example of the water beetle *Dytiscus marginatus*. Do you know it? I'll show it you.'

'I promised I'd tell you his story . . .' Arkady began.

'The story of the beetle?'

'That's enough, Evgeny! No, my uncle's story. You'll see he's not the sort of man you imagine he is. He deserves pity rather than derision.'

'I don't doubt. But why're you so bothered about him?'

'One ought to be just, Evgeny.'

'Why should that follow?'

'No, listen.'

And Arkady told him his uncle's story. The reader will find it in the next chapter.

7

PAVEL PETROVICH KIRSANOV had been educated to start with at home, like his younger brother Nikolai, and then in the Corps of Pages.* From childhood he had been distinguished by remarkable good looks. In addition, being self-confident, slightly facetious in manner and amusingly sardonic, he couldn't help being liked. He began to appear everywhere in society as soon as he became an officer. He was taken up by many people and he made the most of himself, even playing the fool, even giving himself airs; but in his case this seemed attractive. Women went out of their minds about him, while men described him as foppish and secretly envied him. He lived, as has already been said, in an apartment with his brother, of whom he was sincerely fond although he was quite unlike him. Nikolai Petrovich had a limp and small, pleasant, but rather melancholy features, small dark eyes and soft, sparse hair; he was fond of an inactive life, but also fond of reading while shunning society. Pavel Petrovich never spent a single evening at home, was renowned for his boldness and physical prowess (he had wanted to make gymnastics popular among young socialites of the time) and he had never read more than five or six French books. In his twenty-eighth year he was already a captain and a glittering career awaited him. Suddenly everything changed.

At that time occasional appearances were made in St Petersburg society by a lady who has not been forgotten to this day, Princess R. She had a well-educated and decent but rather silly husband, and no children. She would suddenly go abroad, suddenly return to Russia, and in general led a strange life. She was considered a feather-brained coquette, used to devote herself zestfully to all manner of pleasures, would dance herself off her feet and laugh and joke with young men whom she would receive before dinner in the half-light of her drawing-room, while at night she would cry and pray and find no peace of mind anywhere and frequently spend her time till morning wandering about her room sorrowfully wringing her hands or sitting, all pale and cold, over a psalter. Day would dawn and she would be transformed once again into a society lady and once more she would go out and laugh and chatter and literally hurl herself at whatever might afford her the slightest pleasure. She had an astonishing figure. Her tresses, golden in colour and heavy as gold, fell to below her knees, but no one would have called her a beauty. The only beautiful thing about her face were her eyes and not so much the eyes themselves—they were small and grey—but their look, swift and searching, uncaring to the point of recklessness and meditative to the point of melancholy—in short, enigmatic. Some unusual light shone in her look even when her tongue was babbling the most futile nonsense. She always dressed elegantly.

Pavel Petrovich met her one time at a ball, danced a mazurka with her, during which she did not utter a single sensible word, and fell passionately in love with her. Accustomed to making conquests, he achieved his object in this case as well, but the ease of his victory did not cool his ardour. On the contrary, he became even more desperately and powerfully attracted to this woman, in whom, even when she had given herself irretrievably, there still remained, as it were, something sacred and inaccessible to which no one might penetrate. God knows what it was that found its niche in her soul! It was as if she were in the grip of certain secret forces which were unknown even to her. They played with her as they wished. Her limited intelligence was unable to cope with their caprices. Her whole behaviour comprised a succession of absurdities. The only letters which might have aroused the legitimate suspicions of her husband she wrote to a man who was almost a stranger to her, while her love itself always exuded an air of melancholy, so that she tended never to laugh and joke with her chosen partner and always listened to him and looked at him in bewilderment. Sometimes, for the most part in a flash, this bewilderment would change into cold horror and her face would acquire a wild-eyed, deathly look and she would lock herself in her bedroom and her maidservant would be able to hear, with an ear pressed to the keyhole, her stifled sobbing.

More than once, returning home after seeing her, Kirsanov felt within him that lacerating and bitter annoyance which rises in one's heart after ultimate lack of success. What more do I want? he'd ask himself as his heart still ached for her. He once gave her a present of a ring with a sphinx carved in the stone.

'What's this?' she asked. 'Is it a sphinx?'

'Yes,' he answered, 'and the sphinx is you.'

'Me?' she asked and slowly raised her enigmatic eyes to his. 'Do you know that's very flattering,' she added with a slight grin and her eyes gazed at him as strangely as ever.

It was hard enough for Pavel Petrovich even when Princess R. was in love with him. But when she cooled towards him—and this happened fairly quickly—he almost went out of his mind. He was in an agony of jealousy, never gave her a moment's peace and traipsed around after her everywhere. She grew tired of his obsessive pursuit and went abroad. He retired from the army despite the beseechings of friends and the pleas of his superiors and went after the princess. Four years he spent abroad either chasing after her or deliberately losing sight of her. He grew ashamed of himself and angry at his cowardly behaviour, but none of it helped. Her image, that incomprehensible, almost senseless but enchanting image had become too deeply embedded in his soul. In Baden he succeeded in restoring relations with her; it was as if she'd never been so passionately in love with him . . . but within a month everything was over: the fire of passion had burst into flame for a last time and had finally gone out for good. Sensing the inevitable parting, he at least sought to remain her friend, as if friendship with such a woman would ever be possible . . . She slipped out of Baden on the quiet and since then had constantly avoided Kirsanov.

He returned to Russia and attempted to take up his old life, but he couldn't fit in as he'd done before. Like someone who's taken poison, he couldn't settle. He would still go out and about in society and still retained all the habits of a socialite. He could boast of two or three new conquests, but he no longer expected anything particular either from himself or from others and took up no job of any kind. He aged and went grey; spending his evenings sitting at the club being peevishly bored and indifferently arguing about this and that in bachelor company became a necessity for him—and that's a bad sign, as everyone knows. To marriage, it goes without saying, he gave no thought at all. Ten years or so passed in this fashion, colourlessly, fruitlessly and swiftly, appallingly swiftly. Nowhere does time pass as swiftly as in Russia, though they say that in prison it passes even more quickly. On one occasion, while dining in his club, Pavel Petrovich learned of the death of Princess R. She had died in Paris in a state close to insanity. He rose from his table and walked slowly to and fro through the rooms of the club, stopping as if rooted beside the card players, but he did not return home any earlier than usual. Some while later he received a parcel addressed to him. It contained the ring he had given to the princess. She had cut a cross on the sphinx and given orders that he should be told that the cross was the clue to her enigma.

This event occurred at the beginning of 1848 at the very moment when Nikolai Petrovich, after the death of his wife, was on his way to St Petersburg. Pavel Petrovich had scarcely seen his brother since the latter had settled in the country, because Nikolai Petrovich's marriage had coincided with the very first days of Pavel Petrovich's acquaintanceship with the princess. Returning from abroad, he had gone to his brother's with the intention of staying a couple of months there and sharing in his happiness, but had managed to spend only a single week with him. The difference in the two brothers' circumstances had been too great. By 1848 this difference had lessened: Nikolai Petrovich had lost his wife and Pavel Petrovich had lost his memories and after the death of the princess he had tried to forget all about her. But Nikolai had the enduring consolation of a life well spent and a son who was growing up before his very eyes; Pavel, on the contrary, a solitary bachelor, had entered upon that confused and darkling time of life—a time when regrets look like hopes and hopes like regrets—when youth is over but old age has not yet begun.

This time was more difficult for Pavel Petrovich than for anyone, because having lost his past he had lost everything.

'I don't ask you to come to Marino now,' Nikolai Petrovich told him (he called his estate Marino in memory of his wife), 'because you were bored stiff there when my wife was alive and you'll go crazy there now, I think.'

'I was stupid and frivolous in those days,' answered Pavel Petrovich. 'I've grown much calmer since then, even if I haven't grown any wiser. Now, by contrast, if you will allow me, I'm ready to settle down with you there.'

Instead of answering him, Nikolai Petrovich embraced him. But it wasn't until eighteen months after that conversation that Pavel Petrovich decided to put his intention into effect. However, once he'd settled in the country he didn't leave it at all, even during those winters which Nikolai Petrovich spent in St Petersburg with his son. He took up reading more and more in English and in general

modelled his life on English tastes, saw the neighbours only rarely
and drove out only to attend elections,* where he for the most part
said nothing, only occasionally teasing and frightening old-fashioned
landowners with his liberal witticisms and having nothing whatever
to do with members of the younger generation. Both the former and
the latter considered him stuck-up; both also respected him for his
excellent aristocratic demeanour and the rumours about his conquests; for the fact that he dressed superbly and always stayed in the
best room in the best hotel; for the fact that he usually dined well and
that on one occasion he had dined with Wellington while a guest of
Louis-Philippe;* for the fact that he always carried around with him
a silver toilet-case and a portable bath; for the fact that he always
smelled of some extraordinary and astonishingly 'upper-class' scent;
for the fact that he played whist in a masterly way and always lost;
finally, he was respected as well for his irreproachable honesty.
Ladies found him a charming melancholic, but he had nothing to do
with ladies . . .

'So you see, Evgeny,' said Arkady, finishing his account, 'how
unjustly you've judged my uncle! I won't mention how he's more
than once rescued my father from misfortune and given him all his
money—you probably didn't know that the estate wasn't divided
between them—but he's always ready to help anyone and, besides,
always stands up for the peasants. True, when he talks to them he
always screws up his face and sniffs eau de cologne . . .'

'Oh sure—nerves,' Bazarov interrupted.

'Perhaps, except he's very kind-hearted. And he's far from stupid.
He's given me all sorts of good advice . . . especially . . . especially on
dealing with women.'

'Aha! A bit of his own medicine—we know the sort of thing!'

'Well, to put it briefly,' Arkady went on, 'he's deeply unhappy,
believe you me, and it's wrong to despise him.'

'Who's despising him?' Bazarov retorted. 'But I'll tell you this—a
man who's staked everything on the card of a woman's love and
when that card's beaten gets all embittered and sinks to the point
where he's not fit for anything, he's not a man, not a real man. You
say he's unhappy—well, you ought to know, but the stuff and nonsense still hasn't gone out of him completely. I'm sure he thinks he's
up to scratch because he reads that Galignani thing and once a
month saves a peasant from punishment.'

'Think of his education and the period in which he lived,' Arkady remarked.

'His education?' queried Bazarov. 'Each man's got to educate himself—well, as I do, for instance. As for the period—why've I got to depend on it? It'd be better if it depended on me. No, my friend, that's a lot of sloppy thinking, a lot of nonsense! And what's all this about the mysterious relationships between a man and a woman? We physiologists know all about these relationships. Just you study the anatomy of the eye—where's all this enigmatic look, as you call it, come from? It's all romanticism, nonsense, rubbish, artiness. Let's go and have a look at that beetle.'

And both friends went off to Bazarov's room, in which some kind of medicinal, surgical smell had already established itself along with the smell of cheap tobacco.

8

PAVEL PETROVICH was not present for long at the conversation between his brother and the bailiff, a tall and thin man with the sweet voice of a consumptive and the eye of a rogue who responded to all Nikolai Petrovich's remarks with 'Certainly, sir, everyone knows that, sir' and always attempted to make out that the peasants were drunkards and thieves. The newly introduced system of management squeaked like an ungreased wheel and creaked like furniture thrown together out of raw wood. Nikolai Petrovich did not lose heart but was frequently given to sighs and second thoughts because he sensed that without money it wouldn't work, and practically all his money had been used up. Arkady'd told the truth: more than once Pavel Petrovich had helped his brother; more than once, seeing how he was struggling and racking his brains trying to think of a way out, Pavel Petrovich had slowly gone over to the window and, putting his hands in his pockets, had muttered through his teeth: 'Mais je puis vous donner de l'argent' and had given him the money; but that day he'd had nothing with him and so he'd preferred to leave. The fuss and bother of management bored him. In any case, it always seemed to him that Nikolai Petrovich, despite all his keenness and hard work, didn't deal with things as he should have done, although he couldn't really put his finger on where Nikolai Petrovich went wrong. My brother's not practical enough, is what he told himself; they always get the better of him.

By contrast, Nikolai Petrovich always had a high opinion of Pavel Petrovich's practicality and always sought his advice. 'I'm a softy, weak, always lived in the country,' he would say, 'but you've not lived so much among people for nothing, you know them well. You're eagle-eyed, you are.' In response to these words Pavel Petrovich would simply turn away, but he didn't spoil his brother's illusions.

Leaving Nikolai Petrovich in his study, he walked along the corridor separating the front of the house from the back and, on coming to a rather low door, paused in thought, twisted his moustache and knocked.

'Who's there? Come in!' rang out Fenechka's voice.

'It's me,' said Pavel Petrovich and opened the door.

Fenechka jumped up from the chair, on which she'd been seated with her baby, and, handing him to a girl who immediately carried him out of the room, hurriedly adjusted her kerchief.

'Forgive me for troubling you,' Pavel Petrovich began, not looking at her, 'I simply wanted to ask you—they're going into town today, I think—to see that they get some green tea for me.'

'Yes, sir,' replied Fenechka. 'How much do you want?'

'Half a pound will be enough, I think. Ah, I see you've made some changes here,' he added, casting round a brisk glance which also slipped across Fenechka's face. 'The curtains,' he said, seeing that she didn't understand him.

'Yes, sir, the curtains. Nikolai Petrovich let me have them. They've been up a long time.'

'And I haven't been in your room for a long time. Everything you have here looks very pretty.'

'Thanks to Nikolai Petrovich,' whispered Fenechka.

'Are you better here than where you were before, in the wing?' Pavel Petrovich asked politely, not without a slight smile.

'Of course, better, sir.'

'Who's taken your place there?'

'The laundresses are there now.'

'Ah!'

Pavel Petrovich fell silent. He'll be going now, thought Fenechka, but he didn't go and she stood in front of him as if rooted to the ground, weakly twiddling her fingers.

'Why did you have your baby taken away?' asked Pavel Petrovich at last. 'I love children. Show him to me.'

Fenechka went crimson from confusion and joy. She was frightened of Pavel Petrovich because he scarcely ever spoke to her.

'Dunyasha!' she cried. 'Bring in Mitya!' Fenechka addressed everyone in the house in the formal, second-person plural. 'But no, wait a moment, he'll have to have his little jacket on.'

Fenechka went to the door.

'It doesn't matter,' remarked Pavel Petrovich.

'I won't be a moment,' Fenechka said and went out in a hurry.

Pavel Petrovich remained alone and on this occasion looked around him with particular attention. The small, low-ceilinged room in which he found himself was extremely clean and comfortable. It smelled of the recently varnished floor, of camomile and the lemon scent of melissa. Along the walls stood lyre-backed chairs; they had been bought in Poland by the late General on one of his campaigns. In one corner stood a high cot under a muslin curtain, next to a metal-bound travelling trunk with a curved lid. In the opposite corner a small lamp burned in front of a large dark icon of St Nicholas the worker of miracles; a tiny china egg on a red ribbon fastened to his shining halo hung down over the saint's chest. On the window-sills jars of the previous year's jam, all with meticulously tied tops, were shot through with green light and on their paper tops Fenechka herself had written 'GOSEBERRY' in large letters. Nikolai Petrovich was particularly fond of this jam. From the ceiling, on a long cord, there hung a cage containing a short-tailed siskin; it ceaselessly chirruped and jumped about and the cage ceaselessly rocked and shook and hemp seeds pattered down on to the floor. On the wall between the windows, above a small commode, hung a number of rather poor photographs of Nikolai Petrovich in various poses done by a travelling photographer. In the same place hung a photograph of Fenechka herself which was a complete mess—some kind of eyeless face smiled fixedly in a small dark frame and nothing else could be made out; while above Fenechka General Ermolov* in a Caucasian cloak, frowned threateningly towards distant Caucasian mountains from beneath a silk pincushion which had fallen down over his forehead.

About five minutes passed and a rustling and whispering was heard in the next room. Pavel Petrovich took off the commode a rather greasy book, an odd volume of Masalsky's *Streltsy*,* and turned several of the pages. Then the door opened and Fenechka came in with Mitya in her arms. She had dressed him in a little red shirt with a lace collar, brushed his hair and wiped his face. He breathed hard, stretched and strained his whole body and moved his little arms vigorously, as do all healthy babies, but the fancy little shirt evidently pleased him and a look of contentment pervaded his whole chubby little figure. Fenechka had also put her hair in order and adjusted her kerchief, but she could well have left things as they were—for, in fact, is there anything more attractive in the world than a pretty young mother with a healthy child in her arms?

'What a fine fellow,' said Pavel Petrovich patronizingly and tickled Mitya under his double chin with the tip of the long nail of his index finger. The baby fixed his eyes on the siskin and gurgled.

'This is your uncle,' said Fenechka, bending her face towards him and giving him a slight shake, while Dunyasha quietly set down on the windowsill a lighted perfumed taper, placing a half-kopeck piece under it.

'How old is he now?' asked Pavel Petrovich.

'Six months. He'll soon be seven months, on the eleventh.'

'Won't it be eight, Fedosya Nikolaevna?' suggested Dunyasha not without diffidence.

'No, seven. Eight's not possible!' The baby again gurgled, stared at the travelling trunk and suddenly seized his mother's nose and mouth in his little fist. 'Rascal!' said Fenechka, not moving her face away from his fingers.

'He looks like my brother,' remarked Pavel Petrovich.

Who else could he look like? thought Fenechka.

'Yes,' went on Pavel Petrovich, as if talking to himself, 'there's no doubt about the resemblance.' He glanced closely, almost sadly at Fenechka.

'This is your uncle,' she repeated, in a whisper this time.

'Ah! Pavel! That's where you've got to!' suddenly rang out the voice of Nikolai Petrovich.

Pavel Petrovich turned round hurriedly and frowned. But his brother looked at him so happily, with such gratitude, that he couldn't refrain from smiling in return.

'You have a splendid little boy,' he said and looked at his watch. 'I dropped in here to mention about my tea . . .'

And, assuming an indifferent air, Pavel Petrovich at once left the room.

'He came in here of his own accord, did he?' Nikolai Petrovich asked Fenechka.

'Of his own accord, yes. He just knocked and came in.'

'Well, has Arkady been to see you again?'

'No, he hasn't. Wouldn't it be better if I was in the wing, Nikolai Petrovich?'

'Why's that?'

'I thought it might be better to start with.'

'N . . . no,' stammered Nikolai Petrovich and wiped his forehead. 'It had to be like that earlier . . . Hello, little fellow,' he said with sudden vivacity and, drawing close to the baby, kissed him on the cheek. Then he bent slightly and touched his lips to Fenechka's bare arm which was white as milk against Mitya's little red shirt.

'Nikolai Petrovich! What're you doing?' she muttered and lowered her eyes, then calmly raised them again. The expression in her eyes was charming when she looked up from beneath her brows and grinned softly and slightly foolishly.

Nikolai Petrovich became acquainted with Fenechka as follows. On one occasion about three years previously he had had to spend the night at an inn in a distant country town. He was pleasantly struck by the cleanness of his room and the freshness of the bed linen. Is the landlady a German? was the thought that occurred to him, but the landlady turned out to be Russian, a woman of about fifty, neatly dressed, with a handsome, intelligent face and a stately way of speaking. He struck up a conversation with her over tea and liked her very much. At that time Nikolai Petrovich had only just settled into his new estate and, since he didn't want to staff his place with serfs, was looking for hired labour. The landlady, for her part, complained about the small number of visitors to the town and the difficult time she was having. He proposed that she should come to his place as a housekeeper and she agreed. Her husband had died long before, leaving her the one daughter, Fenechka. A couple of weeks later Arina Savishna (such was the new housekeeper's name) arrived in Marino together with her daughter and settled in a small wing of the house. Nikolai Petrovich's choice turned out to be successful. Arina brought order to the house. About Fenechka, who had then just turned seventeen, no one said a word and scarcely anyone saw her, because she kept to herself, leading a quiet life, and only on Sundays would Nikolai Petrovich glimpse in the parish church, somewhere to one side, the delicate profile of her pale face. So a year passed.

One morning Arina came to him in his study and, after bowing low as usual, asked him whether he could help her daughter, who had a spark from the stove in her eye. Nikolai Petrovich, like all longstanding country residents, engaged in looking after the sick and had even ordered homeopathic remedies to be sent to him. He immediately ordered Arina to bring the patient to him. Learning that the master had summoned her, Fenechka had a fit of nerves but did, however, follow in her mother's wake. Nikolai Petrovich led her to the window and took her head in both hands. After meticulously scrutinizing her reddened and inflamed eye, he prescribed her an eye salve, which he made up on the spot, and, tearing his handkerchief into strips, showed her how to apply it. Fenechka listened to him and then wanted to leave. 'Kiss the master's hand, silly,' Arina told her. Nikolai Petrovich did not give her his hand to kiss and instead, in some confusion, kissed her bent head, on the parting. Fenechka's eye soon got better, but the impression she had made on Nikolai Petrovich did not pass so quickly. He found himself continually thinking of her pure, gentle face raised apprehensively and he felt in the palms of his hands the soft hair, saw the innocent, slightly open lips, below which small, pearly teeth glittered moistly in the sunlight. He began looking at her in church with greater attention and tried to strike up a conversation with her. She at first fought shy of him and on one occasion, towards evening, meeting him on a narrow footpath made through a field of rye, she slipped away into the tall, thick rye, overgrown with wormwood and cornflowers, simply to avoid being seen by him. He glimpsed her head through the golden network of ripe ears of rye from which she was peering out like a small wild animal and he called out fondly to her:

'Hello, Fenechka, I don't bite!'

'Good day, sir,' she whispered, not leaving her hiding place.

Bit by bit she became accustomed to seeing him, but she was still shy of him in his presence when suddenly her mother died of cholera. What was to become of Fenechka? She had inherited from her mother a love of order, practical common sense and a sense of propriety, but she was so young, so alone, and Nikolai Petrovich was himself such a kind man and so modest . . . The rest does not need telling.

'So my brother just dropped in on you?' Nikolai Petrovich asked her again. 'Just knocked and came in?'

'Yes, sir.'

'Well, that's wonderful. Let me give Mitya a treat.'

And Nikolai Petrovich began throwing him almost up to the ceiling, to the great delight of the baby and to the alarm of the mother, who stretched out her hands to his bare little legs each time he flew up in the air.

But Pavel Petrovich returned to his elegant room, hung with fine dark-grey wallpaper and decorated with guns fixed on a colourful Persian rug, with walnut furniture upholstered in dark-green veleteen, a Renaissance-style bookcase in old dark oak, bronze statuettes on a magnificent desk and a fireplace. He flung himself on his sofa, folded his hands behind his head and remained there motionless, gazing almost with despair at the ceiling. Whether it was that he wanted to hide from the very walls themselves what was happening to his face, or for some other reason, he stood up, undid the loops holding the heavy window curtains and once again flung himself down on the sofa.

9

BAZAROV got to know Fenechka on that day as well. He was strolling with Arkady in the garden and explaining to him why some of the saplings, particularly the oaks, hadn't taken.

'More silver poplars ought to have been planted here—and firs, too, and limes, say, so as to increase the loam. Look, the arbour's taken well', he added, 'because it's all acacia and lilac—they're good boys, you know, they don't need looking after. Hey, there's someone in there!'

Fenechka was sitting in the arbour with Dunyasha and Mitya. Bazarov stopped and Arkady nodded at Fenechka as if he were an old acquaintance.

'Who's that?' Bazarov asked him as soon as they'd gone past. 'What a pretty girl!'

'Who are you talking about?'

'It's obvious—only one of them's pretty.'

Arkady, not without some confusion, explained to him in a few words who Fenechka was.

'Aha!' cried Bazarov. 'He's got good taste, your father has, I can see that! I like him, I really do! He's a good chap. Still, I must introduce myself,' he added and went back to the arbour.

'Evgeny!' Arkady called after him in fright. 'Be careful, for God's sake!'

'Don't worry,' said Bazarov, 'we know a thing or two, we do, we're not streetwise for nothing.'

Going up to Fenechka, he took off his cap.

'Permit me to introduce myself,' he began, bowing politely, 'I'm a friend of Arkady Nikolaich and a man of peace.'

Fenechka rose from the bench and looked at him in silence.

'What a wonderful baby!' Bazarov went on. 'Never mind, I've never put the evil eye on anyone yet. Why're his cheeks so red? Is he teething?'

'Yes, sir,' said Fenechka, 'he's got four teeth so far and now his gums are swollen again.'

'Let me see . . . Don't be frightened, I'm a doctor.'

Bazarov picked up the baby who, to both Fenechka's and Dunyasha's surprise, did not show the least resistance or fright.

'I see, I see . . . there's nothing wrong, everything's in order, he'll have good strong teeth. If there's anything wrong, tell me. Are you yourself well?'

'I am, thank God.'

'Thank God, that's best of all. And you?' added Bazarov, turning to Dunyasha.

Dunyasha, an austere young woman in the house and a great giggler elsewhere, simply snorted in reply.

'Well, that's fine. Here's your little soldier back, then.'

Fenechka took the baby back into her arms.

'How good he was with you,' she murmured under her breath.

'Children are always good with me,' Bazarov answered. 'I know the secret.'

'Children sense who really loves them,' Dunyasha remarked.

'That's true,' Fenechka agreed. 'Take Mitya, he won't go to anyone he doesn't know well.'

'Will he come to me?' asked Arkady who, after standing some distance away for a while, now came closer to the arbour.

He tried to attract Mitya's attention, but Mitya threw his head back and started crying, which upset Fenechka a great deal.

'Another time, when he's got used to me,' said Arkady to smoothe matters over, and both friends went on their way.

'What's her name, by the way?' asked Bazarov.

'Fenechka . . . Fedosya,' answered Arkady.

'And her father's name? One's got to know that too.'

'Nikolaevna.'

'*Bene*. I'm glad she's not too shy. Someone else might hold that against her. What's the point of that nonsense? Why should she be shy? She's a mother and she's got a perfect right.'

'Oh, she's got a right,' Arkady remarked, 'but you see it's my father . . .'

'He's got a right, too.'

'Well, no, I don't agree.'

'I see, so another little son and heir doesn't really suit us, is that it?'

'You ought to be ashamed to ascribe to me such an idea!' Arkady retorted fiercely. 'I wasn't considering my father wrong from that point of view. I think he ought to have married her.'

'Aha!' Bazarov exclaimed calmly. 'What a highbrow we have here! You are still ascribing significance to marriage. I hadn't expected that from you.'

The friends went several steps in silence.

'I've had a look at all your father's arrangements,' Bazarov began saying again. 'The cattle are in a poor state and the horses are decrepit. The buildings are also needing repair and the workers look like a crowd of inveterate loafers, while the bailiff's either a fool or a rogue, I can't make out which.'

'You're very harsh today, Evgeny Vasilevich.'

'And the good little peasants'll take your father for everything he's got. You know the saying: "The Russian peasant'll gobble up God."'

'I'm beginning to agree with my uncle,' Arkady remarked. 'You really do have a poor opinion of the Russians.'

'Bullshit! A Russian's only any good if he's got the worst possible opinion of himself. What's important is that twice two is four and all the rest's nonsense.'

'Is nature nonsense too?' asked Arkady, gazing thoughtfully into the far distance of multicoloured fields beautifully and softly illuminated by a low sun.

'Nature's also nonsense in the sense in which you understand it. Nature's not a temple but a workshop, and man's the worker in it.'

The slow, prolonged sounds of a cello being played in the house wafted towards them at that instant. Someone was playing Schubert's *'Erwartung'* with feeling, although with an inexperienced touch, and the sweet melody poured out on the air like honey.

'What's that?' asked Bazarov in astonishment.

'That's father.'

'Your father plays the cello?'

'Yes.'

'How old's your father?'

'Forty-four.'

Bazarov suddenly burst out laughing.

'What're you laughing at?'

'For heaven's sake! A grown man of forty-four, a *pater familias*, living in the provinces and playing the cello!'

Bazarov went on laughing, but Arkady, despite the respect in which he held his teacher, on this occasion did not even smile.

10

A COUPLE of weeks passed. Life in Marino flowed along in its usual way with Arkady enjoying a sybaritic life and Bazarov working. Everyone in the house had grown used to him, his brash manners and his uncomplicated and abrupt remarks. Fenechka, in particular, had become so accustomed to him that on one occasion at night she ordered him to be woken up because Mitya had had an attack of convulsions. He came and, half joking, half yawning as was his way, sat with her for a couple of hours and helped the baby. By contrast, Pavel Petrovich loathed Bazarov with all the strength of his spirit. He considered him arrogant, brazen, cynical and common. He suspected that Bazarov didn't respect him, that he might, indeed, almost hate him—him, Pavel Petrovich! Nikolai Petrovich was wary of the young 'nihilist' and felt doubts about the beneficial effect of his influence on Arkady, but he listened to him gladly and gladly attended his physics and chemistry experiments. Bazarov had brought with him a microscope and devoted hours on end to using it. The servants were also attracted to him, although he used to make fun of them. Still, they felt he was one of them, not one of the gentry. Dunyasha would gladly giggle at him and give him sidelong, significant looks as she ran past him all aflutter like a little quail. Peter, an extremely self-regarding and silly man, his brow eternally furrowed by strain, one whose sole accomplishments were that he could look unctuous, read haltingly and give his frock-coat a frequent brushing—even he smirked and brightened up whenever Bazarov deigned to look at him. The small peasant boys ran after the 'docture' like little dogs. Only the old man Prokofich didn't like him, used to serve him at table with a gloomy expression, called him a 'fleecer' and 'freeloader' and swore blind that Bazarov with his sideburns looked just like a pig stuck in a thicket. Prokofich in his own way was just as much of an aristocrat as Pavel Petrovich.

The first days of June began, the best time of year. The weather was settled and beautiful. True, there was once again a distant threat of cholera, but the local inhabitants had already grown used to its visitations. Bazarov would rise very early and walk a couple or so miles, not for the sake of walking—he couldn't stand walking for its own sake—but to collect grasses and insects. Sometimes he took Arkady with him. On their return trips they would usually have an argument and Arkady would usually be defeated despite the fact that he talked more than his companion.

Once they were delayed in returning for some reason. Nikolai Petrovich went out to meet them in the garden and, on drawing level with the arbour, suddenly heard the rapid footsteps and voices of both young men. They were walking on the other side of the arbour and could not see him.

'You don't know my father sufficiently well,' Arkady was saying.

Nikolai Petrovich took cover.

'Your father's a good chap,' said Bazarov, 'but he's out of date, he's sung his swansong.'

Nikolai Petrovich pricked up his ears. Arkady apparently made no reply to this.

The 'out-of-date' man stood stockstill for a couple of minutes and slowly made his way home.

'A couple of days ago I saw him reading Pushkin,' Bazarov was saying meanwhile. 'Please tell him that's no good at all. He's not a child any longer and it's time he gave up that childish nonsense. Fancy being a romantic at the present day! Give him something worthwhile to read.'

'What should I give him?' asked Arkady.

'Well, I think Büchner's *Stoff und Kraft** to start with.'

'I think so, too,' remarked Arkady approvingly. '*Stoff und Kraft* is written in a popular style.'

'You and I, you see,' Nikolai Petrovich said to his brother after dinner as he sat in his study, 'have become out of date, we've sung our swansong. What of it? Perhaps Bazarov's right. But I confess I find one thing hurtful. I'd hoped just at this time to be close friends with Arkady and it turns out I've fallen behind and he's gone on ahead and so we can't understand each other.'

'Why's he gone ahead? And why's he so different from us?' exclaimed Pavel Petrovich impatiently. 'It's everything this signor, this nihilist's been stuffing into his head. I hate this smart-aleck doctor. In my opinion he's just a charlatan. I'm sure that, despite all his frogs, he doesn't know all that much about physics.'

'No, brother, you mustn't say that. Bazarov's clever and knowledgeable.'

'And abominably cocky,' Pavel Petrovich interrupted again.

'Yes,' remarked Nikolai Petrovich, 'he's cocky. But apparently you can't have one without the other. Only there's one thing I can't understand. I thought I was doing everything I could to keep up with the times—fixing things up for the peasants and setting up a farm—so much so that I'm being branded a "red" throughout the province, and I read and study and generally speaking try to keep abreast of contemporary demands, but they're saying I've sung my swansong. And you know, brother, I'm beginning myself to think I have.'

'Why's that?'

'This is why. Today I was sitting and reading Pushkin ... I remember I'd picked up "The Gypsies"* ... Suddenly Arkady comes up to me and silently, with such a look of fond compassion on his face, quietly, as if I were a child, takes away my book and puts in front of me another one, a German book . . . and then he smiles and goes away and takes the Pushkin with him.'

'What on earth! What book did he give you?'

'This one.'

And Nikolai Petrovich took out of the back pocket of his frock-coat the well-known work by Büchner in its ninth edition.

Pavel Petrovich turned it this way and that in his hands.

'Hmm!' he grunted. 'Arkady Nikolaevich is mindful of your education. Well, have you tried reading it?'

'I have.'

'So?'

'Either I'm stupid or it's all nonsense. It must be that I'm stupid.'

'You haven't forgotten your German, have you?' asked Pavel Petrovich.

'I understand German.'

Pavel Petrovich again turned the book over in his hands and glanced at his brother from under his brows. Neither spoke.

'By the way,' Nikolai Petrovich began, evidently wanting to change the subject, 'I've had a letter from Kolyazin.'

'From Matthew Ilich?'

'From him. He's arrived in our local town to make an inspection of the province. He now carries a lot of clout and writes me saying he'd like to see us, since we're relatives, and inviting me and you and Arkady to go to town.'

'You're going?' asked Pavel Petrovich.

'No. Are you?'

'No. I'm not. Lot of good going forty miles or so just to eat some fancy jelly. Mathieu wants to show off for our benefit, damn him! He'll have enough incense of flattery wafted in his direction from the province at large without having ours as well. And what self-importance—his highness a privy councillor, indeed! If I'd gone on with my career, gone slogging along in that stupid way, I'd have been an adjutant-general by now. In any case, you and I are out of date.'

'Yes, brother, the time's come to order our caskets and fold our hands across our breasts,' remarked Nikolai Petrovich with a sigh.

'Well, I'm not giving in all that quickly,' his brother declared. 'We've still got a battle to fight with that doctor fellow, I feel it in my bones.'

The battle occurred that very day at tea-time. Pavel Petrovich came into the drawing-room spoiling for a fight, both irritable and determined. He simply needed a pretext for attacking his enemy, but the pretext was a long time in coming. Bazarov generally spoke little in the presence of 'the li'l ole Kirsanovs' (that's what he called both brothers) and that afternoon he felt out of spirits and drank cup after cup of tea in silence. Pavel Petrovich was burning with impatience. Finally he got what he wanted. The conversation turned to one of the local landowners.

'Rubbish, just an aristo,' remarked of him callously Bazarov, who had come across him in St Petersburg.

'Permit me to ask you', Pavel Petrovich began, his lips quivering, 'whether, according to your ideas, the words "rubbish" and "aristo-crat" mean one and the same thing?'

'I said "just an aristo",' said Bazarov, lazily taking sips of tea.

'Exactly, sir. But I suggest that you are of the same opinion about aristocrats as you are about those who are "just aristos". I consider it my duty to inform you that I do not share that opinion. I am bold enough to say that everyone knows me as a liberal and one who loves progress. But it is precisely for that reason I respect those who are real aristocrats. You should recall, my dear sir,' (at these words Bazarov raised his eyes to Pavel Petrovich) 'you should recall, my dear sir,' he repeated acidly, 'the English aristocrats. They do not retreat one iota from their rights, and for that reason they respect the rights of others. They demand fulfilment of the obligations owing to them and for that reason they themselves fulfil *their* obligations. The aristocracy has given freedom to England and supports it.'

'We've heard that old, old stuff many times,' Bazarov retorted. 'What d'you want to prove by it?'

'*Ectually* I want to prove, my dear sir,' (whenever he grew angry Pavel Petrovich deliberately said 'ectually' and 'ectual', although he knew only too well that they were incorrect. This quaint habit was a hangover from the Alexandrine epoch.* Dandies in those days, on the rare occasions when they spoke Russian, used the terms 'ectually' and 'ectual' as much as to say that 'We, native-born Russians though we are, are at the same time such grandees we're allowed to break school rules!'), '*ectually* I wanted to prove that without a sense of personal dignity, without having a sense of respect for oneself—and in an aristocrat these feelings are highly developed—there can be no firm foundation for the social . . . *bien public*, for the social edifice. Individual personality, my dear sir—that's the chief thing. The human personality must be strong as a rock, because everything is built on it. I know full well, for example, that you are pleased to find my habits amusing, the way I dress, even my neatness, but all this flows from my feeling of self-respect, from my sense of duty, sir, yes, sir, of duty. I live in the country, in the back of beyond, but I do not let myself go, I respect the human person in myself.'

'Permit me to say, Pavel Petrovich,' said Bazarov, 'here you are full of respect for yourself and sitting with your arms folded. What good's that for the *bien public*? You'd be better off not respecting yourself and doing something.'

Pavel Petrovich went pale.

'That's a completely different question. I don't have to explain to you now why I am sitting with my arms folded, as you are pleased to express it. I simply want to say that aristocratism is a principle, and without principles only immoral or empty-headed people can live in our time. I was saying this to Arkady on the day after he arrived and I say it to you now. Isn't that so, Nikolai?'

Nikolai Petrovich nodded.

'Aristocratism, liberalism, progress, principles,' Bazarov had already started saying, 'just think what a lot of foreign . . . and useless words! A Russian wouldn't need them if you gave them to him!'

'What does he need then, in your opinion? To listen to you we're literally no part of humanity, outlaws from it. For heaven's sake, the logic of history demands . . .'

'What do we want that logic for? We can get along without it.'

'How so?'

'It's obvious. You, I trust, don't need logic to put a piece of bread in your mouth when you're hungry. All these abstract terms don't mean a thing to us!'

Pavel Petrovich made a frantic gesture.

'After this I don't understand you. You are insulting the Russian people. How is it possible not to recognize principles and rules! On the strength of what are you acting?'

'I already told you, uncle, that we don't recognize any authorities,' Arkady broke in.

'We are acting on the strength of what we consider useful,' said Bazarov. 'At the present time condemnation is more useful than anything else, so we condemn.'

'Everything?'

'Everything.'

'What?—not only art and poetry but . . . It's terrible to think what else . . .'

'Everything,' Bazarov repeated with inexpressible calmness.

Pavel Petrovich stared at him. He hadn't anticipated this, but Arkady had even gone red with pleasure.

'However, permit me to say this,' Nikolai Petrovich started saying. 'You're condemning everything or, to be more precise, you're pulling everything down, but surely you've got to build something as well.'

'That's not for us to do. First we've got to clear the ground.'

'The contemporary state of the peasantry demands this,' added Arkady self-importantly. 'We must fulfil these needs, we don't have the right to give in to satisfying our personal egoism.'

This last phrase clearly displeased Bazarov. It smacked of philosophizing, that is to say of romanticism, since Bazarov was also given to calling philosophy romanticism, but he didn't consider it necessary to correct his young disciple.

'No, no!' exclaimed Pavel Petrovich with sudden fervour. 'I do not wish to believe that you gentlemen really know the Russian people, that you are spokesmen for their needs and their aspirations! No, the Russian people are not the way you imagine them. They honour tradition as sacred, they are patriarchal, they cannot live without faith . . .'

'I do not dispute that,' Bazarov interrupted. 'I am even prepared to agree that *in that* you are right.'

'So, if I'm right . . .'

'It still doesn't prove anything.'

'Precisely, it doesn't prove anything,' repeated Arkady with the certainty of an experienced chess player who has foreseen an apparently dangerous move by his opponent and is therefore not in the least put out by it.

'Why doesn't it prove anything?' muttered an astonished Pavel Petrovich. 'It means you are going against your own people, doesn't it?'

'What if it does?' exclaimed Bazarov. 'The people believe that when it thunders it's the prophet Elijah driving his chariot through the sky. So what? Must I agree with them? Okay, so they're Russian, but aren't I Russian too?'

'No, you're not Russian after what you've just said! I cannot recognize you as a Russian.'

'My grandfather ploughed the land,' Bazarov responded with haughty arrogance. 'Ask any one of your peasants which of us he recognizes as a fellow Russian—you or me. You don't even know how to talk to them.'

'While you talk to them and despise them at the same time.'

'So what, if they deserve to be despised! You are critical of the direction I take, but whoever told you that it's occurred in me by chance, that it isn't summoned into being by the same national spirit in whose name you are speaking so fiercely?'

'Oh, really! So we're much in need of nihilists!'

'Whether they're needed or not is not for us to decide. After all, you don't consider yourself useless.'

'Gentlemen, gentlemen, please don't get personal!' cried Nikolai Petrovich and rose to his feet.

Pavel Petrovich smiled and, placing a hand on his brother's shoulder, made him sit down again.

'Don't worry,' he said. 'I won't forget myself, precisely on account of that sense of personal dignity which has been made such fun of by Mister . . . Mister doctor. Permit me to ask,' he went on, turning again to Bazarov, 'you may perhaps think your doctrine is new, eh? You are wrong in imagining that. The materialism which you preach has been in fashion more than once and has always turned out to be insupportable . . .'

'Another foreign word!' interrupted Bazarov. He was beginning to lose his temper and his face had acquired a coppery and ugly colour. 'In the first place, we don't preach anything, it's not what we're used to . . .'

'What do you do, then?'

'This is what we do. Previously, in the recent past, we used to speak about how our officials took bribes, that we've got no roads, no commerce, no proper judiciary . . .'

'Well, yes, yes, you're critics of society—that's what I think they're called. I'm in agreement with many of your criticisms, but . . .'

'And then we realized that to chatter and simply go on chattering all the time about our running sores wasn't worth the effort and led only to being banal and doctrinaire. We saw that even the clever ones amongst us, the so-called leading figures in society and the social critics, as they're called, were no bloody good and we were busy talking a lot of nonsense, fussing about with this and that kind of art and unconscious creativity and parliamentarianism and a legal profession and devil knows what, when the real business of life was about one's daily bread, when the grossest superstition was stifling us, when all our joint-stock companies were collapsing simply because there weren't enough honest people, when even the liberation of the serfs, which the government's been so busy with, will scarcely do us any good because our peasants'll be glad to steal from each other simply in order to drink themselves silly down the local pub.'

'I see,' interrupted Pavel Petrovich, 'I see. Meaning you're convinced of all this and have decided for yourselves not to do anything serious about anything.'

'And we've decided not to do anything about anything,' Bazarov repeated sombrely.

He had suddenly grown annoyed with himself for having talked so much in front of this lordly gentleman.

'And just swear at everything?'

'And swear at everything.'

'And that's called nihilism?'

'And that's called nihilism,' Bazarov repeated, this time with particular cockiness.

Pavel Petrovich made a slight face.

'So that's it!' he declared in a strangely calm voice. 'Nihilism's got to come to the aid of all the wrongs in the world and you, you're our saviours and heroes. But why in that case do you abuse others, like those so-called social critics? Don't you chatter on just as much as the rest?'

'We're guilty of most things but not of that,' Bazarov spat out through his teeth.

'Is that so? Are you taking action, then? Are you preparing to act?'

Bazarov did not answer. Pavel Petrovich literally shook with rage, but at once took control of himself.

'Hmm! To take action, to smash things . . .' he went on. 'But how can you smash something without even knowing why you're doing it?'

'We smash things because we're a force,' remarked Arkady.

Pavel Petrovich looked at his nephew and smiled faintly.

'Yes, a force literally doesn't take account of anything,' declared Arkady and sat up straight.

'Oh, you wretch!' yelled Pavel Petrovich. He was positively in no condition to restrain himself any longer. 'If only you'd give a moment's thought to *what* it is in Russia you're supporting with your banal maxim! No, this could try the patience of an angel! Force! There's force in the wild Kalmuck and the Mongol—so what's that to us? Civilization is what's dear to us—yes, indeed, my good sir. Its fruits are dear to us. And don't you tell me that its fruits are worth nothing at all. The meanest dauber, *un barbouilleur*, a chap playing a piano for five copecks an evening—they're all more useful than you are, because they are representatives of civilization and not of brute Mongol force! You imagine you are leaders of society, but all you want to do is live in Kalmuck huts! Force! Just you remember finally, you men of force, that there're only four and a half of you but there are millions of others who won't allow you to trample underfoot their most sacred convictions, who'll stamp you out once and for all!'

'Even if they do stamp us out once and for all, that's the way we're going,' said Bazarov ''Cept you needn't be too sure. There aren't as few of us as you imagine.'

'What? Are you seriously thinking of handling, of dealing with the whole people?'

'From a penny candle, you know, Moscow burned down,' answered Bazarov.

'I see, I see. At first almost satanic arrogance, and after that taking the mickey. So that's how young people are being entertained, that's what the inexperienced hearts of little boys are being subjected to! Take a look, there's one of them sitting beside you, after all he practically worships you . . . Go on, look at him!' (Arkady turned away and frowned.) 'This infection has already spread far and wide. I've been told that in Rome our artists won't so much as set foot in the Vatican. They consider Raphael scarcely better than an idiot because he's one of the so-called authorities, but they're themselves feeble and untalented to the point of crudity and their imaginations can't rise above "A Girl at the Fountain"* no matter what happens! And the girl's usually painted appallingly badly. In your opinion they're fine chaps, eh?'

'In my opinion' retorted Bazarov 'Raphael isn't worth a copper penny and they're no better than he is.'

'Bravo! Bravo! Listen to that, Arkady . . . That's how young people of today should express themselves! It's unthinkable that they shouldn't follow you! Previously young people had been expected to learn. Because they didn't want to appear to be ignoramuses, they worked hard willy-nilly. But now all they have to say is: Everything in the world's nonsense! and that's that. Young people are delighted. The fact is that previously they were simply dunces and now they've suddenly become nihilists.'

'That's it, then, you've been let down by your vaunted sense of personal dignity,' Bazarov remarked phlegmatically, while Arkady fumed and his eyes flashed. 'Our argument has gone too far. It seems better to end it. I'll only be ready to agree with you', he added, getting to his feet, 'when you can mention to me at least one institution in our contemporary life, whether family or social, which should not arouse complete and merciless condemnation.'

'I can mention millions of such institutions!' exclaimed Pavel Petrovich. 'Millions! Take the peasant commune, for example.'

A chilly grin contorted Bazarov's lips.

'Well, when it comes to the peasant commune', he said, 'you'd be better off talking to your dear brother. He's likely now to have practical experience of what the peasant commune is, its joint responsibility, sobriety and suchlike things.'

'The family, then, the family as it exists among our peasants!' cried Pavel Petrovich.

'You'd be better off, I suggest, not looking at that question in detail. I suppose you've heard of the practice of fathers-in-law having it off with their daughters-in-law, haven't you? Listen to me, Pavel Petrovich, give yourself a couple of days to think about it and you'll still be unlikely to come up with anything. Look carefully at all the layers of our society and think well about each one and meanwhile Arkady and I'll . . .'

'Take the mickey out of everything,' Pavel Petrovich chimed in.

'No, go off and dissect frogs. Come on, Arkady! Goodbye, gentlemen!'

Both friends went off. The brothers remained on their own and at first did no more than give each other looks.

'There you have it,' Pavel Petrovich began eventually, 'that's present-day youth for you! There they are—our inheritors!'

'Inheritors!' repeated Nikolai Petrovich with a melancholy sigh. During the course of the dispute he had literally felt himself sitting on hot coals and covertly shot anxious glances from time to time at Arkady. 'Do you know what I've remembered, brother? Once I had a quarrel with our late mother. She was shouting and didn't want to hear a thing from me . . . I finally told her: You can't understand me. I said: We belong to different generations. She was frightfully offended. But I thought, what can I do about it? It's a bitter pill but it's got to be swallowed. So now our turn's come, and our successors can say to us: You're not of our generation, you've got to swallow your pill.'

'You're far too magnanimous and modest,' responded Pavel Petrovich. 'By contrast, I'm certain that you and I are a great deal more in the right than these chaps, although we may express ourselves, perhaps, in a slightly old-fashioned language, *vieilli*, and don't possess their brazen self-conceit . . . Oh, how high-and-mighty the young people are nowadays! You ask one of them which wine he would like, red or white, and he answers in a deep voice: "I have a habit of preferring red", and with such a self-important expression on his face it's as if the whole universe has its eye on him at that moment . . .'

'Would you like some more tea?' asked Fenechka, poking her head into the doorway. She had been reluctant to come into the drawing-room so long as she had heard voices raised in argument.

'No, you can order them to take away the samovar,' answered Nikolai Petrovich and rose to meet her. Pavel Petrovich said '*bonsoir*' to him curtly and went off to his own room.

11

HALF an hour later Nikolai Petrovich went into the garden to his favourite arbour. He was full of gloomy thoughts. For the first time he was clearly aware of the rift between him and his son. He had a foreboding that with each passing day it would become greater and greater. It turned out that he'd spent days on end one winter in St Petersburg reading away at the latest works of fiction all for nothing; all for nothing had he listened to the conversations of the young men; all for nothing had he been overjoyed when he'd succeeded in inserting his own word into their bubbling talk. My brother says we're in the right, he thought, and, setting aside any matter of self-esteem, I myself feel that they're further from the truth than we are, and yet at the same time I feel they've got something we haven't, some sort of superiority over us . . . Is it youth? No, it's not youth by itself. Doesn't their superiority lie in the fact that there are fewer traces of class-consciousness and privilege in them than in us?

Nikolai Petrovich bent his head and drew his hand across his face.

But to reject poetry? he reflected again. To have no sympathy for art and nature?

And he looked around, as if wishing to understand how anyone could fail to appreciate nature. Evening was already approaching; the sun was hidden behind a small aspen wood which lay a quarter of a mile from the garden: the shadow from it stretched endlessly across the motionless fields. A peasant was riding at a trot on a white horse along the dark narrow lane beside the wood. He could be seen quite clearly, even to the patch on his shoulder, despite the fact that he was in the shadow. The legs of his little horse flashed briskly and distinctly by. The sun's rays shot through the wood from the far side and, penetrating into its depths, suffused the trunks of the aspen with such a warm light that they acquired the appearance of pines, while their foliage became almost pine-blue, and above the wood there rose the coldly pale blue sky, slightly flushed by the sunset. Swallows flew high above; the wind had quite died; late bees buzzed lazily and sleepily in the lilac blossoms; midges swarmed in a column above a solitary, outstretched branch.

My God, how marvellous! thought Nikolai Petrovich and favourite verses sprang to his lips. Then he remembered Arkady and *Stoff und Kraft* and fell quiet, but remained sitting where he was and continued to be consumed by the sad and joyous play of his solitary thoughts. He had a fondness for day-dreaming. Life in the country had developed this propensity in him. No matter how long ago it was he'd day-dreamed as he waited for his son at the post-station, since then a change had already occurred and new relations, then as yet unclear, had already defined themselves—and how! He called to mind his dead wife, not as he had known her over so many years, not as a good, homely housewife, but as a young girl with a slender waist, an innocently searching look and a tightly plaited braid hanging over her childishly thin neck. He remembered her as he had seen her for the first time. He had been a student then. He had met her on the stairs of the apartment where he lived and, accidentally bumping into her, turned round, tried to apologize and could only mutter; 'Pardon, monsieur,' while she bowed her head, grinned and suddenly took fright, it seemed, and ran off, but on the turn of the stairs rapidly glanced up at him, assumed a serious expression and went red. And afterwards came the first shy visits, the half-words, the half-smiles and then the bewilderment and the sadness and the passion and, at last, the breathless joy . . . Where had all that gone? She became his wife and he had been happy as few are on this earth. But, he thought, those sweet, first moments, why shouldn't one live with them in undying, eternal life?

He did not attempt to clarify his thought to himself, but he felt that he wanted to hold firm to that blessed time in his life with something stronger than memory. He wanted to re-experience the closeness of his Masha, to feel the warmth of her body and her breath, and he even imagined that she was there standing over him . . .

'Nikolai Petrovich,' Fenechka's voice resounded close to him, 'where are you?'

He shuddered. There was neither pain, nor bad conscience in this reaction. He never allowed even the possibility of any comparison between his wife and Fenechka, but he regretted that she'd decided to look for him. Her voice instantly reminded him of his grey hair, his age and the present time . . . The enchanted world into which he'd already entered, which had just risen from the misty waves of the past, quivered suddenly and vanished.

'I'm here,' he answered, 'I'm coming. You be off.'

Here they are, those traces of class-consciousness and privilege! he thought in a flash. Without saying a word Fenechka peered into the arbour at him and then disappeared and he noted with astonishment that night had already fallen since he'd begun day-dreaming. Everything had grown dark and silent around him, and Fenechka's face had seemed to glide before his eyes, so pale and small. He rose to his feet and made an effort to return to the house, but his heart, grown so tender with reminiscence, could not be calmed in his breast and he started walking slowly up and down the garden, either looking thoughtfully down at his feet or raising his eyes to the sky where stars already swarmed and winked at each other. He walked to and fro a great deal, almost to the point of exhaustion, but the sense of peril within him, a kind of searching, indefinite, melancholy disquiet, would not lessen. Oh, how Bazarov would have laughed at him if he'd known what was going on inside him at that moment! Arkady himself would have condemned him. Tears, pointless tears were forming in his eyes, in the eyes of a man of forty-four, an agronomist and landowner—and that was a hundred times worse than playing the cello!

Nikolai Petrovich continued his walking and remained unable to go back into the house, that peaceful and comfortable nest of his which gazed so welcomingly at him with its lighted windows. He simply did not have the strength to abandon the darkness and the garden and the feeling of fresh air on the face and that sense of peril within him . . .

At a turn in the path he met Pavel Petrovich.

'What's happened to you?' he asked Nikolai Petrovich. 'You're white as a ghost. You must be unwell. Why don't you go to bed?'

In a few words Nikolai Petrovich explained to him what his feelings were and left him. Pavel Petrovich walked to the end of the garden, and also grew thoughtful and also raised his eyes to the sky. But his beautiful dark eyes reflected nothing apart from the light of the stars. He was no born romantic and his dandified, dry and passionate, Frenchified, misanthropic nature did not know how to day-dream.

'D'you know something?' Bazarov said to Arkady that very night. 'I've had an excellent thought. Your father was talking today about an invitation he'd received from your distinguished relative. Your father won't be going, so let's you and I go off to town. After all, your relative's asked you as well. You can see what weather we're having and we'll go on a jaunt, take a look at the town. We'll knock about there for five or six days and that'll be that! *Basta!*'

'And then you'll be coming back here?'

'No, I'll have to go off and see my father. You know he lives about twenty miles from town. I haven't seen him for a long time, nor my mother. I'll have to do right by the old folks. They're nice people, particularly my father—he's really amusing. I'm their only child.'

'Will you spend long with them?'

'I don't know. I'll probably be bored stiff.'

'Will you come back to us on your return journey?'

'I don't know . . . I'll see. Well, shall we? Shall we set off?'

'Okay,' said Arkady reluctantly.

In his heart he was overjoyed at his friend's suggestion, but he considered he was obliged to hide his feelings. He wasn't a nihilist for nothing!

The next day he drove off with Bazarov to the town. The younger members of the household at Marino were sad at their departure—Dunyasha even burst into tears—but the older ones breathed a bit easier.

12

THE town to which our friends had set off was presided over by a governor drawn from among 'the young ones', both a progressive and a despot, as is habitually the case in Russia. In the course of his first year of office he had succeeded in quarrelling not only with the marshal of nobility, a retired captain of the guards, a horse-dealer and *bon viveur*, but also with his own officials. The strife arising on this account had assumed such dimensions in the end that the ministry in St Petersburg had found it necessary to send a trustworthy person to sort out the matter on the spot. The choice had fallen on Matthew Ilich Kolyazin, the son of the Kolyazin under whose guardianship both the Kirsanov brothers had been at one time. He was also one of 'the young ones', that is to say he had just passed forty, but he had set his sights on becoming a statesman and consequently wore a star on each side of his chest. One of them, true, was foreign and far from the best. Like the governor whom he had come to pass judgement on, he was also considered a progressive and, being already a big wheel of sorts, bore no resemblance to the majority of such big wheels. He had the highest opinion of himself. His vanity knew no limits, but he conducted himself simply, gave everyone looks of approval, listened condescendingly and had such a hearty laugh that he could even pass at first for 'a really excellent fellow'. However, on important matters he knew how to 'kick up the dust', as they say. On such occasions he would say: 'What one needs is energy—*l'énergie est la première qualité d'un homme d'état.*' But for all that he usually behaved like a complete idiot and any official with any experience could usually get the better of him.

Matthew Ilich had a way of expressing himself with great admiration for Guizot* and strove to impress upon everyone that he did not belong in the ranks of routine and out-of-date bureaucrats, that he did not leave unnoticed any important manifestation of social life ... Such forms of expression were quite familiar to him. He even followed—true, with a certain majestic casualness—the developments in contemporary literature much as a grown man, encountering a procession of small boys on the street, might sometimes join it himself. In all essentials Matthew Ilich did not differ greatly from those stately politicos of the Alexandrine epoch who, in readiness for an evening at Madame Svechina's, then living in St Petersburg, used to read a page of Condillac* in the morning, except that the way he did things was different, more contemporary. He was skilled in dancing attendance at court, a great schemer and that was all; he had no head for business, no mind of his own, but knew how to look after his own interests. No one could curb him in that—and that's the main thing.

Matthew Ilich received Arkady with the heartiness of an enlightened man of state—let's say even with playfulness. However, he was surprised when he learned that his relatives had remained in the country. 'Your father was always a bit odd,' he remarked, tossing up and down the tassels of his magnificent velvet dressing-gown, and suddenly, turning to a young official in a uniform jacket that had been buttoned up in the most scrupulously loyal fashion, exclaimed with a look of concern: 'What?' The young man, whose lips had become stuck together through prolonged disuse, got to his feet and looked at his superior in bewilderment. But, having browbeaten his inferior, Matthew Ilich then ignored him. Generally speaking, our senior officials love browbeating their inferiors. The means they employ to achieve this are pretty varied. The following means, which is often used, 'is quite a favorite',* as the English say. A high official suddenly stops understanding the simplest words and pretends to be deaf. He will ask, for example:

'What day is it?'

He is informed with the utmost courtesy: 'Today is Friday, your ex-x-x-cellency.'

'Eh? What? What's that? What're you saying?' the high official repeats tensely.

'Today is Friday, your ex-x-cellency.'

'Whazzat? What? What's Friday? Which Friday?'

'Friday, your ex-x . . . x-x-x . . . x-x-x . . . xcellency, a day in the week.'

'We-e-ell, we-e-ell, so you've decided to teach me a thing or two, have you?'

Matthew Ilich was after all a high official, even though he was considered a liberal.

'I advise you, my friend, to pay a visit to the governor,' he told

Arkady. 'I'm not advising you to do this, you understand, because I uphold any old-fashioned ideas about the need to pay one's respects to the authorities but simply because the governor's a good chap. In any case, you'd probably like to get to know local people—you're not an unsociable bear, I hope? And he's giving a large ball the day after tomorrow.'

'Will you be going to the ball?' Arkady asked.

'He's giving it in my honour,' said Matthew Ilich almost with regret. 'Do you dance?'

'I do dance, only badly.'

'That's too bad. There are good-looking ladies here and a young man should be ashamed not to dance. Again I say this not on the strength of any old-fashioned ideas. I don't for a moment suppose that a man's mind should be found only in his feet, but Byronism is ludicrous, *il a fait son temps.*'

'It wasn't, uncle, out of Byronism that I . . .'

'I'll introduce you to the local young ladies and I'll take you under my wing,' Matthew Ilich interrupted and gave a self-satisfied laugh. 'That'll hot things up for you, eh?'

A servant entered and announced the arrival of the president of the revenue department, an old man with honeydew eyes and wrinkled lips who was excessively fond of nature, particularly on a summer day when, in his own words, 'every little bee takes its own little fee from every flower so wee . . .'. Arkady left.

He found Bazarov in the inn where they were staying and spent a long time persuading him to go and see the governor. 'There's no escaping!' said Bazarov at last. 'In for a penny, in for a pound! We've come to gawp at the landowning class, so let's go and gawp at them!' The governor received the young men politely but did not offer them seats and did not sit down himself. He constantly fussed over things and rushed about. He had a habit of putting on a tight uniform jacket in the morning and an extremely tight cravat and never finishing a meal or a drink and spending all his time on administration. They called him Bourdaloue in the province, hinting not at the well-known French Jesuit* but at the 'loo' in his name. He invited Kirsanov and Bazarov to his ball and a couple of minutes later invited them a second time, already mistaking them for brothers and calling them Kaisarov.

As they returned home from the governor's there suddenly leapt from a passing droshky a small man in a Slavophile jacket* who, with a shout of 'Evgeny Vasilich!', flung himself at Bazarov.

'Ah, it's Herr Sitnikov,' said Bazarov, still striding along the sidewalk. 'What brings you here?'

'Imagine, pure chance!' the latter answered and, turning to the droshky, waved his hand almost half-a-dozen times and shouted: 'Follow behind us, follow! My father has business here,' he went on, skipping over the ditch next to the sidewalk, 'so he asked me to, well ... I learned today you'd arrived and I've already been to where you're staying . . .' (In fact, the friends, on returning to their room, had found there a dog-eared visiting card with the name Sitnikov on one side in French and on the other in elaborate Slavonic script.) 'I hope you're not coming from the governor, are you?'

'Don't hope any such thing, we've just come from him.'

'Ah! In that case I'll go and see him too . . . Evgeny Vasilich, introduce me to your . . . your . . .'

'Sitnikov, Kirsanov,' Bazarov barked out without stopping.

'I'm most delighted,' Sitnikov began, sidling up fawningly and hurriedly pulling off his far too elegant gloves, 'I've heard so much . . . I'm an old friend of Evgeny Vasilich's and I can even say I'm a pupil of his. It's to him I owe the fact that I've been reborn . . .'

Arkady glanced at this Bazarov pupil. An anxious and vacant expression could be discerned in the small, quite pleasant features of his well-scrubbed face. His little eyes, which looked as if they'd literally been hammered into place, gazed out fixedly and uncomfortably, and he also had a way of laughing uncomfortably with an abrupt, wooden laugh.

'Believe me,' he went on, 'the first time Evgeny Vasilich said in my presence that there was no need to believe in authorities, I felt such excitement it was literally as if I'd had a vision! There, I thought, at last I've found a real man! In any case, Evgeny Vasilich, you absolutely must go and see one of the local ladies who is completely capable of understanding you and for whom a visit from you would be a real treat. I think you may have heard of her.'

'Who's that?' asked Bazarov unwillingly.

'Kukshina, Eudoxie, Evdoksiya Kukshina. She's a remarkable character, *emancipée* in the true sense of the word, a socially advanced woman. You know what? Let's all go and see her right now. She lives only a couple of steps away. We'll have lunch there. You've not had lunch, have you?'

'Not yet.'

'Well, that's splendid. She's split up with her husband, you understand, and doesn't depend on anyone.'

'Is she good-looking?' broke in Bazarov.

'N . . . no, I can't say she is.'

'Then for what diabolical reason are you taking us there?'

'Oh, you're a real joker, you are! She'll offer us champagne.'

'So that's it! You're a practical man, one can tell that at once. By the way, your father's still tax-farming,* is he?'

'Still tax-farming,' said Sitnikov in a hurry and gave vent to a shrill laugh. 'So what's it to be? Is it on?'

'I don't know, I'm sure.'

'You wanted to gawp at the locals, so let's go,' Arkady remarked under his breath.

'And you, Mister Kirsanov, what about you?' chimed in Sitnikov. 'We can't go without you.'

'How can we all suddenly descend on her?'

'That doesn't matter. Kukshina's a marvel.'

'There'll be a bottle of champagne, will there?' asked Bazarov.

'Three!' cried Sitnikov. 'I can vouch for that!'

'With what?'

'My own head.'

'It'd be better with your dad's money-bags. Still, let's be off.'

13

THE small upper-class house in the Moscow manner in which Avdotya Nikitishna (or Eudoxie) Kukshina lived was situated in one of the recently burnt-out streets of the town. It is a well-known fact that our provincial towns burn down once every five years. At the front door, above a crooked visiting card, the bell-handle could be seen and in the porch the new arrivals were met by someone who was part-servant, part-lady companion wearing a cap—a sure sign of the progressive proclivities of the lady of the house. Sitnikov asked if Avdotya Nikitishna was at home.

'Is that you, Victor?' came a shrill voice from a neighbouring room. 'Come in.'

The woman in the cap vanished at once.

'I'm not alone,' said Sitnikov, swiftly divesting himself of his Slavophile jacket beneath which was revealed a cross between a tight-fitting coat and one loose as hopsack, and casting a lively glance at Arkady and Bazarov.

'It doesn't matter,' the voice answered. '*Entrez.*'

The young men went in. The room in which they found themselves was more like a workroom than a sitting-room. Papers, letters and so-called Russian 'fat journals', for the most part uncut, lay about the place on dusty tables and everywhere one could see white discarded cigarette-ends. On a leather divan, in a semi-upright position, was sitting a woman who was still young, fair-haired, slightly dishevelled, in a rather crumpled silk dress, sporting large bracelets on her short little hands and an embroidered lace kerchief on her head. She rose from the divan and, casually tugging round her shoulders a small velvety coat of yellow ermine, announced languidly: 'Hello, Victor,' and shook Sitnikov's hand.

'Bazarov, Kirsanov,' he barked in imitation of Bazarov.

'My pleasure,' replied Kukshina and, fixing on Bazarov her round eyes, between which a small red turned-up nose shone with a slightly orphaned air, added: 'I know you,' and shook his hand as well.

Bazarov frowned. The small and unprepossessing figure of the *emancipée* was not in the least ugly, but the expression on her face had an unpleasant effect on someone looking at her. One felt like asking her: 'What's wrong with you? Are you hungry? Are you bored? Are you shy? What are you all tensed up about?' Like Sitnikov, she was always in a state. She had a way of talking and moving that was both very free and easy and at the same time very inept. She evidently considered herself a good-natured and simple creature, and yet no matter what she did she always gave the impression that she'd done precisely what she'd not wanted to do. As children say, everything with her seemed 'made up', meaning it wasn't simple, wasn't natural.

'Yes, yes, I know you, Bazarov,' she repeated. (She had a habit, common to many provincial and Moscow ladies, of addressing men from the first day of their acquaintance by their surnames.) 'Would you like a cigar?'

'It doesn't matter about cigars,' broke in Sitnikov, who had succeeded in flinging himself into an armchair with one leg stuck up in the air, 'but let's have lunch, we're absolutely famished. And have a bottle of champagne brought up for us.'

'Sybarite!' said Evdoksiya and laughed. (When she laughed, her upper gum was revealed above her teeth.) 'Isn't it true, Bazarov, that he's a sybarite?'

'I enjoy the comforts of life,' said Sitnikov self-importantly. 'That doesn't stop me being a liberal.'

'But it does, it does!' exclaimed Evdoksiya and then, however, gave an order to her maidservant for lunch to be served and the champagne. 'What do you think about it?' she added, turning to Bazarov. 'I'm sure you share my opinion.'

'Well, no,' retorted Bazarov. 'A piece of meat is better than a piece of bread even from a chemical point of view.'

'So you're keen on chemistry? It's my passion. I've even invented a new mastic.'

'A new mastic? You?'

'Yes, me. And do you know why? To make dolls with heads that can't break. You see, I'm practical as well. But it's not all quite ready yet. I've still got to read some of Liebig. By the way, have you read Kislyakov's article about female labour in *Moscow News*?* Please read it. You're interested in the woman question, aren't you? And in schools?* What's your friend keen on? What's his name?'

Mrs Kukshina literally *shed* her questions one after another with excessively feminine casualness, without waiting for answers, in the way that spoilt children talk to their nannies.

'My name is Arkady Nikolaich Kirsanov,' said Arkady, 'and I'm not keen on anything.'

Evdoksiya burst out laughing.

'Oh, isn't that charming! What, aren't you smoking? Victor, I'm annoyed with you, you know.'

'Why?'

'I've heard you've again started saying nice things about George Sand. She's an out-of-date woman and nothing more! You can't compare her with Emerson! She's got no ideas about education or physiology or anything else. I'm sure she's never heard of embryology and in our time how can you get along without it?' (Evdoksiya even spread out her hands.) 'Ah, what an astonishing article Elisevich* has written on the subject! He's a mister of genius!' (Evdoksiya constantly used the word 'mister' instead of 'man'.) 'Bazarov, take a seat beside me on the divan. Perhaps you don't know it, but I'm terribly afraid of you.'

'Why is that, may I inquire?'

'You're a dangerous mister. You're such a critic. Oh, my God, I can't help laughing! I'm sounding just like some female landowner from the steppes! Mind you, I really am a landowner. I manage an estate on my own and, believe it or not, my head man Erofei is an amazing type, just like Cooper's Pathfinder.* There's something absolutely direct about him! I've finally settled down here—an impossible town, don't you think? But that can't be helped!'

'It's just a town,' Bazarov remarked with icy composure.

'They've all got such shallow interests, that's what's so awful! Earlier I used to spend my winters in Moscow . . . but now my one and only, my Monsieur Kukshin, lives there. What's more, Moscow's now—oh, I don't know—it's not what it was. I'm thinking of going abroad. I was on the point of going last year.'

'To Paris, I suppose?' asked Bazarov.

'To Paris and Heidelberg.'

'Why Heidelberg?'

'Good heavens, Bunsen's there!'*

Bazarov found nothing to say to this.

'*Pierre* Sapozhnikov, do you know him?'

'No, I don't.'

'What, you don't know *Pierre* Sapozhnikov! He still spends all his time at Lidiya Khostatova's.'

'I don't know her either.'

'Well, he took it upon himself to be my companion. Thank God, I'm free, I've no children . . . What was that I said: *thank God!* Still, it doesn't matter.'

Evdoksiya rolled a cigarette with her nicotine-stained fingers, ran her tongue along one edge, sucked at it and lit up. A maid came in with a tray.

'Ah, here's lunch! Would you like a bite to eat? Victor, open the bottle, that's your thing!'

'My thing, my thing,' muttered Sitnikov and once more gave vent to his shrill laugh.

'Are there any good-looking women round here?' asked Bazarov on his third glass.

'There are,' answered Evdoksiya, 'but they're all so empty-headed. For instance, *mon amie* Odintsova isn't bad-looking. It's a pity that her reputation's a bit . . . Of course, that wouldn't matter if it weren't that there's no real freedom of viewpoint there, no breadth of view, nothing of that kind. The whole system of education's got to be changed. I've been thinking about this. Our women are very poorly educated.'

'You won't do a thing with them,' broke in Sitnikov. 'They ought to be treated with contempt, and I do treat them with contempt, utterly and completely!' (The opportunity to feel such contempt and express it was a most pleasant sensation for Sitnikov; he was especially persistent in his attacks on women without suspecting that, in a few months' time, he would have to go crawling on all fours in front of his wife simply because she was a high-born Princess Durdoleosova.) 'Not one of them would be able to understand our conversation. Not one of them would be worth us talking about her, serious men that we are!'

'Anyhow they've got no need to understand our conversation,' said Bazarov.

'Who are you talking about?' put in Evdoksiya.

'Good-looking women.'

'I see! So you share Proudhon's* opinion, do you?'

Bazarov straightened up haughtily. 'I don't share anyone's opinions. I have my own.'

'Down with authorities!' shouted Sitnikov, delighted by the chance to express himself sharply in the presence of a man before whom he fawned.

'But Macaulay* himself . . .' Kukshina started saying.

'Down with Macaulay!' thundered Sitnikov. 'Are you standing up for all these silly women?'

'Not for silly women, no, but for the rights of women, which I've vowed to defend to the last drop of my blood.'

'Down with . . .!' But at this point Sitnikov stopped abruptly. 'But I'm not really condemning them,' he announced.

'Yes, I can see you're a Slavophile!'

'No, I'm not a Slavophile, although of course . . .'

'Yes, yes, yes, you're a Slavophile. You're a devotee of the *Domostroi*:* You'd like to have a whip in your hand!'

'A whip's no bad thing,' remarked Bazarov. 'Only we're down to our last drop now . . .'

'Of what?'

'Champagne, dearest Avdotya Nikitishna, champagne—not of your blood.'

'I cannot be indifferent when I hear women being attacked,' went on Evdoksiya. 'It's terrible, terrible! Instead of attacking them, you'd be better off reading Michelet's *De l'amour*.* It's marvellous! Misters, let's talk about love,' added Evdoksiya, languidly letting her hand fall on a crumpled cushion of the divan.

A sudden silence ensued.

'No, there's no point in talking about love,' said Bazarov, 'though you've just mentioned an Odintsova . . . Isn't that what you called her? Who is this lady?'

'A delight! A delight!' squeaked Sitnikov. 'I'll introduce you. Clever, rich and a widow. Unfortunately she's not sufficiently developed yet. She ought to get to know our Evdoksiya better. I drink your health, Eudoxie! Let's clink glasses! "*Et toc, et toc, et tin-tin-tin! Et toc, et toc, et tin-tin-tin!!*"'*

'Victor, you're playing the fool!'

The lunch went on a long time. The first bottle of champagne was followed by another, then a third and even a fourth. Evdoksiya chattered away unceasingly and was aided and abetted by Sitnikov. They spent a great deal of time debating whether marriage was a prejudice or a crime, whether all people were born identical and what precisely individuality was. At last a point was reached when Evdoksiya, red in the face from so much wine and pounding with her flat-cut finger-nails on the keys of an out-of-tune piano, set about singing in a hoarse voice some gypsy songs and then the romance of Seymour Schiff 'When Sunny Granada lies a-dreaming'* and Sitnikov wound a scarf round his head and acted the role of the dying lover at the words:

> 'And may your lips with mine
> Blend in a burning kiss.'

Arkady by this time had had enough. 'Gentlemen, it's just like Bedlam here,' he remarked aloud.

Bazarov, who had only made the odd sarcastic contribution to the conversation, being much keener on the champagne, yawned loudly, stood up and, without saying goodbye to his hostess, walked out of the house along with Arkady. Sitnikov dashed out after them.

'Well, what about her, what about her?' he asked, running fawningly on either side of them to right and left. 'Didn't I tell you? A remarkable personality! We need more women like her! In her own way, she's a highly moral phenomenon.'

'Is that establishment belonging to your *darling* father over there also a highly moral phenomenon?' asked Bazarov, pointing a finger at the tavern they were just passing.

Sitnikov once more went off into shrill laughter. He was very embarrassed by his origins and did not know whether to consider himself flattered or insulted by Bazarov's unexpected reference to his *darling* father.

14

A FEW days later the ball took place at the governor's. Matthew Ilich was a real '*beau* of the ball', the marshal of nobility announcing to one and all that he had come purely out of respect for him, while the governor even during the ball itself, even when he was standing still, continued to 'administrate'. The affability assumed by Matthew Ilich in his behaviour could only be rivalled by the grandness of his manner. He was the soul of politeness to everyone—to some with a hint of aversion, to others with a hint of respect. He was profusely flattering to the ladies '*en vrai chevalier français*' and ceaselessly gave vent to a large, resonant, solitary laugh as befitted a true grandee. He slapped Arkady on the back and loudly proclaimed him 'my young relative', bestowed on Bazarov, decked out in an old-fashioned frock-coat, a distracted yet condescending sidelong glance, together with some vague mumbling of a greeting in which it was only possible to distinguish 'I' and '. . . stremely.' He offered a finger to Sitnikov and gave him a smile after already turning away. Even to Kukshina, who arrived at the ball without a crinoline petticoat and in dirty gloves, but with a bird of paradise in her hair, even to Kukshina he said: '*Enchanté.*' There were crowds of people and no shortage of eligible men for dancing. The civilians preferred to crowd together along the walls, but the military danced conscientiously, especially one of them who had spent six weeks in Paris where he had learned various racy exclamations such as '*Zut*', '*Ah fichtrrre*', '*Pst, pst, mon bibi*' and so on. He pronounced them to perfection, with real Parisian *chic*, and yet at the same time he would say '*si j'aurais*' instead of '*si j'avais*' and use '*absolument*' in the sense of 'certainly' and generally express himself in that Great Russian-French dialect which the French make such fun of when they don't feel the need to assure our brother Russians that they speak their language like angels, '*comme des anges*'.

Arkady danced badly, as we know, and Bazarov didn't dance at all. They both settled themselves in a corner and Sitnikov joined them. His face a picture of contemptuous mockery, delivering himself of poisonous jibes, he darted glances boldly round him and to all appearances seemed to be genuinely enjoying himself. Suddenly his face changed and, turning to Arkady, he announced in some embarrassment: 'Odintsova's arrived.'

Arkady looked round and saw a tall woman in a black dress who had stopped in the doorway of the ballroom. She stunned him by the dignity of her bearing. Her bare arms lay beautifully against her elegant waist and fine sprays of fuchsia drooped beautifully from her brilliant hair on to her sloping shoulders. Her bright eyes shone calmly and intelligently—calmly, it has to be said, and not pensively—from beneath her slightly pronounced white temples and her lips smiled a scarcely discernible smile. Her face shone with a kind of soft and alluring strength.

'Are you acquainted with her?' Arkady asked Sitnikov.

'Closely. Would you like me to introduce you?'

'Please. When the quadrille's over.'

Bazarov also turned his attention to Odintsova.

'What sort of a figure's that?' he said. 'She's not like the other birds.'

Waiting until the end of the quadrille, Sitnikov led Arkady up to Odintsova, but it was scarcely the case that he was closely acquainted with her because he found himself tongue-tied and she gazed at him with a certain astonishment. However, her face acquired a look of pleasure when she heard Arkady's surname. She asked whether he was the son of Nikolai Petrovich.

'I am.'

'I've met your father twice and heard a great deal about him,' she went on. 'I'm very glad to make your acquaintance.'

At that moment some adjutant or other flew up to her and invited her to take part in a quadrille. She agreed.

'Do you dance, then?' Arkady inquired respectfully.

'I do. Why do you think I don't? Or do you feel I'm too old?'

'Forgive me, I didn't mean that . . . In which case allow me to invite you to join me in the mazurka.'

Odintsova gave a condescending smile.

'If you like,' she said and looked at Arkady not so much in a superior way as in the way that married sisters look at very young brothers.

Odintsova was slightly older than Arkady—she was almost twenty-nine—but in her presence he felt just like a schoolboy or a student, as if the difference in their ages was considerably greater.

Matthew Ilich came up to her full of majestic looks and obsequious remarks. Arkady withdrew but continued to watch her, never for a moment taking his eyes off her during the quadrille. She chatted just as freely with her partner as she had with the grandee, calmly making a play of turning her head and eyes and once or twice calmly laughing. Her nose was a little large, as is the case with most Russians, and her complexion was not entirely pure. Despite this Arkady decided that he'd never in his life encountered such a charming woman. He couldn't get the sound of her voice out of his ears and the very folds of her dress, it seemed, hung on her differently from all others, more elegantly and abundantly, and her movements were particularly smooth and, at the same time, natural.

Arkady sensed a certain diffidence in his heart when, at the first sounds of the mazurka, he sat down beside his partner and, ready to start a conversation, did no more than run his hand through his hair and was unable to find a single word to say. But he was not diffident or embarrassed for long. Odintsova's calmness communicated itself to him and a quarter of an hour had scarcely passed before he was talking freely about his father and his uncle and life in St Petersburg and in the country. Odintsova listened to him with polite interest, slightly opening and closing her fan. Their chat was interrupted when others asked her for dances and Sitnikov, besides, asked her twice. Whenever she returned she once more took her seat and picked up her fan, but her bosom gave no sign of breathing faster and Arkady would once more set about chattering, overwhelmed by happiness at being so close to her and talking to her and looking in her eyes and at her beautiful forehead and at the whole of her charming, serious and intelligent face. She herself spoke little, but whatever she said showed a knowledge of life and from several of her remarks Arkady concluded that here was a young woman who had already managed to experience a great deal emotionally and mentally in her life.

'Who were you standing with', she asked him, 'when Mr Sitnikov brought you up to me?'

'Ah, you noticed him, did you?' Arkady asked in his turn. 'He's got a splendid face, hasn't he? He's someone called Bazarov, my friend.'

Arkady proceeded to talk about his friend.

He spoke about him in such detail and with such enthusiasm that

Odintsova turned towards him and looked at him attentively. Meanwhile, the mazurka drew to a close. Arkady felt regret at having to part with his partner—after all, he'd spent such a happy hour or more with her! True, he had constantly felt in the course of this time that she had been condescending to him and that he should have been grateful to her for doing so . . . But young hearts are not disconcerted by feelings of that kind.

The music stopped.

'*Merci*,' said Odintsova, rising. 'You have promised to visit me, so bring along your friend as well. I shall be very interested to see a man who has the boldness not to believe in anything.'

The governor approached Odintsova, announced that supper was served and with a preoccupied face offered her his arm. On the way out she turned in order to smile and nod towards Arkady for the last time. He bowed low, glanced at her (how elegant her waist seemed to him, swathed in a greyish shimmer of black silk!) and, telling himself that at that moment she'd probably forgotten about his existence, felt in his heart a kind of refined humility . . .

'So how did it go?' Bazarov asked Arkady as soon as he'd returned to him in his corner. 'Did you receive satisfaction? One gent was just telling me that that lady was *oy-oy-oy*! but then he seemed a fool. Well, what d'you think, is she really *oy-oy-oy*?'

'I don't quite understand that description,' Arkady answered.

'Really! What an innocent!'

'In that case I don't understand your gentleman friend. Odintsova is very charming, there's no doubt about that, but she is so cool and so sternly self-assured that . . .'

'Still waters—you know what they say!' put in Bazarov. 'You say she's cool. That's what's tasty about her. You like ice-cream, don't you?'

'Perhaps,' said Arkady, 'I can't judge that. She'd like to get to know you and asked me to bring you along when we visit her.'

'I can just imagine what picture you painted of me! Still, you did the right thing. Take me along. Whoever she is, just a provincial lioness or an *emancipée* like Kukshina, she's still got the best shoulders I've seen for a long time.'

Arkady was repelled by Bazarov's cynicism, but, as often happens, he reproached his friend not for what he liked least about him.

'Why don't you want to allow the idea of freedom of thought among women?' he asked under his breath.

'Because, mate, in my view, the only ones among women who think freely are bloody freaks.'

Their conversation ended at that. Both young men left immediately after supper. Kukshina in a nervy, malicious way, but not without diffidence, started laughing at their departure, her self-esteem having been deeply hurt by the fact that neither the one nor the other had paid any attention to her. She stayed on longer than anyone else at the ball and by nearly four in the morning danced a polka-mazurka with Sitnikov in the Parisian fashion. This edifying spectacle concluded the governor's party.

15

'LET'S see what species of mammal this personage belongs to,' Bazarov said to Arkady the next day as he accompanied him up the stairs of the hotel in which Odintsova was staying. 'My nose tells me there's something not quite right here.'

'I'm astonished at you!' cried Arkady. 'How on earth? You, you, Bazarov, maintaining the kind of narrow-minded morality which . . .'

'Oh, don't be silly!' Bazarov casually cut him short. 'Don't you know that in our lingo and for chaps like us "not quite right" means "quite right". It means there's something to be made out of it. Didn't you yourself tell me this morning she made a strange marriage although, in my opinion, to marry a rich old man isn't strange at all, but is, on the contrary, a sensible thing to do. I don't believe the town rumours, but I'd love to think, as our educated governor says, that they had some justice in them.'

Arkady did not respond to this and knocked on the door of her room. A young servant in livery led both friends into a large room which was poorly furnished, as are all rooms in Russian hotels, but filled with flowers. Odintsova herself soon appeared in a simple morning dress. By the light of the spring sunshine she looked even younger. Arkady introduced her to Bazarov and with secret amazement noticed that he appeared a little embarrassed, while Odintsova remained completely calm, as she had been the previous evening. Bazarov was aware that he had been embarrassed and grew annoyed with himself. 'Well, I never! Scared of a woman!' he thought and, lounging in an armchair no worse than Sitnikov, started speaking with exaggerated abandon while Odintsova never for a moment took her crystal-clear eyes off him.

Anna Sergeevna Odintsova was the daughter of Sergei Nikolae-vich Loktev, famous for his looks, his affairs and his gambling who, after leading a boisterous life in St Petersburg and Moscow for some fifteen years, ended by losing everything and was forced to settle in the country where, in any case, he soon died, leaving a tiny sum to his two daughters, the twenty-year-old Anna and the twelve-year-old Katya. Their mother, from an impoverished princely line, had already died in St Petersburg when her husband had been at the height of his powers. Anna's position after the death of her father was very difficult. The brilliant education which she had received in St Petersburg did not fit her for looking after house and home and also did not fit her for a dull country life. She knew absolutely no one in the whole locality and had no one she could turn to. Her father had tried to avoid seeing his neighbours. He had despised them and they had despised him, both in their different ways.

However, she didn't lose her head and at once sent off for her mother's sister, a Princess Avdotya Stepanovna Kh ... ya, a malicious and arrogant old woman who, once settled in her niece's house, grabbed all the best rooms for herself, groused and complained from morning to night and never even took a stroll in the garden without the company of her sole peasant servant, a dour-looking footman in threadbare pea-green livery with sky-blue braid and a tricorn hat. Anna patiently put up with all her aunt's eccentricities, covertly occupied herself with her sister's education and grew reconciled, it seemed, to the idea of wasting away in the depths of the country. But fate had something else in store for her.

She chanced to be noticed by a certain Odintsov, a very wealthy man of forty-six, an odd sort of chap, a hypochondriac, portly, ponderous and sarcastic, but no fool and not a bad man. He fell in love with her and proposed to her. She consented to become his wife and he lived with her for half-a-dozen years and, on his death, left her everything he owned. For a year after his death Anna did not leave the countryside. Then she went abroad with her sister, but only visited Germany, was bored by it and returned to take up residence in her beloved Nikolskoe which was some thirty miles or so from the town. There she had a magnificent, splendidly furnished house and a fine garden with an orangery (the late Odintsov had denied himself nothing). Anna Sergeevna visited the town very rarely, for the most part on business, and never stayed long. She was not liked in the province, a frightful fuss and to-do was made about her marriage to Odintsov, all manner of stories were told about her and it was averred that she used to assist her father in his card-sharping practices and had not gone abroad for nothing, but in order to conceal certain unfortunate consequences ... 'You know what I mean, don't you?' the gossipers would conclude. 'She's been through fire and water,' they would say of her, and a certain well-known local joker usually added: 'And through copper pipes as well.' All these rumours reached her, but she let them pass: she had a character that was independent and resolute enough.

Odintsova sat leaning against the back of her armchair and listened to Bazarov with one hand resting on the other. Contrary to his normal behaviour, he did a good deal of talking and evidently tried to impress his listener, something which surprised Arkady. He couldn't decide whether Bazarov had succeeded. It was hard to tell from Anna Sergeevna's face what her impressions were because her face retained the same friendly, sensitive look all the time and her beautiful eyes glowed with attention, but an attention that was not rebellious. Bazarov's brashness at the beginning of the visit had had an unpleasant effect on her, like a bad smell or a sharp noise, but she understood at once that he'd been embarrassed and this even flattered her. It was only the vulgarly mediocre that repelled her and no one would have accused Bazarov of mediocrity.

Arkady had much to be surprised at that day. He had expected that Bazarov would treat Odintsova as an intelligent woman and talk about his convictions and opinions, because she had expressed a wish to meet a man 'who has the boldness not to believe in anything', but instead Bazarov talked about medicine and homeopathy and botany. It turned out that Odintsova had not been wasting her time in her isolation. She had read several good books and was used to expressing herself in good Russian. She directed the conversation to music but, noticing that Bazarov did not recognize art, gently returned to the subject of botany, although Arkady had been on the point of saying something about the significance of folksong. Odintsova still treated him as a younger brother, as if she valued in him the goodness and straightforwardness of youth and nothing more. The conversation lasted more than three hours, being unhurried, varied and lively.

At last the friends stood up and said goodbye. Anna Sergeevna looked fondly at them, held out to both of them her beautiful white hand and, after a pause for thought, said with an indecisive but friendly smile:

'Gentlemen, if you're not afraid of being bored, come and visit me in Nikolskoe.'

'Delighted, Anna Sergeevna,' cried Arkady, 'I'd consider it a special pleasure . . .'

'And you, Monsieur Bazarov?'

Bazarov did not more than bow, and Arkady was obliged to feel surprise for the last time when he noticed that his friend had gone red.

'Well?' he asked him out on the street, 'are you still of the opinion that she's *oy-oy-oy*?'

'Who the hell knows! You saw how frosty she could be!' retorted Bazarov and added after a moment's silence: 'What a duchess she is, right-royal an' all! She just needs a long train behind her and a crown on her head!'

'Our duchesses don't speak Russian like that,' remarked Arkady.

'She's seen changes, mate. She's had a taste of living like us.'

'Still, she's charming,' said Arkady.

'What a sumptuous body she's got!' Bazarov continued. 'I'd just love to get her into an anatomical theatre.'

'Stop it, for God's sake, Evgeny! You're impossible!'

'All right, calm down, chum. I've told you—she's the tops. We've got to go and see her.'

'When?'

'Let's go the day after tomorrow. There's not a lot to do here! Drink champagne with Kukshina? Listen to that relative of yours, that liberal grandee? Let's be done with all this the day after tomorrow. Besides, my father's little place isn't far from there. Nikolskoe's on the *** highway, isn't it?'

'Yes.'

'*Optime.* Don't let's hang about. Only fools hang about—and clever dicks. I tell you, what a sumptuous body!'

A couple of days later both friends were off on their way to Nikolskoe. The day was bright and not too hot, and the fat little post-horses trotted along in unison, slightly wagging their twisted and plaited tails. Arkady gazed at the road and smiled, unsure why.

'Congratulate me,' Bazarov suddenly exclaimed, 'today's June 22nd, the day of my guardian angel. Let's see how he looks after me. They're expecting me home today,' he added, lowering his voice. 'Well, they'll just have to wait, it's no big deal!'

16

THE estate where Anna Sergeevna lived stood on a bare sloping hill a short distance from a yellow stone church with a green roof, white pillars and a fresco painting over the main entrance depicting 'The Resurrection of Christ' in a so-called Italian manner. Particularly remarkable for his rounded contours was a swarthy warrior in a spiked helmet spreadeagled in the foreground. Behind the church a long village stretched out in two row of houses with chimneys visible here and there among the straw roofs. The manor house was built in the same style as the church, a style known among us as belonging to the age of Alexander I. The house was also painted yellow and had a green roof, white pillars and a pediment bearing a coat of arms. The provincial architect had built both buildings with the approval of the late Odintsov who couldn't tolerate any futile and self-serving novelties, as he called them. The dark trees of an ancient garden hemmed in the house on both sides and an avenue of neatly trimmed firs led up to the entrance.

Our friends were met in the hall by two hefty liveried footmen, one of whom instantly ran off to inform the head butler. The head butler, a stout man in a black frock-coat, appeared at once and led the guests up a carpeted staircase into a specially prepared room containing two beds and all the necessary toilet requisites. Tidiness evidently reigned in the house: everything was clean and everywhere there was a pleasant smell, just as in the waiting-rooms of government ministries.

'Anna Sergeevna requests you to come and see her in half-an-hour,' the head butler announced. 'Have you any orders for me in the meantime?'

'No orders, O most respected one,' Bazarov replied. 'Except you might be good enough to bring a tot of vodka.'

'Certainly, sir,' said the head butler not without some bewilderment and went out with a scraping of shoes.

'What high style!' remarked Bazarov. 'Isn't that what you call it? She's a duchess right enough.'

'Some duchess', retorted Arkady, 'to have invited at a glance such powerful aristocrats as you and me to stay with her!'

'Particularly me, a future medic and son of a medic as well as being grandson of a sexton. You know I'm a grandson of a sexton, don't you?'

'Like Speransky,'* Bazarov added after a short pause and curling his lip. 'Still, she's one for creature comforts, milady is, isn't she? Don't you think we ought to put on white tie and tails?'

Arkady simply responded with a shrug, but even he felt some embarrassment.

Half an hour later Bazarov and Arkady went down to the drawing-room. It was a high, spacious room furnished fairly luxuriously but without particular taste. Heavy and expensive furniture stood in the usual pompous fashion up against walls hung with gold-patterned brown wallpaper. The late Odintsov had ordered it from Moscow through his friend and agent, a wine merchant. Above a centrally placed divan hung a portrait of a fleshy, blond man who appeared to look down on the guests with hostility. 'That must be *him*,' Bazarov whispered to Arkady and, wrinkling his nose, added: 'Should we do a bunk?' But at that moment their hostess entered. She was wearing a dress of light barège material and her hair, brushed back smoothly behind the ears, endowed her clear, fresh features with a girlish look.

'Thank you so much for keeping your word,' she began. 'Be my guests: you'll not find it all that bad here. I'll introduce you to my sister, she plays the piano well. That won't mean much to you, Monsieur Bazarov, but you, Monsieur Kirsanov, are fond of music, I think. Apart from my sister, I have an old aunt living with me and a neighbour sometimes visits to play cards. That's the sum total of our society. Now let's sit down.'

Odintsova uttered the whole of this little speech in a particularly precise way as if she had learned it by heart. Then she turned to Arkady. It transpired that her mother had known Arkady's mother and she had even been let in on the secret of her love for Nikolai Petrovich. Arkady started talking very warmly about his late mother, while Bazarov busied himself with looking at some albums 'What a tame thing I've become,' he thought.

A beautiful borzoi hound wearing a blue collar ran into the room with a pattering of feet on the floor and behind it came a girl of about eighteen, dark-haired and swarthy, with a rather round but pleasant face and small dark eyes. She was carrying a basket full of flowers.

'Ah, here's my Katya,' said Odintsova, nodding in her direction.

Katya slightly curtsied, took a seat next to her sister and proceeded to sort out the flowers. The borzoi hound, whose name was Fifi, approached both of the guests in turn, wagging her tail, and pushed her cold nose into their hands.

'Did you pick all these yourself?' Odintsova asked.

'I did,' Katya answered.

'Will auntie be joining us for tea?'

'She will.'

When Katya spoke, she smiled very charmingly, shyly and openly, and raised her eyes upwards in an engagingly severe way. Everything about her was still girlishly fresh and untouched—her voice and the light down of her complexion and her rosy hands with the whitish markings on her palms and the ever so slight narrowness of her shoulders. She had a way of constantly blushing and quickly catching her breath.

Odintsova turned to Bazarov.

'You are studying those little pictures out of politeness, Evgeny Vasilich,' she began. 'It doesn't interest you. Join us here and let's have a talk about something.'

Bazarov drew closer.

'What would you like us to talk about, ma'am?' he asked.

'Whatever you like. I warn you, I'm frightfully argumentative.'

'You are?'

'Yes, me. That seems to surprise you. Why?'

'Because, so far as I can judge, you have a calm and cool temperament, but for argument one needs passion.'

'How can you have managed to get to know me so quickly? In the first place, I'm impatient and like having my own way—you'd better ask Katya. In the second place, I get carried away very easily.'

Bazarov looked at Anna Sergeevna.

'Maybe you know best. Okay, so you want an argument, let's have one. I was looking at views of the Meissner Hochland in your album and you said that it couldn't be interesting to me. You said that because you assume that I have no artistic sense—and I really don't have any. But those views could be of interest to me from a geological point of view, from the point of view of the formation of mountains, for instance.'

'Forgive me, but as a geologist you would far rather have a book, a specialist work, and not a picture.'

'A picture shows me at a glance what would take up all of ten pages in a book.'

Anna Sergeevna was silent for a moment.

'So you really haven't got a drop of artistic sense?' she remarked, leaning on the table and by this very movement bringing her face closer to Bazarov's. 'How on earth can you get on without it?'

'Why is it necessary, may I ask?'

'If only to know how to understand people and study them.'

Bazarov laughed.

'In the first place, experience of life exists for that purpose. And in the second place, I assure you it's not worth studying people separately. All people are alike in their bodies as in their souls. Each one of us has a brain, a spleen and lungs made in the same way and the so-called moral qualities are the same in all of us. The minor variations don't mean anything. One human example is sufficient to judge all the rest. People are like trees in a forest. No botanist is going to be concerned with each individual birch tree.'

Katya, who had been slowly sorting through the flowers, raised her eyes in bewilderment to look at Bazarov and, encountering his rapid and negligent glance, blushed right up to her ears. Anna Sergeevna gave a shake of the head.

'Like trees in a forest,' she repeated. 'So, according to you, there's no difference between a silly man and a sensible one, between a good one and a bad one?'

'Yes, there is, just as there's a difference between a sick man and a healthy one. The lungs of a consumptive are not in the same state as yours or mine, though they're made the same. We know approximately what causes physical ailments, while moral diseases derive from poor education, from all the rubbish with which people's heads are filled from birth onwards—in short, from the shocking state of society. Reform society and there'll be no more disease.'

Bazarov said all this with a look on his face which gave the impression he'd been thinking to himself all the time. Believe me or not, it's all the same to me! He slowly ran his long fingers through his sideburns and his eyes darted about.

'So you suppose,' said Anna Sergeevna, 'that when society is reformed there'll be no more stupid or bad people?'

'At least in a properly organized society it'll be completely irrelevant whether someone is stupid or clever, good or bad.'

'Yes, I see—we'll all have the same kind of spleen.'

'Precisely so, your ladyship.'

Odintsova turned to Arkady.

'What is your opinion, Arkady Nikolaich?'

'I agree with Evgeny,' he answered.

Katya gave him a glance from beneath her brows.

'You astonish me, gentlemen,' said Odintsova, 'but we'll discuss this with you another time. Now I hear auntie coming to have tea with us. We must spare her ears.'

Anna Sergeevna's aunt, Princess Kh . . . ya, a tiny, wizened woman with a face like a tightly clenched little fist and wicked, fixed eyes under a grey wig, came into the room and with scarcely a bow towards the guests sat down in a wide, velvet-covered armchair in which no one, apart from herself, had a right to sit. Katya placed a stool under her feet. The old woman did not thank her and didn't even glance at her, but simply fidgeted with her arms beneath a yellow shawl which covered practically all her diminutive body. The Princess loved yellow and there were bright yellow ribbons on her cap.

'How did you sleep, auntie?' Odintsova asked, raising her voice.

'That dog's here again,' the old woman complained in response and, noting that Fifi took a couple of indecisive steps in her direction, cried out: 'Shoo! Shoo!'

Katya called Fifi and opened the door for her.

Fifi dashed joyously out in the hope that she would be taken for a walk but, finding herself abandoned on the other side of the door, started scratching and whining. The Princess frowned and Katya was on the point of going out.

'I think tea's ready, isn't it?' said Odintsova. 'Gentlemen, let's go. Auntie, it's time for tea.'

The Princess rose silently from her armchair and was the first to leave the drawing-room. All of them followed her into the dining-room. A liveried page-boy noisily moved away from the table a special armchair laden with cushions, into which the Princess lowered herself. Katya, who poured out the tea, handed her the first cup, one decorated with a coat of arms. The old woman stirred honey into her cup (she found it sinful and expensive to have sugar with her tea, although she herself never spent a penny on anything) and suddenly asked in a hoarse voice:

'What does *Preence* Ivan write?'

No one answered her. Bazarov and Arkady soon realized that no one paid any attention to her although they all treated her with respect. 'It's all for the sake of show they keep her, because she's of a princely line,' Bazarov thought. After tea Anna Sergeevna proposed that they all go for a walk, but it started to rain and, with the exception of the Princess, they all returned to the drawing-room. The neighbour arrived, the one who was fond of cards, Porfiry Platonich by name, a stoutish, rather grey-haired man with shortish little legs, seemingly sharpened to a point, very polite and fun-loving. Anna Sergeevna, who spent most of her time talking to Bazarov, asked him whether he'd like to try his chances with them in an old-fashioned way by playing préférence.* Bazarov agreed, saying he'd have to have some practice for his future career as a country doctor.

'Take care,' Anna Sergeevna remarked. 'Porfiry Platonich and I'll beat you hollow. And you, Katya,' she added, 'you play something for Arkady Nikolaich. He's fond of music and we can listen as well.'

Katya approached the grand piano unwillingly and Arkady, although fond of music, followed her equally reluctantly. It seemed to him that Odintsova was sending him away while his heart, like the heart of any young man at his age, was bubbling with a kind of restless and tiresome sensation akin to a premonition of love. Katya raised the lid of the grand piano and, without looking at Arkady, asked in a small voice:

'What shall I play for you?'

'Whatever you like,' Arkady answered negligently.

'What kind of music do you like best?' Katya asked again, not changing her position.

'Classical,' Arkady answered in the same negligent voice.

'Do you like Mozart?'

'I like Mozart.'

Katya got out Mozart's C minor Sonata-Fantasia. She played very well, although rather stiffly and drily. Her eyes fixed on the notes and her lips tight shut, she sat upright and still and it was only towards the end of the sonata that her face grew flushed and a small lock of dishevelled hair dropped on her dark eyebrow.

Arkady was particularly struck by the last part of the sonata, the part in which, amidst the engaging joyousness of the light-hearted tune, there suddenly arise bursts of such bitter, almost tragic grief . . . But the thoughts roused in him by the sounds of Mozart did not relate to Katya. Watching her, he simply thought: 'The girl doesn't play at all badly and she's not bad-looking either.'

When the sonata was over, Katya asked, without taking her fingers off the keys: 'Is that enough?' Arkady declared that he didn't dare ask her to do any more and began talking to her about Mozart, asking her whether she'd chosen the sonata herself or had it recommended to her. But Katya replied in monosyllables. She literally 'went into hiding', disappeared into herself. Whenever this happened to her she took a long time to re-emerge. Even her face acquired a stubborn, almost sullen expression. She was not so much shy as mistrustful and a little frightened of the sister who had taught her, something which, it goes without saying, the latter did not suspect at all. Arkady ended by calling to him Fifi, who had returned, and starting for appearance's sake, with an amiable smile, to stroke her head. Katya once more set about arranging her flowers.

Meanwhile, Bazarov went on losing game after game. Anna Sergeevna played cards masterfully. Porfiry Platonich could also stand up for himself. Bazarov ended by being in debt, though not greatly, but it was still not exactly pleasant for him. Over supper Anna Sergeevna again directed the conversation to botany.

'Let's go for a walk tomorrow morning,' she said to him, 'I want to know the Latin names of field flowers and their characteristics.'

'What do you want to know their Latin names for?' asked Bazarov.

'One must be tidy in all things,' she answered.

'What a marvellous woman Anna Sergeevna is!' exclaimed Arkady when he was alone with his friend in the room which had been allocated to them.

'Yes,' said Bazarov, 'a woman with brains. Oh, and she's seen a thing or two.'

'In what sense do you say that, Evgeny Vasilich?'

'In the best sense, the best, Arkady Nikolaich, my dear old fellow! I'm sure she runs her estate splendidly. But she's not the marvel, the marvel's her sister.'

'What? That little dark girl?'

'Yes, that little dark girl. There's one who's fresh and untouched and apprehensive and not talkative and everything you want. That's one to get busy on. You could make whatever you like out of her. But the other, she's hardbaked.'

Arkady did not say anything to Bazarov in response and each of them went to bed with his own particular thoughts in his head.

And that evening Anna Sergeevna thought about her guests. She liked Bazarov for his absence of pretension and the very sharpness of his judgements. She saw in him something new, which she'd never encountered before, and she was curious about him.

Anna Sergeevna was a fairly strange creature. Having no prejudices, not even having any strong beliefs, she was not accustomed to yield to anything and was not on her way to discovering anything. She had a clear idea of many things, many things interested her, and nothing satisfied her entirely. What is more, she scarcely sought complete satisfaction. Her mind was keenly inquiring and indifferent at one and the same time because her doubts never diminished to the point of forgetfulness and never increased to the point of causing alarm. Had she not been rich and independent, she would have perhaps thrown herself into the struggle and come to know the meaning of passion. But she had an easy life, although she had occasional bouts of boredom, and she went on spending day after day without hurry and only rarely experiencing excitement. Rainbow hues would now and then shine before her eyes, but she felt relieved when they subsided and didn't regret their passing. Her imagination would even soar beyond the bounds of what would be permitted by the laws of ordinary morality, but even then the blood would flow as calmly as ever in her attractively elegant and untroubled body. It could happen that, on stepping out of a fragrant bath, all hot and luxuriant, she would fall to day-dreaming about the futility of life, its grief and hardness and evil and her soul would be filled with sudden boldness and bubble with noble aspirations, but a draught would come from a half-open window and Anna Sergeevna would shrink into herself and complain and almost lose her temper and need only one thing at that moment: no more beastly draught blowing at her.

Like all women who had not succeeded in falling in love, she sought for something without knowing precisely what. Personally she wanted nothing, although it seemed to her that she wanted everything. She had hardly been able to stand the late-lamented Odintsov (she had married him for his money, although she would probably not have agreed to become his wife if she hadn't considered him a kind man) and had acquired a secret aversion to all men, whom she regarded as nothing more than untidy, ponderous and flabby, feebly importunate creatures. Once, when she'd been somewhere abroad, she'd met a handsome young Swede with the face of a knight-errant and honest blue eyes beneath a frank, open forehead. He had produced a strong impression on her but that had not stopped her from returning to Russia.

What a strange man that doctor is! she thought, lying in her magnificent bed, on lace pillows, beneath a light silk cover. Anna Sergeevna had inherited from her father something of his love of luxury. She had been very fond of her errant but kind-hearted father, while he had worshipped her and amiably joked with her as an equal, entrusted everything to her and listened to her advice. Her mother she could scarcely remember.

He's strange, that doctor! she repeated to herself. She stretched, smiled, put her arms behind her head, then ran her eyes over a couple of pages of a silly French novel, dropped the book and fell asleep, all clean and cool in clean and fragrant bed linen.

The next morning Anna Sergeevna went off botanizing with Bazarov immediately after breakfast and returned just before lunch. Arkady went nowhere and spent an hour or so in Katya's company. He was not at all bored being with her and she herself offered to play yesterday's sonata for him again, but when Odintsova returned eventually and when he caught sight of her, his heart contracted momentarily.

She came through the garden with a slightly tired walk. Her cheeks glowed red and her eyes glittered more brightly than usual under a round straw hat. She twisted in her fingers the thin stalk of a field flower, a light mantle had slipped down to her elbows and the broad grey ribbons of her hat were clinging to her bosom. Bazarov walked along behind her, self-assured and uncaring as ever, but the look on his face, though happy and even fond, did not please Arkady. Muttering 'Hello!' through his teeth, Bazarov went off to his room while Odintsova distractedly shook Arkady's hand and also walked past him.

'Why hello?' thought Arkady. 'Haven't we seen each other so far today?'

17

TIME (as is well known) sometimes flies like a bird, sometimes crawls like a worm. But a man feels particularly happy when he doesn't even notice whether it's passing quickly or quietly. Arkady and Bazarov spent fifteen days at Odintsova's in precisely this way. This was partly assisted by the tidiness which she maintained both in her house and in her life. She kept to it firmly herself and made others submit to it. Everything during the day occurred at a fixed time. In the morning, on the stroke of eight o'clock, the entire company assembled for tea; between tea and lunch each one did as he or she wished and the lady of the house was usually busy with the estate manager (the peasants on the estate paid quit-rent), the head butler or the chief housekeeper. Before dinner the company again assembled for conversation or for reading; the evening was dedicated to walks, cards and music; at half-past ten Anna Sergeevna would retire to her room, give orders for the next day and go to bed.

Bazarov did not like the measured, rather solemn orderliness of life each day. 'It's like running on rails,' he claimed. The liveried footmen and obsequious butlers offended his sense of democracy. He found that, if you'd gone as far as that, then you ought to dine in the English fashion, in white tie and tails. He expressed himself on one occasion about this to Anna Sergeevna. Her manner was such that everyone felt able to express their opinion in her presence without hesitation. She heard him out and said: 'From your point of view you're right, and perhaps in this instance I'm really behaving like a grand lady, but you simply cannot live without tidiness in the country or boredom'll get the better of you'—and she went on doing things her own way. Bazarov grumbled, but his and Arkady's life at Odintsova's was so easy because everything in her house 'ran on rails'. Despite this, a change had occurred in both young men since the first days of their stay at Nikolskoe. Bazarov, whom Anna Sergeevna clearly liked, although she rarely agreed with him, began to show signs of a hitherto nonexistent unease. He was easily irritated, talked unwillingly, looked angry and couldn't stay in one place for long, as if something were constantly bothering him; while Arkady

who had finally decided for himself that he was in love with
Odintsova, began to give way to quiet despair. However, this despair
did not prevent him from getting to know Katya and even helped
him to establish fond and friendly relations with her. *She* doesn't
think anything of me! So be it! But here's someone kind who doesn't
turn me away, he thought, and his heart once more tasted the sweet-
ness of feelings of magnanimity. Katya was vaguely aware that he
was looking for some sort of comfort in her society and didn't refuse
either him or herself the innocent pleasure of a friendship that was
half bashful, half confident. In Anna Sergeevna's presence they did
not talk to each other because Katya always felt embarrassed under
her sister's keen eye and Arkady, as was appropriate to someone in
love, in the presence of his beloved couldn't turn his attention to
anything else, but he enjoyed being alone with Katya. He felt he
wasn't strong enough for Odintsova; he was shy and at a loss whenever he found himself alone with her and she didn't know what to
say to him because she felt he was too young for her. By contrast, he
felt at home with Katya. He condescended to her and didn't stop her
talking about the impressions aroused in her by music, the reading of
novels and poetry and other nonsense, either not noticing or unaware
that such 'nonsense' appealed to him as well. For her part Katya
didn't interfere with his need to feel sorry for himself. Arkady got on
with Katya. Odintsova with Bazarov and so it usually turned out that
both pairs, after spending a short while together, went off each on
their separate ways, especially when it was time for walks. Katya
simply *worshipped* nature and Arkady loved it as well, although he
didn't dare admit it. Odintsova was pretty indifferent to it, just as
was Bazarov. The almost constant separation of our friends did not
remain without consequences and the relations between them began
to change. Bazarov stopped talking to Arkady about Odintsova
and even stopped scolding her 'aristocratic manners'. True, he sang
Katya's praises as before and did no more than advise a curb on
her tendency to be sentimental, but his praises were hastily given
and his advice was dry and generally he talked with Arkady a great
deal less than he had previously. It was as if he were avoiding him,
as if he were shy of him . . .

Arkady took note of all this, but kept his remarks to himself.

The real cause of this 'change' was the feeling evoked in Bazarov
by Odintsova, a feeling which tormented him and drove him mad

and which he'd instantly have denied with a contemptuous laugh and cynical abuse had anyone hinted to him, even remotely, what was happening to him. Bazarov was a great admirer of women and women's beauty, but love in an ideal—or as he expressed it—a romantic sense he described as rubbish, unforgivable stupidity, and he considered chivalrous feelings something freakish or diseased and more than once expressed surprise why Toggenburg* along with all the minnesingers and troubadours hadn't been locked up in a madhouse. 'If you like a woman', he was fond of saying, 'then try and get what you can. If you can't, well, no matter, give her up—there are plenty of fish in the sea.' He liked Odintsova. The widespread rumours about her, the freedom and independence of her ideas and her undoubted fondness for him—all this, it seemed, was to his advantage, but he quickly realized that he couldn't 'get what he wanted' with her and, to his amazement, he found he hadn't the strength to 'give her up'. His blood was set on fire as soon as he thought about her. He would have easily come to terms with his hot blood, but something else had taken root in him, something he would never have allowed, about which he had always made jokes and which hurt his pride. In discussions with Anna Sergeevna he expressed his indifference and contempt for everything romantic more emphatically than ever, but when on his own he recognized with disgust the romantic in himself.

At such times he would set off for the forest and stride through it breaking what branches got in his way and hurling abuse at her and at himself. Or he'd climb up on a haystack, in a haybarn and, stubbornly shutting his eyes, would force himself to sleep, in which, of course, he didn't always succeed. Suddenly he would imagine that those wholesome arms would some time or other entwine themselves round his neck, that those proud lips would respond to his kisses, that those intelligent eyes would gaze with tenderness—yes, with tenderness—into his eyes, and her head would spin and he'd forget himself for an instant—until disgust flared up in him again. He caught himself thinking all kinds of 'shameful' thoughts, just as if some devil or other were teasing him. On occasion it even seemed to him that a change was occurring in Odintsova as well, that the expression on her face showed something special that might perhaps . . . But at this thought he would stamp his foot or grind his teeth and shake his fist at himself.

Yet Bazarov wasn't entirely mistaken. He had stirred Odintsova's imagination. He preoccupied her and she thought a great deal about him. She wasn't bored in his absence and didn't wait for his return, but his appearance at once enlivened her. She would gladly remain by herself with him and gladly talk to him, even when he annoyed her or insulted her tastes and her elegant habits. It was as if she wanted to test him and get to know herself better.

On one occasion, while strolling in the garden with her, he suddenly announced in a sombre voice that he was intending to go off soon to see his father in the country. She went as pale as if she'd been stabbed in the heart, and it was such a stabbing feeling that she was astonished and for a long time afterwards wondered what it meant. Bazarov had not announced his departure with any intention of testing her or seeing how she would react. He never 'told stories'. The morning of that day he'd met his father's bailiff who'd looked after him as a child, Timofeich. This Timofeich, a careworn and nimble little old fellow, with faded yellow hair, a weatherbeaten red face and puckered eyes full of tiny teardrops, unexpectedly appeared before Bazarov in his shortish jacket of thick blue-grey cloth tied with a leather thong and in tarred boots.

'Hello, old chap!' Bazarov exclaimed.

'Good morning, Evgeny Vasilich, sir,' the little old man began and smiled with joy, at which his whole face was suddenly covered in wrinkles.

'Why're you here? Did they send you after me?'

'Oh, sir, what a thing to say!' Timofeich stammered (he was mindful of the strict orders received from his master on setting out). 'We was goin' into town on business an' we 'eard you were 'ere, sir, so we turned in 'ere, sir, on the way—to take a look at you—not wantin' to be a nuisance, mind!'

'Well, you're an old liar,' Bazarov interrupted him. 'This isn't the way to the town, is it?'

Timofeich looked nonplussed and said nothing.

'Is father well?'

'God be praised, yessir.'

'And mother?'

'An' Arina Vlasevna is too, sir.'

'They're expecting me, are they?'

The old man bent his little head to one side.

'Ah, Evgeny Vasilich, what a long wait it's been, sir! Lookin' at 'em, your poor parents, one's 'eart aches, in God's name it does!'

'Well, all right, all right! Don't lay it on too thick! Tell 'em I'll be there soon.'

'Yessir,' answered Timofeich with a sigh.

On leaving the house he pulled his cap down over his head with both hands, climbed on to a wretched racing droshky which he had left at the gates and set off at a trot, but not in the direction of the town.

That evening Odintsova was sitting in her room with Bazarov while Arkady walked up and down the hall listening to Katya's playing. The Princess had gone up to her room. In general she couldn't stand guests and in particular she couldn't stand these 'newfangled' ones, as she called them. In the main rooms of the house she did no more than huff and puff, but in her own room, in front of her chambermaid, she would sometimes let fly such abuse that her bonnet would jump up and down along with her wig. Odintsova knew all about this.

'So you're about to be on your way,' she began, 'but what about your promise?'

Bazarov gave a start. 'What promise?'

'Have you forgotten? You wanted to give me some lessons in chemistry.'

'Nothing doing, ma'am! My father's expecting me. I can't hang about any more. Besides, you can read Pelouse et Frémy, *Notions générales de chimie*.* It's a good book and clearly written. You'll find everything you need there.'

'But don't you remember you assured me that a book can't take the place of—I've forgotten how you put it, but you know what I mean—don't you remember that?'

'Nothing doing, ma'am!' Bazarov repeated.

'Why go?' asked Odintsova, lowering her voice.

He glanced at her. She had thrown back her head against the back of the armchair and crossed her arms, bare to the elbows, across her bosom. She looked paler by the light of the single lamp hung with a fishnet-style cut-out paper shade. A full white dress covered her whole figure in soft folds. The tips of her feet, also crossed, were scarcely to be seen.

'And why stay?' answered Bazarov.

Odintsova turned her head slightly.

'Why do you say why? Aren't you happy here with me? Or do you think no one'll miss you here?'

'I'm convinced of it.'

Odintsova was silent a while.

'You're wrong to think that. Besides, I don't believe you. You can't have been serious.' Bazarov continued to sit motionless. 'Evgeny Vasilich, why don't you say something?'

'What've I got to say? It's not worth missing people in general and me in particular.'

'Why's that?'

'I'm a positive chap, uninteresting. I don't know how to talk.'

'You're fishing for compliments, Evgeny Vasilich.'

'That's not my sort of thing. Don't you yourself know that the elegant aspect of life, the one you are so keen on, isn't accessible to me?'

Odintsova bit the corner of her handkerchief.

'Think what you like, but I'll be bored when you've gone.'

'Arkady'll be here,' remarked Bazarov.

Odintsova gave a slight shrug.

'I'll be bored,' she repeated.

'Really? In any case, you won't be bored for long.'

'Why do you think that?'

'Because you yourself have told me that you get bored whenever your tidy life is upset. You've arranged your life so infallibly tidily that there's no place in it for boredom, regrets . . . or any difficult feelings.'

'You find I'm infallible—that I've arranged my life as tidily as that?'

'Certainly! For example, in a few minutes ten o'clock will strike and I know you'll drive me away.'

'No, I won't, Evgeny Vasilich. You can stay. Open the window, I feel hot in here.'

Bazarov stood up and pushed at the window. It opened instantly with a loud crack. He hadn't expected it to open so easily. Moreover, his hands were shaking. The soft dark night looked into the room with its almost jet-black sky, faintly rustling trees and the fresh scent of pure open air.

'Let down the blind and sit down,' said Odintsova. 'I want to chat with you before you go. Tell me something about yourself. You never talk about yourself.'

'I try to talk to you about useful things, Anna Sergeevna.'

'You're very modest . . . Still, I'd like to know a bit about you and your family and your father, for whose sake you're leaving us.'

Why's she saying such words? Bazarov thought. 'All that's not in the least interesting,' he said aloud, 'particularly for you. We're a dull lot . . .'

'While, in your opinion, I'm an aristocrat?'

Bazarov raised his eyes to Odintsova.

'Yes,' he said, exceptionally sharply.

She smiled.

'I see you don't know me well, although you assure me that all people are similar to one another and there's no point in studying them. Some time or other I'll tell you about my life, but now you tell me yours.'

'I don't know you well,' Bazarov repeated. 'Perhaps you're right. Maybe everyone is just that—an enigma. Take you, for example— you fight shy of society, you find it irksome, and yet you've invited a couple of students to come and stay with you. Why do you, with your intelligence and your beauty, why do you live in the country?'

'What? What did you say?' Odintsova picked him up animatedly. 'With my . . . beauty?'

Bazarov frowned.

'That's neither here nor there,' he said. 'I meant that I don't understand properly why you've settled in the country.'

'You don't understand it . . . However, you must explain it to yourself somehow, surely?'

'Yes. I suppose, you see, that you stay constantly in one place because you've become spoiled, because you're very fond of comfort and comfortable things and are extremely indifferent to everything else.'

Odintsova again smiled.

'You definitely don't want to believe that I'm capable of being distracted by anything, do you?'

Bazarov glanced at her from under his brows.

'By curiosity, say, but not otherwise.'

'Really? Well, now I see why we've got on so well. You're the same as I am.'

'We've got on . . .' said Bazarov under his breath.

'Yes! Still, I'd forgotten you want to leave.'

Bazarov stood up. The lamp glowed faintly in the midst of the darkened, fragrant, secluded room and through the occasionally restless blind poured the vexing freshness of the night and its mysterious whisperings. Odintsova did not stir in the very slightest, but a strange excitement gradually crept over her. It conveyed itself to Bazarov. He suddenly felt that he was alone with a young and beautiful woman.

'Where are you going?' she asked slowly.

He didn't reply and sat down again.

'So you consider me an unemotional, molly-coddled, spoiled creature,' she went on in the same tone of voice, not taking her eyes off the window. 'But what I do know about myself is that I'm very unhappy.'

'You're unhappy! Why? You surely can't ascribe any importance to a lot of rubbishy rumours.'

Odintsova frowned. She was annoyed that he'd understood her in that way.

'Such rumours don't even amuse me, Evgeny Vasilich, and I'm too proud to let them affect me. I'm unhappy because . . . because I've no desire, no wish to live. You're giving me doubting looks, you're thinking—that's the "aristocrat" speaking who wears lace and sits in a velvet armchair. I can't hide the fact that I love what you call "comfort", and yet at the same time I have little desire to live. Reconcile that contradiction how you will. Besides, in your eyes it's all romanticism.'

Bazarov shook his head.

'You're healthy, independent and wealthy—what more do you want? What exactly do you want?'

'What do I want?' repeated Odintsova and sighed. 'I'm so tired and I'm old and I feel I've been living a very long time. Yes, I'm old,' she added, gently drawing the ends of her lace mantilla over her bare shoulders. Her eyes met Bazarov's and she coloured very slightly. 'Behind me there are already so many memories—life in St Petersburg, wealth, then poverty, then the death of my father, my marriage, then going abroad as one is expected to . . . Lots of memories, but no point in remembering them, and ahead of me a long, long road with nothing to aim for . . . I just don't want to go along it.'

'Are you that disillusioned?' Bazarov asked.

'No,' said Odintsova, pausing between the words, 'but I'm dissatisfied. I think, if only I could feel a strong attachment to something or other . . .'

'You want to fall in love,' Bazarov interrupted, 'but you can't—that's why you're unhappy.'

Odintsova took to studying the sleeves of her mantilla.

'Do you really think I can't fall in love?' she said.

'Of course not! It's simply that I was wrong to call you unhappy. On the contrary, when that sort of thing happens to someone that person deserves rather to be pitied.'

'When what happens?'

'Falling in love.'

'How do you know that?'

'It's what I've been told,' said Bazarov angrily.

You're flirting, he thought. You're bored and you're having a bit of fun with me out of boredom, while I . . . His heart was actually on the point of breaking.

'Still, perhaps you're too demanding,' he said, leaning forward with his whole body and playing with the fringe of his armchair.

'Perhaps. For me it's either all or nothing. A life for a life. If you've taken what's mine, then you've got to give up what's yours and then there won't be any regrets or going back. There's no better way than that.'

'Is that so?' remarked Bazarov. 'That's justice all right, and I'm only surprised you haven't so far found what you wanted.'

'So you think it's easy to give yourself up completely to whatever you want?'

'It's not easy if you start thinking about it and playing for time and giving yourself a high price—making much of yourself, that is. But if you do it without thinking, it's easy to give yourself to something.'

'How can one not make much of oneself? If I'm not worth anything, who needs my loyalty?'

'That's not my business. It's for the other person to decide what I'm worth. The main thing is to know how to give yourself.'

Odintsova raised herself away from the back of her armchair. 'You say this', she began, 'as if you've experienced it all yourself.'

'A good point, Anna Sergeevna, but it's all, you know, not in my line.'

'But you would know how to give yourself?'

'I don't know. I don't want to boast.'

Odintsova said nothing and Bazarov fell silent. The sounds of the piano floated to them from the drawing-room.

'Katya's playing so late,' remarked Odintsova.

Bazarov stood up. 'Yes, it really is late now. Time you were in bed.'

'Wait a moment, where're you off to . . . I want to say something.'

'What?'

'Wait a moment,' whispered Odintsova. Her eyes were fixed on Bazarov as if she were studying him closely.

He strode about the room, then suddenly approached her, hurriedly said goodbye, squeezed her hand so tightly she almost gave a cry and then went out. She raised her squashed fingers to her lips, blew on them and instantaneously, impulsively rose from the armchair and took rapid steps to the door as if wanting to bring Bazarov back.

A chambermaid came into the room with a carafe on a silver tray. Odintsova stood stockstill, ordered her to go and again sat down and once more grew thoughtful. Her plait unwound and fell like a dark snake on her shoulder. The lamp went on burning for a long time in Anna Sergeevna's room and for a long time she remained motionless, only occasionally running her fingers over her arms which were being slightly nipped by the night cold.

Meanwhile, Bazarov, after a couple of hours, returned to his bedroom with boots wet from dew, looking dishevelled and sullen. He found Arkady sitting at the writing-desk with a book in his hands dressed in a coat buttoned up to the top.

'You're not in bed yet?' he queried, apparently annoyed.

'You spent a long time with Anna Sergeevna this evening,' said Arkady without answering the question.

'Yes, I was with her the whole time you and Katya were playing the piano.'

'I wasn't playing . . .' Arkady began and then stopped. He felt tears rising in his eyes and he had no wish to start crying in front of his mocking friend.

18

THE next day when Odintsova came down to her breakfast tea Bazarov spent a long time bent over his cup and then he suddenly glanced at her. She turned towards him just as if he'd given her a nudge and it seemed to him that her face had grown a shade paler in the course of the night. She quickly left to go to her own room and appeared only for lunch. Throughout the morning the weather had been rainy and there had been no opportunity to go out for a walk. The entire company assembled in the drawing-room. Arkady picked up the latest number of a journal and began reading aloud. The Princess, as was her custom, started by looking surprised at this, as if he was doing something improper, and then took to staring at him irritably. But he paid no attention to her.

'Evgeny Vasilich,' said Anna Sergeevna, 'come to my room . . . I want to ask you something. Yesterday you mentioned a certain textbook . . .'

She rose and went to the door. The Princess glared round her with the kind of look which declared 'Can't you just see how astonished I am!' and then she once more fixed her eye on Arkady, but he raised his voice and, exchanging looks with Katya, whom he was sitting next to, went on with his reading.

Odintsova walked briskly to her room. Bazarov followed swiftly behind her without raising his eyes and simply catching by ear the soft whistle and rustle of the silk dress which glided before him. Odintsova sank into the same armchair that she had sat in the previous evening and Bazarov occupied his place of the night before.

'So what's that book called?' she asked after a brief silence.

'Pelouse et Frémy, *Notions générales* . . .' answered Bazarov. 'Among others I could also recommend Ganot,* *Traité élémentaire de physique expérimentale.* In this work the illustrations are better and in general this textbook . . .'

Odintsova stretched out her hand.

'Evgeny Vasilich, forgive me, but I haven't asked you to come here to talk about textbooks. I wanted to renew last night's conversation. You left so suddenly . . . Will this bore you?'

'I'm at your service, Anna Sergeevna. But what exactly were you and I talking about last night?'

Odintsova cast a sidelong glance in Bazarov's direction.

'We were talking, I think, about happiness. I was telling you about myself. Anyhow, I mentioned the word happiness. Tell me why is it that even when we are enjoying music, for example, or a fine evening or conversation with people we like, why does it all seem to be a hint of some limitless happiness existing somewhere else rather than a real happiness, the kind, that is, we possess ourselves? Why is this? Or perhaps you don't feel anything of the kind?'

'You know the saying, "Next door's grass is always greener",' Bazarov retorted. 'In any case, you said yesterday that you weren't satisfied. You're right, though—such thoughts don't enter my head.'

'Perhaps they seem to you ridiculous.'

'No, but they don't enter my head.'

'Really? You know I'd much like to know what you do really think about.'

'In what way? I don't understand you.'

'Listen, I've long wanted to have things out with you. There's no point in your saying—you know this as well as I do—that you're not out of the ordinary. You're still young and you've got your whole life ahead of you. What are you preparing yourself for? What sort of future awaits you? I mean, what purpose do you want to achieve, where are you going, what's on your mind? In short, who are you, what are you?'

'You astonish me, Anna Sergeevna. You know perfectly well I am interested in the natural sciences, but as for who I am . . .'

'Yes, who are you?'

'I've already told you that I'm a future country doctor.'

Anna Sergeevna made an impatient gesture.

'Why do you talk like that? You don't believe it yourself. Arkady might talk to me that way, but not you.'

'What's Arkady got to do . . .'

'Stop it! I can't see it's possible that you'd be satisfied with such a modest career, especially as you yourself are always insisting that so far as you're concerned there's no such thing as medicine. You— with your ambition—a country doctor! You tell me that just to keep me at arm's length, because you don't trust me. But you know, Evgeny Vasilich, I could learn to understand you because I was once poor and ambitious like you. Perhaps I've gone through just the same testing times as you.'

'That's all very well, Anna Sergeevna, but you must forgive me . . . I'm not at all accustomed to expressing my feelings and between the two of us there's such a distance . . .'

'What distance? You'll be telling me again I'm an aristocrat, will you? Enough of that, Evgeny Vasilich, I thought I'd proved to you . . .'

'Yes, and besides that,' Bazarov interrupted, 'what's the point of talking and thinking about the future which for the most part doesn't depend on us? If the opportunity arises to do something—great, and if it doesn't at least you'll be glad you didn't chatter about it beforehand.'

'You call a friendly conversation chatter . . . Or perhaps you don't consider me as a woman worthy of your trust? You probably despise us all.'

'I do not despise you, Anna Sergeevna, and you know that.'

'No, I don't know anything of the sort . . . but let's suppose I understand your reluctance to talk about your future career. As for what's occurring inside you now . . .'

'Occurring!' echoed Bazarov. 'It's as if I'm some kind of political state or society! In any case it's not in the least interesting. And, anyhow, is a man always able to proclaim loudly what is "occurring" inside him?'

'I don't see why it's impossible to express everything that's on one's mind.'

'*You* can?' Bazarov asked.

'I can,' answered Anna Sergeevna after slight hesitation.

Bazarov bent his head.

'You're luckier than I am.'

Anna Sergeevna gave him a questioning look.

'As you wish,' she went on, 'but something tells me that it's not just luck that's made us get on so well, that we'll be good friends. I'm sure that your—how can I put it?—your tenseness, your self-control will vanish evetually, won't it?'

'So you've noticed my self-control, my—as you put it—tenseness?'

'Yes.'

Bazarov stood up and went to the window.

'And would you like to know the cause of this self-control, would you like to know what is *occurring* inside me?'

'Yes,' repeated Odintsova with a certain apprehension that was as yet unclear to her.

'And you won't be angry?'

'No.'

'No?' Bazarov stood with his back to her. 'Then you should know that I love you, stupidly, madly . . . So now you've got what you wanted.'

Odintsova stretched out both hands in front of her, but Bazarov pressed his forehead to the glass of the window. He took in deep breaths. His whole body was visibly quivering. But it was not the quivering of boyish shyness, nor was it the sweet horror of first confession that possessed him. It was passion that beat within him, strong and laboured, passion that resembled anger and was probably akin to it. Odintsova grew both alarmed and sorry for him.

'Evgeny Vasilich,' she said and, despite herself, her voice resounded with tenderness.

He quickly turned round, cast a devouring look at her and, seizing both her hands, drew her suddenly to him.

She did not free herself from his embrace at once, but a moment later she was already standing far away in a corner and gazing at Bazarov from there. He rushed towards her.

'You've not understood me,' she whispered in hurried alarm. It seemed that had he taken another step she would have screamed . . . Bazarov bit his lip and left the room.

Half an hour later a maid gave Anna Sergeevna a note from Bazarov. It consisted of only one line: 'Must I leave today or can I stay till tomorrow?' 'Why leave? I couldn't understand you and you didn't understand me,' was Anna Sergeevna's answer to him, but to herself she thought: I couldn't even understand myself.

She did not appear until dinner-time and spent the whole while pacing to and fro in her room, her hands behind her back, occasionally stopping either by the window or in front of the mirror and slowly drawing a handkerchief across her neck on which she imagined she had a spot that was burning hot. She constantly asked herself what had made her 'get what she wanted', as Bazarov had put it, about his true feelings and whether she hadn't suspected something of the kind. 'I'm to blame,' she said aloud, 'but I couldn't have .

foreseen it.' She grew thoughtful and went red when she recalled Bazarov's almost bestial face as he flung himself at her.

'Or else?' she declared suddenly and stopped and shook her curls. She caught sight of herself in the mirror. Her head thrown back and the mysterious smile in her half-closed, half-open eyes and on her lips seemed to tell her something at that instant from which she herself flinched in embarrassment.

'No,' she decided at last. 'God knows where it might have led. You've got to be serious about this. Peace of mind is still the best thing on earth.'

Her peace of mind had not been shaken. But she grew sad and even shed a few tears, not knowing herself why, only not from any insult inflicted on her. She did not feel insulted; rather, she felt she was to blame. Under the influence of various vague feelings—an awareness of life slipping away, a desire for novelty—she had made herself go as far as a certain point and even forced herself to look beyond it and glimpsed there not even a bottomless pit but no more than emptiness . . . or sheer ugliness.

19

No matter how self-controlled Odintsova was, and no matter how far above every kind of prejudice, she still felt awkward when she appeared in the dining-room for dinner. However, the meal passed off fairly happily. Porfiry Platonich arrived and had various anecdotes to recount, since he'd just returned from the town. Among other things he informed them that the governor, Bourdaloue, had ordered his officials on special assignments to wear spurs in case he sent them somewhere in haste on horseback. Arkady held discussions under his breath with Katya and diplomatically fawned on the Princess. Bazarov was stubbornly and sullenly silent. Odintsova glanced a couple of times—directly and not covertly—at his stern and bitterly surly face, with its lowered eyes and the mark of contemptuous resoluteness in every feature, and thought: 'No . . . no . . . no . . .'. After dinner she went off into the garden with the entire company and, seeing that Bazarov wanted to have a word with her, took several steps to one side and stopped. He approached her, but even at that point did not raise his eyes and said huskily:

'I must apologize to you, Anna Sergeevna. You cannot fail to be angry with me.'

'No, I'm not angry with you, Evgeny Vasilich,' Odintsova answered, 'but I'm disappointed.'

'So much the worse. I am duly punished in every way. My position—you will probably agree with this—is a very stupid one. You wrote to me: Why leave? But I cannot stay and I don't want to. Tomorrow I will be off.'

'Evgeny Vasilich, why do you . . .'

'Why am I leaving?'

'No, I didn't mean that.'

'You can't bring back the past, Anna Sergeevna . . . but sooner or later this would be bound to happen. Consequently I must leave. I am aware of only one condition which would make me stay, but that condition can never be. After all, forgive my boldness, you don't love me, do you, and you never will?'

Bazarov's eyes glittered for an instant beneath his dark brows.

Anna Sergeevna did not respond to him. 'I'm frightened of this man,' was the thought that flashed through her head.

'Goodbye, ma'am,' said Bazarov, as though he'd guessed what she was thinking, and set off in the direction of the house.

Anna Sergeevna followed quietly after him and, calling Katya to her, took her by the hand. She did not part from her until that evening. She did not play cards and took to laughing more and more, which certainly did not go well with her pale and embarrassed look. Arkady was puzzled and watched her in the way that young people watch—that is to say, constantly asking himself what it all meant. Bazarov locked himself in his room; at tea-time, however, he returned. Anna Sergeevna wanted awfully to speak kindly to him but she did not know how to begin.

An unexpected event relieved her of the trouble: the butler announced the arrival of Sitnikov.

It is hard to convey in words how, quail-like, the young 'progressive' flew into the room. Having decided, with his customary impertinence, to travel to the country to see a lady whom he scarcely knew and who had never invited him, but with whom there were staying, judging by all he'd been able to gather, such close and clever friends of his, he nevertheless felt shy to the marrow of his bones and, instead of uttering the apologies and greetings he'd rehearsed earlier, muttered some rubbish about Eudoxie, meaning Kukshina, having sent him to enquire about Anna Sergeevna's health and that Arkady Nikolaevich also was always singing him the highest praises of . . . At which point he faltered and so lost his way that he sat down on his own hat. Yet, since no one drove him away and Anna Sergeevna even presented him to her aunt and sister, he quickly recovered and started trilling away to his heart's content. The appearance of mediocrity is often useful in life because it weakens tautly strung strings and sobers up people's self-confident or self-forgetful feelings, reminding them how close they are to mediocrity as well. With Sitnikov's arrival everything became duller—and a lot simpler. Everyone even ate an unusually full dinner and went to bed half-an-hour earlier than usual.

'I can now repeat to you', said Arkady, lying in his bed, to Bazarov, who had also got undressed, 'what you once said to me: "Why do you look so solemn? Have you really just performed some sacred duty?"'

Between the two young men a kind of spuriously free-and-easy mickey-taking had recently become the established practice, which is always a sign of covert dissatisfaction or unstated suspicions.

'I'm off to see my old man tomorrow,' said Bazarov. Arkady raised himself and leaned on one elbow. He was both surprised and for some reason delighted.

'Ah!' he said. 'And that's what makes you solemn, is it?'

Bazarov yawned.

'Too much learning'll make you prematurely old.'

'And what about Anna Sergeevna?' Arkady went on.

'What about Anna Sergeevna?'

'I mean will she let you go?'

'I'm not one of her employees.'

Arkady grew thoughtful and Bazarov lay back and turned his face to the wall.

Several minutes passed in silence.

'Evgeny!' Arkady exclaimed suddenly.

'What?'

'I'll be leaving with you as well tomorrow.'

Bazarov said nothing.

''Cept I'll be going home,' Arkady continued. 'We'll go together as far as the Khokhlov houses and there you can get horses at Fedot's. I'd have been glad to get to know your parents but I'm afraid I might get in their way and yours. You'll be coming back to us afterwards, won't you?'

'I've left my things with you,' answered Bazarov, not turning round.

Why doesn't he ask me why I'm leaving? And just as suddenly as he is? thought Arkady. In fact, why am I leaving and why is he? he continued his musings. He could not answer his own question satisfactorily and his heart filled with bitterness. He felt it would be difficult for him to say goodbye to this life to which he'd become so used, but the idea of staying here alone was somehow odd. Something's happened between them, he told himself, so why should I stick out like a sore thumb round here after he's gone? She'll get bored stiff with me and I'll lose everything. He started imagining Anna Sergeevna and then other features gradually arose in place of the beautiful image of the young widow.

'I'll miss Katya!' Arkady whispered into his pillow, on which a teardrop fell. He suddenly threw back his hair and said loudly:

'What in the devil's name made the idiot Sitnikov turn up?'

Bazarov at first stirred in his bed and then he uttered the following:

'Look, mate, I see you're still bloody silly. We need Sitnikovs. I—know what I mean?—I need such cretins. It's not for the Gods, in fact, to bake the pots!'

Aha! thought Arkady—and it was only at this moment that the entire limitless depth of Bazarov's conceit was revealed to him—So you and I are the Gods, are we? That's to say, you're the God and maybe I'm the cretin?

'Yes,' Bazarov repeated sullenly, 'you're still bloody silly.'

Odintsova showed no particular surprise the next day when Arkady told her that he was leaving with Bazarov. She seemed distracted and tired. Katya looked at him quietly and seriously and the Princess even made the sign of the cross beneath her shawl in such a way that he couldn't not see it. By contrast, Sitnikov was flabbergasted. He had only just come down to breakfast in a new stylish—this time non-Slavophile—outfit. The previous evening he had astonished the manservant assigned to him by the enormous quantity of linen he had brought with him—and suddenly his comrades were abandoning him! He did a little bit of impatient foot-tapping, dashed about a bit like a hunted hare at the edge of a wood—and then suddenly, almost in a panic, almost shouting, announced that he intended to leave too. Odintsova did not try to detain him.

'I have a very well-sprung carriage,' added the unfortunate young man, turning to Arkady. 'I could give you a lift and Evgeny Vasilich can take your tarantass, that would be more convenient still.'

'But it's quite out of your way and I live a long way off.'

'It's nothing, nothing at all. I've got a lot of free time and in any case I've got things to do in those parts.'

'Tax-farming?' asked Arkady rather too contemptuously.

But Sitnikov was so desperate that, contrary to habit, he didn't even laugh.

'I assure you my carriage is extraordinarily comfortable,' he muttered, 'and everyone will have somewhere to sit.'

'Don't offend Monsieur Sitnikov by refusing,' said Anna Sergeevna.

Arkady glanced at her and gave a slow meaningful nod.

The guests left after breakfast. Saying goodbye to Bazarov, Odintsova stretched out her hand to him and said:

'We will see each other again, won't we?'

'Whatever you say,' answered Bazarov.

'In that case we'll see each other.'

Arkady was the first to go down the front steps; he climbed into Sitnikov's carriage. A butler respectfully helped him into his seat, but he would gladly have hit him or burst into tears. Bazarov took his seat in the tarantass. Having reached the Khokhlov houses, Arkady waited while Fedot, the keeper of the post-station, harnessed the horses and, going up to the tarantass, said to Bazarov with his earlier smile:

'Evgeny, take me with you. I'd like to go to your place.'

'Get in,' said Bazarov through his teeth.

Sitnikov, who had been strolling about around the wheels of his carriage, whistling vigorously, simply let his mouth fall open on hearing these words, but Arkady cold-bloodedly removed his things from his carriage, sat down next to Bazarov and, bowing politely to his former travelling companion, shouted: 'Let's be off!' The tarantass set off and was soon lost from sight.

Sitnikov, conclusively confounded, looked at his coachman, but he was playing his whip over the tail of the trace-horse. Then Sitnikov jumped into the carriage and, thundering at two passing peasants: 'Put your hats on, you fools!', chased off to the town, where he arrived very late and where the next day, at Kukshina's, he had strong words to say about the 'two repellently arrogant ignoramuses'.

Seating himself in the tarantass next to Bazarov, Arkady pressed his hand firmly and did not speak for a while. It seemed that Bazarov understood and was appreciative of both the pressure on his hand and the silence. He had not slept at all the previous night and not smoked and had eaten practically nothing for several days. His drawn, lean profile stood out despondently and sharply from beneath his pulled-down cap.

'Look, mate,' he said at last, 'give me a cigar. See, my tongue's yellow, isn't it?'

'It is,' answered Arkady.

'Well, that's it—the cigar's got no taste. The machinery's come unstuck.'

'You really have changed recently,' Arkady remarked.

'It's nothing! We'll soon get right. One thing's a bore—my mother's great at fussing, so if I haven't got a bloated stomach and don't eat ten times a day she's worried sick. As for my father, he's all right, he's been all over the place and taken some knocks in his time. No, I can't smoke!' he added and flung his cigar into the dust of the road.

'Twenty miles, is it, to your estate?' asked Arkady.

'About twenty. Ask this wiseacre here.'

He pointed to the peasant, one of Fedot's men, sitting on the box. But the wiseacre answered, 'Who the 'ell knows, t'ain't no miles marked round 'ere' and went on scolding the shaft-horse for ''acking wi' 'is noddle', meaning jerking his head.

'Yes, indeed,' Bazarov began, 'let that be a lesson to you, my young friend, a really edifying example. The devil knows what nonsense it is! Every single man hangs by a thread, a bottomless pit can open beneath him any minute, and yet he still goes on thinking up unpleasantnesses for himself and making a mess of his life.'

'What are you hinting at?' asked Arkady.

'I'm not hinting at anything, I'm saying straight out that you and I've behaved in a bloody silly way. There's no point talking about it! But I've already noted in clinical work that when someone gets angry at his pain he'll be certain to get the better of it.'

'I don't quite understand you,' said Arkady. 'It seems to me you didn't have anything to complain about.'

'If you don't quite understand me, I'll inform you of the following: in my opinion it's better to break stones working on a road than to let a woman control so much as the tip of your finger. That's all . . .' Bazarov was about to utter his favourite word— 'romanticism'—but desisted and said: '. . . nonsense! You won't believe me now, but I'm telling you that you and I've been in the society of women and we've enjoyed it, but to give up that society is just like having a bucketful of cold water poured over you on a hot day. A man shouldn't concern himself with such trivia. A man must be fierce, says an excellent Spanish proverb. Hey, you there,' he added, addressing the peasant sitting on the box, 'you, wiseacre, have you got a wife?'

The peasant turned to both friends his flat and dull-eyed face.

'A wife? Sure I 'ave. Who 'asn't?'

'Do you beat her?'

'My wife? Can do. Not wi'out a reason, mind.'

'Great! So does she ever beat you?'

The peasant jerked the reins. 'What a thing to say, sir! You're fond o' jokin', you are . . .' He was evidently offended.

'Listen to that, Arkady Nikolaevich! But you and I have been well and truly beaten—that's what it means to be educated people!'

Arkady gave a forced laugh, while Bazarov turned away and kept his mouth shut for the rest of the journey.

The twenty miles seemed a whole fifty to Arkady. But then, on descending a low hill, the small village where Bazarov's parents lived finally came into view. Next to it, enclosed by a young birch plantation, could be glimpsed a small manor house with a straw roof. At the first hut in the village two peasants in hats were standing and exchanging insults. 'You're a great big pig,' one said to the other, 'and worse than a little piglet.' 'And your wife's a witch,' the other retorted.

'In view of the lack of restraint in their forms of address', Bazarov remarked to Arkady, 'and the playfulness of their turns of speech, you can judge that my father's peasants aren't unduly oppressed. Oh, look, there he is coming out on to the porch of his residence! He's probably heard our harness bells. It's him, it's him—I recognize him! Hey! Hey! Still, how grey he's grown, poor old chap!'

20

BAZAROV leaned out of the tarantass and Arkady stretched his head round the back of his comrade and saw on the porch of the small manor house a tall, spare man with dishevelled hair and a thin, aquiline nose, dressed in an old army tunic which was hanging open. He was standing with his legs apart smoking a long-stemmed pipe and screwing up his eyes against the sun.

The horses came to a stop.

'So you've finally got here,' his father said to Bazarov, still continuing to smoke, although his pipe literally jumped up and down in his fingers. 'Come on, get down, get down, let me hug you.'

He had no sooner started embracing his son than 'Enyushka darling, Enyushka!' resounded from a wavering female voice. The front door was flung open and out on to the porch came a little round squat old woman in a white cap and a short colourful blouse. She cried out, appeared about to collapse and would certainly have fallen if Bazarov hadn't caught her. Her plump little arms instantly wound themselves round his neck and she pressed her head to his chest and everything suddenly went quiet. The only sounds were her intermittent sobbings.

Bazarov senior breathed deeply and screwed up his eyes even tighter.

'Well, that's enough, that's enough, Arisha! Stop it!' he began, exchanging a glance with Arkady who was standing motionless by the tarantass, while even the peasant on the box turned away his eyes. 'It's not necessary at all! Please stop it!'

'Ah, Vasily Ivanich,' muttered the old woman, 'for what ages I've been without my dear boy, my darling, my little Enyushka . . .' and, without relaxing her hold on him, she withdrew her wrinkled and delighted face, still wet with tears, from Bazarov, looked at him with eyes full of adoration and laughter and once more let her head drop on to his chest.

'Well, yes, of course, it's all in the nature of things,' said Vasily Ivanich, 'only it'd be better if we went indoors. Look, a guest has arrived with Evgeny. Forgive us,' he added, turning to Arkady and slightly shuffled one foot. 'A woman's frailty, you understand. Well, a mother's heart as well . . .'

But even his lips and eyebrows quivered and his chin shook, though he evidently sought to fight down his emotions and appear more or less indifferent. Arkady bowed.

'Really, let's go in, mother,' said Bazarov and led the exhausted old lady into the house. Having seen her into an easy chair, he once more hurriedly exchanged embraces with his father and introduced him to Arkady.

'Sincerely glad to make your acquaintance,' declared Vasily Ivanich, 'only please forgive me, everything here's done in a simple way, on a military footing. Arina Vlasevna, be quiet, there's a good thing. Why such emotionalism? Our gentleman guest will be bound to hold it against you.'

'Sir,' said the old lady through her tears, 'I don't have the honour to know your name and patronymic . . .'

'Arkady Nikolaich,' Vasily Ivanovich said to her seriously in a stage whisper.

'Forgive me, silly thing that I am.' The old lady blew her nose and, tilting her head first to the right, then to the left, carefully wiped one eye after the other. 'You must forgive me. You know, I literally thought I'd die without seeing my da-a-a-rling, da-a-a-rling boy again.'

'And so you've seen him, dear lady,' interrupted Vasily Ivanovich. 'Tanyushka . . .' He turned to a barefooted girl of about thirteen, in a bright-red cotton dress, who was peering in fright round the door '. . . bring the mistress a glass of water—on a tray, mind, do you hear?—and you, gentlemen,' he added with a kind of olde-worlde playfulness, 'allow me to invite you into the study of a retired veteran.'

'Enyushka dear, let me kiss you just one more time,' implored Arina Vlasevna. Bazarov bent down to her. 'Oh, what a handsome man you've become!'

'Well, it doesn't matter whether he's handsome or not,' remarked Vasily Ivanovich, 'but he's a man, an *homme fait*, as they say. And now I hope, Arina Vlasevna, having sated your mother's heart to the full, you'll think about sating our dear guests because, as you know, even nightingales can't live on songs alone.'

The old lady rose from the armchair.

'This very minute, Vasily Ivanich, the table'll be laid. I'll run into the kitchen myself and order the samovar got ready, and everything'll be ready, everything. But after three whole years of not seeing him, not having food ready for him, not getting him something to drink, you think it's easy, do you?'

'Well, see to it, then, like a good housewife, get along with you and don't let us down. While you, gentlemen, I ask you to follow me. Timofeich's here to pay his respects, Evgeny. And I dare say he's delighted, the old rascal. What? He's delighted, the old rascal, isn't he? Please come this way.'

And Vasily Ivanovich walked ahead fussily, scraping and shuffling his down-at-heel slippers.

His entire small house consisted of no more than six tiny rooms. One of them, into which he led our friends, was called the study. A thick-legged table, piled high with papers black with age-old dust, looking like soot, occupied the entire wall-space between the two windows. The walls were hung with Turkish guns, whips, a sabre, a couple of maps, some anatomical drawings and a portrait of Hufeland,* a monogram made of hair in a black frame and a diploma under glass. A leather sofa, torn and partly collapsed, was set between two enormous cupboards of Karelian birch. Shelves were crowded with a jumble of books, boxes, stuffed birds, jars and phials. In one corner stood a broken electric machine.

'I warned you, my dear visitor,' Vasily Ivanich began, 'that we live here, so to speak, in a bivouac manner . . .'

'Stop it. What're you apologizing for?' interrupted Bazarov. 'Kirsanov knows full well that we're not Croesuses and that you haven't got a palace. Where'll we put him? That's the question.'

'Of course, Evgeny—you see I've got a splendid room in the small wing. He'll be very comfortable there.'

'So you've had a small wing added, have you?'

'Yes, sir, where the bath-house is, sir,' Timofeich put in.

'Next to the bath-house, that is,' Vasily Ivanovich hurriedly concluded. 'Now it's summer it's . . . I'll just dash over there and see to it. Meanwhile, you, Timofeich, bring their things over. It goes without saying, Evgeny, that I leave my study at your disposal. *Suum cuique.*'*

'There you have it! He's the most entertaining old fellow and extremely kind,' added Bazarov, as soon as Vasily Ivanovich had left.

'Just as odd as yours, except in a different way. He just goes on and on about things a lot.'

'And I think your mother's marvellous,' said Arkady.

'Yes, there's no nonsense about her. Just you see the kind of dinner she'll give us.'

'They weren't expecting you today, sir. No beef's been delivered,' said Timofeich who was just dragging in Bazarov's trunk.

'We'll get by without beef—that can't be helped. Poverty, they say, isn't a sin.'

'How many serfs does your father have?' Arkady suddenly asked.

'The estate's not his but mother's. I remember about fifteen serfs.'

'Twenty-two in all now,' remarked a dissatisfied Timofeich.

There was the slap-slap of slippers approaching and Vasily Ivanovich reappeared.

'In a few minutes your room will be ready to receive you,' he exclaimed triumphantly, 'Arkady . . . It's Nikolaich, isn't it? I think that's how you like to be addressed, isn't it? And here's a servant for you,' he added, pointing to a boy who came in with him, his hair close-cropped, dressed in a blue caftan which was out at the elbows and someone's else's boots. 'He's called Fedka. Once again I repeat, though my son forbids me to, you mustn't hope for too much. Still, he knows how to fill a pipe. You smoke, don't you?'

'I smoke mostly cigars,' Arkady answered.

'And very sensible, too. I myself give preference to cigars, but in our isolated parts the obtaining of them is extraordinarily difficult.'

'Come off it, that's enough sackcloth and ashes,' Bazarov interrupted again. 'You'd be better off sitting on that sofa and letting us have a look at you.'

Vasily Ivanovich laughed and sat down. He looked very like his son, except that his forehead was narrower and less high and his mouth a little broader and he ceaselessly moved about and shrugged his shoulders just as if his clothing was too tight for him and blinked and coughed and drummed his fingers, while his son differed from him in a kind of unforced immobility.

'Sackcloth and ashes!' echoed Vasily Ivanovich. 'Evgeny, don't you get the idea that I'm trying, so to speak, to bring tears to our guest's eyes at the idea that we're living in such a back of beyond. On the contrary, I'm of the opinion that for a thinking man there's no such thing as a back of beyond. At least I've been trying as far as possible not to let the grass grow under my feet, not to fall behind the times.'

Vasily Ivanovich drew out of his pocket a new yellow handkerchief which he'd managed to pick up on his trip to Arkady's room and, waving it about in the air, went on saying:

'I'm not saying a thing, for example, about the fact that it isn't without hurtful sacrifices to myself that I've transferred my peasants to quit-rent and I've gone halves with them over my land. I considered it my duty and common sense itself demanded it in this instance, although other landowners haven't even so much as given it a thought. I'm referring to the common sense of science, of education.'

'Yes, I see you've got a copy of *The Friend of Health** for 1855,' Bazarov remarked.

'An old comrade of my acquaintance sent it to me,' said Vasily Ivanovich hurriedly, 'but we have some understanding, for instance, of phrenology,' he added, turning, however, more towards Arkady and pointing to a plaster cast of a head covered in numbered squares which was standing on top of a cupboard, 'and Schönlein* has not remained unknown to us, nor has Rademacher.'*

'So they still believe in Rademacher in this province of ours, do they?' asked Bazarov.

Vasily Ivanovich gave a cough.

'In this province of ours . . . Of course, gentlemen, you're better informed. How can we keep up with you? After all, you're here to take over from us. Even in my time a humoralist like Hoffmann* or a Brown* with his vitalism seemed very comic, although in their time they'd been famous. Somebody new has taken over from Rademacher in your view, you worship him, but in twenty years, no doubt, they'll be laughing at him as well.'

'It'll be a comfort to you to know', said Bazarov, 'that nowadays in general we laugh at medicine and worship nobody.'

'How d'you mean? You want to be a doctor, don't you?'

'I do, but the one doesn't prevent the other.'

Vasily Ivanovich stuck his third finger into his pipe bowl where a little burning ash still remained. 'Well, maybe, maybe, I'm not going to argue about that. After all, what am I? A retired army doctor, *voilà tout*, now turned agronomist. I served in your grandfather's brigade . . .' he addressed himself again to Arkady '. . . yes, sir, yes, indeed. I've seen some sights in my time. And the sorts of society I've been in, the people I've known! I myself, the very same person you see sitting here before you, I have felt the pulse of Prince Wittgenstein* and of Zhukovsky!* Those who were serving in the southern army on the 14th,* you know what I mean . . .' here Vasily Ivanovich pursed his lips meaningfully '. . . I knew every single one of them. Still, my business wasn't with them. For me it was—know how to wield your lancet and forget about the rest! But your grandfather was a very well-respected man, a true soldier.'

'Admit it, he was thick as a plank,' Bazarov drawled tiredly.

'Ah, Evgeny, the things you say! Heavens above! . . . Of course, General Kirsanov didn't belong among the . . .'

'Oh, forget about him!' Bazarov interrupted. 'As I was coming here I was real pleased by your little birch plantation and glad to see how it had spread out so well.'

Vasily Ivanovich grew excited at this.

'Just you take a look at how my little garden's doing now! I planted every sapling myself. I've got fruit trees and berries and all kinds of medicinal herbs. No matter how clever you young chaps are, still Paracelsus* uttered a sacred truth when he said '*in herbis, verbis et lapidibus* . . . After all, you know, I've given up practice, but a couple of times a week I find I've got to shake up the old grey cells. People come for advice and you can't drive them away. It can happen that the poor ask for my help. And there aren't any other doctors round here at all. One near neighbour, just imagine, a retired major, he also goes in for healing. I asked whether he'd studied medicine, and was told: No, he hadn't studied it, he just did it more out of philanthropy . . . Ha! Ha! Out of philanthropy! I ask you! Ha! Ha! Ha! Ha!'

'Fedya, fill me a pipe!' instructed Bazarov severely.

'And there used to be another doctor round here who made a visit to a sick man,' Vasily Ivanovich went on with a kind of desperation, 'but his patient had already gone *ad patres* and the servant wouldn't let the doctor in, saying there wasn't any need for him now. The doctor hadn't expected that and he asked in confusion: "Did your master hiccup before he died?" "Yes, sir, he did, sir." "Did he hiccup a lot?" "A lot, yes." "That's all right, then." And back he went home. Ha! Ha! Ha!'

The old man was the only one to laugh. Arkady permitted himself a smile. Bazarov simply inhaled. The conversation went on in this fashion for about an hour. Arkady managed to extricate himself and go to his room, which turned out to be part of the bath-house entrance, but very comfortable and clean. Finally little Tanya came in and announced that dinner was ready.

Vasily Ivanovich was the first to get up.

'Let's go, gentlemen! Be good enough to forgive me if I've bored you. Very likely my wife's entertainment'll satisfy you more than mine.'

The dinner, which had been prepared so quickly, turned out very well and was even sumptuous. Only the wine was, as they say, absolute plonk—an almost black type of sherry bought by Timofeich in town off a merchant of his acquaintance which tasted like a mixture of copper and resin. The flies were also a nuisance. Normally a servant-boy would keep them away with a large leafy branch, but on this occasion Vasily Ivanovich sent him away out of fear of being censured by the younger generation. Arina Vlasevna had found the time to smarten herself and had put on a tall cap with silk ribbons and a light-blue patterned shawl. She again burst into tears on seeing her darling Enyushka, but her husband had no occasion to scold her because she rapidly wiped away her tears so as not to spoil the shawl.

Only the young men ate, their hosts having dined long ago. Fedka served them, obviously encumbered by his unfamiliar boots, and he was assisted by a woman with a mannish face and only one eye, Anfisushka by name, who also performed the functions of house-keeper, poultry-keeper and laundress. Throughout the meal Vasily Ivanovich strode up and down the room and with a completely happy and even beatific look on his face spoke of the serious misgivings which he felt at Napoleonic politics and the complexities of the Italian question. Arina Vlasevna paid no attention whatever to Arkady and made no effort to be hospitable. With her little fist supporting her round face, to which the puffy, cherry-red lips and little birthmarks on her cheeks and above her eyebrows lent a very kindly, homely expression, she never took her eyes off her son and sighed again and again. She was dying to know how long he'd come for, but was frightened to ask. What if he says only for a couple of days? she thought and her heart went dead.

After the main course Vasily Ivanovich vanished for a short while and returned with an open half-bottle of champagne. 'See,' he exclaimed, 'although we live in the back of beyond, at times of celebration we know how to enjoy ourselves!' He poured out three wineglasses and a vodka glass, toasted the health of the 'inestimable visitors' and in true military fashion tossed back his glass while Arina Vlasevna was obliged to drink up her tot's worth of wine to the last drop. When the sweet course arrived, Arkady, who couldn't stand anything sweet, none the less considered it his duty to have a bit of four different sorts, all freshly made, more especially since Bazarov refused outright and immediately lit up a cigar. Then came the turn of tea with cream, butter and pretzels. Afterwards Vasily Ivanovich led everyone out into the garden to admire the beauty of the evening. Passing by a bench, he whispered to Arkady:

'This is the place where I love to philosophize as I watch the sun go down. It suits an old hermit like me. And there, a little farther off, I've put in a few of the trees beloved of Horace.'

'What trees are they?' asked Bazarov, overhearing him.

'Why, what else? Acacias.'

Bazarov began to yawn.

'I suppose it's time our travellers yielded to the arms of Morpheus,' remarked Vasily Ivanovich.

'You mean it's time to sleep!' declared Bazarov. 'That judgement is correct. It *is* time.'

Saying goodbye to his mother, he kissed her on the forehead, while she embraced him and secretly, behind his back, made the sign of the cross three times. Vasily Ivanovich conducted Arkady to his room and wished him 'the very same beneficial relaxation as I used to enjoy at your happy time of life.' And in fact Arkady did sleep extremely well in his bathroom entrance because it had a smell of mint and a couple of crickets took it in turns to chirrup away soporifically behind the stove. Vasily Ivanovich left Arkady, went to his study and, perching on the divan at his son's feet, would have liked to have chatted to him, but Bazarov at once sent him away, saying he wanted to sleep although he did not fall asleep until morning. His eyes wide open, he gazed irritably into the darkness because, if memories of childhood held no sway over him, he still had not managed to rid himself of his most recent bitter impressions. Arina Vlasevna at first said her prayers to her heart's content, then she conversed for a long, long time with Anfisushka who, standing as if rooted in front of her mistress and impaling her with her single eye, conveyed to her in a

mysterious whisper all her observations and thoughts concerning
Evgeny Vasilevich. The old lady's head had been completely turned
by the joy and the wine and the cigar smoke. Her husband had
wanted to have a word with her and gave up.

Arina Vlasevna was a real Russian noblewoman of former times.
She should have lived a couple of centuries before in the times of the
old Muscovy. She was extremely devout and emotional and believed
in all manner of omens, soothsayings, incantations and premonitory
dreams. She believed in those who were considered fools in God's
name, in spirits of the hearth and home, in forest spirits, in unlucky
encounters, in witchcraft and the evil eye, in folk remedies, in the
cure-all properties of Maundy salt and in the imminent end of the
world. She believed that, if on Easter Sunday the candles did not go
out at the midnight service, there would be a good buckwheat harvest, and that if a human eye should see a mushroom it would cease
growing. She believed that the devil always liked to be near water
and that every Jew had a blood-red birthmark on his chest. She was
frightened of mice, snakes, frogs, sparrows, leeches, thunder, cold
water, draughts, horses, goats, red-haired humans and black cats and
considered crickets and dogs unclean. She did not eat veal, pigeon,
crayfish, cheese, asparagus, artichokes, rabbit or melon, because a
severed melon resembled the severed head of John the Baptist. She
could not speak of oysters without shuddering. She was very fond of
eating, but was strict in her fasting. She would sleep ten hours out of
the twenty-four, but wouldn't go to bed at all if Vasily Ivanovich had
a headache. She had never read a book in her life apart from *Alexis,
or the Cottage in the Forest** and she wrote one—at most two—letters
a year, but she was clever at running a house, drying produce for
storage and making preserves, although she never touched anything
with her own hands and in general liked to remain sedentary. Arina
Vlasevna was very kind and in her own way not at all stupid. She
knew that there are those in the world who have to give orders and
the simple folk who must obey them, so she was not averse to signs of
servility in others, nor to the habit of bowing down to the ground,
but she always treated subordinates nicely and considerately and
never let a beggar pass by without giving him something and never
condemned anyone outright, gossip though she might from time to
time. In her youth she had been very good-looking, had learned to
play the clavichord and could speak a little French, but in the course

of many years of travelling about with her husband, whom she had married against her wishes, she had put on weight and forgotten about music and French. She adored and feared her son unspeakably; she left the running of the estate to Vasily Ivanovich and made no effort to involve herself, groaning and waving a handkerchief and raising her eyebrows ever higher and higher in horror the moment her old man started on about the forthcoming changes and his own plans. She was nervy, constantly anticipated some great misfortune or other and instantly burst into tears whenever she recalled something sad. Such ladies are already few and far between. God knows whether one should be glad of that fact!

21

RISING from his bed, Arkady flung open the window and the first thing he saw was Vasily Ivanovich. Dressed in a Bokhara dressing-gown tied at the waist with a large handkerchief, the old man was busily engaged in digging the kitchen garden. He noticed his young guest and, leaning on his spade, cried out:

'Good health to you! How did you sleep?'

'Splendidly,' answered Arkady.

'And I am here, as you can see, like a kind of Cincinnatus,* digging out a bed for some late turnips. The time has now come—and thank God it has!—for each one of us to obtain our means of survival with our own hands and not rely on others. One's got to do one's own work. It turns out that Jean-Jacques Rousseau* was right. Half an hour ago, my good sir, you'd have seen me in a completely different position. For one woman, who was complaining of the cramps—that's what they call it, but to us it's dysentery, I—how can I best express it?—I doled out opium. For another one I pulled out a tooth. I offered her some ether, only she refused. I do it all gratis—*en amateur*. Besides, it's nothing unusual for me because I'm a man of the people, a *homo novus*, not from a hereditary line, like my trouble and strife . . . Wouldn't you like to come out here into the shade, to breathe in some fresh air before we have tea?'

Arkady joined him outside.

'Welcome once again!' declared Vasily Ivanovich, raising his hand in a military salute to the greasy skull-cap on his head. 'I know you are accustomed to luxury and to pleasure, but even the great men of this world are not averse to spending a short while beneath a cottage roof.'

'I say,' retorted Arkady, 'what sort of a great man of this world am I? And I'm not accustomed to luxury.'

'Have it your way, please,' responded Vasily Ivanovich with a friendly grimace. 'I may be put on the shelf now, but I've also been about the world a bit and I can tell what a bird is from its flight. I'm also a bit of a psychologist, after my fashion, and a physiognomist. If I hadn't had such a gift, I dare say, I'd have been done for long ago. Being a small man, they'd have wiped the floor with me. I can tell you without compliments that the friendship which I note between you and my son genuinely pleases me. I've just seen him. As is his habit, no doubt well known to you, he got up very early and has dashed around the whole place. May I be so curious as to ask—have you known my son long?'

'Since last winter.'

'I see. Allow me to ask you—but you'll sit down, won't you?— allow me as a father to ask you in all sincerity, what's your opinion of my Evgeny?'

'Your son is one of the most remarkable men I have ever met,' answered Arkady animatedly.

Vasily Ivanovich's eyes opened wide suddenly and his cheeks went slightly pink. The spade fell from his grasp.

'So you assume . . .' he began.

'I am sure', broke in Arkady, 'that there is a great future waiting for your son, that he will make your name famous. I was convinced of this at our first meeting.'

'How . . . how was that?' Vasily Ivanovich was scarcely able to ask. A delighted smile parted his wide lips and remained fixed there.

'You'd like to know how we met?'

'Yes . . . and all about . . .'

Arkady began telling his story and speaking about Bazarov with even greater warmth and even greater fondness than on the evening when he had danced the mazurka with Odintsova.

Vasily Ivanovich listened and listened, blew his nose, rolled his handkerchief between his hands, coughed, ruffled his hair and finally it all became too much for him, he bent towards Arkady and kissed him on the shoulder.

'You have made me a completely happy man,' he pronounced, still smiling broadly. 'I must tell you that I . . . I simply worship my son. I can't say anything about my old woman—you know what mothers are!—but I do not dare to show my feelings in his presence, because he doesn't like that kind of thing. He's opposed to all outpourings of emotion. Many even condemn him for such severity of character and see in it a sign of arrogance and lack of feeling. But you can't apply ordinary rules to people like him, can you? For example, someone else in his place would have gone on asking more and more of his parents, but in our case—can you believe it?—he's never taken a single extra penny, by God he hasn't!'

'He's an unselfish, honest man,' remarked Arkady.

'That's it—he's unselfish. And, Arkady Nikolaich, I not only simply worship him but I am proud of him, and my one ambition is that in time the following words should appear in his biography: "The son of a simple regimental doctor who, however, early recognized his ability and spared nothing to ensure his education . . ."' The old man's voice broke off.

Arkady squeezed his hand.

'What d'you think,' asked Vasily Ivanovich after a short silence, 'is it in a medical career that he'll achieve the fame you predict for him?'

'Perhaps not in a medical career, although in this respect he'll be among the leading scientists.'

'In what, then?'

'It's hard to say at present, but he will be famous.'

'He will be famous!' repeated the old man and fell into deep thought.

'Arina Vlasevna asks you to come and have tea,' announced Anfisushka, passing by with an enormous dish of ripe raspberries.

Vasily Ivanovich shook himself out of his thoughts. 'Will there be chilled cream with the raspberries?'

'Yes, sir.'

'Chilled cream as well, see to it! Don't be shy, Arkady Nikolaich, take some more. Why isn't Evgeny here?'

'I'm here,' cried Bazarov's voice from the direction of Arkady's room. Vasily Ivanovich quickly turned round.

'Aha! You wanted to visit your friend! But you're too late, *amice*, he and I've already had an extended conversation. Now it's time to go and have our tea—your mother's summoned us. Besides, I wanted to have a word with you.'

'About what?'

'There's a little fellow here, a peasant, he's suffering from icterus . . .'

'Do you mean jaundice?'

'Yes, chronic and very obstinate icterus. I prescribed centaury and St John's wort, made him eat carrot and dosed him with soda, but these are merely *palliatives* and something more effective is needed. Although you laugh at medicine, I'm sure you could give me some practical advice. But we'll talk about that later. Now let's go and drink some tea.'

Vasily Ivanovich jumped up from the bench and broke into the song from the opera *Robert le Diable*:*

> 'We'll set ourselves a law, a law
> To live for joy for evermore!'

'Astonishing vivacity!' exclaimed Bazarov, withdrawing from the window.

Midday approached. The sun burned down from behind a thin layer of solid whitish cloud. Everything went quiet and only cocks crowed vigorously in the village, arousing in all who heard them a strange sensation of drowsiness and ennui. Somewhere high above in the tips of the trees the unceasing screech of a fledgling hawk rang out plaintively. Arkady and Bazarov lay in the shade of a small hay-stack, having spread out beneath them armfuls of dry and rustling, though still green and fragrant hay.

'That aspen over there', Bazarov began, 'reminds me of my child-hood. It's growing at the edge of a hole which is all that remains of a brick barn, and in those days I was sure that that hole and that aspen possessed special magic powers, because I was never bored when I was near them. I didn't understand then that I wasn't bored because I was a child. Now I'm grown-up the special magic powers don't work any more.'

'How much time did you spend here in all?' asked Arkady.

'A couple of years in a row. Then we'd come back here from time to time. We led a vagrant life. Most of the time we were mucking about in towns.'

'Has this house been here long?'

'A long time. My grandfather built it, my mother's father.'

'Who was he, your grandfather?'

'The devil only knows. An adjutant-major or something. Served under Suvorov* and talked all the time about crossing the Alps. It must've been a lot of nonsense.'

'That's why a portrait of Suvorov is hanging in your sitting-room. I love little houses like yours, they're so old and cosy. And they've got a special smell.'

'It gives off lamp-oil and sweet clover,' declared Bazarov with a yawn. 'As for the flies in such charming little houses—Phew!'

'Tell me,' began Arkady after a short silence, 'were they strict with you as a child?'

'You see what parents I have. They're not strict folk.'

'Do you love them, Evgeny?'

'I love them, Arkady.'

'They love you so much!'

Bazarov did not speak for a while.

'You know what I'm thinking?' he said eventually, putting his hands behind his head.

'No, I don't. What?'

'I'm thinking my parents have pretty good lives! There's my father at sixty busying himself with this and that, talking about "palliatives", helping to cure people, being all grand and magnanimous with his peasants and generally having a whale of a time. And there's my mother, her day so packed with various activities, with so many "oh's" and "ah's", that she never gives herself time to think. But as for me . . .'

'You?'

'What I'm thinking is: here I am, lying under a haystack . . . The tiny little place I occupy is so small in relation to the rest of space where I am not and where it's none of my business; and the amount of time which I'll succeed in living is so insignificant by comparison with the eternity where I haven't been and never will be . . . And yet in this atom, in this mathematical point, the blood circulates, the brain works and even desires something as well . . . What sheer ugliness! What sheer nonsense!'

'Allow me to remark that what you're saying can be applied generally to all people . . .'

'You're right,' broke in Bazarov. 'What I meant to say was that they—my parents, that's to say—are busy and don't worry about their own insignificance, they don't care a shit about it . . . but I . . . I feel merely boredom and anger.'

'Anger? Why anger?'

'Why? Whadya mean why? Have you forgotten?'

'I remember everything, but I don't recognize your right to be angry. You're unhappy, I agree, but . . .'

'Hey! Yes, I can see, Arkady Nikolaevich, you understand love like all the most modern young people as "Come on, come on, come on, little chick", but as soon as the little chick starts approaching you're off like a shot! I'm not like that. But enough of this. What can't be helped shouldn't be talked about.' He turned on his side. 'Aha!

Look! Here's an ant pulling along a half-dead fly. Go on, mate, pull away! Don't bother about the fact that she's resisting you, make use of the fact that you, as an animal, have the right not to recognize feelings of pity, not like people like us, we who've busted ourselves!'

'You shouldn't say that, Evgeny! When did you bust yourself?'

Bazarov raised his head.

'That's the only thing I've got to be proud of. I haven't bust myself, so no woman's going to bust me. Amen! Enough said! You won't hear another word from me about this.'

Both friends lay for a time in silence.

'Yes,' began Bazarov, 'a man's a strange creature. When you squint from a distance at the dull life our honoured "fathers" live here, you think: What could be better? You eat and you drink and you know you're behaving in the most proper, the most rational manner. But no—the boredom of it'll kill you. You start to want people round, even if it's just to swear at, but there must be people round you.'

'Life has to be arranged in such a way that each moment of it should be important,' Arkady declared thoughtfully.

'Listen who's talking! The important can be false and sugar-coated, and one can even reconcile oneself to the unimportant . . . but squabbles, squabbles—they're bloody awful!'

'Squabbles don't exist for someone if he simply ignores them.'

'Hmm . . . What you've just said is a back-to-front commonplace.'

'What? What're you calling that?'

'Look, it's like this: to say, for example, that education is useful is a commonplace, but to say that education is harmful is a back-to-front commonplace. It seems fancier but in fact it's the same.'

'Where's the truth, on which side?'

'Where is it? I'll answer you with the same question: where is it?'

'You're in a melancholy mood today, Evgeny.'

'Is that so? The sun must have got to my brain and I shouldn't have eaten so many raspberries.'

'In that case it'd be good to have a doze,' Arkady remarked.

'Maybe. Only don't you look at me. A person's face always looks silly when he's asleep.'

'Are you all that bothered what people think about you?'

'I don't know what to say. A real man shouldn't bother about it. A real man is one you don't think about but one you've got to obey or detest.'

'That's strange! I don't detest anyone,' said Arkady after a moment's reflection.

'But I detest lots of people. You're a softy, you're wishy-washy, there's no point in you detesting anyone! You're all shy and retiring, you couldn't rely on yourself much . . .'

'Whereas you,' Arkady interrupted, 'you can rely on yourself, eh? You have a high opinion of yourself, do you?'

Bazarov was silent for a while.

'When I meet a man who can stand up to me', he said, emphasizing each word, 'then I'll change my opinion about myself. Detest! Look, for example, today you said, as we went past the hut of our village bailiff Philip—the fine, white one—you said: "Russia will only reach perfection when the very last peasant will have a dwelling like that and each of us has got to help to bring this about . . .". But, you know, I absolutely loathed that very last peasant, that Philip or Sidor, for whom I've got to work my fingers to the bone and who won't even give me a thankyou—and why the hell should he? Well, so he'll live in his white hut while I'll be pushing up the daisies . . . Well, so what?'

'That's enough, Evgeny . . . To listen to you today one would be bound to agree with those who reproach us for not having any principles.'

'You're talking like your uncle. In general there are no principles—to think you haven't grasped that yet!—but there are feelings. Everything depends on them.'

'Why's that?'

'Because it does. Take me, for example, I advocate a negative point of view—on the strength of my feelings. I like being negative, that's the way my brain works—and that's all there is to it! Why do I like chemistry? Why do you like apples? It's on the strength of your feelings, too. It's all one and the same. People'll never get deeper than that. It isn't everyone'll tell you this, and even I mightn't tell you this another time.'

'What d'you mean? Is even honesty just a feeling?'

'Of course!'

'Evgeny!' Arkady began in a sad tone of voice.

'Eh? What? That's not to your taste, eh?' Bazarov interrupted. 'No, mate, once you've decided to mow everything down, you might as well knock yourself off your feet as well! Still, we've done enough philosophizing. "Nature induces the silence of sleep", said Pushkin.'

'He never said anything of the kind,' said Arkady.

'Well, if he didn't say it, then he could and should have said it, in his capacity as a poet. Besides, he must have done military service.'

'Pushkin was never a soldier!'

'For heaven's sake, on every page he's got "To fight! To fight! For Russia's honour!"'

'What fairy-tales you do think up! Anyhow, that's a slander.'

'Slander? Big deal! There's a big word you've thought up just to frighten me! No matter what slander you do to a man, in fact he deserves twenty times worse.'

'Let's go to sleep!' announced Arkady with annoyance.

'With the greatest pleasure,' Bazarov answered.

But neither the one nor the other was able to sleep. An almost hostile feeling took possession of the hearts of both young men. After about five minutes they opened their eyes and silently exchanged glances.

'Look,' Arkady suddenly said, 'a dry maple leaf has broken loose and is falling to the ground. Its movement is exactly like the flight of a butterfly. Isn't that odd? What is saddest and dead bears a resemblance to what is most joyous and living.'

'Oh, Arkady Nikolaich, my friend,' exclaimed Bazarov, 'I ask one thing of you: Don't talk fancy!'

'I talk the way I know . . . Anyhow, you're becoming a dictator. A thought came into my head, so why shouldn't I express it?'

'I see. But why shouldn't I also express my thought too? I think that fancy talk is improper.'

'So what's proper? Swearing?'

'Aha! Yes, I can see you're determined to follow in your uncle's footsteps. How that idiot would be delighted if he heard you now!'

'What did you call Pavel Petrovich?'

'I called him what he deserves to be called—an idiot.'

'But this is intolerable!' cried Arkady.

'Aha! There speaks family feeling,' Bazarov said calmly. 'I've noticed it's very firmly rooted in people. A man will give up every-thing, repudiate every prejudice, but to admit, for example, that his brother who steals other people's handkerchiefs is a thief is beyond his powers. It's really a case of *my* brother, *mine*—not whether he's a genius . . . Can that be right?'

'In my case it wasn't family feeling, but a simple sense of justice,' Arkady retorted. 'But because you don't understand that sense, because you haven't got that *feeling*, you can't pass judgement on it.'

'In other words, Arkady Kirsanov is too elevated for my understanding, so I bow down before you and hold my tongue.'

'That's enough, please, Evgeny. We'll end up by quarrelling.'

'Ah, Arkady, do me a favour! Let's quarrel once and for all—to the death, to the bitter end!'

'But if we do, surely we'll end by . . .'

'By having a fight?' butted in Bazarov. 'So what? Here, in the hay, in such idyllic surroundings, far from the world and human eyes, it won't mean a thing! But you'd never get the better of me. I'd get you by the throat straight off . . .'

Bazarov extended his long, hard fingers, while Arkady turned and prepared to defend himself, if only in fun. But so full of hatred was his friend's face, so very unfunny the threat he perceived in his twisted grin and burning eyes, that Arkady felt a momentary timidity regardless . . .

'Ah! That's where you've got to!' rang out the voice of Vasily Ivanovich at that instant, and there rose before the two young men the figure of the old regimental doctor, wearing a home-made linen jacket and with a straw hat, also home-made, on his head. 'I was looking for you everywhere. But you've chosen a splendid place and you've devoted yourselves to a marvellous occupation. Lying on the "earth" and looking up at "heaven" . . . You know, that means something really special, doesn't it?'

'I look up to heaven only when I want to sneeze,' said Bazarov bluntly and, turning to Arkady, added under his breath: 'A pity he interrupted.'

'Well, that's enough,' whispered Arkady and squeezed his friend's hand surreptitiously. But no friendship can withstand such confrontations for long.

'I look at you, my young conversationalists,' Vasily Ivanovich was saying in the meantime, shaking his head and leaning with hands crossed on a cleverly twisted stick of his own design, with the carving of a Turk for a handle, 'I look at you and I can't help admiring you. What strength there is in you, what youth in full flower, what ability, what talent! You are quite simply a . . . a Castor and Pollux!'

'Would you believe it—he's gone off into mythology!' declared Bazarov. 'It's obvious you were a powerful Latinist in your time! I'm right in thinking, aren't I, that you were awarded a silver medal for composition, eh?'

'O Dioscuri, Dioscuri!' repeated Vasily Ivanovich.

'Still, father, that's enough showing off.'

'At a certain time of life a little showing-off's permitted,' muttered the old man. 'Besides, gentlemen. I was looking for you not in order to pay you compliments but, first of all, to inform you that we'll be having dinner shortly and, secondly, I wanted to warn you, Evgeny . . . You're a sensible chap, you know how people are, and you know what women are, and consequently you'll forgive them if . . . Your mother wanted to hold a church service to mark your return home. You mustn't imagine that I'm asking you to attend the service. Anyhow, it's already over. But Father Aleksei . . .'

'The priest?'

'Well, yes, the member of the clergy. He'll be . . . He'll be having dinner with us . . . I didn't expect that and I even advised against it . . . But that's how it's worked out . . . He misunderstood me . . . Well, Arina Vlasevna also . . . In any case, he's a very kind and sensible chap . . .'

'He won't eat my portion at dinner, will he?' Bazarov asked.

Vasily Ivanovich laughed. 'For heaven's sake, what are you saying!'

'I don't ask anything more. I'm ready to sit down and eat with anyone.'

Vasily Ivanovich adjusted his hat.

'I was sure beforehand,' he said, 'that you were above all kinds of prejudice. Take me now, an old man, sixty-two years old, I don't even have any.' (Vasily Ivanovich did not dare admit that he had himself wanted a church service; he was no less devout than his wife.) 'But Father Aleksei very much wanted to make your acquaintance. You'll like him, you'll see. He's not averse to a game of cards and he even—but this is just between ourselves—he even smokes a pipe.'

'Is that so? We'll sit down after dinner for cards and I'll beat him.'

'Ha-ha-ha, we'll see! You can't be too sure.'

'Really? You're not stirring it all up, are you?' asked Bazarov with a special emphasis.

The bronzed cheeks of Vasily Ivanovich went a dark red.

'You ought to be ashamed of yourself, Evgeny. What's past is over and done with. Well, yes, I am ready to admit in front of our friend here that I had a passion for cards when I was young—that's true. Yes, and I paid for it, sure enough! Still, how hot it is! May I join you? I'm not disturbing you, am I?'

'Not in the least,' answered Arkady.

Vasily Ivanovich lowered himself into the hay with a grunt and a wheeze.

'I am reminded by your present lodging, my dear sirs,' he began, 'of my bivouac army life and the dressing stations, also in a place like this next to a haystack and by God we were glad they were.' He heaved a sigh. 'I've experienced a very great deal in my time. For example, if you'll permit me, I'll tell of a curious episode during the plague in Bessarabia.'

'For which you received the Vladimir,* didn't you?' Bazarov broke in. 'We know, we know. In any case, why don't you wear it?'

'I've told you, after all, that I haven't any prejudices,' muttered Vasily Ivanovich (he had only the day before ordered the red ribbon to be taken off his jacket) and started telling his story about the plague. 'And after all that he's gone to sleep,' he whispered suddenly to Arkady, pointing at Bazarov and giving a jovial wink. 'Evgeny, up you get!' he added loudly. 'We must go and have dinner . . .'

Father Aleksei, a large and impressive man, with thick, meticulously groomed hair and an embroidered belt worn round his violet silk cassock, turned out to be very skilful and resourceful. He was the first to make a point of offering his hand to Arkady and Bazarov, as if aware they weren't in need of his blessing, and in general he behaved in an agreeably unconstrained manner. He did not let himself down and did not belittle others. Whenever appropriate, he laughed at seminar Latin and stood up for his bishop. He drank two glasses of wine and refused a third. He accepted a cigar from Arkady, but did not smoke it, saying that he would take it home. He had only one not entirely pleasant habit, which was that from time to time he would slowly and carefully raise his hand to swat flies on his face and sometimes managed to squash them.

He took his place at the green card-table with a measured

expression of pleasure and ended by winning two roubles and fifty copecks in notes off Bazarov, the reason being that Arina Vlasevna had no understanding of how to count in silver coins. As usual she sat next to her son (she never played cards), as usual she had her cheek resting on her little fist and she only stood up in order to see that a new dish was served. She was frightened of making any display of affection for Bazarov and he didn't encourage her or invite any fondness from her, and Vasily Ivanovich had in any case advised her not to 'disturb him too much'. 'Young people don't like that kind of thing,' he insisted to her. (As for the dinner that day, there were no complaints: Timofeich had himself in person galloped off at the crack of dawn to obtain some special Circassian beef and the bailiff had gone off in another direction to get freshwater burbot, ruff and crayfish, while simply for mushrooms alone peasant women had received forty-two copper copecks.) But Arina Vlasevna's eyes, directed constantly at Bazarov, expressed not merely devotion and fondness; they could also be seen to contain sadness mixed with curiosity and fear, and a certain meek reproach.

However, Bazarov was in no mood to analyse exactly what his mother's eyes expressed. He rarely turned to her and then only with a short question. He asked her once for her hand 'to bring me luck' and she calmly placed her soft little hand in his broad, hard-skinned palm.

'Well,' she asked after a moment, 'did that help?'

'Made it even worse,' he replied with a dismissive laugh.

'He is playing an almighty risky game,' declared Father Aleksei, as if with some regret, and stroked his fine beard.

'A Napoleonic rule, father. Napoleonic,' chimed in Vasily Ivanovich and led with an ace.

'That rule got him to St Helena,' said Father Aleksei and trumped the ace.

'Wouldn't you like a blackcurrant drink, Enyushka darling?' asked Arina Vlasevna.

Bazarov merely shrugged his shoulders.

'No!' he told Arkady the next day. 'I'll be leaving tomorrow. I'm bored. I want to work, but it's impossible here. I'll go back to your estate. I've left all my things there. At least at your place I can lock my door. Here my father goes on insisting "My study's at your disposal, no one'll disturb you there," but he never leaves me alone for a moment. And I feel bad about locking him out. And my mother, too. I hear her sighing on the other side of the wall and go out and see her—and I can't think of a thing to say.'

'She'll be very upset,' said Arkady, 'and he will be as well.'

'I'll be coming back.'

'When?'

'When I'm off to St Petersburg.'

'I'm particularly sorry for your mother.'

'Why's that? She's been plying you with berries, has she?'

Arkady lowered his eyes.

'You don't know your mother, Evgeny. She's not only a splendid woman, she's very clever—and I mean it. This morning she talked to me for about half an hour and so sensibly, so interestingly.'

'Was she on about me the whole time?'

'It wasn't only about you.'

'Perhaps you're right. You can see things as an outsider. If a woman can conduct a half-hour conversation, that's a good sign. But I'm still going to leave.'

'It won't be easy for you to give them this news. They're talking all the time about what we'll be doing in a couple of weeks.'

'It won't be easy, no. The devil wound me up today to have a bit of fun at father's expense. He recently had one of his quit-rent peasants flogged—and a good thing, too—you don't have to look at me with such horror!— and a good thing, too, because he was a thief and a frightful drunkard. Only father'd never expected that I'd become, as they say, apprised of the fact. He was extremely put out, and now I've got to annoy him with this in addition . . . It doesn't matter! He'll get over it!'

Bazarov said 'It doesn't matter!' but a whole day passed before he could bring himself to tell his father of his intention. Finally, while saying good-night to him in his study, he announced with a protracted yawn:

'Yes, and I'd almost forgotten to mention . . . Please tell them tomorrow to have our horses sent to Fedot's for going away.'

Vasily Ivanovich was astonished.

'Is Mr Kirsanov leaving us?'

'Yes, and I'm going with him.'

Vasily Ivanovich swung round on the spot.

'You're leaving us?'

'Yes, I've got to. Please arrange about the horses.'

'Good,' the old man started muttering, 'for going away . . . Good . . . Only, er, only why?'

'I've got to travel to his place for a short while. Afterwards I'll come back here again.'

'Ah! For a short while! Good.' Vasily Ivanovich took out his handkerchief and, giving a sneeze, almost bent down to the ground. 'So that'll be all, will it? I'd thought you'd spend a bit longer with us. Three days . . . After three years that's . . . that's not very much, it's not very much, Evgeny!'

'Well, I'm telling you I'll be back soon. But I've got to.'

'Got to . . . So be it, you've got to do your duty, that must come first. So I'll send off the horses, shall I? Right. Arina and I haven't expected this, of course. She's asked for some flowers from a neighbour to make your room look nice.' (Vasily Ivanovich did not mention the fact that each morning, as soon as it was light, standing barefoot in his slippers, he had had discussions with Timofeich and, taking out one torn banknote after another with trembling fingers, he had ordered him to make various purchases, laying particular stress on delicacies to eat and on red wine which, so far as could be observed, the young men enjoyed very much.) 'The main thing is freedom. That's always been my rule. You mustn't impose restraints . . . You mustn't . . .'

He suddenly fell silent and went off towards the door.

'We'll be seeing each other again soon, father, we really will.'

But Vasily Ivanovich, without turning round, simply gave a wave of the hand and went out. On returning to his bedroom, he found his wife already in bed and began to say his prayers in a whisper so as not to disturb her. However, she woke up.

'Is that you, Vasily Ivanovich?' she asked.

'It's me, my dear.'

'Have you just come from seeing Enyushka? Do you know, I'm afraid it may not be nice for him sleeping on that sofa. I've asked Anfisushka to lay out your little travelling mattress and new pillows. I'd have given him our feather one, but then I remembered he never liked sleeping on anything soft.'

'It doesn't matter, my dear, don't worry. He's all right. Oh, Lord, forgive us, sinners that we are,' he went on with his prayer in a subdued voice. Vasily Ivanovich took pity on the old woman who was his wife. He did not want to tell her that night what sorrow awaited her.

Bazarov and Arkady left the next day. From morning onwards everything in the house was touched by gloom. A dish fell out of Anfisushka's hands. Even Fedka was at a loss and ended by taking off his boots. Vasily Ivanovich fussed about more than ever, evidently trying to keep his spirits up by talking loudly and stamping his feet, but his face had a puckered, pinched look and he constantly avoided meeting his son's eyes. Arina Vlasevna cried softly. She would have completely broken down and lost control of herself had not her husband spent two whole hours in the early morning dissuading her. When Bazarov, after frequent promises that he would be back within a month, finally tore himself away from the embraces which held him and took his seat in the tarantass; when the horses had set off and the harness-bell had begun tinkling and the wheels had started turning—and there was nothing left to see, the dust having settled and Timofeich, all bent and tottering, having crept back into his cramped room; and when the old couple were left alone in their own suddenly equally cramped and decrepit house, Vasily Ivanovich, who had still kept up a brave pretence outside on the porch of waving his handkerchief in the air for a few moments, sank into a chair and let his head drop on to his chest.

'He's left us, he's given us up,' he muttered, 'given us up . . . He got bored with being here. Now I'm alone, utterly alone! Just like this finger!' He repeated this several times and each time he held up his index finger.

Then Arina Vlasevna went up close to him and, leaning her grey head against his grey head, said:

'There's nothing for it, Vasya! Our son's cut off from us. He's a falcon, like a falcon he wanted to come and he flew here, then he wanted away and he flew away. But you and I, we're just a couple of old mushrooms, we are, stuck in the hollow of a tree, sitting side by side and never moving. Except that I'll always remain the same for you for ever and ever, just as you will for me.'

Vasily Ivanovich took his hands away from his face and suddenly embraced his wife, his true friend, more tightly even than he'd been used to embrace her in his youth, for she had comforted him in his misery.

22

IN silence, only occasionally exchanging a few unimportant words, our friends travelled to Fedot's. Bazarov was not entirely satisfied with himself. Arkady was dissatisfied with him. In addition, he felt in his heart that pointless sadness which is familiar only to those who are very young. The coachman changed the horses and, climbing on to his box, asked which way: right or left?

Arkady gave a shudder. The road to the right led towards town and then home; the road to the left led to Odintsova's.

He glanced in Bazarov's direction.

'Evgeny,' he asked, 'do we go left?'

Bazarov turned away.

'What sort of stupidity is this?' he muttered.

'I know what sort of stupidity it is,' Arkady answered. 'Still, what's it matter? It's not the first time, is it?'

Bazarov shoved his cap down over his forehead.

'You know best,' he said eventually.

'Left!' shouted Arkady.

The tarantass rolled off in the direction of Nikolskoe. But having decided on such 'stupidity', the friends maintained an even more obstinate silence than before and even seemed angry.

As soon as the head butler met them on the steps of the Odintsov house, the two friends could guess that they had behaved foolishly in yielding to such a sudden whim. They were evidently not expected. They cooled their heels for a fairly long time in the drawing-room and wore fairly silly looks on their faces. Eventually Odintsova came out to see them. She greeted them with her usual cordiality, but was surprised by their quick return and, in so far as it was possible to judge from her unhurried gestures and remarks, she was none too pleased by it. They hastened to make clear that they had only called by on their way and in four hours or so would be off again in the direction of the town. She limited herself to a slight exclamation, asked Arkady to convey her greetings to his father and sent for her aunt. The Princess appeared just having woken up, a fact which lent even greater malice to the expression on her old and wrinkled face. Katya was unwell and did not leave her room. Arkady suddenly realized that he had wanted to see Katya at least as much as he had wanted to see Anna Sergeevna. The four hours or so passed in inconsequential chat about this and that. Anna Sergeevna both listened and spoke without smiling. Only at the moment of their departure did the former fondness seem to stir in her heart.

'You find me in a depressed state today,' she said, 'but you shouldn't pay any attention to that and you must come again—I say this to both of you—in a short while.'

Both Bazarov and Arkady answered her with wordless bows, took their places in their carriage and, without stopping anywhere at all, set off home, to Marino, which they reached safely on the following evening. Throughout the entire journey neither the one nor the other so much as mentioned Odintsova's name. Bazarov, in particular, hardly opened his mouth and spent all the time staring to one side, away from the road, with a kind of embittered intensity.

In Marino everyone was extraordinarily excited at their arrival. The prolonged absence of his son had begun to worry Nikolai Petrovich. He gave a shout, did a little jig and jumped up and down on the sofa when Fenechka came running into him with shining eyes and announced the arrival of 'the young gentlemen'. Pavel Petrovich himself felt a certain pleasant excitement and smiled condescendingly as he shook hands with the returned travellers. Discussion and questions ensued. Arkady talked more than anyone, particularly at dinner, which went on until after midnight. Nikolai Petrovich ordered several bottles of porter, recently delivered from Moscow, to be served, and drank so much that his cheeks became red as raspberries and he laughed continually with a mixture of childishness and nervousness. The general exhilaration spread to the servants as well. Dunyasha ran to and fro like a mad thing and was constantly banging doors, and Peter at three o'clock in the morning was still trying to master a Cossack-style waltz on his guitar. The strings rang out plaintively and pleasantly on the still air, but, with the exception of a few initial grace-notes, nothing came of the efforts of the perfectly trained gentleman's gentleman, for nature had denied him a gift for music as it had denied him a gift for everything else.

Meanwhile, life had not been running too smoothly at Marino and things were going badly for poor Nikolai Petrovich. Worries about the farm increased day by day and they were unhappy, senseless worries. The fuss and bother with the hired workers had become intolerable. Some demanded a settling of accounts or bonuses while others left after having received payment in advance. The horses fell ill. Harnesses were used up so quickly it was as if they'd been burned up. All the work was done negligently. The threshing-machine ordered from Moscow turned out to be useless due to its weight. Another was put out of commission the first time it was used. Half the cattle shed burned down because one blind old woman, a house-serf, had gone in windy weather to delouse her cow with a burning ember . . . True, according to this same old woman, the entire mis-fortune was due to the fact that the master had had the idea of introducing hitherto unheard-of cheeses and dairy products. The farm bailiff suddenly grew thoroughly lazy and even began to put on weight, just as every Russian puts on weight once he's in clover. Seeing Nikolai Petrovich from some distance, he'd throw a stick at a piglet running by or threaten some half-naked little boy, in order to make a show of doing his job zealously, but he spent most of his time sleeping. The peasants who had been transferred to quit-rent didn't pay their dues on time and stole wood. Almost every night watch-men caught—and sometimes seized by force—peasant horses which had been grazing in the farm meadows. Nikolai Petrovich tried to introduce monetary fines for such infringements, but the matter usually ended with the horses being returned to their owners after they had spent a day or two out to grass on the master's land. To crown everything, the peasants began squabbling among themselves. Brothers began to demand redivision of their allotments because their wives couldn't get on together in the same house. Fights would suddenly break out and all would suddenly be on their feet, as if at a command, and all would rush to the office steps, often drunk and with smashed-up faces, and plead to see the master and demand justice and retribution and there'd be noise and commotion and the shrill shrieks of the women would mingle with the loud swearing of the men. The warring sides had to be sorted out, which meant shouting until one was hoarse, knowing beforehand that it was almost impossible to reach the right decision. There weren't enough hands for the harvest. A local farmer with the most benign counten-ance had undertaken to supply reapers at a commission of a couple of roubles an acre and had then cheated in an utterly unscrupulous fashion. The farm's own women workers had put up their charges to an unheard-of degree and the crops meanwhile were running to seed, and then there was the fact that the mowing was behindhand, and then again the Council of Trustees was making threats and demanding the immediate and full payment of interest . . .

'I haven't any strength left!' Nikolai Petrovich cried more than once in desperation. 'I can't knock their heads together on my own, my principles don't allow me to send for the local policeman, but without fear of punishment you can't do a damned thing!'

'*Du calme, du calme,*' Pavel Petrovich responded to this, while humming and hawing, frowning and pulling at his moustache.

Bazarov kept himself apart from these 'squabbles' and in any case, as a guest, it was not for him to meddle in other people's affairs. The day after his arrival at Marino he set about dealing with his frogs, his infusorians and chemical compounds and spent the whole time busy with them. Arkady, by contrast, considered it his duty if not to help his father, then at least to give the appearance of being willing to help. He listened patiently to him and on one occasion offered advice, not so that it should be taken but simply to indicate his interest. Running an estate did not arouse any revulsion in him. He even dreamed with pleasure about dealing with farming matters, but at that time his head was swarming with other thoughts.

To his own astonishment, Arkady found himself ceaselessly thinking about Nikolskoe. Previously he would simply have shrugged his shoulders if someone had suggested he might be bored living under the same roof with Bazarov—and what a roof at that! His own roof after all!—but he *was* bored and he wanted out. He conceived the idea of walking to the point of exhaustion, but that did not help. Talking on one occasion to his father, he learned that Nikolai Petrovich had in his possession several rather interesting letters which had been written by Odintsova's mother to his late wife, and he pestered him until he'd obtained these letters, in search of which Nikolai Petrovich was obliged to rummage about in twenty or so different boxes and trunks. Having obtained possession of these half-decayed pieces of paper, Arkady seemed to grow calmer, as if he saw before him now an aim that he could pursue. ' "I say this to both of you"— that's what she herself added,' he whispered to himself all the while. 'The devil take it, I'll go! I'll go!' But he recalled the last visit, the cool reception and his former awkwardness—and shyness got the better of him. Still, a youthful sense of 'What the hell!', a secret wish to try his luck and put his own powers to the test on his own without anyone else's help finally gained the upper hand. Scarcely ten days after his return to Marino, on the pretext of studying the working of local Sunday schools,* he galloped off to the town and from there to Nikolskoe. Ceaselessly urging his driver on, he travelled there like a young officer off to battle, overwhelmed by fear and joy and hardly able to breathe with excitement. 'The chief thing is not to think,' he constantly repeated to himself. His driver turned out to be mad on driving fast and stopped at every inn on the route, saying 'One for the road, eh?' or 'What about one?' but, having 'had one', did not spare the horses. At last the tall roof of the familiar house came in sight. 'What on earth am I doing?' was the thought that flashed through Arkady's head. 'But I can't turn back now!' The troika of horses raced along at full tilt and the driver shouted and whistled. The little bridge thundered beneath the hooves and wheels and the avenue of neatly trimmed firs grew closer and closer . . .

A girl's pink dress flickered in the dark green of the foliage and a young face looked out from beneath the light fringe of a parasol. He recognized Katya and she recognized him. Arkady ordered the driver to stop the frantically galloping horses, jumped down from the carriage and went towards her. 'So it's you!' she cried and gradually blushed all over. 'Let's go and see my sister, she's here in the garden. She'll be glad to see you.'

Katya led Arkady into the garden. The meeting with her seemed to him a particularly happy omen. He was delighted at seeing her, as if she were a close relative. Everything was working out so splendidly, without any head butler or need for him to be announced. At a turn in the path he caught sight of Anna Sergeevna. She was standing with her back to him. Hearing his footsteps, she calmly turned round.

Arkady was once again on the point of being embarrassed, but the first words she uttered calmed him at once.

'Hello, you runaway!' she said in her level, fond voice and walked towards him, smiling and screwing up her eyes against the sun and the breeze. 'Where did you find him, Katya?'

'Anna Sergeevna,' he began, 'I have brought you something quite unexpected . . .'

'You've brought yourself, that's best of all.'

23

HAVING said goodbye to Arkady with mock regret and letting him know that he was not deceived in the least about the real object of his journey, Bazarov was finally left on his own. He was possessed by a fever of work. He no longer quarrelled with Pavel Petrovich, all the more so since the latter, in his presence, adopted an excessively aristocratic look and expressed his opinions more by sounds than by words. Only on one occasion was Pavel Petrovich on the point of crossing swords with the 'nihilist' over the then fashionable question of the landowners in the Baltic provinces,* but he stopped himself, declaring with cold politeness:

'However, we are unable to understand one another. I, at least, have the honour not to understand you.'

'Really!' exclaimed Bazarov. 'Man is in a position to understand everything—both the vibration of the ether and what happens on the sun, but how another man can sneeze differently from the way he sneezes he's in no position to understand.'

'Eh? Are you trying to be clever?' Pavel Petrovich asked, and walked off.

However, he sometimes asked permission to be present at Bazarov's experiments and once even lowered his fragrant face, washed with the finest of soaps, close to the microscope to inspect a transparent infusorian swallowing a speck of green dust and carefully masticating it with tiny, very busy, fist-like retractors in its throat. Much more frequently than his brother it was Nikolai Petrovich who visited Bazarov, coming every day, as he put it, to 'learn something' if the cares of managing the estate did not prevent him. He would never get in the young natural scientist's way and always took a seat somewhere in the corner of the room and watched attentively, now and then permitting himself to ask a safe question. During meal-times he always tried to direct the conversation to physics, geology or chemistry, because all other subjects, even those relating to estate management, not to mention political ones, could lead, if not to confrontation, then to mutual dissatisfaction. Nikolai Petrovich was aware that his brother's hatred for Bazarov had not diminished in the least. An unimportant event, among many others, confirmed him in this. Cholera began to break out in the surrounding area and even 'carried off' two people from Marino itself. One night Pavel Petrovich suffered from a particularly violent attack. He was tortured with pain until morning, but he did not turn to Bazarov for help and, on seeing him the next day, in answer to his question why he hadn't sent for him said, still pale, but clean-shaven and with his hair perfectly brushed: 'Surely you said yourself, don't you remember, that you don't believe in medicine?' So the days passed one by one. Bazarov worked on stubbornly and grimly. But meanwhile there was someone in Nikolai Petrovich's house to whom he could not exactly open his heart but with whom he was glad to chat. That person was Fenechka.

He used to meet her chiefly early in the morning, in the garden or in the yard. He never went to her room and she only came and knocked on his door once, when she wanted to ask whether or not she should give Mitya a bath. Not only did she trust him, not only did she not fear him, she behaved with him a lot more freely and openly than with Nikolai Petrovich. It is hard to say why this was. It was perhaps because she subconsciously sensed in Bazarov the absence of anything aristocratic and of any of that superiority which can both attract and frighten. In her eyes he was both an excellent doctor and an unassuming man. She busied herself with her baby unbothered by his presence and, on one occasion, when she suddenly felt giddy and had a headache, she accepted a spoonful of medicine from his hands. Whenever Nikolai Petrovich was about she seemed to fight shy of Bazarov. She did this not out of guile but out of a feeling of decency. Pavel Petrovich she feared more than ever. He had taken recently to watching her closely and would suddenly put in an appearance, literally rising from the earth behind her back dressed in his English suit, with his watchful, immobile face and his hands in his pockets. 'It makes you go all cold,' Fenechka would complain to Dunyasha and the latter would respond with a sigh and think about another 'unfeeling' man. Bazarov, without suspecting it, had become the 'cruel tyrant' of her heart.

Fenechka liked Bazarov. But he also liked her. Even his face would change whenever he spoke to her. It would assume a clear, almost kindly expression and a certain fun-loving attentiveness became mixed in with his usual casual manner. Fenechka grew prettier as each day passed. There is a time in the life of every young woman when she suddenly begins to blossom and flower like a summer rose. This time had come for Fenechka. Everything contributed to it, even the July heat which was then at its height. Dressed in a white summer dress, she herself looked whiter and more summery than ever. She did not go brown, but the heat, from which she could not protect herself, brought a slight pinkness to her cheeks and ears and, softly relaxing her whole body, was reflected by her pretty eyes in a dreamily languorous look. She could hardly bring herself to work at anything. Her hands would constantly slip down into her lap. She could scarcely walk about and only did so with groans and complaints at her funny feeling of weakness.

'You should go bathing more often,' Nikolai Petrovich told her.

He had set up a large bathing-place, covered with canvas, in one of the ponds which still had some water in it.

'Oh, Nikolai Petrovich! The heat'll kill you getting to the pond and it'll kill you coming back! There's no shade anywhere in the garden!'

'It's true there's no shade,' answered Nikolai Petrovich and wiped his eyebrows.

On one occasion, at seven in the morning, Bazarov, while returning from a stroll, came across Fenechka in a bower of lilac which had long ceased flowering but was still thick and green. She was sitting on a bench, having as usual put a white kerchief over her head. Beside her lay a whole heap of red and white roses still damp with dew. He greeted her.

'Ah! Evgeny Vasilich!' she exclaimed and lifted the edge of the kerchief to look at him, in doing so baring her arm as far as the elbow.

'What are you doing here?' asked Bazarov, sitting down beside her. 'Are you making a bouquet?'

'Yes, for the breakfast table. Nikolai Petrovich likes it.'

'But breakfast's not for a while yet. What a heap of flowers!'

'I've been picking them now, because it'll get so hot it'll be impossible to go outside. This is the only time I can breathe. I've got completely weak from this heat. I'm frightened I might be falling ill.'

'What an imagination you've got! Let me feel your pulse.' Bazarov took her hand, sought out the evenly beating vein and did not even bother to count the heartbeats. 'You'll live a hundred years,' he declared, letting go of her hand.

'Oh, God preserve us!' she exclaimed.

'What? Don't you want to live a hundred years?'

'A hundred years! My grandma was eighty-five or so and what a misery she was! Gone all black-looking, deaf and bent and coughing all the time—she was a burden to herself. That's no sort of life!'

'So it's better to be young?'

'Why not?'

'Why's it better? You tell me that!'

'Why? Look at me now, I'm young, I can do everything I want—I can go and come and carry what I like and I don't have to ask anyone to do things for me . . . What more could you ask?'

'But to me it's all the same whether I'm young or old.'

'How can you say it's all the same? It's not possible, what you're saying.'

'Yes, well, you judge for yourself, Fedosya Nikolaevna, what my youth is worth to me? I live by myself, quite on my own . . .'

'That's always up to you.'

'Not entirely up to me! There's got to be someone to take pity on me.'

Fenechka gave Bazarov a sideways glance but said nothing.

'What's that book?' she asked after a moment's silence.

'This one? It's a solemn scientific book.'

'Why do you study all the time? Aren't you bored? I'd've thought you knew everything already.'

'As you can see, I don't. Try and read some of it yourself.'

'I won't understand a thing in it. Is it in Russian?' Fenechka asked, taking the volume with its heavy binding in both hands. 'How big it is!'

'Yes, it's in Russian.'

'Still, I won't understand any of it.'

'I didn't ask you so you'd understand it. I wanted to watch you while you read. When you read, the tip of your nose wiggles very charmingly.'

Fenechka, who had tried under her breath to make sense of an article on creosote, burst out laughing and cast the book aside. It slid down from the bench on to the ground.

'I also like it when you laugh,' said Bazarov.

'That's enough!'

'I like it when you talk. It's just like a babbling brook.'

Fenechka turned her head away. 'The things you say!' she cried, running her fingers through the flowers. 'And what do you want to listen to me for? You've had talks with such clever women.'

'Fedosya Nikolaevna, believe me, all the clever women in the world aren't worth your little elbow!'

'Oh, there's another fib!' Fenechka whispered and clasped her hands together.

Bazarov picked up the book from the ground.

'This is a medical book. Why did you throw it down?'

'A medical book, is it?' repeated Fenechka and turned towards him. 'You know something? Ever since you gave me those drops— remember?—Mitya is sleeping so well! I can't think how to thank you. You really have been very kind.'

'In actual fact doctors have got to be paid,' Bazarov remarked with a grin. 'As you know yourself, doctors are a mercenary lot.'

Fenechka raised to Bazarov eyes that seemed even darker as a result of the whitish reflection falling on the upper part of her face. She did not know whether he was joking or not.

'If you'd like that, we will with pleasure . . . I'll have to ask Nikolai Petrovich . . .'

'Do you think I want money?' Bazarov interrupted her. 'No, it's not money I want from you.'

'What, then?' asked Fenechka.

'What?' repeated Bazarov. 'You guess.'

'I'm no good at guessing!'

'So I'll tell you: I want . . . one of those roses.'

Fenechka again burst out laughing and even clasped her hands tightly, so funny did Bazarov's request seem to her. She laughed and simultaneously felt she'd been sweet-talked into it. Bazarov was looking intently at her.

'Please, please,' she said at last and, bending down to the bench, started sorting through the roses. 'Which would you like, a red or a white one?'

'A red one, and not too large.'

She straightened up.

'Here, take it,' she said, but instantly withdrew her outstretched hand and, biting her lip, glanced towards the entrance of the bower and then pricked up her ears.

'What is it?' said Bazarov. 'Is it Nikolai Petrovich?'

'No, no . . . He's ridden off into the fields . . . No, I'm not frightened of him, but it's Pavel Petrovich . . . I thought for a moment . . .'

'What?'

'I thought it was *him* walking by. No . . . No, it's no one. Take it.'
Fenechka handed Bazarov a rose.

'Why on earth are you frightened of Pavel Petrovich?'

'He gives me the shivers. It's not what he says, it's his way of
looking at you. After all, you're not fond of him, are you? Remember
how you used to quarrel with him all the time? I don't know what the
quarrelling was all about, but I saw you could twist him round your
little finger . . .'

Fenechka demonstrated with her hands what she meant when she
said Bazarov twisted Pavel Petrovich round his little finger. Bazarov
smiled.

'If he started to get the better of me,' he asked, 'would you stand
up for me?'

'Why should I need to stand up for you? No one'll get the better of
you.'

'You think that, do you? But I know a hand that could knock me
down with one finger if it wanted to.'

'What hand is that?'

'You mean you don't know? Just smell the fragrance of the rose
you've given me.'

Fenechka craned her slender neck and brought her face close to
the rose. The kerchief slipped from her head on to her shoulders and
revealed a soft mass of black, shining, slightly dishevelled hair.

'One moment, I'd like to smell the rose as well,' said Bazarov, bent
forward and kissed her strongly on her open lips. She reacted with a
start, pressed both her hands against his chest, but her pressure was
weak and he was able to renew and prolong his kiss.

From the other side of the lilacs came a dry cough. Fenechka
instantly shifted to the other end of the bench. Pavel Petrovich
appeared, gave a slight bow and said with a kind of malicious des-
pondency: 'You are here, I see,' and walked on. Fenechka at once
picked up all the roses and left the bower. 'You shouldn't have done
that, Evgeny Vasilevich,' she whispered as she went out. There was
nothing pretend about her whispered reproach.

Bazarov recalled another recent scene and felt both conscience-
stricken and annoyed to the point of self-hatred. But he immediately

gave a shake of the head, ironically congratulated himself on being 'formally admitted into the ranks of the world's womanizers'* and went off to his room.

Meanwhile, Pavel Petrovich left the garden and, walking at a slow pace, made his way as far as a wood. He remained there a fairly long time and when he returned for breakfast Nikolai Petrovich asked him in a worried voice whether he was well, because his face had become so sombre.

'You know how I sometimes suffer from an excess of bile,' Pavel Petrovich answered him calmly.

24

ABOUT two hours later he tapped on Bazarov's door.

'I must apologize for disturbing you at your scientific pursuits,' he began, taking a seat by the window and leaning both his hands on a beautiful walking-stick with an ivory handle (he usually walked without a stick), 'but I am bound to ask you to allow me five minutes of your time—no more.'

'All my time is at your disposal,' answered Bazarov, whose face had shown a rapid change of expression as soon as Pavel Petrovich had stepped into his room.

'Five minutes is all I need. I have come to put you a question.'

'A question? About what?'

'Please be good enough to listen. At the beginning of your stay in my brother's house, when I still did not deny myself the pleasure of conversing with you, I happened to hear your opinions on many matters, but so far as I can recollect, neither between us nor in my presence, did what was said ever touch on duels or duelling in general. Allow me to know what your opinion is on this subject.'

Bazarov, who had been on the point of rising to greet Pavel Petrovich, seated himself on the edge of the table and folded his arms.

'This is my opinion,' he said. 'From a theoretical point of view a duel is a nonsense. But from a practical point of view—well, that's another matter.'

'You mean, I take it, if I have understood you, that no matter what your theoretical view of duels may be, in practice you would not allow yourself to be insulted without demanding satisfaction?'

'You have fully fathomed my thought.'

'Very well, sir. I am very pleased to hear you say this. Your words relieve me of the need to know . . .'

'Of the need to decide, you mean.'

'It makes no difference, sir. I say things so that I may be understood. I am no seminar creep. Your words relieve me of a certain sad necessity. I have decided to fight a duel with you.'

Bazarov's eyes popped out of his head.

'With me?'

'Exactly, sir, with you.'

'Why, for heaven's sake?'

'I could explain to you my reason,' began Pavel Petrovich, 'but I prefer not to speak of it. You, according to my tastes, are superfluous here. I cannot stand you, I hate you, and if that isn't enough . . .'

Pavel Petrovich's eyes glittered. Bazarov's flashed also.

'Very good, sir,' he said. 'Further explanations are unnecessary. You've taken it into your head to try out on me your spirit of knight errantry. I could refuse you that pleasure, but so be it!'

'I am sincerely obliged to you,' answered Pavel Petrovich, 'and I can hope now that you will accept my challenge without making me resort to violent measures.'

'That is, leaving allegories aside, without resort to your stick?' remarked Bazarov coldly. 'That is completely right. You'd gain nothing by inflicting injury on me. It also might not be entirely safe for you. You can remain a gentleman . . . I accept your challenge also in a gentlemanly spirit.'

'Splendid,' said Pavel Petrovich and stood his stick in the corner. 'We'll now say a few words about the conditions of our duel. But I'd like to know first—do you consider there's any need to resort to the formality of a small quarrel which could provide a pretext for my challenge?'

'No, it'd be better without formalities.'

'I myself think so, too. I assume it would also be inappropriate to go into the real reasons for our confrontation. We cannot stand each other. What more is needed?'

'What more?' repeated Bazarov ironically.

'So far as the actual conditions of the duel are concerned, since there won't be any seconds—after all, where'll we find them?'

'Precisely—where'll we find them?'

'So I have the honour to propose the following: that we fight early tomorrow, say, at six o'clock, behind the grove, using pistols. The distance will be ten paces . . .'

'Ten? All right, we can hate each other at that distance.'

'It could be eight,' remarked Pavel Petrovich.

'Eight—so be it!'

'Two shots each. In any case, each of us should have a letter in his pocket which puts the blame for his death on himself.'

'No, I'm not entirely in agreement with that,' said Bazarov. 'It smacks too much of a French novel, a bit fanciful.'

'Perhaps. Still, you'd agree, wouldn't you, that it would not be nice to be suspected of murder?'

'I agree. But there is a way of avoiding that sad fate. We may not have seconds, but we could have a witness.'

'Who precisely, may I ask?'

'Peter.'

'What Peter?'

'Your brother's manservant. He is a man at the very summit of contemporary refinement and will undertake his role with all the *comme il faut* necessary in such circumstances.'

'I think you must be joking, my good sir.'

'Not in the least. Having given my proposal some thought, you will be convinced that it is informed with common sense and a lack of complication. There's no hiding the truth. I will take it upon myself to prepare Peter in a suitable fashion and bring him to the site of the carnage.'

'You will go on joking about it,' uttered Pavel Petrovich as he rose from his chair. 'But after the admirable readiness which you have shown I have no right to impose on you . . . So everything is settled . . . By the way, have you any pistols?'

'What on earth would I have pistols for, Pavel Petrovich? I am not a military man.'

'In that case, I offer you mine. You can be sure that I haven't used them for five years.'

'That's very comforting news.'

Pavel Petrovich picked up his walking-stick.

'So, my good sir, it simply remains for me to thank you and let you get back to your pursuits. My humble respects.'

'A pleasant goodbye, my good sir,' said Bazarov, seeing his guest out.

Pavel Petrovich went out, but Bazarov stood for a moment at the door and suddenly cried out:

'Bloody hell! What a lot of fine words and what nonsense! What a comedy we've got involved in! Like a couple of dogs trained to prance about on their hind legs. But I couldn't refuse. I mean, he'd very likely have hit me, and then . . .' (Bazarov paled at the very idea; all his pride literally reared up.) 'Then I'd have had to throttle him like a kitten.'

He went back to his microscope, but his heart was beating too fast and the calm needed for research had vanished. 'He must have seen us today,' he thought, 'but surely he's not doing this on his brother's behalf? Just a kiss—big deal! There's something else. Ha! Is he in love with her himself? It goes without saying—he's in love with her, it's clear as daylight! What a tangle, just think! It's bad, though,' he decided eventually, 'bad, no matter what way you look at it! Firstly, I'll have to offer my forehead to an adversary's bullet and in any case I'll have to leave. Then there's Arkady to think about . . . and that jolly old bug, Nikolai Petrovich. It's bad, bad!'

The day passed particularly quietly and flatly. It was as if Fenechka simply no longer existed, sitting in her own room quiet as a mouse in its hole. Nikolai Petrovich had a worried look. He had been told that in the wheat, on which he had placed special hopes, rust had appeared. Pavel Petrovich oppressed everyone, even Prokofich, with his icy politeness. Bazarov began a letter to his father and then tore it up and threw it under the table. 'If I die', he thought, 'they'll learn soon enough. But I'm not going to die. No, I'll be sticking around on this earth a long while yet.' He ordered Peter to come to him the next day at first light for an important matter. Peter imagined that he wanted to take him to St Petersburg. Bazarov went to bed late and spent the whole night tormented by crazy dreams. Odintsova spun round and round him, but she turned out to be his mother, and behind her came a little kitten with black whiskers and she turned out to be Fenechka. Pavel Petrovich appeared to him as an enormous forest with which he still nevertheless had to fight a duel. Peter awoke him at four o'clock and he immediately dressed and went out with him.

The morning was marvellous and fresh. Small dappled clouds formed a fleece against the pale clear blue. A fine dew was scattered on leaves and grass and glittered like silver on spiders' webs. The damp dark earth still seemed to retain within it the rosy pinkness of the sunrise. The whole sky was filled with the singing of larks. Bazarov made his way as far as the grove, sat down in the shade at the edge of it and only then revealed to Peter what he expected of him. The perfectly trained gentleman's gentleman was scared to death. But Bazarov allayed his fears with the assurance that all he had to do was stand at a distance and watch, and that he would not be held responsible for anything. 'Anyhow,' he added, 'think what an important role you're going to play!' Peter made a gesture of despair, hung his head and leaned back against a silver birch, green in the face.

The road from Marino went round the little grove. A light coating of dust lay on it, as yet untouched since the previous day by wheel-marks or footprints. Bazarov couldn't help glancing along this road while he pulled off blades of grass and chewed at them and all the while repeated to himself: 'How bloody silly!' The morning chill made him shiver a couple of times. Peter glanced at him despondently, but Bazarov simply grinned back at him. He was no coward.

The sound of horses' hooves came from the roadway. A peasant appeared from behind the trees. He was driving in front of him a couple of horses harnessed together and, as he went past Bazarov, looked at him somewhat oddly without removing his cap, which evidently struck Peter as a bad omen. He's up early, thought Bazarov, and at least he's about his business, but what are we doing here?

'I think he's coming, sir,' hissed Peter suddenly.

Bazarov raised his head and saw Pavel Petrovich. Dressed in a checked summer jacket and trousers white as snow, he was walking briskly along the road. Under his arm he carried a box wrapped in a green cloth.

'Forgive me, I seem to have kept you waiting,' he said, bowing first to Bazarov, then to Peter, whom he invested at that moment with the authority of a second. 'I did not wish to disturb my valet.'

'That's quite all right,' responded Bazarov. 'We've only just arrived ourselves.'

'Ah, so much the better!' Pavel Petrovich glanced round him. 'No one in sight, no one to trouble us . . . We can begin?'

'We can begin.'

'You don't want any further discussion, I presume?'

'No.'

'Would you like to do the loading?' asked Pavel Petrovich, removing the pistols from the box.

'No, you do the loading. I will start measuring out the paces. My legs are longer,' added Bazarov with a grin. 'One, two, three . . .'

'Evgeny Vasilich,' babbled Peter with difficulty (he was shaking as if in a high fever), 'if you'll permit me I'll withdraw.'

'Four . . . five . . . Withdraw, my dear chap, withdraw. You can even go and stand behind a tree and cover your ears, only don't close your eyes. And if someone falls, run and help him up.

Six . . . seven . . . eight . . .' Bazarov stopped. 'Is that enough?' he said, turning to Pavel Petrovich. 'Or shall I add another couple?'

'As you wish,' said the latter, ramming home a second bullet.

'Well, I'll take a couple more.' Bazarov made a mark on the ground with the toe of his boot. 'That's the barrier marked out. By the way, how many paces do each of us take back from the barrier? It's important to know. There was no discussion about this yesterday.'

'Ten, I suggest,' answered Pavel Petrovich, offering Bazarov both pistols. 'Please be good enough to choose.'

'I will be good enough . . . You will agree with me, Pavel Petrovich, that our duel is so unusual as to be comical. Just take a look at the physiognomy of our second.'

'You still want to make a joke of it,' replied Pavel Petrovich. 'I do not deny the oddness of our duel, but I consider it my duty to warn you that I intend to fight seriously. *A bon entendeur, salut!* He who has ears to hear, let him hear.'

'Oh, I don't doubt we are determined to exterminate each other. But why not laugh and combine *utile dulci*, the useful with the pleasant? You see—you use French to me, I use Latin to you.'

'I will fight seriously,' repeated Pavel Petrovich and took up his position. Bazarov for his part counted out ten paces from the barrier and stopped.

'You are ready?' asked Pavel Petrovich.

'Completely.'

'Then we can approach.'

Bazarov calmly moved forward and Pavel Petrovich walked towards him, with his left hand in his pocket and with the other gradually raising the barrel of his pistol. He's aiming straight at my nose, thought Bazarov, and how intently he's screwing up his eyes, the villain! Still, it's a very unpleasant sensation. I'll fix my eyes on his watch chain . . .

Something whizzed sharply past Bazarov's ear and the same instant a shot rang out.

I've heard it, he managed to think, so nothing's happened. He took a step forward and, without aiming, squeezed the trigger.

Pavel Petrovich staggered slightly and grabbed at his thigh. A trickle of blood appeared through his white trousers.

Bazarov flung his pistol aside and approached his opponent.

'Are you wounded?' he asked.

'You have the right to summon me to the barrier,' said Pavel Petrovich, 'and this is nothing. The condition is that each of us still has another shot.'

'Well, forgive me, that can wait for another time,' Bazarov replied and seized hold of Pavel Petrovich, who had begun to grow pale. 'I'm no longer a duellist but a doctor and must first of all inspect your wound. Peter! Come here, Peter! Where's he got to?'

'All this is nonsense . . . I'm . . . not . . . in . . . need . . . of . . . any help,' said Pavel Petrovich, stopping between each word. 'I . . . have to . . . once more . . .' He tried to tweak his moustache, but his hand failed him, his eyes rolled up and he lost consciousness.

'Here's something else! A fainting fit! What next!' Bazarov cried, lowering Pavel Petrovich into the grass. 'Let's see what it's all about.' He took out a handkerchief, wiped away the blood and searched around the wound. 'No bones broken,' he muttered through his teeth. 'The bullet passed through without going deep and one muscle, the *vastus externus*, has been hit. He'll be doing a jig in three weeks! But going into a dead faint! Oh, these nervy people! Just look how delicate his skin is.'

'Is he dead, sir?' croaked the quavering voice of Peter just behind him.

Bazarov glanced round.

'Go and get some water, my dear chap, quick as you can. He'll outlive both of us.'

But the perfect gentleman's gentleman appeared not to understand a word that was said and did not budge. Pavel Petrovich slowly opened his eyes. 'It's the end!' whispered Peter and began to make the sign of the cross.

'You're right . . . What a silly physiognomy!' said the wounded gentleman with a forced smile.

'The devil take you, go and get some water!' shouted Bazarov.

'It's all right . . . It was a momentary *vertige* . . . Help me up . . . That's right . . . This scratch simply needs something wrapping round it and I'll make my way home on foot, or failing that they can send the droshky for me. The duel, if you agree, will not be renewed. You have behaved with nobility . . . today, today—take note of that.'

'There's no point in harping on the past,' retorted Bazarov, 'and as for the future, there's no point in busting your head over that either, because I intend to get the hell out of here. Come on, I'll bandage up your leg now. Your wound isn't dangerous, but the best thing is to staunch the bleeding. First of all, though, I must bring this creature to his senses.'

Bazarov shook Peter by the scruff of the neck and sent him to fetch the droshky.

'See you don't alarm my brother,' Pavel Petrovich told him. 'And don't you dare tell him anything about this.'

Peter dashed off and while he ran for the droshky the two opponents sat on the ground and kept silent. Pavel Petrovich tried not to look at Bazarov. He had no wish to be reconciled with him. He was ashamed of his arrogance and his failure, ashamed of the whole enterprise, although he also felt it couldn't have ended in a more satisfactory way. At least he won't be seen around here any longer, he comforted himself, and one can be thankful for that. The silence continued, oppressive and awkward. Both of them felt in the wrong. Each of them knew that the other understood him. For friends this knowledge is pleasant, and for enemies it is particularly unpleasant, especially when there can be neither explanations, nor any chance of escaping from each other.

'Have I tied your bandage too tight?' Bazarov asked at last.

'No, that's all right, it's splendid,' answered Pavel Petrovich and then added a moment later: 'You won't fool my brother. We'll have to tell him that we quarrelled over politics.'

'Very good,' said Bazarov. 'You can say that I was rude about Anglophiles.'

'Splendid. What do you suppose that man thinks about us now?' Pavel Petrovich went on, pointing at the very same peasant who, a few minutes before the duel, had driven the harnessed horses past Bazarov and, returning back along the roadway, took off his cap and 'tugged his forelock' at the sight of his 'masters'.

'Who the hell knows!' answered Bazarov. 'More than likely he doesn't think anything at all. The Russian peasant is just like the mysterious stranger about whom Mrs Radcliffe* used to write so often. Who can understand him? He can't understand himself.'

'Ha! You've hit the nail on . . .' Pavel Petrovich was on the point of saying more and suddenly cried: 'Just look what your silly idiot Peter's gone and done! There's my brother galloping towards us!'

Bazarov turned and saw the pale face of Nikolai Petrovich who was sitting in the droshky. He jumped down before the vehicle had come to a stop and rushed towards his brother.

'What's this mean?' he asked in an excited voice. 'Evgeny Vasilich, for heaven's sake, what is this?'

'It's nothing,' answered Pavel Petrovich. 'There was no reason for you to be bothered about this. Mr Bazarov and I had a small disagreement and I am a little in his debt.'

'But what was the cause of all this, for God's sake?'

'How can I put it? Mr Bazarov made a disrespectful remark about Sir Robert Peel.* I hasten to add that I alone am to blame for this and Mr Bazarov has behaved admirably. It was I who issued the challenge.'

'But you're bleeding, for heaven's sake!'

'Did you suppose that I had water in my veins? But this blood-letting could even do me good. Isn't that true, doctor? Help me into the droshky and don't go all melancholy. I'll be all right tomorrow. That's right. Splendid. Drive on, coachman!'

Nikolai Petrovich walked off behind the droshky. Bazarov would have remained behind, but Nikolai Petrovich said to him: 'I must beg you to take care of my brother until another doctor can be brought from town.'

Bazarov nodded without saying a word.

An hour later Pavel Petrovich lay in bed with an expertly bandaged leg. The whole house was in an uproar. Fenechka complained of being unwell. Nikolai Petrovich wrung his hands on the quiet, while Pavel Petrovich laughed and made jokes, especially with Bazarov. He put on a fine white linen shirt, a fashionable short morning coat and a fez, did not permit the blinds to be lowered over the windows and enjoyed complaining about the need to refrain from food.

Towards evening, however, he grew feverish and his head began to ache. The doctor came from town. (Nikolai Petrovich had not listened to his brother and Bazarov himself had not wanted it otherwise. He had spent the whole day in his room, all jaundiced and angry, and he had only paid the shortest of visits to his patient; on a couple of occasions he had happened to encounter Fenechka, but she had run away from him in horror.) The new doctor prescribed cooling drinks and, besides, gave his backing to Bazarov's assurances that there was no danger of any kind. Nikolai Petrovich told him that his brother had wounded himself through carelessness, to which the doctor answered 'Hmm!' But having had his palm crossed with twenty-five roubles in silver coinage he said: 'You don't say! Exactly, that often happens.'

No one in the house went to bed and no one undressed. Nikolai Petrovich spent the whole time going to and fro to his brother on tiptoe. The latter would drop off, groan slightly, tell him in French: '*Couchez-vous*' and then ask for a drink. Nikolai Petrovich made Fenechka take him a glass of lemonade. Pavel Petrovich looked at her intently and drank the glass down to the last drop. The fever grew a little worse towards morning and he became slightly delirious. At first Pavel Petrovich started talking disconnectedly. Then he suddenly opened his eyes and, seeing his brother beside his bed, leaning anxiously over him, said:

'Don't you think it's true, Nikolai, that Fenechka has something in common with Nelly?'

'With what Nelly, Pasha?'

'Why do you ask that? With Princess R. . . . Particularly in the upper part of her face. *C'est de la même famille.*'

Nikolai Petrovich did not reply, but for his own part he was astonished at the way old feelings can survive in a man. So that's come to the surface again, he thought.

'Oh, how much I love that empty creature!' groaned Pavel Petrovich, sadly folding his hands behind his head. 'I won't tolerate some brazen cad daring to get his hands on her,' he babbled a few moments later.

Nikolai Petrovich did no more than sigh. He did not suspect who these words referred to.

The next day Bazarov came to him about eight o'clock. He had managed to pack all his things away and set free all his frogs, insects and birds.

'Have you come to say goodbye?' asked Nikolai Petrovich, rising to greet him.

'I have, sir.'

'I understand you and entirely approve of what you're doing. My poor brother is of course to blame and he's had to pay for it. He told me himself that he placed you in an impossible position. I'm sure you couldn't avoid this duel which . . . which is to be explained to some extent simply by the ongoing antagonism in your mutual views.' (Nikolai Petrovich found it hard to put what he meant into words.) 'My brother is a man of the old school, excitable and stubborn . . . Thank God, it's all over now. I've taken every possible measure to prevent news of it leaking out . . .'

'I'll leave you my address in case something happens,' Bazarov remarked casually.

'I hope nothing'll happen. Evgeny Vasilich . . . er, I'm very sorry your stay in my house has had to have such a . . . such a conclusion. It's all the more grievous to me that Arkady . . .'

'I'll very likely be seeing him,' responded Bazarov, in whom 'explanations' and 'declarations' of any kind always evoked feelings of impatience. 'In the event that I don't, I would ask you to give him my respects and ask him to accept my expressions of regret.'

'And I would ask you . . .' Nikolai Petrovich answered, bowing. But Bazarov did not wait for the end of his sentence and left the room.

Learning of Bazarov's departure, Pavel Petrovich wanted to see him and shook him by the hand. But Bazarov remained cold as ice even at this, realizing that Pavel Petrovich sought to make a display of his magnanimity. He did not manage to say goodbye to Fenechka, simply exchanged glances with her through the window. Her face seemed to him to look melancholy. She'll be done for, very likely! he thought. Still, she'll get out of it somehow! Meanwhile, Peter was so overcome with emotion that he cried on Bazarov's shoulder until the latter cooled his sentimental outpourings by asking him: 'Are you always wet round the eyes?' And Dunyasha had to run away into the grove to hide her feelings. The cause of all this misery climbed into the carriage, lit up a cigar and, a couple or so miles on, at a turn in the road where for the last time the Kirsanov estate came into view, all stretched out in a line with its new manor house, he simply spat and muttered: 'Damned aristos!' and wrapped himself more tightly in his coat.

Pavel Petrovich quickly improved, but he still had to stay in bed about a week. He endured what he called his 'incarceration' fairly patiently, save that he fussed a great deal over his dress and constantly begged for his room to be fumigated with eau-de-cologne. Nikolai Petrovich would read him journals and Fenechka would serve him as she had done before, bringing him bouillon, lemonade, soft-boiled eggs and tea, but a secret horror would take possession of her each time she went into his room. Pavel Petrovich's extraordinary conduct had frightened everyone in the house and her most of all. Only Prokofich was unmoved and expressed the opinion that even in his time the masters were given to fighting duels, 'only it was gentlemen of the nobility who did so, while upstarts of the likes of *them*'d be given a floggin' in the stables for their insolence.'

Fenechka's conscience hardly pricked her, but from time to time she was tormented by the thought of the real cause of the quarrel. And Pavel Petrovich had such a strange way of looking at her, so that even when she had her back to him she still felt his eyes on her. She grew thin from constant inner agitation and, as often happens, she looked even more charming.

On one occasion—it was in the morning—Pavel Petrovich felt better and had moved from his bed to a divan and Nikolai Petrovich, after enquiring about his health, had gone to see how the threshing was going. Fenechka brought in a cup of tea and, after leaving it on a little table, was on the point of going out. Pavel Petrovich detained her.

'Where are you off to in such a hurry, Fedosya Nikolaevna?' he began. 'Surely you've got nothing to do, have you?'

'No, sir . . . I mean, yes, sir . . . I have to pour the tea.'

'Dunyasha'll do that without you. Sit for a little while with an invalid. Besides, there's something I must talk to you about.'

Fenechka sat down on the edge of an armchair in silence.

'Listen,' said Pavel Petrovich and tweaked his moustache, 'I've long wanted to ask you why you seem to be frightened of me?'

'Me, sir?'

'Yes, you. You never look at me directly, just as if you didn't have a clear conscience.'

Fenechka went red, but she glanced at Pavel Petrovich. He seemed to her to have a kind of odd look and her heart began to quiver slightly.

'Your conscience is clear, isn't it?' he asked her.

'Why shouldn't it be?' she whispered.

'Why not indeed! Besides, to whom would you be culpable? Me? Hardly. Other people here in the house? That's hardly feasible either. Surely not my brother? You love him don't you?'

'I love him.'

'With all your heart, with all your soul?'

'I love Nikolai Petrovich with all my heart.'

'Really and truly? Look at me, Fenechka.' (It was the first time he had called her that.) 'You know it is a great sin to tell lies.'

'I am not telling lies, Pavel Petrovich. If I didn't love Nikolai Petrovich, there'd be nothing left for me to live for.'

'And you wouldn't change him for anyone else?'

'Who could I change him for?'

'For anyone you like! Say for the gentleman who's just left here.'

Fenechka stood up.

'My God, Pavel Petrovich, why are you so cruel to me? What have I ever done to you? How can you say such things?'

'Fenechka,' said Pavel Petrovich sorrowfully, 'didn't I see . . .'

'What did you see, sir?'

'There . . . in the bower.'

Fenechka went red up to the roots of her hair and her ears.

'And why was I to blame for that?' she asked with difficulty.

Pavel Petrovich raised himself a little.

'You weren't? No? Not in the least?'

'Nikolai Petrovich is the only person in the world I love and I will love him for the rest of my life!' Fenechka cried while sobs literally rose in her throat. 'And what you saw I will say on the day of judgement was none of my fault and never will be, and it would be better if I died this very moment rather than someone suspect I might do to my benefactor Nikolai Petrovich . . .'

But at this point her voice betrayed her and simultaneously she felt Pavel Petrovich seize and squeeze her hand. She glanced at him and went cold as stone. He had become paler than ever, his eyes glistened and—still more astonishingly—a single heavy tear rolled down his cheek.

'Fenechka!' he exclaimed in a marvellously resonant whisper. 'Love my brother! Love him! He's such a kind, good man! Don't give him up for anyone else on earth! And don't listen to what anyone says! Just think what could be worse than to love and not to be loved! Don't ever abandon my poor Nikolai!'

Fenechka's eyes had dried and her fear had vanished, so great was her astonishment. But it became still greater when Pavel Petrovich, Pavel Petrovich himself, pressed her hand to his lips and leaned towards her, not kissing her but simply sighing from time to time convulsively . . .

Good Lord! she thought. Is he about to have a fit?

At that instant the whole of his ruined life trembled within him.

The staircase creaked beneath rapid steps. He pushed her away instantly and let his head drop back on the pillow. The door was flung open and in rushed Nikolai Petrovich, happy, fresh and pink-looking. Mitya, just as fresh and pink as his father, bounced up and down on his chest dressed only in a little shirt and clinging by his bare little feet to the large buttons of his country overcoat.

Fenechka simply flung herself at him and, winding her arms round both him and her son, pressed her head against his shoulder. Nikolai Petrovich was astonished because Fenechka, always shy and modest, had never shown affection for him in the presence of a third person.

'What's happened to you?' he asked and, glancing at his brother, handed over Mitya to her. 'You're not feeling worse, are you?' he enquired, going over to Pavel Petrovich.

The latter buried his face in his cambric handkerchief.

'No . . . It's nothing . . . nothing. On the contrary, I feel a lot better.'

'You were in too great a hurry to move to the divan. And where are you off to?' added Nikolai, turning to Fenechka. But the door had already banged to behind her. 'I'd wanted to show you my fine champion of a boy, he was so longing to see his uncle. Why did she take him away like that? Still, what's wrong with you? Has something happened to you?'

'Brother!' Pavel Petrovich declared solemnly.

Nikolai Petrovich shuddered. He felt frightened, but he could not understand why.

'Brother,' repeated Nikolai Petrovich, 'give me your word that you will meet a request of mine.'

'What request? Tell me.'

'It is a very important one. The way I see it, all your happiness in life depends on it. I've spent the whole time mulling over what I want to say to you now . . . Brother, meet your responsibility, the responsibility of an honest and noble man and put an end to the licentiousness and bad example which you are setting, you, the best of men.'

'What do you mean, Pavel?'

'Marry Fenechka. She loves you, she's the mother of your son . . .'

Nikolai Petrovich took a step back and flung out his arms.

'Is it you, Pavel, saying this? You, whom I've always considered the most unswerving opponent of such marriages! You are saying this! But surely you knew that it was purely out of my respect for you that I didn't do what you rightfully call my duty!'

'You were wrong to respect me in this instance,' replied Pavel Petrovich with a weak smile. 'I am beginning to think that Bazarov was right when he reproached me for my aristocratism. No, my dear brother, we've done enough putting on airs and thinking how society'll react. We're already old and staid and it's time we put all vanity on one side. Let us, as you say, do our duty. You wait and see, we may even obtain happiness into the bargain.'

Nikolai Petrovich rushed to embrace his brother.

'You've opened my eyes at last!' he cried. 'It's not for nothing that I've always said you were the kindest and cleverest man in the world and now I see that you're as sensible as you are magnanimous.'

'Take care, take care,' Pavel Petrovich interrupted him. 'Don't damage the leg of your magnanimous brother who at almost fifty years of age fought a duel like some junior lieutenant. So it's decided—Fenechka'll be my, er, *belle-sœur*.'

'My dear Pavel! But what'll Arkady say?'

'Arkady? He'll be overjoyed, of course he will! Even if marriage may be against his principles, his feeling of equality will be flattered. In fact, what do class differences matter *au dix-neuvième siècle*?'

'Ah, Pavel, Pavel, let me give you another kiss! All right, I'll be careful.'

The brothers embraced.

'What do you think, shouldn't you announce your intention to her right away?' asked Pavel Petrovich.

'What's the rush?' objected Nikolai Petrovich. 'You didn't have words, did you?'

'Words? Us? *Quelle idée!*'

'Well, that's splendid. You get well, that's the first thing. As for this matter, it won't go away, we'll have to give it a lot of thought and consideration . . .'

'But surely you've made up your mind, haven't you?'

'Of course I've made up my mind and I thank you with all my heart. I'll leave you alone now. It's time you had a rest. Excitement is bad for you, but we'll talk about this later. Go to sleep, there's a good chap, and God grant you good health!'

What's he thanking me for? thought Pavel when he was left alone. As if it didn't depend on him! But as soon as he gets married I'll go somewhere far away, to Dresden or Florence, and I'll live there till I'm dead as a Dodo.

Pavel Petrovich moistened his temples with eau-de-cologne and closed his eyes. Illuminated by the bright daylight, his handsome, gaunt head lay on the white pillow like the head of a dead man. Indeed, he was dead as a Dodo.

25

IN the garden of Nikolskoe, in the shade of a tall ash-tree, Katya and Arkady were seated on a turf seat. On the ground beside them lay Fifi, having lent her long body that elegant curve known among sportsmen as 'a hare's lie'. Both Arkady and Katya were silent. He held in his hand a half-opened book while she picked out of a basket some last crumbs of white bread and threw them to a small family of sparrows which, with their characteristic cowardly impudence, jumped about twittering at her feet. A faint breeze, rustling in the leaves of the ash-tree, set in calm to-and-fro motion, both over the dark path and along Fifi's yellow spine, a series of pale golden patches of light. Uninterrupted shade engulfed Arkady and Katya, save that from time to time a bright strand would catch alight in her hair. They were both silent, but it was precisely in the fact of their silence and their sitting together that a trusting closeness reigned. Each seemed not to be thinking about the other, but was secretly delighted by the other's nearness. And their faces had changed since we last saw them, Arkady's seeming calmer and Katya's more lively and bolder.

'Don't you find', Arkady began, 'that the "ash" is very well named. No other tree is so light and glimmers in the air so "ashenly" as it does.'

Katya raised her eyes and said 'Yes' while Arkady thought: She doesn't reproach me for talking 'fancy'.

'I don't like Heine', Katya broke in, directing her eyes at the book in Arkady's hand, 'when he's laughing or when he's crying, I only like him when he's thoughtful and sad.'

'And I like him when he laughs,' Arkady remarked.

'That's the old traces of your satirical approach . . .'

(Old traces! thought Arkady. If only Bazarov had heard that!) 'Just you wait, we'll soon change you.'

'Who'll change me? You will?'

'Who? My sister will and Porfiry Petrovich, with whom you've now stopped quarrelling, and my auntie, whom you accompanied to church the day before yesterday . . .'

'I couldn't say no! And as for Anna Sergeevna, she herself, you remember, was in agreement with Evgeny over many things.'

'My sister was then under his influence, just as you are.'

'Just as I am! Haven't you noticed that I've already freed myself from his influence?'

Katya did not speak.

'I know', Arkady went on, 'that you never liked him.'

'I can't judge what he's like.'

'You know something, Katerina Sergeevna, every time I hear that kind of answer I don't believe it. There isn't a person about whom you can't pass a judgement! That's simply an excuse.'

'Well, then, I'll tell you that it's not so much that I don't like him but I feel he's alien to me and I'm alien to him . . . and you're alien to him too.'

'Why's that?'

'How can I put it? He's untamed, but you and I are hand-reared.'

'I'm hand-reared, too, am I?'

Katya nodded. Arkady scratched his ear.

'Listen, Katerina Sergeevna, basically I think that's hurtful.'

'Would you really rather be untamed?'

'Untamed, no, but strong and energetic.'

'You can't rather be that . . . Look, your friend wouldn't rather be that, but he simply has it in him.'

'Hmm! So you think he had a strong influence on Anna Sergeevna, do you?'

'Yes. But no one can ever get the better of her for long,' Katya added in a soft voice.

'Why do you think that?'

'She's very proud . . . No, I didn't mean that . . . She's very keen on her independence.'

'Who isn't?' asked Arkady, but instantly there flashed into his mind the question: What's she mean? and the same thought occurred to Katya. Young people when they are frequently together as friends tend constantly to have identical thoughts.

Arkady smiled and, moving slightly closer to Katya, said in a whisper:

'Admit that you're a little frightened of *her*.'

'Of whom?'

'*Her*,' Arkady repeated meaningfully.

'Aren't you?' Katya asked in turn.

'Me too. Note that I said: Me *too*.'

Katya wagged a threatening finger at him.

'I'm astonished,' she began. 'My sister has never been so well disposed to you as she is now and a great deal better than on your first visit.'

'I see!'

'Haven't you noticed it? Doesn't it please you?'

Arkady grew thoughtful.

'What's made me deserve Anna Sergeevna's goodwill? Is it that I brought her your mother's letters?'

'That, and other reasons which I won't tell you.'

'Why?'

'I won't.'

'Really! I know that you're very stubborn.'

'I am stubborn.'

'And observant.'

Katya gave Arkady a sideways glance.

'Perhaps that annoys you? What are you thinking about?'

'I'm wondering where that gift for observation, which you really have inside you, came from. You're so timid and mistrustful and frightened of everyone . . .'

'I've lived a lot on my own and so you start to think about things regardless. But am I really frightened of everyone?'

Arkady cast in Katya's direction a look of gratitude. 'That's all very well,' he went on, 'but people in your position—I mean with your income—rarely possess this gift. The truth finds it as hard to reach them as it does to reach the thrones of kings.'

'But I'm not rich.'

Arkady was amazed and did not understand Katya immediately. And then it occurred to him that in fact the estate belonged entirely to her sister. This was not, for him, an unpleasing thought.

'How well you said it!' he said out loud.

'What?'

'You said it so well—so simply, without being ashamed and without showing off. You see, I imagine there must be something special, a special kind of show-off vanity in the feelings of someone who knows he's poor and says he is.'

'I have never had any such feelings—thanks to my sister. I mentioned my income simply because it seemed appropriate.'

'Right. But you must admit that even you've got a bit of that vanity in you which I've just mentioned.'

'For example?'

'For example, you wouldn't—forgive the question—you wouldn't marry a rich man, would you?'

'If I loved him very much . . . No, I don't think I would even then.'

'Ah, you see!' cried Arkady and, after a moment's pause, added: 'Why wouldn't you?'

'Because it's as popular songs say, it wouldn't be equal.'

'Perhaps you want the authority or . . .'

'Oh, of course not! Why should I? On the contrary, I'm ready to take second place, except that inequality's unbearable. To respect oneself while taking second place, that I can understand. That's being happy. But a subservient existence . . . No, there's enough of that as it is.'

'There's enough of that as it is,' Arkady echoed Katya's words. 'Yes, yes,' he went on, 'you're not of the same blood as Anna Sergeevna for nothing, you're just as independent as she is, but you're more reticent. I'm sure you'd never be the first to express what you feel, no matter how strongly you felt it or how sacred the feeling was . . .'

'What would I do instead?' asked Katya.

'You're just as clever and you've got as much, if not more, character than she has . . .'

'Don't compare me with my sister, please,' Katya interrupted hurriedly, 'it's too much to my disadvantage. You seem to have forgotten that my sister is both beautiful and clever and . . . and, what's more, you in particular, Arkady Nikolaich, shouldn't be saying such things, and with such a serious face as well.'

'What do you mean by "you in particular"? What makes you think I'm joking?'

'Of course you are.'

'Do you really think so? And what if I'm convinced of what I'm saying? What if I feel I haven't yet expressed myself sufficiently strongly?'

'I don't understand you.'

'Really? Well, I can see now I rated your powers of observation too highly.'

'Why?'

Arkady said nothing and turned away while Katya searched in her basket for a few more crumbs and began throwing them to the sparrows, but her hand moved too abruptly and they flew away before they'd had a chance of pecking.

'Katerina Sergeevna!' Arkady suddenly began. 'It probably won't mean a thing to you, but you ought to know that I wouldn't change you not only for your sister but for anyone else in the world!'

He stood up and quickly walked away, as if frightened of the words which had just been torn from his tongue.

Katya let both her hands and her basket drop into her lap and, with her head bent, followed Arkady for a long while with her eyes. Slowly a crimson flush stole over her cheeks. But her lips did not form a smile and her dark eyes expressed bewilderment and some other, as yet nameless feeling.

'Are you here by yourself?' Anna Sergeevna's voice resounded beside her. 'I thought you came into the garden with Arkady.'

Katya slowly directed her eyes towards her sister (elegantly, even stylishly dressed, she was standing on the path and stroking Fifi's ears with the tip of her open parasol) and slowly she said:

'I'm by myself, yes.'

'I can see that,' the other answered with a laugh. 'He's gone to his room, has he?'

'Yes.'

'Were you reading together?'

'Yes.'

Anna Sergeevna took Katya by the chin and raised her face.

'You didn't quarrel, I hope?'

'No,' said Katya and calmly moved her sister's hand away.

'How solemnly you answer! I thought I'd find him here and ask him to come for a walk with me. He's always been begging me to do this. Your shoes have come from the town, go and try them on. I noticed yesterday that your old ones were worn out. In general you don't take enough care about such things, and you have such pretty little feet! Your hands are nice, only they're too big. You must make the most of your feet. But I know you're no coquette.'

Anna Sergeevna walked off along the path, making a slight rustling with her beautiful dress. Katya rose from the bench and, picking up her Heine, also walked off— only not to go and try on shoes.

Beautiful little feet, she thought, slowly and lightly ascending the sunbaked stone steps of the terrace, beautiful little feet, you say . . . Well, he'll be at my beautiful little feet, won't he!

But she was instantly ashamed of such a thought, and she ran briskly up the steps.

Arkady went along the corridor towards his room and a butler caught up with him and announced that a Mr Bazarov was sitting there waiting for him.

'Evgeny!' muttered Arkady almost in fright. 'Has he been here long?'

'He's just this moment arrived and asked that he shouldn't be announced to Anna Sergeevna, but demanded that he be shown directly to your room.'

Has there been some accident at home? wondered Arkady and, racing swiftly up the stairs, flung open the door to his room. The sight of Bazarov at once calmed his fears, although a more experienced eye would probably have perceived in the as-ever vigorous but pinched-looking figure of his unexpected guest signs of inner excitement. With a dusty greatcoat over his shoulders and a cap on his head, he was sitting on the windowsill. He did not stand up even when Arkady flung himself on his shoulder with loud cries of welcome.

'What a surprise! Fancy you being here!' he repeated again and again, posturing about the room like someone who imagines and wants to show how overjoyed he is. 'Is everything all right at home, everyone well, I hope?'

'Everything's all right at your place, but not everyone's well,' said Bazarov. 'And stop all that gabbing, order me some kvass, sit down and listen to what I've got to tell you in a few but, I hope, fairly emphatic phrases.'

Arkady stopped chattering at once, while Bazarov told him about his duel with Pavel Petrovich. Arkady was extremely astonished and even saddened, but he did not consider there was any need to show it. He simply asked whether his uncle's wound was really serious and on receiving the answer that it was very interesting, though not in a medical sense, he gave a forced smile, while in his heart he felt both horrified and rather ashamed. Bazarov seemed to understand him.

'Yes, mate,' he said, 'that's what it means to live among feudal lords. You drop in on feudal lords and you find yourself taking part in knightly tournaments. So, you see, I've decided to go to my real "fathers",' Bazarov concluded, 'and on the way I've turned in here—to give an account of all this, I would have said, if I didn't think such a useless lie was sheer stupidity. No, God knows why I turned in here. You see there are times when a man finds it useful to take himself by the scruff of the neck and pull himself out of where he is, like pulling a radish out of a vegetable bed. That's what I did a day or so ago . . . But I simply wanted to take one last look at what I was leaving behind, at the cosy vegetable bed I'd been in.'

'I hope that these words don't refer to me,' Arkady retorted with feeling. 'I hope you aren't thinking of leaving *me* behind.'

Bazarov looked at him intently, almost penetratingly.

'Would that upset you all that much? It strikes me that it's *you* who's left *me* behind. You look all fresh-faced and shiny clean—your affair with Anna Sergeevna must be going well.'

'What affair with Anna Sergeevna?'

'Wasn't it because of her that you came here from the town, my little fledgling? By the way, how are the Sunday schools getting on there? You're in love with her, aren't you? Or have you gone all coy about it now?'

'Evgeny, you know I've always been open with you. I can assure you, I can swear to you, that you're wrong.'

'Hmm! That's a new word,' Bazarov remarked under his breath. 'But you've no need to get hot and bothered, it's all quite the same to me. A romantic would have said: "I feel that our paths are beginning to diverge", but all I say is that we've got fed up with each other.'

'Evgeny . . .'

'My dear fellow, it's no great calamity, the world's full of things you can get fed up with! But now, I think, isn't it time to say goodbye? Ever since arriving here I feel just bloody awful, just as if I'd been reading over and over again Gogol's letters* to the wife of the Governor-General of Kaluga. Besides, I ordered them not to unhitch the horses.'

'Good heavens, you can't!'

'Why not?'

'I'm not even talking of myself, but it'll be the height of rudeness to Anna Sergeevna, who will certainly want to see you.'

'Well, that's where you're wrong.'

'On the contrary, I'm sure I'm right,' retorted Arkady. 'And why are you pretending? If it comes to that, didn't you come here simply to see her?'

'Maybe that's true, but you're still wrong.'

But Arkady was right. Anna Sergeevna did want to see Bazarov and issued an invitation to him through her butler. Bazarov changed before going to see her. It turned out that he had packed a change of clothes where he could easily lay his hands on it.

Odintsova received him not in the room where he had so unexpectedly confessed his love to her, but in the drawing-room. She charmingly stretched out towards him the tips of her fingers, but her face expressed an involuntary tension.

'Anna Sergeevna,' Bazarov hastened to say, 'I must begin by calming your fears. You see before you a mortal man who has long ago come to his senses and hopes that others have also forgotten the stupid things he has done. I will be going off on a long journey and you will agree that, though I am no softy, I would be unhappy to carry away with me the thought that you remember me with repugnance.'

Anna Sergeevna heaved a deep sigh, like someone who has just climbed to the top of a high mountain, and her face was enlivened by a smile. She offered her hand to Bazarov a second time and responded to his handshake.

'Let bygones be bygones,' she said, 'all the more so since, in all honesty, I was also to blame then, if not for flirting then for something else. Just let's say we'll be friends as we were before. That was a dream, wasn't it? And who remembers dreams?'

'Who remembers them? In any case, love is such a . . . such an overblown emotion.'

'Is it really? I am very pleased to hear that.'

That was how Anna Sergeevna expressed herself and how Bazarov expressed himself. They both thought they were telling the truth. Was the truth, the whole truth, in their words? They themselves didn't know, no more than the author does. But their ensuing conversation gave the impression that they were completely sure of each other.

Anna Sergeevna asked Bazarov, among other things, what he had been doing at the Kirsanovs. He was on the point of telling her about the duel with Pavel Petrovich, but hesitated at the thought that she might think he was showing off and answered that he had spent the whole time working.

'And I', said Anna Sergeevna, 'started off by being in a black mood, God knows why, and even planned to go abroad, just imagine! Then that mood passed. Your friend Arkady Nikolaich arrived and I again adopted my old habits, assumed my former role.'

'What role is that, may I ask?'

'The role of an aunt, instructress, mother, call it what you will. Besides, you should know that previously I didn't have a clear understanding of your close friendship with Arkady Nikolaich. I found him fairly insignificant. But now I know him much better and I'm convinced that he's clever . . . Chiefly, though, he's young, young . . . not like you and me, Evgeny Vasilich.'

'Is he still as shy as ever in your presence?' asked Bazarov.

'Surely not . . .' Anna Sergeevna began saying but after a moment's thought she added: 'Now he's got much more confident and is prepared to talk to me. Previously he used to avoid me. However, I never sought his company. He's great friends with Katya.'

Bazarov was annoyed by this. There's not a woman who can't pretend! he thought.

'You say he used to avoid you,' he declared with a cold smile, 'but it's probably no secret to you that he was in love with you?'

'What? He was too?' burst from Anna Sergeevna.

'He was too,' repeated Bazarov with a restrained bow. 'You can't mean you didn't know this and that I've told you something new?'

Anna Sergeevna lowered her eyes.

'You are wrong, Evgeny Vasilich.'

'I don't think so. But perhaps I shouldn't have mentioned this.' Just don't go on pretending, he added, speaking to himself.

'Why shouldn't you have mentioned it? But I suggest that in this case you are ascribing far too much importance to a momentary impression. I am beginning to suspect that you are inclined to exaggerate.'

'We'd better not talk any more about this, Anna Sergeevna.'

'Why not?' she responded and then herself changed the course of the conversation. She still felt awkward with Bazarov, even though she had told him and she had assured herself that everything was forgotten. In exchanging the simplest of remarks with him, even while joking with him, she felt a slight constraint of fear. In the same way people aboard ship, out at sea, talk and laugh without a care, exactly as if they were on dry land. But should there be the slightest hitch, the slightest sign of something unusual, immediately every face wears an expression of special alarm, bearing witness to a constant awareness of ever-present danger.

Anna Sergeevna's conversation with Bazarov did not go on for long. She began to think of other things and answer distractedly and finally proposed to him that they should go into the main room, where they found the Princess and Katya. 'And where's Arkady Nikolaich?' asked the hostess and, learning that he had not been seen for more than an hour, sent for him. He couldn't be found at once. He had made his way into the very depths of the garden and, his chin resting on his clasped hands, was sitting lost in thought. They were deep and important these thoughts, but they weren't sad. He knew that Anna Sergeevna was alone with Bazarov and he felt no jealousy, as had happened before. On the contrary, his face had brightened quietly and it seemed that he was amazed at something and delighted by it and had made up his mind about it.

26

THE late lamented Odintsov disliked innovations, but he was not averse to what he called 'a certain play of elevated taste' and as a consequence of this had erected in his garden, between the greenhouse and the pond, a structure resembling a Grecian portico built of Russian brick. In the rear wall of this portico or gallery six niches had been made for statues which Odintsov had intended to order from abroad. These statues were to have represented Solitariness, Silence, Contemplation, Melancholy, Modesty and Sensitivity. One of them, the Goddess of Silence, with a finger to her lips, had actually been delivered and set in place, but on the very same day little boys from the manor house had knocked off the nose and, although a local plasterer had undertaken to give her a nose 'twice as good as the original', Odintsov ordered her to be removed and she was found a place in the corner of the threshing barn where she stood for many long years, giving rise to superstitious horror among the peasant women. The façade of the portico had long since become overgrown with thick vegetation and only the capitals of the columns were visible above the solid greenery. Within the portico itself it was cool, even at midday. Anna Sergeevna did not like visiting the place ever since she had seen a grass-snake there, but Katya often went there to sit on a large stone seat which had been set below one of the niches. Surrounded by freshness and shade, she used to take her work there and read or give herself up to that feeling of complete tranquillity which is probably familiar to everyone and whose charm consists in a scarcely conscious, silent attentiveness to the broad wave of life which ceaselessly rolls both around us and within us.

The day after Bazarov's arrival Katya was sitting on her favourite seat and Arkady was once again seated beside her. He had asked her to join him in the portico.

About an hour remained before lunch. Dewy morning had already given way to the heat of the day. Arkady's face retained its expression of the previous day, while Katya had a worried look. Her sister had summoned her into her private study immediately after breakfast and, having paid her compliments to start with (something which always alarmed Katya a little), had advised her to be more cautious in

her conduct with Arkady and particularly to avoid the solitary conversations with him which had apparently been the subject of comment by her auntie and the whole household. Apart from that, the
previous evening Anna Sergeevna had not been in a good mood and
Katya herself, what's more, had experienced a kind of bewilderment,
just as if she had been to blame for something. In acceding to
Arkady's request she had told herself that it was to be the last time.

'Katerina Sergeevna,' he began with a certain shy expansiveness,
'ever since I have had the good fortune to stay in the same house as
you, I've discussed many things with you but there is still one very
important question—important to me, that is—which I haven't yet
touched on. You remarked yesterday that I've been changed by being
here,' he added, both catching and avoiding the querying glance
Katya directed at him. 'In fact, I've changed a great deal and you
know this better than anyone else—you, to whom in all essentials I'm
obliged for this change.'

'I? Me?' queried Katya.

'I'm not now the arrogant boy I was when I came here,' Arkady
went on. 'I'm not now twenty-three for nothing. I still want to be
useful, I still want to dedicate all my strength to the pursuit of truth,
as I did before. But I'm no longer looking for my ideals where I
sought them before. They now seem to me much . . . much closer.
Until now I hadn't understood myself, I'd given myself tasks which
were beyond my strength . . . Recently my eyes have been opened,
thanks to a certain feeling . . . I'm not expressing myself absolutely
clearly, but I hope you'll understand what I mean . . .'

Katya said nothing, but she had stopped looking at Arkady.

'I suppose,' he began again in a more excited voice, just as a
chaffinch in the birch foliage above him launched casually into song,
'I suppose it's the duty of any honest man to be entirely candid with
those . . . with those who . . . with people close to him, I mean . . .
and so I, er, intend . . .'

But at this point Arkady's eloquence failed him. He broke off,
grew tongue-tied and had to pause for a short while. Katya still did
not raise her eyes. It seemed she did not understand what he was
leading up to and was still expecting something.

'I foresee that I'll surprise you,' began Arkady, again mustering
his strength. 'All the more since this feeling has to do to a certain
extent—to a certain extent, mind—with you. If you remember, you

reproached me yesterday for a lack of seriousness,' went on Arkady with the look of a man who has walked into a bog and feels that with each step he is sinking further and further in and still keeps on rushing forward in the hope that he'll eventually make his way through. 'That reproach is frequently directed at . . . frequently heaped on . . . young men even when they've ceased to deserve it. And if I had more self-confidence . . .' (Help me! Help me! thought Arkady in desperation, but Katya still did not so much as turn her head.) 'If I could hope . . .'

'If only I could be sure of what you're saying . . .' resounded Anna Sergeevna's clear voice at that moment.

Arkady stopped instantly and Katya went pale. Just by the shrubbery which concealed the portico ran a path. Anna Sergeevna was walking along it in company with Bazarov. Katya and Arkady could not see them, but heard every word, the rustle of her dress and even the sound of her breathing. They took a few steps and, as if intentionally, stopped right in front of the portico.

'You can see, can't you,' Anna Sergeevna went on, 'that you and I were wrong. We're neither of us in the first flush of youth, particularly me. We've lived out our lives and grown tired. We're both— why pretend otherwise?—clever, so we started by being interested in each other, our curiosity was aroused . . . and then . . .'

'And then I blew it,' interrupted Bazarov.

'You know that wasn't what made us part. But whatever it was, we didn't need each other, that was the main thing. There was too much—how can I put it?—too much that was the same about us. We didn't realize this to start with. On the contrary, Arkady . . .'

'You're still in need of him, are you?' asked Bazarov.

'That's enough of that, Evgeny Vasilich. You say he's not indifferent to me and I've always thought he liked me. I know I could pass for his aunt, but I don't want to hide from you that I've begun to think of him more and more. In that kind of youthful and fresh feeling there is a certain charm . . .'

'The word *allure* is more applicable in such circumstances,' interrupted Bazarov. A seething irritability was audible in his calm but hollow voice. 'Arkady wasn't very forthcoming with me yesterday and didn't say a word about you or your sister. That's an important symptom.'

'He's like a brother to Katya,' said Anna Sergeevna, 'and that's what I like about him, although maybe I shouldn't allow such closeness between them.'

'You're speaking as a . . . as a sister?' drawled Bazarov.

'Of course . . . But why are we standing here? Let's go on. What a strange conversation we're having, aren't we? Could I ever have expected that I'd be talking to you like this? You know I'm frightened of you, don't you? And at the same time I trust you, because in fact you're a very kind, good man.'

'In the first place, I'm not a kind, good man at all. And secondly I've lost for you whatever meaning I may have had, and that's why you say I'm kind and good. It's much the same as laying a wreath of flowers on the head of a dead man.'

'Evgeny Vasilich, we're not given the power to . . .' Anna Sergeevna started to say, but a wind sprang up, set the leaves rustling and carried off her words.

'Surely you're free . . .' Bazarov declared a short while afterwards. Nothing more could be heard. Their footsteps died away and everything grew quiet.

Arkady turned to Katya. She was sitting in the very same position; except that she had dropped her head even lower.

'Katerina Sergeevna,' he said in a trembling voice, his hands clasped tightly together, 'I love you eternally and irrevocably and I love no one but you. I wanted to tell you this, discover what your own thoughts were and ask for your hand, because I'm not a rich man and I feel I'm ready to make any kind of sacrifice . . . Why don't you say something? Don't you believe me? Do you think I'm not being serious? But just think of these last few days! Haven't you become convinced long ago that everything else—you know what I mean—everything, everything else has long ago vanished without trace? Look at me, say just one word to me . . . I love . . . I love you . . . Believe me now!'

Katya turned on Arkady a solemn and bright look and, after a long pause for thought, with hardly a smile, said:

'Yes.'

Arkady jumped up from the seat.

'Yes! You've said yes, Katerina Sergeevna! What's that word mean? Is it that I love you and that you believe me . . . or . . . or . . . I daren't say more . . .'

'Yes,' repeated Katya and this time he understood her. He took hold of her large beautiful hands and, sighing with joy, pressed them to his heart. He could scarcely remain on his feet and went on repeating 'Katya . . . Katya . . .' while she quite innocently started crying, laughing quietly to herself at her own tears. He who has not seen such tears in the eyes of a loved one has not yet experienced to what extent, though totally consumed by gratitude and shame, a man can be happy on this earth.

The next day, early in the morning, Anna Sergeevna summoned Bazarov to her private study and with a forced laugh handed him a folded sheet of writing paper. It was a letter from Arkady. In it he asked for her sister's hand.

Bazarov quickly ran through the letter and made an effort not to show the desire to gloat which instantly ignited in his heart.

'I see,' he said, 'and you, it seems, no longer ago than yesterday were saying he loves Katerina Sergeevna with a brotherly love. What do you intend to do now?'

'What do *you* advise?' asked Anna Sergeevna, still laughing.

'I suggest,' replied Bazarov, also with a laugh, although he did not feel happy at all and had no desire to laugh, just as she didn't, 'I suggest you should give your blessing to the young couple. It's a good match in every respect. Kirsanov's circumstances are reasonable, he's his father's only son and his father's a good man, he won't have any objections.'

Odintsova paced about the room. Her face went alternately pale and pink.

'Do you think so?' she said. 'All right, then, I can't see anything in the way. I'm pleased for Katya . . . and for Arkady Nikolaich. It goes without saying that I'll wait until I receive a reply from his father. I'll send him in person to him. But now it turns out, you see, that I was right yesterday when I told you we were neither of us in the first flush of youth . . . Why on earth didn't I see any of this? It astonishes me!'

Anna Sergeevna again laughed and at once turned away.

'The youth of today has become extremely good at pretending,' remarked Bazarov and also laughed. 'Goodbye,' he began again after a short silence. 'I wish you the pleasantest of outcomes to this business, while I will enjoy it from afar.'

Odintsova swiftly turned to him.

'Surely you're not leaving? Why shouldn't you stay *now*? Stay . . .

I enjoy talking to you ... it's like walking along the edge of a precipice. At first it's frightening and then you gain courage from somewhere or other. Do stay.'

'Thank you for the suggestion, Anna Sergeevna, and for your flattering opinion of my conversational talents. But I find that I've already spent too long in a sphere that is foreign to me. Flying fish can keep in the air for a short while, but they're bound to flop back into the water pretty quickly. Allow me to flop back into my element.'

Odintsova looked at Bazarov. A bitter smile made her pale face work. This man loved me! she thought. And she pitied him and stretched out a hand to him in fellow feeling.

But he had understood her.

'No!' he said and took a step back. 'I may be a poor man, but I've never in my life accepted charity. Goodbye and good health to you!'

'I'm sure we're not seeing each other for the last time,' said Anna Sergeevna with an involuntary movement.

'Anything may happen in this life!' answered Bazarov, bowed and went out.

'So you've decided to make a nest, have you?' he said that very day to Arkady, squatting on his heels to pack his travelling trunk. 'Well, it's a good thing to do. Only you needn't have been so crafty. I'd expected you to take a completely different direction. Or perhaps you were disconcerted by that yourself?'

'I literally hadn't expected anything like this when I said goodbye to you,' answered Arkady, 'but why are you being so crafty yourself and talking about it being a "good thing" as if I didn't know your opinion of marriage?'

'Oh, my dear good friend!' exclaimed Bazarov. 'The things you say! You see what I'm doing—there's an empty space in my trunk and I'm stuffing hay into it. It's the same with the luggage of our own lives. It doesn't matter what you fill it with so long as there's no empty space. Don't be offended, please. You probably remember the opinion I always had of Katerina Sergeevna. Other young ladies only pass for clever because they've got such a clever way of sighing, but yours'll stand up for herself, and she'll do it so cleverly she'll have you under her thumb—well, that's as it should be.' He slammed shut the lid of the trunk and stood up. 'But now I'm telling you again in farewell ... because there's no point in pretending: We're saying goodbye for ever and you know it yourself . . . You've behaved sensibly. You're not made for the bitter, sour-tasting, rootless life of people like me. You haven't got the daring, you haven't got the anger, all you've got is youthful courage and youthful fervour—and that's not enough for what I've got to do. Aristos like you'll never go beyond noble humility or noble indignation and that's all nonsense. You, for example, won't fight—and yet you think you're fine chaps—but people like us, we want to fight. And we will! The dust we kick up'll eat out your eyes, our mud'll get all over you, but you—you're not as grown up as we are, you can't help admiring yourselves, you think it's pleasant to give yourselves a hard time. But to us that's all a yawn. Give us other people! I say. We've got others to destroy! You're a marvellous fellow, but you're still just a little softy liberal gent—*ey volatoo*, as my parent would say.'

'You're saying goodbye to me for ever, Evgeny,' said Arkady sadly, 'and you've got no other words for me?'

Bazarov scratched the back of his neck.

'I've got other words, Arkady, only I won't say them, because it'd be romanticism—it'd mean going all syrupy. Just you get married as soon as you can and fix up your nest round you and have more and more kids. They'll be the clever ones because they'll have been born at the right time, not like you and me. Aha! I see the horses are ready. It's time to go! I've already said goodbye to everyone else . . . Well, shall we? Shall we hug each other?'

Arkady flung himself on the shoulder of his former mentor and friend and tears literally burst from his eyes.

'What it means to be young!' declared Bazarov calmly. 'Yes, all my hopes are on Katerina Sergeevna. Just you wait and see what a comfort she'll be to you!'

'Goodbye, old mate!' he said to Arkady when he'd already climbed into the cart and, pointing to a pair of jackdaws sitting side by side on the stable roof, added 'There's a lesson for you! Learn from them!'

'What's that mean?' asked Arkady.

'What? You can't be all that poor at natural history! Or have you forgotten that the jackdaw is the most respectable family bird? Let them be your example! Farewell, *signor*!'

The cart gave a shudder and rolled off on its way.

Bazarov had told the truth. In conversation that evening with Katya, Arkady had completely forgotten about his mentor. He was already beginning to submit to her and Katya sensed this and was not surprised. The following day he had to travel to Marino to see Nikolai Petrovich. Anna Sergeevna had no wish to stand in the way of the young people's happiness and it was only out of a sense of what was proper that she did not leave them too long on their own. Out of the goodness of her heart she kept away the Princess, whom news of the forthcoming marriage had reduced to a veritable storm of tears. To start with, Anna Sergeevna had been frightened that the sight of their happiness would seem rather tiresome to her as well, but it turned out completely the opposite. The sight not only did not oppress her, it intrigued her and finally it mellowed her. Anna Sergeevna was both overjoyed and saddened by this. Evidently Bazarov was right, she thought. It was all a matter of curiosity, just curiosity, and love of a quiet life, and egoism . . .

'Children!' she exclaimed loudly. 'Tell me, is love an overblown emotion?'

But neither Katya nor Arkady had any idea what she meant. They were apprehensive of her because the accidentally overheard conversation had not gone from their thoughts. However, Anna Sergeevna soon reassured them, which was not difficult, because she had become reassured in herself.

27

BAZAROV'S old parents were all the more overjoyed at their son's sudden arrival since it was all the more unexpected. Arina Vlasevna was so flustered and ran about the house so much that Vasily Ivanovich compared her to 'a wee grouse-hen' and the docked tail of her short blouse actually did give her rather a bird-like look. While all he did was make low humming sounds and chew on the amber mouthpiece of his pipe and, seizing his neck in his fingers, turn his head this way and that just as if he were testing whether it was screwed on properly and then suddenly open his wide mouth and laugh without emitting a sound.

'I've come to stay with you for a whole six weeks, old man,' Bazarov told him. 'I want to work, so please don't get in my way.'

'You'll literally forget my physiognomy, that's how much I'll get in your way!' answered Vasily Ivanovich.

He kept his promise. Having surrendered his study to his son as before, he all but vanished from his sight and he made his wife desist from any unnecessary expressions of fondness. 'You and I, my old dear,' he told her, 'wore out our Evgeny a wee bit on his first visit. Now we've got to be more sensible.' Arina Vlasevna agreed to what her husband said but gained little from it because she only saw her son at meal-times and finally became frightened to talk to him at all. 'Enyushka darling,' she'd say to him, and he'd scarcely have time to glance in her direction when she'd start fingering the laces of her handbag and mutter: 'Nothing, nothing, I was just . . .' and then she'd go off to Vasily Ivanovich and ask him, leaning her cheek on her hand: 'How can I find out, my dear, what darling Enyushka'd like for dinner, cabbage soup or borshch?' 'Why haven't you asked him yourself?' 'But I'd bore him!' However, Bazarov soon stopped locking himself in because the fever of work had 'jumped off him' (as he put it) and been replaced by a wearisome boredom and a dull restlessness. A strange lethargy marked his every movement, even his way of walking, usually firm and decisively bold, underwent a change. He stopped going for walks on his own and began to look for company. He took his tea in the sitting-room, strolled around the kitchen garden with Vasily Ivanovich and shared a quiet pipe or two

with him. Once he even enquired about Father Aleksei. To start
with, Vasily Ivanovich was delighted with this change, but his joy did
not last long. 'Our Enyushka breaks my heart,' he complained in a
low voice to his wife. 'It's not that he's dissatisfied or angry, that
wouldn't mean a thing. He's embittered, he's sad—that's what's
awful. He never says a word. If only he'd scold the two of us, but he
just gets thinner and his face is such a poor colour.' 'Oh, Lordy,
Lordy!' whispered the old woman. 'I'd love to hang an amulet round
his neck but he wouldn't let me.' Vasily Ivanovich tried several times
in the most cautious way to broach with Bazarov the question of his
work, his health and Arkady, but Bazarov always responded unwillingly and negligently and on one occasion, noting that his father in
conversation was slowly leading up to something, said to him in
annoyance: 'Why're you always tiptoeing round me? This manner is
worse than your old one.' 'No, no, I didn't mean anything!' the poor
Vasily Ivanovich answered hurriedly. Just as fruitless were his
attempts to raise political matters. Having mentioned once, in connection with the imminent Emancipation of the serfs, the question
of progress, he had hoped to arouse his son's sympathies, but the
other said indifferently: 'Yesterday I was walking beside a fence and
I heard the local peasant boys, instead of singing some folksong,
bellowing out "Now the true time has come, My heart is full of
love" . . . That's progress for you.'

Sometimes Bazarov would go into the village and, as usual in
mock serious fashion, would strike up a conversation with some
peasant or other. 'Well,' he would say to him, 'expound to me your
views on life, there's a good chap. They say all the strength and
future of Russia resides in you. With you there'll be a new epoch in
history—you'll give us both a real language and proper laws.' The
peasant either wouldn't answer or would utter words like 'Ahrr, er,
we're able, like . . . also dependin' like, you know . . . what land we
got, see . . .' 'Just you explain to me how your peasant world* is run,
will you?' Bazarov would interrupt him. 'And is it the very same
world that rests on three fishes?'

'It's the earth, sir, what rests on three fishes,' explained the peasant reassuringly in a self-righteous patriarchal sing-song, 'but
against the way our world runs, that is, there's the will o' the landowners, as everyone knows, 'cos you're our lords and masters. An'
the more stern-like the master is, the better the peasant likes it.'

Having heard this kind of thing, Bazarov on one occasion shrugged his shoulders contemptuously and turned away, but the peasant wandered off about his business.

'What was he wantin'?' asked another peasant of mature years and gloomy appearance from a distance, standing on the doorstep of his hut and having been present during the other's conversation with Bazarov. 'Was he on about the arrears, eh?'

'Not about arrears he weren't, mate!' answered the first peasant, and there was no trace in his voice of any patriarchal sing-song, but, by contrast, there was an audibly dismissive harshness. 'Just talkin' some bloody nonsense. Wanted to wag 'is tongue a bit. Like all them masters, you know, he doesn't understand nuthin', does he?'

'Not a bloody thing!' responded the other peasant and, shoving caps back on their heads and giving their belts a tug, they both fell to discussing their own matters and needs. Alas, the contemptuously shrugging Bazarov, who knew how to talk to the peasants (as he had boasted in his quarrel with Pavel Petrovich), this self-assured Bazarov didn't even suspect that in their eyes he had something of the look of a village idiot.

However, he finally found an occupation for himself. One time in his presence Vasily Ivanovich was bandaging a peasant's wounded leg, but the old man's hands were shaking and he couldn't manage the strips of cloth. His son helped him and from that moment forward began to participate in his medical practice, never ceasing for an instant to make fun of the treatments which he himself prescribed and his father who immediately put them into effect. But Bazarov's mockery didn't upset Vasily Ivanovich in the least; he was even comforted by it. Holding his greasy dressing-gown across his stomach with two fingers and smoking his pipe, he would listen with enjoyment to Bazarov and the more vicious were his remarks, the more ebulliently did his overjoyed father roar with laughter and display his rows of blackened teeth right down to the very last one. He would even repeat these sometimes pointless or silly remarks and, for example, spent several days saying over and over again for no good reason: 'Well, that's your nine times table for you!' simply because his son, learning that he'd been to the morning service, had used this expression. 'Thank God, he's stopped being depressed!' he whispered to his wife. 'The way he kidded me along today— marvellous!' What's more, the fact that he had such an assistant brought him to a state of ecstasy and filled him with pride. 'Yes, indeed,' he told some woman or other dressed in a heavy peasant overcoat and a horned headdress as he handed her a phial of Goulard Water* or a jar of white ointment, 'you ought, my dear, to give thanks to God every minute of the day for the fact that my son is staying in my house. You are receiving treatment by the latest and most scientific method, do you understand that? The emperor of the French, Napoleon, even he doesn't have a better doctor.' But the woman, who had come to complain that she felt as though 'she'd been lifted up on pricks' (the meaning of these words, however, she was herself unable to explain), merely bowed and put her hand in her bosom where she had four eggs tied up in a piece of towelling.

Bazarov once even extracted a tooth from an itinerant cloth sales-man and, although the tooth was quite ordinary, Vasily Ivanovich treasured it as a rarity and, on showing it to Father Aleksei, insis-tently repeated:

'Just look at those roots! What strength Evgeny's got! The sales-man chap literally flew up in the air . . . I think if it'd been an oak tree, that'd have flown up too!'

'Admirable!' said Father Aleksei when it was all over, not knowing how to react and how to extricate himself from this old man who had gone into such raptures.

On one occasion a little peasant from a neighbouring village brought Vasily Ivanovich his brother who was ill with typhus. Lying prone on a straw litter, the unfortunate man was dying. Dark blotches covered his body and he had been unconscious for some time. Vasily Ivanovich expressed his regret that no one had thought of turning to the aid of medicine sooner and announced that there was nothing he could do. In fact, the little peasant did not even get his brother home: he died then and there in the cart.

About three days later Bazarov came into his father's room and asked if he had any lunar caustic.

'I have. What d'you want it for?'

'I must, er, cauterize a cut.'

'Whose?'

'Mine.'

'Yours! How's that? What sort of a cut? Where is it?'

'Here, on my finger. I went over to the village today—you know, the one where the peasant with typhus came from. For some reason an autopsy'd been decided on and I hadn't had any practice for a long time.'

'Well?'

'Well, I asked the local doctor if I could—and I cut myself.'

Vasily Ivanovich suddenly went pale and, without another word, dashed into his study, whence he instantly returned with a small piece of caustic in his hand. Bazarov was on the point of taking it and leaving.

'In God's name', announced Vasily Ivanovich, 'let me do that myself!'

Bazarov grinned. 'What a demon you are for keeping in practice!'

'Don't joke, please. Show me your finger. The cut's not large. Does it hurt?'

'Press harder, don't be afraid.'

Vasily Ivanovich stopped. 'What do you think, Evgeny, wouldn't it be better if we burnt it with a hot iron?'

'That should have been done earlier. To be realistic, now even lunar caustic's no good. If I'm infected, it's too late now anyhow.'

'How . . . too late . . .' Vasily Ivanovich could scarcely bring himself to utter the words.

'Of course it is! It's more than four hours since it happened.'

Vasily Ivanovich still proceeded with a little more cauterizing of the cut. 'Surely that local doctor had some caustic, didn't he?'

'No, he didn't.'

'My God, what a thing! A doctor—and he doesn't have such an essential item!'

'You should've seen his lancets!' declared Bazarov and went out.

Until the evening of that day and throughout the course of the next Vasily Ivanovich resorted to all sorts of pretexts to go into his son's room and although he not only made no allusion to the cut but even tried to talk about quite secondary matters, he still looked so intently into his eyes and watched over him so anxiously that Bazarov lost patience and threatened to leave. Vasily Ivanovich gave him his word that he wouldn't show his anxieties, all the more so since Arina Vlasevna, from whom he had naturally kept everything secret, had begun to pester him with questions about why he wasn't sleeping and what was wrong with him. For a couple of days he kept it up, although the look of his son, whom he covertly scrutinized all the while, did not please him very much at all, but on the third day at dinner he could not go on with the pretence. Bazarov sat at the table looking down at his plate and did not touch any of the food.

'Why aren't you eating, Evgeny?' he asked, lending his face a most relaxed expression. 'I think the food's been nicely prepared.'

'I don't want it, so I'm not eating.'

'Have you lost your appetite? Your head,' he added tentatively, 'is it aching?'

'It's aching. So what?'

Arina Vlasevna sat up straight and took notice.

'Please, Evgeny, don't be offended,' Vasily Ivanovich went on, 'but why don't you let me feel your pulse?'

Bazarov rose. 'I can tell you without feeling my pulse that I've got a fever.'

'Did you have the shivers?'

'I had the shivers. I'll go and lie down and you can send me in some lime tea. I've caught a cold, that's what it must be.'

'I thought I heard you coughing last night,' said Arina Vlasevna.

'I've caught a cold,' Bazarov repeated and left them.

Arina Vlasevna set about preparing tea from lime flower while Vasily Ivanovich went into the next room and silently tore his hair.

Bazarov did not get up again that day and spent the whole night in a heavy, semi-conscious doze. At one o'clock in the morning, opening his eyes with an effort, he glimpsed above him in the lamp light the pale face of his father and ordered him to go away. The latter obeyed, but immediately returned on tiptoe and, half-hidden by the small doors of a cupboard, gazed relentlessly at his son. Arina Vlasevna also did not go to bed and, opening the study door slightly, continually went to listen to 'the way our Enyushka's breathing,' as she put it, and then to see how Vasily Ivanovich was. She could see only his bent, motionless back, but even that afforded her a certain relief. In the morning Bazarov tried to get up. His head spun and he had a nose bleed and lay down again. Vasily Ivanovich made his medical check-up in silence. Arina Vlasevna went in to him and asked him how he was feeling. He answered: 'Better' and turned his face to the wall. Vasily Ivanovich shooed his wife away with both hands. She bit her lips to stop herself from crying and went out.

Everything in the house suddenly went dark. Everyone had long faces and a strange quiet descended. A noisily crowing cock was removed from the yard and carted off to the village, quite unable to understand why it was being treated in this way. Bazarov went on lying with his face pressed to the wall. Vasily Ivanovich tried to ask him a few questions but they were tiring to Bazarov and the old man sank back into his armchair, doing no more than crack his fingers from time to time. He would then go out into the garden for a moment or two and stand there rooted like a statue, as if struck dumb by an inexplicable astonishment (a look of astonishment never left his face the entire time) and then he would go back in to his son, trying to avoid being pestered by his wife. She finally seized him by the arm and asked all aquiver, almost threateningly: 'What's wrong with him?' There and then he came to his senses and made himself smile at her in reply, but to his own horror, instead of a smile a laugh came to his lips. He had sent for a doctor first thing that morning. He thought he ought to tell his son about this, so that he wouldn't be annoyed.

Bazarov suddenly turned over on the divan, looked intently and bluntly at his father and asked for a drink.

Vasily Ivanovich handed him some water and took the opportunity to feel his brow. It was literally burning with fever.

'Old man,' Bazarov began in a drawling, hoarse voice, 'my case is hopeless. I'm infected and in a few days you'll be burying me.'

Vasily Ivanovich was staggered, just as if he'd been knocked off his feet.

'Evgeny!' he muttered. 'What a thing to say! God help you! You've caught a cold . . .'

'Enough of that,' Bazarov calmly interrupted him. 'That's no sort of talk for a doctor. There are all the signs of infection and you know it.'

'Where are these signs . . . of infection, Evgeny? For heaven's sake!'

'So what's this?' asked Bazarov and, drawing back his shirtsleeve, showed his father the malignant and protuberant red blotches.

Vasily Ivanovich shuddered and went cold with fright. 'Granted,' he said at last, 'granted . . . if . . . if it's something in the nature of . . . of an infection . . .'

'Pyaemia,' his son prompted.

'Well, yes . . . in the nature of an . . . an epidemic . . .'

'*Pyaemia*,' Bazarov repeated sternly and precisely. 'Or have you forgotten all your textbooks taught you?'

'Well, yes, yes, yes, if that's what you want to call it . . . But we can still get you right!'

'No way you can't. But that's not the problem. I hadn't expected I'd die so soon. It's, truth to tell, a not very pleasant occurrence. Mother and you must now make the most you can of the fact that your religion is strong. Here's a chance for you to put it to the test.' He drank a little more water. 'Meanwhile, I want to ask you to do one thing for me, just so long as my brain is still in my control. Tomorrow or the day after, as you know, it'll go into retirement. I'm not even quite sure now that I'm expressing myself clearly. While I've been lying here I seem to have had red dogs running about all round me and you've been taking aim at me as if I were a woodcock. It was just as if I'd been drunk. Do you understand what I'm saying?'

'For heaven's sake, Evgeny, you're talking perfectly properly.'

'So much the better. You told me you'd sent for a doctor . . . That may have been comfort to yourself . . . Now comfort me: send someone for . . .'

'Arkady Nikolaich?' asked the old man.

'Who's Arkady Nikolaich?' asked Bazarov as if lost in thought. 'Oh, yes! That fledgling! No, don't you bother him. He's grown into a jackdaw. Don't be shocked, I'm not delirious yet. But you send someone for Odintsova, Anna Sergeevna, she's a landowner in these parts . . . Do you know her?' (Vasily Ivanovich nodded.) 'Tell him to say Evgeny Bazarov sends his greetings and wants it to be known he is dying. Will you do that?'

'I'll do it . . . Only it can't be right that you're going to die, Evgeny . . . I mean, judge for yourself! Where will there be any justice in the world after that?'

'I don't know. Just you send someone.'

'I'll send someone this minute and I'll write a letter.'

'No, there's no point. Just tell him to convey my greetings, there's no need for anything else. And now I'll go back to my dogs. It's a strange thing! Here I am trying to fix my thoughts on death and nothing comes of it. All I can see is some kind of faint spot . . . and nothing else.'

He again turned heavily back to the wall and Vasily Ivanovich left the study and went to his wife's bedroom and literally collapsed on his knees in front of the icon.

'Pray, Arina, pray!' he groaned. 'Our son is dying.'

The doctor, the very same country doctor who had had no caustic, arrived and, after looking at the sick man, came out with the advice that a waiting method of treatment should be maintained and then had a few words to say about the chances of recovery.

'Have you ever seen people in my condition who have *not* been despatched to the Elysian fields?' asked Bazarov and, suddenly seizing hold of the leg of a heavy table standing beside the divan, shook it and made it move.

'My strength, my strength,' he said, 'it's all still there, but I've still got to die! An old man, he can at least have managed to get tired of life, but I . . . Yes, just you try and deny death. It'll deny you and that's that! Who is that crying?' he added after a moment. 'Is it mother? Poor thing! Who'll she be able to feed her marvellous borshch to after this? And you, Vasily Ivanovich, you're sniffling as well, aren't you? Well, if Christianity doesn't help, be a philosopher, a stoic! After all, you used to boast you were a philosopher, didn't you?'

'I'm no philosopher!' wailed Vasily Ivanovich and tears just poured down his cheeks.

Bazarov grew worse with each hour that passed. The illness took a rapid course, which usually happens with surgical poisonings. He had not yet lost his memory and still understood what people were saying to him. He was putting up a struggle. 'I don't want to become delirious,' he whispered, clenching his fists, 'it'd be such a lot of nonsense!' And then and there went on: 'Well, subtract eight from ten, what do we get?' Vasily Ivanovich wandered about practically out of his mind and proposed one treatment, then another and yet all he did was cover his son's legs. 'Wrap him in cold sheets . . . give him an emetic . . . hot jars on the stomach . . . some bloodletting,' he kept on saying with great intentness. The doctor, whom he had begged to stay, backed him up in everything and plied the sick man with lemonade while for himself he asked for pipes to smoke or 'something strengthening and warming' meaning vodka. Arina Vlasevna sat on a little low bench beside the door and only occasionally went off to say her prayers. A few days before a little mirror on her dressing-table had slipped out of her hands and broken and she had always considered this a bad omen. Even Anfisushka didn't know what to say to her. Timofeich had been despatched to fetch Odintsova.

The night was a bad one for Bazarov. He was tortured by a cruelly high fever. By morning he felt better. He begged Arina Vlasevna to do his hair, kissed her hand and drank a couple of mouthfuls of tea. Vasily Ivanovich cheered up a little.

'Glory be!' he repeated over and over. 'The crisis has come . . . the crisis has gone.'

'Just imagine it,' murmured Bazarov 'what a word can mean! You've found it, said it, the word "crisis"—and you're happy! It's astonishing how a man can still believe in words. If you tell someone, for example, he's a fool and you don't beat him, he'll be bitterly disappointed. Call him clever but don't give him any money and he'll be perfectly satisfied.'

This little speech by Bazarov, so reminiscent of his former witticisms, brought Vasily Ivanovich to a state of elation.

'Bravo! Splendidly said! Splendid!' he cried, pretending to applaud.

Bazarov smiled sadly.

'So what's your opinion,' he asked, 'has the crisis come or gone?'

'I see you're better, that's what delights me,' answered Vasily Ivanovich.

'Well, that's great! It's always a good thing to be delighted. Have you sent someone to her—remember who I mean?'

'Someone's been sent, of course.'

The change for the better did not last long. The onslaughts of illness were renewed. Vasily Ivanovich sat beside Bazarov. It was obvious that the old man was particularly worried by something. He made an effort to speak about it several times and failed.

'Evgeny!' he uttered at last. 'My son, my dear, dear son!'

This unusual form of address had its effect on Bazarov. He turned his head a little and, evidently trying to break free of the burden of unconsciousness which was settling on him, uttered the words:

'What, father?'

'Evgeny,' Vasily Ivanovich went on and fell on his knees before Bazarov although the latter didn't open his eyes and couldn't see him, 'Evgeny, you're better now and, God willing, you'll get better, but do please make the most of this time, make your mother and me happy and do your duty as a Christian! It's dreadful that I have to say this to you, but still more dreadful . . . after all, it's for ever, Evgeny . . . Just you think what it means . . .'

The old man's voice broke completely and across his son's face, although he still lay there with closed eyes, passed an odd sort of look.

'I won't refuse if it'll make you happy,' he said eventually, 'but I don't think there's any need for hurry. You yourself say I'm better.'

'You are better, Evgeny, you are. But who knows, it's all up to God, and by doing your duty . . .'

'No, I'll wait a while,' Bazarov interrupted him. 'I agree with you that the crisis has come. But if we've both made a mistake, so what? They give the last unction to the unconscious, don't they?'

'For heaven's sake, Evgeny . . .'

'I'll wait. Now I'd like to sleep. Don't disturb me.'

And he laid his head back where it had been.

The old man climbed to his feet, sat in an armchair and, seizing hold of his chin, started biting his fingers.

The creak of carriage springs, that noise which is so especially noticeable in the depth of the countryside, suddenly broke upon his hearing. Ever closer and closer rolled the sound of lightweight wheels. By the time the snorting of the horses could be heard Vasily Ivanovich had jumped up and dashed to a little window. A twin-seat carriage, drawn by four horses, was driving into the courtyard of his small house. Without giving himself a chance to consider what this could mean, in a rush of senseless joy, he ran out on to the porch steps. A liveried footman was opening the little carriage doors. A woman in a black veil and black mantilla was getting out.

'I am Odintsova,' she said. 'Is Evgeny Vasilich still alive? Are you his father? I've brought a doctor with me.'

'Benefactress!' cried Vasily Ivanovich and, seizing her hand, pressed it quiveringly to his lips as the doctor brought by Anna Sergeevna, a small, bespectacled man with a German face, climbed unhurriedly down from the carriage. 'He is still alive, my Evgeny is still alive and now he will be saved! Wife! Wife! An angel from heaven has come to us . . .'

'My God, what is it?' babbled the old woman, rushing out of the sitting-room and, not understanding a thing, right there in the entrance way flung herself at Anna Sergeevna's feet and began to kiss her dress as if she were quite out of her mind.

'What on earth! What on earth!' Anna Sergeevna said over and over, but Arina Vlasevna didn't hear her and Vasily Ivanovich could only repeat: 'Angel! Angel!'

'Wo ist der Kranke? Und vere iz ze patient?' asked the doctor finally, not without a certain indignation.

Vasily Ivanovich came to his senses. 'Here, here, please follow me, *werthester Herr Kollege*,' he added, calling to mind a phrase from his past.

'Ach!' pronounced the German and grinned sourly.

Vasily Ivanovich led him into his study.

'A doctor is here from Anna Sergeevna Odintsova,' he said, bending down to his son's ear, 'and she is here as well.'

Bazarov suddenly opened his eyes. 'What did you say?'

'I said that Anna Sergeevna Odintsova is here and has brought with her this gentleman, a doctor.'

Bazarov searched around with his eyes.

'She's here . . . I want to see her.'

'You'll see her, Evgeny, but first of all we have to have a few words with the doctor. I'll tell him the full story of the illness, because Sidor Sidorych' (that was the local doctor's name) 'has gone and we'll need to have a short consultation.'

Bazarov glanced at the German. 'Well, get on with your few words, only not in Latin. After all, I understand what *jam moritur* means.'

'Der Herr scheint des Deutschen mächtig zu sein,' began the new devotee of Aesculapius, turning to Vasily Ivanovich.

'*Ikh . . . gabe . . .* It'd be better if you spoke Russian,' said the old man.

'Ach, ach! *Zo eet vill be . . .* Pleassse . . .'

And the consultation began.

Half an hour later Anna Sergeevna accompanied Vasily Ivanovich into the study. The doctor had managed to whisper to her that there was no point in thinking about the patient's recovery.

She glanced at Bazarov and stood stock-still in the doorway, so shocking to her was the sight of the inflamed and simultaneously corpse-like face with its glazed eyes directed at her. She was quite simply seized by a chill and enervating terror. The thought that she would not have felt such terror if she had really loved him flashed for a moment through her mind.

'Thank you,' he forced himself to say, 'I hadn't expected this. It's an act of kindness. You see, we are seeing each other again, as you promised.'

'Anna Sergeevna was kind enough . . .' Vasily Ivanovich began.

'Father, leave us. You don't object, Anna Sergeevna? It seems by now . . .'

He indicated by a nod of the head his outstretched, enfeebled body.

Vasily Ivanovich went out.

'Well, thank you,' Bazarov repeated. 'It's right royal of you. I've been told that royalty also visit the dying.'

'Evgeny Vasilich, I hope . . .'

'Oh, Anna Sergeevna, let's start by speaking the truth. It's the end for me. I've been run over. And it turns out it's pointless to think about the future. Death may be an old joke, but for each of us it's as new as ever. So far I've faced up to it . . . But unconsciousness is on its way and then—*phut*!' (He feebly waved his hand.) 'Well, what've I got to tell you is . . . I loved you! That didn't have any meaning then and it's got even less now. Love is just a form of being and now my own form is already disintegrating. I'll say rather—what a wonderful person you are! And now here you are standing in front of me looking so beautiful . . .'

Anna Sergeevna shuddered despite herself.

'It doesn't matter, don't be anxious . . . Do sit down over there . . . Don't come close to me. After all, my illness is infectious.'

Anna Sergeevna rapidly crossed the room and sat down in an armchair beside the divan on which Bazarov was lying.

'Kindness itself!' he whispered. 'Oh, how close you are, and how young and fresh and clean . . . in this foul room! Well, goodbye! Live a long life, that's best of all, and enjoy it while there's time. You can see what an ugly spectacle I am, a half-crushed worm and still showing off. And I used to think, after all, I'll do a whole mass of things, I'll not die, no way! There's a task to be done and I'm a giant! And now the giant's only task is to die decently, although no one cares a damn about that . . . Still, I won't start wagging my tail.'

Bazarov fell silent and started to feel with his hand for his glass. Anna Sergeevna gave him something to drink, fearful to breathe and without taking off her glove.

'You'll forget me,' he started saying again. 'The dead are no companions for the living. My father'll say to you, Just look what a man Russia is losing! That's all nonsense, but don't disillusion the old man. Whatever gives a child comfort—you know what I mean.

And be kind to my mother. After all, people like them you won't find the world over though you search with a torch by daylight . . . I'm needed by Russia . . . No, obviously I'm not needed. And who is needed? The shoemaker's needed, the tailor's needed, the butcher . . . he sells meat . . . the butcher . . . Stop, I'm losing my way . . . There's a forest here . . .'

Bazarov placed his hand on his forehead.

Anna Sergeevna bent over him.

'Evgeny Vasilich, I'm here . . .'

He instantly seized her hand and raised himself up.

'Goodbye,' he said with sudden force and his eyes glittered with a final brilliance. 'Goodbye . . . Listen . . . You know I never kissed you then . . . Blow on the dying lamp and then let it go out . . .'

Anna Sergeevna pressed her lips to his forehead.

'And that's enough!' he said and dropped back on to the pillow. 'Now . . . darkness . . .'

Anna Sergeevna went out quietly.

'How is he?' asked Vasily Ivanovich in a whisper.

'He's gone to sleep,' she answered scarcely audibly.

Bazarov was not destined to wake up again. Towards evening he succumbed to complete unconsciousness and the next day he died. Father Aleksei conducted the religious rites over him. As extreme unction was being administered, when the consecrated oil touched his breast, one of his eyes opened and it seemed that at the sight of the priest in his vestments, the smoking censer and the candle before the icon something like a look of horror was momentarily reflected in the deathly features. When, finally, he expelled his last breath and general lamentation filled the house, Vasily Ivanovich was seized by a sudden frenzy. 'I said I'd repudiate,' he cried out hoarsely, with a burning, contorted face, shaking his fist in the air as if he were threatening someone, 'and I do repudiate, I do!' But Arina Vlasevna, her face awash with tears, leaned on his shoulder and the two of them fell on their knees together. 'It was just', Anfisushka used to relate afterwards in the servants' quarters, 'as if they'd hung their dear heads side by side like little lambs at midday . . .'

But the heat of midday passes, and evening draws in and night comes on and then it is time for a return to the quiet haven where sweet sleep awaits all who travail and are heavy laden . . .

28

SIX months passed. White winter with the cruel silence of cloudless frosts, thick, squeaky-hard snow, rosy hoarfrost on the trees, pale emerald skies, cloud-caps of smoke above chimneys, columns of steam rising from momentarily opened doors, the fresh-looking, literally nipped-at faces of humans and the busy trotting of little horses perished by the cold—white winter was everywhere. A January day was already coming to an end. The chill of evening tightened its grip on the still air and the blood-red sunset rapidly waned. Lights were lit in the windows of Marino. Prokofich in black frock-coat and white gloves was particularly solemnly laying the table for seven. A week before, in the small parish church, two weddings had taken place quietly and almost without witnesses: Arkady to Katya and Nikolai Petrovich to Fenechka. That very January day Nikolai Petrovich was giving a farewell dinner for his brother, who was departing for Moscow on business. Anna Sergeevna had also gone off there immediately after the wedding, having provided generously for the young couple.

Precisely at three o'clock everyone gathered round the table. Mitya was also given a place. He had arrived in the company of a nanny wearing a tall brocade peasant headdress. Pavel Petrovich took his place between Katya and Fenechka and the 'husbands' were seated next to their wives. Our friends had changed in recent times. They all seemed to have grown better-looking and more confident. Only Pavel Petrovich had grown thinner, which, however, endowed his expressive features with even more elegance and made him look even more like a *grand seigneur* . . . And Fenechka had also changed. In a fresh silk dress, with a broad velvet band in her hair and a gold necklace round her neck, she sat in respectful immobility, respectful of herself and of everything around her and smiled as though she wanted to say: 'You must forgive me, I'm not to blame for being so lovely.' And she wasn't the only one—the others all smiled as well and also seemed to offer their apologies, because they all felt a little awkward, a little sad and, in all essentials, very happy. They were all attentive to each other with good-humoured solicitude just as if they'd all agreed to take part in an enjoyable comedy. Katya was the calmest of all. She continuously looked confidently around her and it was noticeable that Nikolai Petrovich was already out of his mind about her. Just before the end of the meal he rose and, taking his glass in his hand, turned to Pavel Petrovich.

'You are leaving us . . . You are leaving us, dear brother,' he began, 'of course, not for long. But I'm still unable to express to you what I . . . what we . . . how much I . . . how much we . . . The whole trouble is that I'm no good at making speeches! Arkady, you say something.'

'No, dad, I've not prepared anything.'

'And I made all sorts of preparations! Brother, let me simply embrace you and wish you the best! And come back to us as soon as you can!'

Pavel Petrovich exchanged kisses with everyone, not excluding little Mitya of course. What is more, in Fenechka's case he kissed her hand, which she did not know how to offer properly, and, draining a second glassful of wine, declared with a deep sigh:

'Be happy, my friends! Farewell!'

The last word, uttered in English, passed unnoticed, but everyone was touched.

'In memory of Bazarov,' Katya whispered in her husband's ear and clinked glasses with him. Arkady responded by giving her hand a firm squeeze, but he did not decide to propose this toast out loud.

That would seem to be the end, wouldn't it? But maybe some of our readers would like to know what each of our characters is doing now, at this very time.* We are ready to satisfy their curiosity.

Anna Sergeevna recently got married, not for love but out of conviction, to one of Russia's future statesmen, a very clever man, a member of the judiciary, with strong practical sense, strength of will and a remarkable way with words, someone still young, kindly and cold as ice. They are living in great harmony with one another and will doubtless live long enough to find happiness . . . perhaps even to find love. Princess Kh . . . ya has died, forgotten on the very day of her death. The Kirsanovs, father and son, have settled in Marino. Their affairs are beginning to set themselves to rights. Arkady has become an enthusiastic proprietor and the 'farm' is already making a fairly significant profit. Nikolai Petrovich has become an arbitrator* and is up to his ears in work. He ceaselessly travels to and fro over his district and delivers long speeches (he is of the opinion that the peasants 'have to be made to see sense', meaning that by frequent repetition of the very same words they are to be driven to distraction) and yet, truth to tell, he fails to satisfy fully either the educated nobility, those who talk about the Emancipation either with *chic*, or about the '*man*cipation' in a melancholy way (pronouncing the '*an*' with nasal emphasis), or the uneducated nobility, those who swear unceremoniously at 'the bloody *mun*cipation'. For both the one and the other he is being far too mild.

Katerina Sergeevna has given birth to a son, Kolya, and Mitya is already running about like a real little boy and chattering away busily. Fenechka, Fedosya Nikolaevna, apart from her husband and Mitya adores no one so much as her sister-in-law and, whenever the latter sits down at the piano, is happy to remain at her side the whole day long. A word also about Peter. He has become quite paralytic with stupidity and self-importance, pronouncing every 'e' as 'u'— *prusuntly*, *ussuntially*, but he has also got married and taken a considerable dowry for his bride, the daughter of a town vegetable-gardener, who refused two good suitors because they didn't have a watch, whereas Peter not only had a watch, he also had patent-leather boots.

In Dresden, on the Brühl Terrace,* between two and four in the afternoon, the most fashionable time for taking a stroll, you could encounter a man of about fifty, already quite grey and apparently suffering from gout, but still handsome, elegantly dressed and with that particular air about him which is acquired by a man only through long acquaintance with the higher strata of society. This is Pavel Petrovich. He left Moscow to go abroad to improve his health and stayed to reside in Dresden, where he consorts mostly with Englishmen and visiting Russians. With the English he behaves simply, almost modestly, but not without dignity, and they find him a little boring, but they respect him for being 'a perfect gentleman'. With Russians he is less straitlaced, gives rein to his bilious wit, makes fun of himself and of them, but all this in his case comes out very charmingly, casually and politely. He upholds Slavophile views: in high society, as is well-known, such a thing is considered *très distingué*. He does not read anything in Russian, but on his writing-table he has a silver ashtray in the shape of a peasant's bast shoe. Our tourists are very keen on him. Matthew Ilich Kolyazin, finding himself 'in temporary opposition',* grandly paid him a visit on his way to take the Bohemian waters, while the locals, with whom, however, he has very little to do, almost worship the ground he treads on. No one can obtain a ticket for the court chapel, the theatre and so on more easily and quickly than *der Herr Baron von Kirsanoff*. He still does good works, in so far as he can. He still cuts a bit of dash in society because he was not at one time a social lion for nothing. But he finds life hard . . . harder than he'd suspected. One only has to glance at him in the Russian church when, leaning sideways against the wall, he falls into deep thought and does not stir for a long while, his lips pursed tightly together in bitterness, and then suddenly remembers himself and begins to make the sign of the cross almost imperceptibly . . .

Kukshina has also gone abroad. She is now in Heidelberg and studying not the natural sciences but architecture, in which, according to her, she has discovered new laws. As formerly she hangs out with students, particularly with young Russian physicists and chemists who have crowded into Heidelberg and who, astonishing their naïve German professors at first with their sober view of things, end by astonishing those very same professors with their complete inactivity and absolute laziness. With two or three student chemists who cannot tell oxygen from nitrogen but are self-opinionated and full of negative criticism, as well as with the great Elisevich, Sitnikov, who is also preparing for greatness, is knocking about in St Petersburg and continuing, so he asserts, the 'cause' of Bazarov. Rumour has it that he recently received a thumping from someone, but he didn't remain at a loss for long. In an obscure little article in an obscure little journal he hinted that the man who had thumped him was a coward. He calls this irony. His father calls him every kind of name as before and his wife considers him silly . . . and a *littérateur*.

There is a small village graveyard in one of the remote corners of Russia. Like almost all our graveyards it has a melancholy appearance with its surrounding ditches long since overgrown, its grey wooden crosses bent and rotting beneath their once painted roofs, the headstones all lopsided as if someone had given them a shove, two or three wretched trees scarcely giving the barest shade and sheep wandering unperturbed among the graves . . . But among them is one that no man has dared lay his hands on and which no animal has trampled. Only birds alight on it and sing at sunrise. An iron railing surrounds it; two young pine saplings have been planted at either end: Evgeny Bazarov is buried in this grave. To it, from the nearby village, there frequently comes a frail old couple, man and wife. Supporting each other, they approach with a heavy step; they go up to the railing and fall down on their knees and cry long and bitterly, and long and attentively they gaze at the silent gravestone beneath which their son lies; they exchange a few brief words, they dust the gravestone and adjust the branch of a sapling and again they pray and cannot make themselves leave this place where it seems to them they are closer to their son and to their memories of him . . .

Can their prayers and their tears be fruitless? Can love, sacred, devoted love, not be all-powerful? Oh, no! No matter how passionate, sinning, rebellious is the heart hidden in the grave, the flowers growing on it look at us serenely with their innocent faces; they speak to us not only of that eternal peace, of that great peace of 'impassive' nature; they speak to us also of eternal reconciliation and of life everlasting . . .

APPENDIX: TURGENEV'S SKETCHES
FOR *FATHERS AND SONS*

THE following translation of part of these sketches is based on the text and invaluable notes given in Patrick Waddington's article 'Turgenev's sketches for *Ottsy i deti* (*Fathers and Sons*)', *New Zealand Slavonic Journal*, 1984, pp. 33–76; and also on the text as emended in I. S. Turgenev, *Polnoe sobranie sochinenii*, second complete revised edition (*Sochineniya*, vol. 12, Moscow, 1986, pp. 563–75). Because most of the material which Turgenev prepared in sketch form for his novel was actually used during its composition, to avoid duplication only the more significant sections— the first list of characters, the character sketch of Bazarov and the outline of the story—are translated here.

It is noteworthy that the characters appear to have been conceived in August 1860, in Ventnor, while the story was not conceived until October at Courtavenel, the Viardot residence east of Paris. Equally noteworthy is how little both characters and story differ in these preliminary sketches from the form they finally acquired. Place-names undergo changes— Odintsovo to Nikolskoe, 'New Place' to Marino; very minor changes occur to characters' names (e.g. Fenichka to Fenechka, Skoropilov to Elisevich); more significantly, the important ideological quarrel between Bazarov and Pavel Petrovich Kirsanov seems to have been brought forward, from Bazarov's second visit to the Kirsanov estate to his first; and neither the love story between Bazarov and Odintsova, nor the tragedy surrounding his death seem to have been anticipated. Otherwise what we have here is a remarkably accurate outline blueprint for a masterpiece.

The statements contained within square brackets [. . . : . . .] are Professor Waddington's annotations (italicized, in English) prior to the colon and translations of the Russian text after the colon.

No 1

Curricula vitae of the characters of the new story.   Ventnor (on the Isle of Wight).   August 1860.

[*reverse of title page*] Piotr Kirsanov *1806* Aglaida   his wife b.1765. + 1840. b. – 1774. + 1840

35·   35·

The characters

The action takes place in 1859.

1.) Nikolai Petrovich Kirsanov
  44—born in 1815

2.) Pavel Petrovich Kirsanov
  his brother, 48: born in 1811

3.) Arkady Nikolaevich, son of N. P.
  22—born in 1837

4.) Evgeny Vasilevich Bazarov
  29—born in 1830

5.) Viktor Fomich Sitnikov
  24—born in 1835

6.) Fedosya Ivanovna—(Fenichka)
  24—born in 1835

7.) Mitya—2. born in 1857

8.) Anna Sergeevna Odintsova,
  widow—28. born in 1831

9.) Katerina Sergeevna Lokteva,
  her sister—20. born in 1839

10.) Avdotya Nikitishna Kukshina,
  31—born in 1828

11.) Peter, a servant—30.

12.) Dunyasha, a maid—25.

13.) [*name crossed out*] Prokofich, a servant, 65.

14.) [*name crossed out*] Matthew Ilich Kalyazin
  Privy Councillor—56—1813.

. . .   .

4. Evgeny Bazarov.—

Son of a doctor, who was himself the son of a priest.—Father's a lively, bilious and original materialist with a small medical practice.—Was an army doctor (in General Kirsanov's brigade and elsewhere), played cards, liked drink, had *omnes fortunas*, officers were fond of him and a little fearful of his tongue.—He married a quiet landowner's daughter with 25 serfs.—Evgeny's tall, thin, with a sharp nose, broad temples, thin lips—dark fair hair. Eyes [*added in margin*: and teeth] greenish, small, but pleasant—[*added in margin*: freckles] manly voice, quick, ~~very~~ agile though rather angular movements. Large hands, large feet.—At university studied natural sciences, philosophy—not without cynicism, special remarks and real capabilities.—A nihilist. Self-assured, speaks abruptly and little—hard-working.—(A mixture of Dobrolyubov, Pavlov and Preobrazhensky.) Lives the life of an unattached young man; doesn't want to be a doctor, is waiting for an opening.—Knows how to talk to the peasantry, although in his heart he despises them. Has no artistic element in his make-up and doesn't recognize any.—Loves making use of women—and influencing men.—Knows a good deal—is energetic, can please with his free-and-easy ways.—In essence a most sterile creature—the antipode of Rudin[1]—because he is without any enthusiasm and faith. Understands German and French well—but speaks badly.—Gets on very well with his father; not without sarcasm so far as his mother is concerned.—An independent soul—and haughtiness of the first order. Large sideburns.

---

about Kirsanov—
'He's sung his swansong

. . .

[1] Rudin was the hero of Turgenev's first novel.   On his first mentioning the character of Bazarov to a friend on the Isle of Wight, presumably N. Ya. Rostovtsev (1831–97), the latter remarked (according to Turgenev's reminiscences): 'But surely you, it seems, have already presented a similar type . . . in Rudin?' 'I was at a loss for words,' Turgenev wrote, 'What was there to say?   Rudin and Bazarov—one and the same type!'

No 2

Brief Outline of the Story of the new novel

Courtavenel. October. 1860.

The Story

At the post-station (like the Dalmatovsky one)—25th May Nikolai Kirsanov is waiting for his son from St Petersburg.—Impatience—scenes outside the window—(piglets, etc.). The weather is beautiful. Finally his son
arrives. But he's not alone: Evg. Bazarov is with him. The meeting—
embarrassment—great haste, needless running about.—Ark. introduces
his father to his friend. [*Added in margin*: (big-beard)]. Baz. very
unrestrained, talks in a carelessly lively way with the coachmen. They get
in the tarantass.—Baz. on the box [*?*].—From the post-station to the
estate is about 10 miles.

The estate's in the latest taste: a farm.—Everything's still very bad and
new and creaks along. In the garden there are sickly trees, the pond
which has been excavated has got salty-tasting water. Father and son's
conversation on the way. The father shyly feels his way and is delighted
and excited. Resolves to tell him about Fenichka. The son receives the
confession very calmly—as is becoming to a progressive—and even in his
soul is somehow content. On the first evening—sticky meetings, etc. The
appearance of the *brother*: a dandy, accustomed to making an impression,
etc. Bazarov talks as if he's at home—freely, but without being cynical . . .
quickly understands all and everyone—but out of carelessness doesn't
think before he speaks. The brother takes a strong dislike to him—and he
slightly frightens *Nikolai*. The talk between Bazarov and Arkady at
night sitting on the bed.

Life in the country begins the next day.—Kirsanov wants to introduce
his son into what is going on—Bazarov knocks him and everyone out of
every kind of rut (like a comet). He dashes about everywhere, socializes
freely and gets to know Fenich. slightly in the garden.—A.'s conversation
with his father—the uncle is silent for the most part—or if he takes part—
then rather irritably and essentially in an old-fashioned way—although
elegantly and keenly. A. is a bit ashamed of his father (although he loves
him very much) because of his out-of-date romanticism. Carefully (on the
urging of Bazarov) he takes Pushkin out of his hands and replaces it with
"*Stoff und Kraft*". ~~After~~ the conversation [*Continued on the right-hand
side*:] with B. in the garden, of which K. hears only the words: 'He has

sung his swansong.'—[*Added in margin*: Comparison of a kind between N. Kirsanov and the servant Prokofich, who complains about the new order of things—both are behind the times.] [*Continued on the left-hand side*:] Scene at night. Bitter-sweet play of romantic feelings—N. goes up to Fenichka's window—then goes into the garden and comes across his brother who then remains alone etc. A feeling of being drawn towards something.—Something new has to be undertaken. Bazarov has already familiarized himself with everything, even with Fenichka.—[*In margin*: 8th June.] A letter arrives from Kolyazin in the local town—he's been sent to inspect the province and would like to see the K—s—invites them to the town where the governor has been arranging receptions for him.— Both Kirsanovs refuse—but Arkady, prompted by Bazarov, goes off there.—(Feeling of relief felt by everyone after their departure.)

—Provincial town. The Governor's ball and his house. Kolyazin shows off.—At a musical evening at the Gov.'s—Baz. and Ark. meet Odintsova [*inserted*: and her sister.]—(They had already met Sitnikov on the street.) Odintsova makes a very strong impression on both of them—in their different ways—Bazarov wants to have her, Ar. is struck by her intelligence and her grace. She invites them to her estate.—[*In margin*: 13th June.] They go there—The estate is 30 [*? Turgenev seems to have hesitated between 20, 30 and 50*] versts[2] from the town. (N.B. Sitnikov must tell them Od.'s story at the ball.)

Description of A. S.'s house.—*Grand genre*—but with signs of neglect. The luxury left over from her husband's times is without great taste.— Life at Odintsova's.—Odintsova is attracted by Bazarov—almost to the point of love; Katya falls seriously in love with Ark.—And he feels gently drawn to her, although he doesn't even suspect it. Charming musical evenings—impatient complaints and outbursts by Bazarov.—The estate where his mother and father live (poor and modest) is 25 versts from Odintsovo.—They know that he's there, but can't make up their minds to get in touch in order not to offend him. Only once, pretending to be on his way to town, old man Bazarov's servant drops by—but without any letter from him. B. who has only just missed having Odints.—suddenly feels vexed and impatient—(this life's already been going on for 2 weeks)—and ~~proposes to go~~ announces to Ar. that he wants to leave. The latter also leaves, all the more because Sitnikov had arrived 3 days before with Kukshina—the emancipée.—Sitnikov proposes to accompany them in his own tarantass—he wants to travel home with Ark.—but at a crossroads— B. sets off to his own home in a cart. [*In margin*: 25th June.] They set

---

[2] A verst is 1.07 kilometres or .66 of a mile and has been rendered in this translation of *Fathers and Sons* by an approximate figure in miles.

off—but at the crossroads with [*sic*] Ark. joins B. in the cart (their own tarantass had gone off to the provinc. town)—and they leave Sitnikov, who returns to Odintsovo.—A. S. drives him out of there along with Kukshina.

[*In margin*: 26th and 27th.] B. and A. spend 2 days at *his parents*. Describe this diligently and so it comes out touchingly and a bit humorously, but truthfully.—Old man B. is frightfully glad to see his son—but pretends to be busily indifferent; the mother pines in silence etc. They are bitterly sad that their son leaves so soon—but they restrain their feelings.—

[*The whole of the paragraph which follows was originally placed after the one here given below it. Turgenev switched them by numbering them 1 and 2. In the margin*: 2nd July. *Also in the margin, but apparently quite independent of the text, Turgenev wrote in large block letters*: PANAEF.[3]]

A. and B. leave in order to travel home—but suddenly (at the crossroads) an overwhelming force draws them towards Odintsovo—Ar. asserts that he is drawn to O., B.—argues that women like her are quite unnecessary—but the real charmer is Katya—but each in his heart feels quite the opposite . . . They arrive . . . O-a receives them rather strangely and they decide, after about 3 days, to go off to 'New Place'. O-a was confused—she'd wanted to have a rest after the unexpectedly close acquaintanceship with B.—and a feeling for Ark. had begun to stir in her.

Return to the Kir. estate. Naïve joy [*inserted*: pity (?)] of F. . . And the father is delighted, although life is again full of problems.—Enormous and cheerless worries over the farm.—Not enough hands for the harvest—the peasants aren't paying their dues.—Nonsense!!—Bazarov suddenly isolates himself and starts working with frenzied devotion. Arkady is bored and fretful; something draws him to Odintsovo—he can't make up his mind to say so—but he invents a pretext for going to the town. B. remains behind unperturbed—besides, because he's working, he is not in anyone's way. He is visited by N. K. and even his brother in order to observe his experiments with infusorians etc.—sits by himself in his room, goes for walks—and various thoughts concerning F. enter his head—He conducts intellectual-nihilistic discussions with the brothers, smashes to smithereens the aristocratism and [*added in margin*: isolated]

---

[3] I. I. Panaev (1816–62), writer and journalist, co-editor with Nekrasov of the journal *The Contemporary* and close friend of Turgenev, though by 1860 Turgenev had abandoned his association with the journal due to the hostility of Chernyshevsky and Dobrolyubov towards him. It is very likely that the name written in block letters is associated with the letter which Turgenev wrote to Panaev from Paris on 13 October 1860, formally dissociating himself from the journal.

dandyism of the one and the practical strivings and romanticism of the other—but himself puts nothing in their place—because he doesn't believe in anything.—(Meanwhile Ark. is living in Odintsovo—and growing ever closer to Katya—and arouses in Odintsova a half-maternal, half-passionate feeling.—

Finally comes the scene of the kiss, which B. gives F. must work on this. Pyotr [*sic*] K. discovers them (he's long been secretly in love with F. though she [?] doesn't love B.—) and his jealousy's aroused—he gives the impression he's seen nothing—and on no pretext at all challenges B. to a duel.

Describe this duel.—[*In margin*: 20th July.] Kirs. slightly wounded in the thigh. [*Added in margin*: (deer going into water).] B. bandages him to the accompaniment of slightly ironic but friendly remarks. Pavel is very ashamed and annoyed.—They agree how ~~to safeguard~~ to explain his wound—and B. transports him home, having laid him down beneath a tree ([*Crossed out*: Prokofich] Peter was second to both of them.) Kirsanov is brought home and put to bed.—[*Crossed out*: He stays there] Fenichka comes to do things for him. The scene between him and her.—Fenichka cries and is frightened —Nikol. K. comes in with his son in his arms and fusses [*sic*] over him and is delighted. F. kisses him tenderly, takes her son and goes out. P. Kir. thinks and thinks and decides to persuade his brother to get married. This scene must come out exceptionally well or it'll go to the devil.—A Christianly moral feeling must be aroused in Pavel and in Nikolai.—He decides to get married—(but Pav. [*added in margin*] decides (on his own) to go abroad.

And Bazarov frees all his birds, frogs, etc. and goes to Odintsovo. He feels awkward staying at the Kir.s . . . He wants to be with A. S.—

His arrival.—He finds Arkady there. Not entirely happy encounter. 1st evening is a bit difficult.—Must write it well.—(He is observant, he suspects . . .)

How they all pass the night—not one of all 4 of them sleeps, though not one suspects this of the other.

Arkady's early morning walk in the garden with Katya.—They confess their love—and sit silently on a bench lost in bliss.—Footsteps are heard. B. and O. approach. A. wants to get up and go to them but K. holds him back.—O. and B. walk past—[*added in margin*: they return 2 times]—their conversation—. . . She admits to B. that she's fallen in love with Arkady. He is silent, doesn't believe her, proves to her she couldn't be, she hasn't got the *strength* to love—but it's very hard for him. They move off . . . both A. and K. move off too . . . They'd exchanged looks during the conversation and squeezed each other's hands tightly.—(O-a ~~says~~ thinks

Ark. has fallen in love with her; Baz. wants to disabuse her of this and hints at K.—but stops.—)

A. writes O. a letter, in which he asks for her sister's hand.—She summons Baz. and shows him the letter. "You want to ask me when I am leaving?" says Bazarov. "This very day. First let's give our blessing to the young pair."—That's what happens.—O. agrees—but it is very hard for her.—Bazarov travels home and Ark. goes to his father, from whom he wants to ask permission.—

B.—arrives home.—His occupations—hunt for distraction.— Melancholy suddenly appears in him.—A precursor of something frightful and final. He starts wandering about the neighbourhood; indulging in half-humorous relationships with the peasants and the womenfolk, to whom he gives medical treatment. (His relations with his mother and father.).—Has to undertake a difficult operation.—He consults his father—about which of them—and as an example—dissection of a corpse—cuts his finger—and is infected. No way of saving himself.—In 48 hours he dies.—The final conversation with his father.—It'll have to be done as well as possible.—The father in deep despair . . . "What a man Russia is losing!" (—What B. tells his mother on this score.) [*In the margin*: dies 25th August.]

At this time there take place absolutely on the quiet the marriages between Kir. and F. and Ark. and Katya.—The dinner—with *smiles* all round. P. goes abroad— and lives in Dresden—like Rosset.[4] Odintsova marries a future politician like Unkovsky.[5]

Sitnikov returns to St Pet. and "together with *Skoropilov*"[6] continues the *cause* of Bazarov.—Kukshina hangs out with chemistry students in Heidelberg.—The Kirsanovs live peacefully and quietly in the country.

---

[4] Possibly Arkady Osipovich Rosset (1812–81) or Klementy Osipovich Rosset (1811– 66). Turgenev does not appear to have known either of them, although he knew their sister, A. O. Smirnova (*née* Rossett) (1809–82), and in his first novel *Rudin* based the character of Darya Lasunskaya on her.

[5] A. M. Unkovsky (1828–93), well-known liberal of the period of the Emancipation of the serfs.

[6] The name, possibly invented, was changed to Elisevich in the final text.

EXPLANATORY NOTES

The following notes are drawn in part from the editions of Turgenev's works cited above in the Note on the Text.

1 *Belinsky*: V. G. Belinsky (1811–48) first became closely associated with Turgenev in 1843. The most influential literary critic of his day and a leading Westernist, he served to epitomize for Turgenev both the progressive, liberal, European orientation of the first generation of the Russian intelligentsia and the earnestness of the largely self-taught intellectual from a modest and underprivileged background (his father was a naval doctor). Both in the fierceness of his convictions and in his anti-establishment cast of mind, Vissarion Belinsky can be said to have served as a role model for the fictional Bazarov.

5 *1848*: the toppling of thrones throughout Europe and the Paris revolution of 1848 (of which Turgenev was an eyewitness) led to a 7-year period of extreme reaction in Russia (1848–55) which culminated in the Crimean War and was only ended by the death of Nicholas I and the accession to the throne of Alexander II, who initiated a reforming process.

12 *Catherine the Great*: proclaimed Empress in 1762, Catherine reigned until 1796 and succeeded in realizing Peter the Great's dream of extending the Russian empire to the Black Sea. In Turgenev's works her period is frequently treated as idyllic, characterized, however, by an old-fashioned quaintness.

13 *How sad to me . . . What—*: *Evgeny Onegin* (by A. S. Pushkin, 1799–1837), ch. VII, stanza 2.

16 *'shake hands'*: in English, in this form, in the original text.

17 *s'est dégourdi*: 'has become a live wire' (Fr.).

forthcoming governmental measures: a reference to the preparatory work initiated by the tsarist administration in connection with the emancipation of the serfs.

18 *Hambs*: French furniture maker (1765–1831) who resided in St Petersburg.

Galignani's Messenger: a liberal newspaper published in Paris since 1804.

23 *good health and the rank of general*: Pavel Petrovich is quoting from Act II of the famous comedy *Woe from Wit* (*Gore ot uma*, 1824) by A. S. Griboedov (1795–1829).

26 *no more haemorrhoids!*: it is very likely that Bazarov's joke refers to two works popular in Russia in the 1840s, firstly *The Art of Making Money by a simple and pleasant means accessible to everyone* by Baron Rothschild, translated from the French (St Petersburg, 1849); secondly, *No More*

Haemorrhoids by a Dr Mackenzie, translated from the German (St Petersburg, 1846).

Liebig: Justus Liebig (1803–73), German chemist, one of the founders of agronomical chemistry.

29 *Corps of Pages*: founded in 1759, an exclusive military academy in St Petersburg (Sadovaya ulitsa) with pupils limited to an annual entry of about 20 or so at age 12. Enjoying tsarist patronage, they were expected to serve at Court and, on leaving, they were granted commissions.

33 *elections*: a reference to the right of the nobility to elect their own officials to their organs of corporate self-government. This right was always subject to the control of the provincial governor and the Ministry of the Interior.

Wellington . . . Louis-Philippe: Arthur Wellesley, 1st Duke of Wellington (1769–1852), English military commander at the battle of Waterloo (1815) and later Prime Minister (1828–30); Louis-Philippe (1773–1850), French monarch, deposed as a result of the February revolution of 1848.

37 *General Ermolov*: A. P Ermolov (1772–1861), Russian general, a hero of the war of 1812, renowned as a diplomat and army commander in the Caucasus.

Streltsy: a 4-volume historical novel by K. P. Masalsky (1802–61), which came out in 1832.

46 *Stoff und Kraft*: a Russian translation of this popular work by Friedrich Büchner (1824–99) appeared in 1860. The title was actually *Kraft und Stoff* (Force and Matter).

47 *'The Gypsies'*: written in 1824, this was an important transitional work in Pushkin's poetic career, notable for the 'realistic' treatment of gypsy life and the dilemma of the Byronic hero, Aleko.

49 *the Alexandrine epoch*: during the reign of Alexander I (1801–25), Francophilia, despite the Napoleonic invasion, was all the rage; but there is the oblique suggestion that Pavel Petrovich was imitating the manner of the Decembrists, aristocratic revolutionaries who in December 1825, on the death of Alexander, attempted to overthrow the autocracy and establish a constitutional monarchy. See note to p. 117 on 'the southern army on the 14th'.

54 *'A Girl at the Fountain'*: the reference is not to any particular painting. Turgenev's poor opinion of the Russian painters in Rome dates from his visit in 1857.

61 *Guizot*: François Guizot (1787–1874), French historian and politician.

62 *Condillac*: Etienne Bonnot de Condillac (1715–80), leading French representative of the Enlightenment, a deist and advocate of philosophical sensualism.

'is quite a favorite': the phrase is in English, with that spelling, in the original.

63 *the well-known French Jesuit*: Louis Bourdaloue (1632–1704), French preacher, whose works were translated into Russian at the beginning of the nineteenth century.

64 *a Slavophile jacket*: Slavophilism was an anti-Western, ultra-patriotic, politically conservative movement which flourished in Russia between 1840 and 1880. Some of its adherents affected a special Russian form of dress. Sitnikov's jacket superficially demonstrated his patriotism, although in other respects he strove equally superficially to be Western, liberal and progressive.

65 *tax-farming*: leasing from the authorities the right to the profits of taxes on spirits, a lucrative but disreputable occupation in nineteenth-century Russia.

67 *Kislyakov ... Moscow News*: the name Kislyakov is probably one invented by Turgenev. The *Moscow News* was an official newspaper published between 1756 and 1917.

   schools: the question of schools also exercised Turgenev. While he was in Ventnor on the Isle of Wight in August 1860, he conceived—as well as his novel—a plan for a 'Society for the Propagation of Literacy and Primary Education' in Russia.

68 *George Sand ... Elisevich*: George Sand (1805–76), French novelist and friend of Turgenev; Ralph Waldo Emerson (1803–82), American writer and philosopher; Elisevich is probably a name invented by Turgenev from the names of two leading progressive journalists who contributed to *The Contemporary*, G. Z. Eliseev and M. A. Antonovich.

   Pathfinder: the hero of several novels by the American writer Fenimore Cooper (1789–1851).

   Bunsen's there!: R. W. Bunsen: (1811–99), German chemist.

69 *Proudhon's*: P. J. Proudhon (1809–65), French writer, economist and sociologist who was opposed to female emancipation.

70 *Macaulay*: Thomas Babington Macaulay (1800–59), English historian.

   Domostroi: a sixteenth-century Russian work in 64 chapters describing an extremely rigid system of household management.

   De l'amour: a work of 1859 by the French writer and historian Jules Michelet (1798–1874).

   'Et toc, et toc ... tin-tin-tin!': quoted from a song by Béranger, 'L'ivrogne et sa femme'.

71 *'When Sunny Granada lies a-dreaming'*: the reference is to a song 'Night in Granada' by K. A. Tarnovsky.

82 *Speransky*: M. M. Speransky (1772–1839), leading statesman of the reign of Alexander I, the first of such men in Russia to rise from humble origins.

86 *préférence*: a card game similar to whist. It was usually a three-handed game played with a pack of 32 cards, all those below the seven being

discarded. The game could include an auction in which the highest bidder declared the contract and selected trumps or the preference could be established by the player opposite the dealer shuffling a pack to be cut by his right-hand neighbour, who would turn up a card. The suit of the same colour would be styled the second preference; the other two would be common suits.

92 *Toggenburg*: the romantic hero of a ballad by Schiller.

94 *Notions générales de chimie*: by T. J. Pelouse (1807–67) and E. Frémy (1814–94), first published in Paris in 1853.

100 *Ganot*: A. Ganot (1804–87), French professor of physics and mathematics, whose *Traité* was first published in Paris in 1851.

114 *Hufeland*: C. W. Hufeland (1762–1836), German scientist, famous for a work of 1796 on the science of prolonging human life, or Macrobiotics.

Suum cuique: 'to each his own' (Lat.).

116 *The Friend* of *Health*: a newspaper for the medical profession published in St Petersburg from 1833 to 1869.

Schönlein: J. L. Schönlein (1793–1864), German doctor and professor.

Rademacher: J. G. Rademacher (1772–1849), German medical scientist and devotee of Paracelsus.

Hoffmann: F. Hoffmann (1660–1742), German medical scientist who, as a humoralist, advocated the view that illness is the result of an imbalance of juices in the organism.

Brown: J. Brown (1735–88), influential English doctor.

117 *Prince Wittgenstein*: P. Kh. Wittgenstein (1768–1842), Russian field marshal, participated in the war of 1812 against Napoleon and commanded the southern army (1818–28), in which the Southern Society of the Decembrists was formed. See note below.

Zhukovsky: V. A. Zhukovsky (1783–1852), leading Russian poet and representative of romanticism, particularly noteworthy as a translator.

the southern army on the 14th: a reference to the members of the Southern Society of the Decembrists, whose leader and principal spokesman was P. I. Pestel (1793–1826). Decembrism refers to those revolutionary insurgents, mostly guards officers belonging to the Northern Society in St Petersburg, who on 14 December 1825 marched their troops into the Senate Square in defiance of orders to swear allegiance to the new tsar, Nicholas I. After some parleying, cannon was brought up and the insurgent troops were scattered, many of them dying in the icy Neva. Among those hanged in 1826 as ringleaders of the revolt was Pestel. More than a hundred other upper-class Decembrists were exiled to Siberia.

Paracelsus: P. A. Paracelsus (Theophrastus Bombastus von Hohenheim) (1493–1541), Swiss physician and alchemist, who advocated the use of specific treatments for particular illnesses 'through herbs, words and minerals.'

120 *Alexis, or the Cottage in the Forest*: sentimental novel (1788) by the French writer Ducray-Duminil (1761–1819). Published in Russian translation in 1794, 1800 and 1804.

122 *Cincinnatus*: Lucius Quinctius *Cincinnatus* (?519–438 BC), Roman patrician and statesman, who retired to a simple life of cultivation on his farm after the crises of 458 and 439 BC.

    Jean-Jacques Rousseau: Rousseau (1712–78) advocated—among many other attributes of a simple life—the health-giving and educational merits of physical labour.

125 *Robert le Diable*: opera (1831) by Meyerbeer (1791–1864).

    Suvorov: Count A. V. Suvorov (1730–1800), greatest of Russian military commanders, whose final achievement was a brilliantly executed retreat across the Alps in 1799.

132 *the Vladimir*: the Holy Order of Vladimir, a military decoration and order founded by Catherine the Great in 1792. Its award conferred nobility status on the recipient.

141 *Sunday schools*: intended initially for the encouragement of literacy among adults, these began to become popular in 1859, the year of the novel's setting.

142 *landowners in the Baltic provinces*: exploitation of their peasants by the German landowners in the Baltic provinces (now Lithuania, Latvia and Estonia) and their opposition to the proposed reforms elicited much critical comment in the press.

148 *the world's womanizers*: in the Russian, admission 'into the ranks of the Céladons'. Céladon was the notoriously womanizing hero of *L'Astrée*, by the French writer d'Urfé (1568–1625).

156 *Mrs Radcliffe*: Ann Radcliffe (1764–1823), very popular English 'Gothic' novelist.

157 *Sir Robert Peel*: English conservative statesman (1788–1850).

171 *Gogol's letters*: this refers to the letter of the famous writer N. V. Gogol (1809–52) to A. O. Smirnova of June 1846, originally included in his ultra-conservative and sententious work *Selected Passages from a Correspondence with Friends* (1847), but forbidden by the censor. It received its first publication under the heading 'What is a Governor's wife?' only in 1860. Bazarov, speaking presumably in 1859, is hardly likely to have read it.

184 *your peasant world*: Bazarov makes fun of the peasant here by playing on the word *mir*, which can mean both 'world' and 'peasant commune'. The peasant quickly assures him that it's the earth (as old folk wisdom averred) which rests on three fishes, not the commune.

186 *Goulard Water*: a medical preparation (*Aqua vegetomineralis Goulardii*) named after a French doctor, Thomas Goulard (d. 1784).

198 *at this very time*: i.e. late 1861 and early 1862, after the Emancipation of the serfs in February 1861.

an arbitrator: in Russian: *mirovoi posrednik*, an official position created after the Emancipation of the serfs to regulate relations between the peasants and their former masters.

199 *the Brühl terrace*: on the former castle battlements of Dresden, above the Elbe; named after Heinrich Brühl (1700–63), Minister to August III, King of Poland.

'in temporary opposition': a reference to the temporary reaction against the reforms of the period in certain quarters of the tsarist administration. In other words, Kolyazin's 'liberal' attitudes were shortlived.

The Oxford World's Classics Website

www.worldsclassics.co.uk

- Information about new titles
- Explore the full range of Oxford World's Classics
- Links to other literary sites and the main OUP webpage
- Imaginative competitions, with bookish prizes
- Peruse the Oxford World's Classics Magazine
- Articles by editors
- Extracts from Introductions
- A forum for discussion and feedback on the series
- Special information for teachers and lecturers

www.worldsclassics.co.uk

American Literature
British and Irish Literature
Children's Literature
Classics and Ancient Literature
Colonial Literature
Eastern Literature
European Literature
History
Medieval Literature
Oxford English Drama
Poetry
Philosophy
Politics
Religion
The Oxford Shakespeare

A complete list of Oxford Paperbacks, including Oxford World's Classics, Oxford Shakespeare, Oxford Drama, and Oxford Paperback Reference, is available in the UK from the Academic Division Publicity Department, Oxford University Press, Great Clarendon Street, Oxford OX2 6DP.

In the USA, complete lists are available from the Paperbacks Marketing Manager, Oxford University Press, 198 Madison Avenue, New York, NY 10016.

Oxford Paperbacks are available from all good bookshops. In case of difficulty, customers in the UK can order direct from Oxford University Press Bookshop, Freepost, 116 High Street, Oxford OX1 4BR, enclosing full payment. Please add 10 per cent of published price for postage and packing.